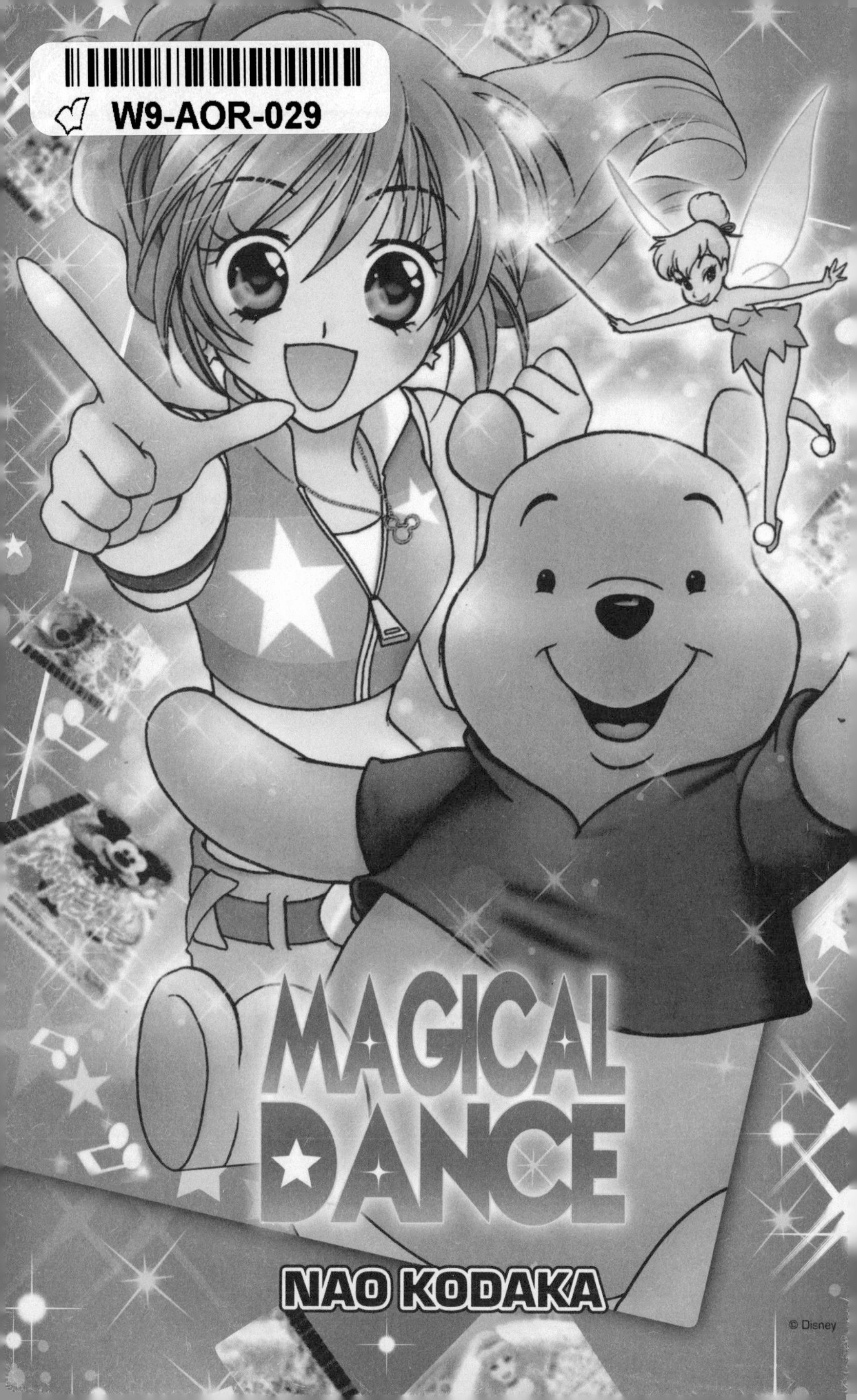
MAGICAL DANCE
NAO KODAKA
© Disney

IN THE LAST VOLUME OF MAGICAL DANCE!

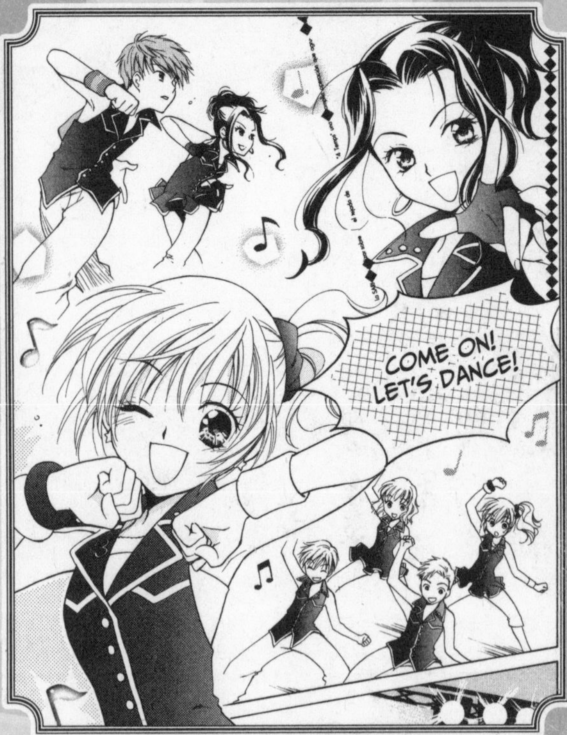
COME ON! LET'S DANCE!

"Wanting nothing more than to be a dancer, Rin joins a troupe with her fellow students and soon realizes that she has two left feet. She practices and practices, but is discouraged by the lack of results and almost gives up on her dreams. Impressed by her passion and dedication, Tinker Bell appears to give her a little encouragement in the form of a little Disney magic! With the help of Tinker Bell's magic cards, Rin calls upon the help of her favorite Disney characters and dances her way to her dreams!"

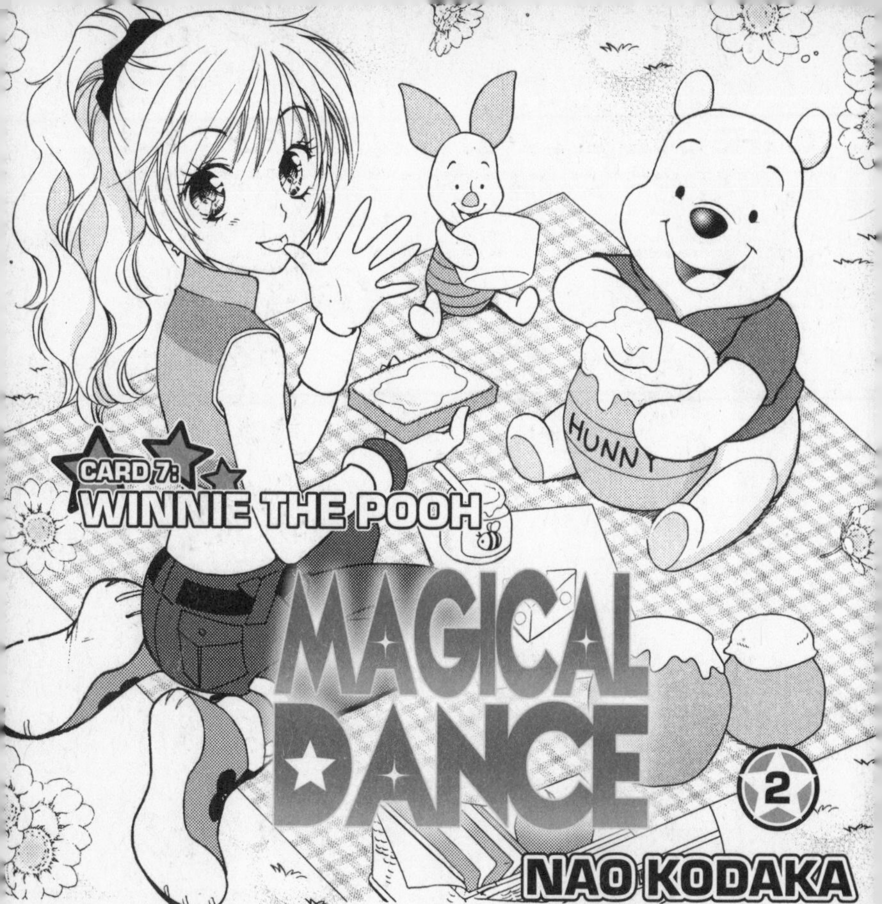
CARD 7:
WINNIE THE POOH
HUNNY
MAGICAL DANCE
2
NAO KODAKA

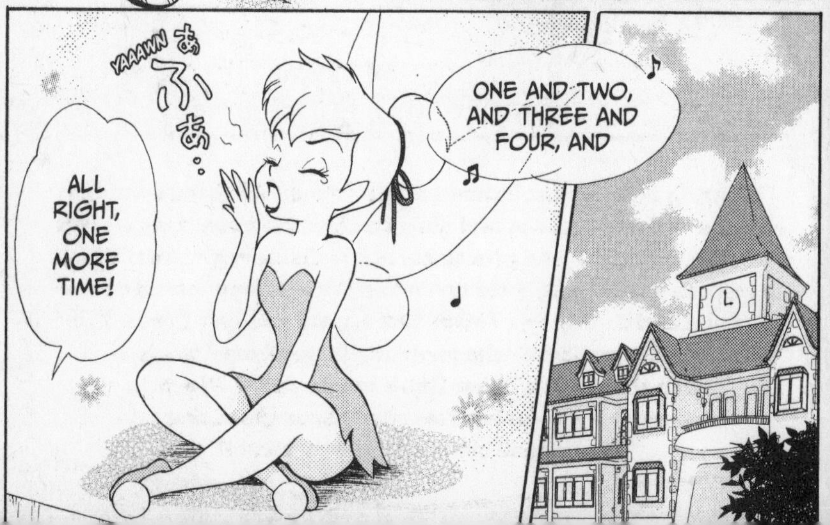
ONE AND TWO, AND THREE AND FOUR, AND
YAAAWN あふあ。。
ALL RIGHT, ONE MORE TIME!

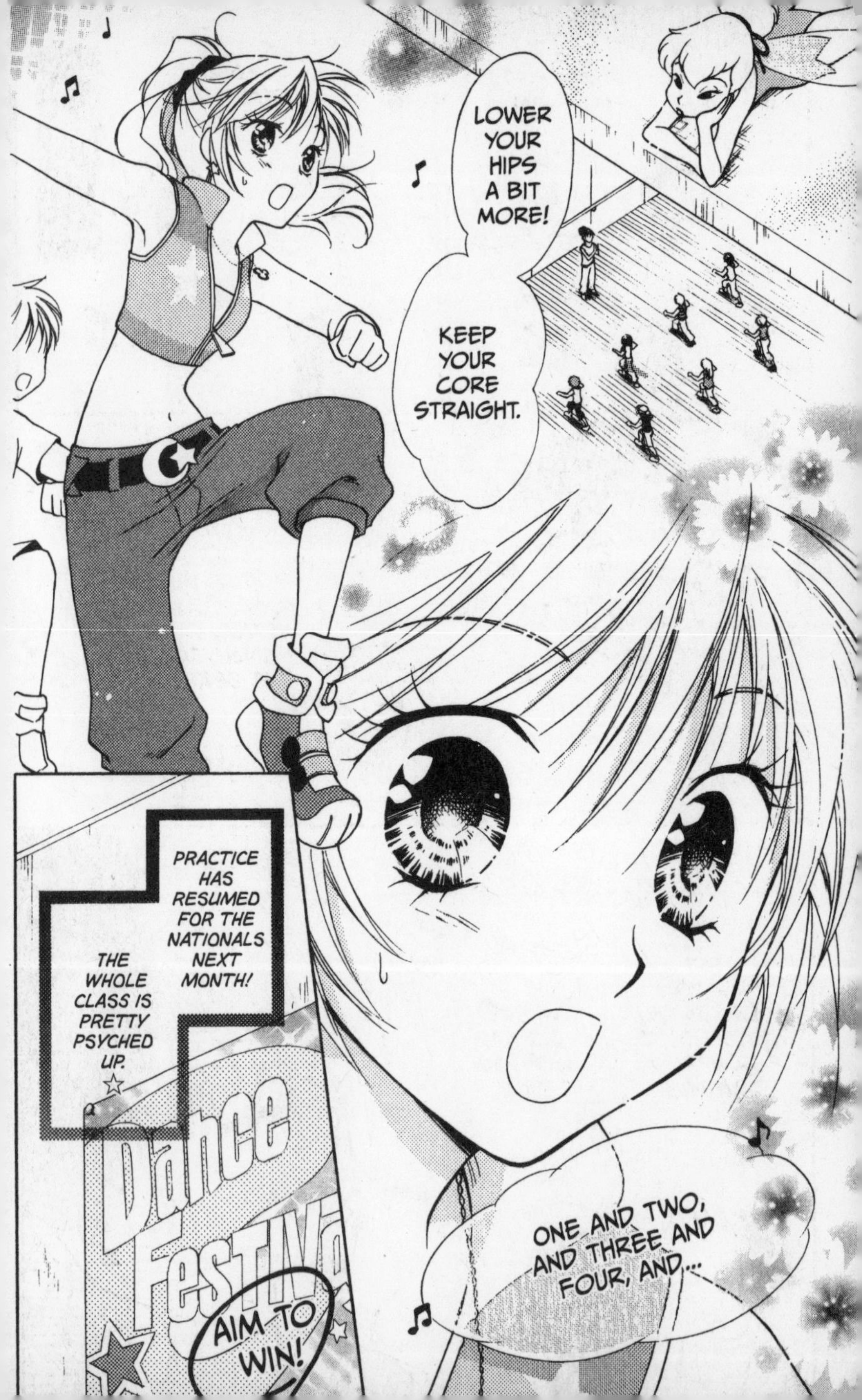
LOWER YOUR HIPS A BIT MORE!
KEEP YOUR CORE STRAIGHT.
PRACTICE HAS RESUMED FOR THE NATIONALS NEXT MONTH!
THE WHOLE CLASS IS PRETTY PSYCHED UP. ☆
ONE AND TWO, AND THREE AND FOUR, AND...
Dance
AIM TO WIN!

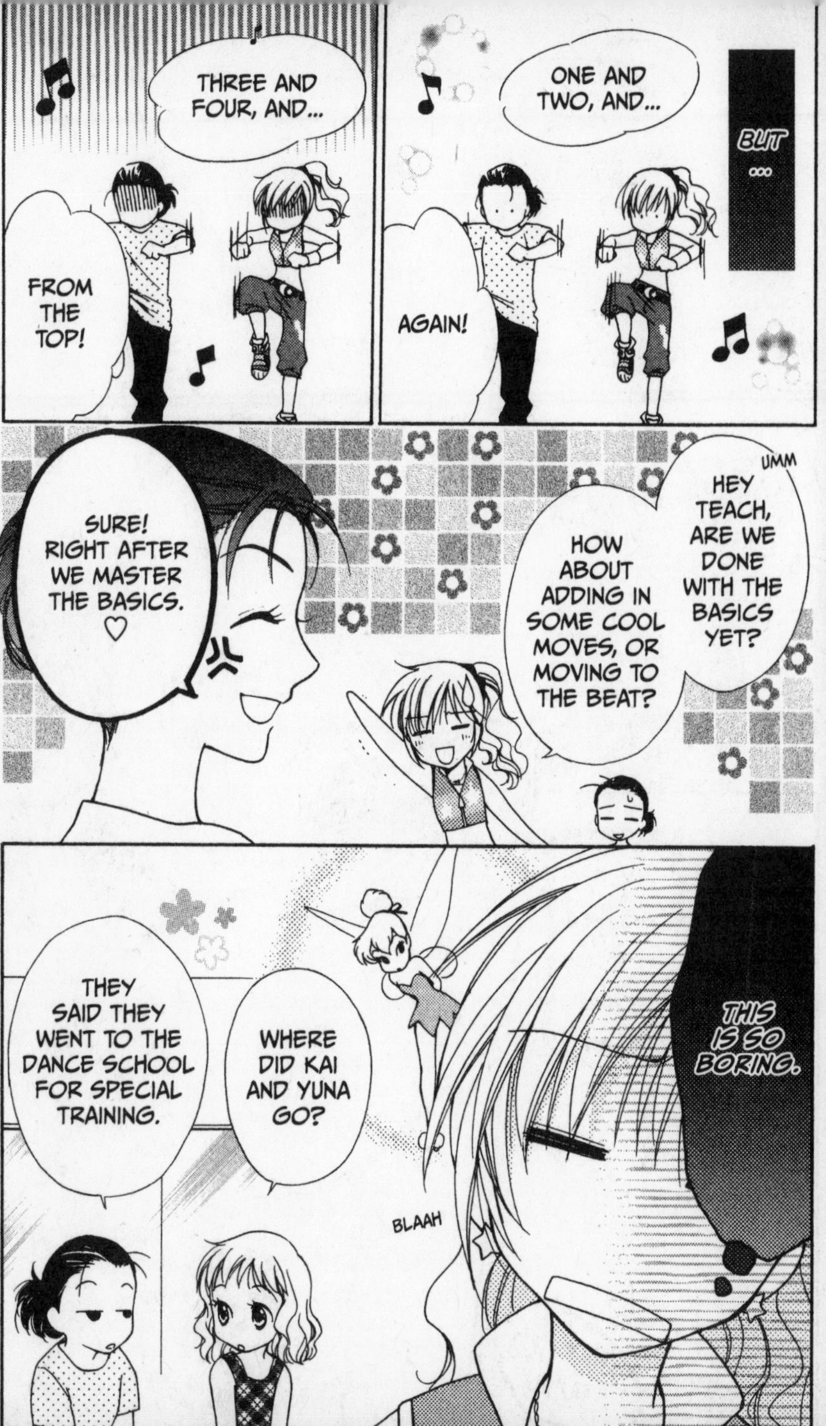
BUT ...
ONE AND TWO, AND...
AGAIN!
THREE AND FOUR, AND...
FROM THE TOP!
UMM
HEY TEACH, ARE WE DONE WITH THE BASICS YET?
HOW ABOUT ADDING IN SOME COOL MOVES, OR MOVING TO THE BEAT?
SURE! RIGHT AFTER WE MASTER THE BASICS. ♡
THIS IS SO BORING.
BLAAH
WHERE DID KAI AND YUNA GO?
THEY SAID THEY WENT TO THE DANCE SCHOOL FOR SPECIAL TRAINING.

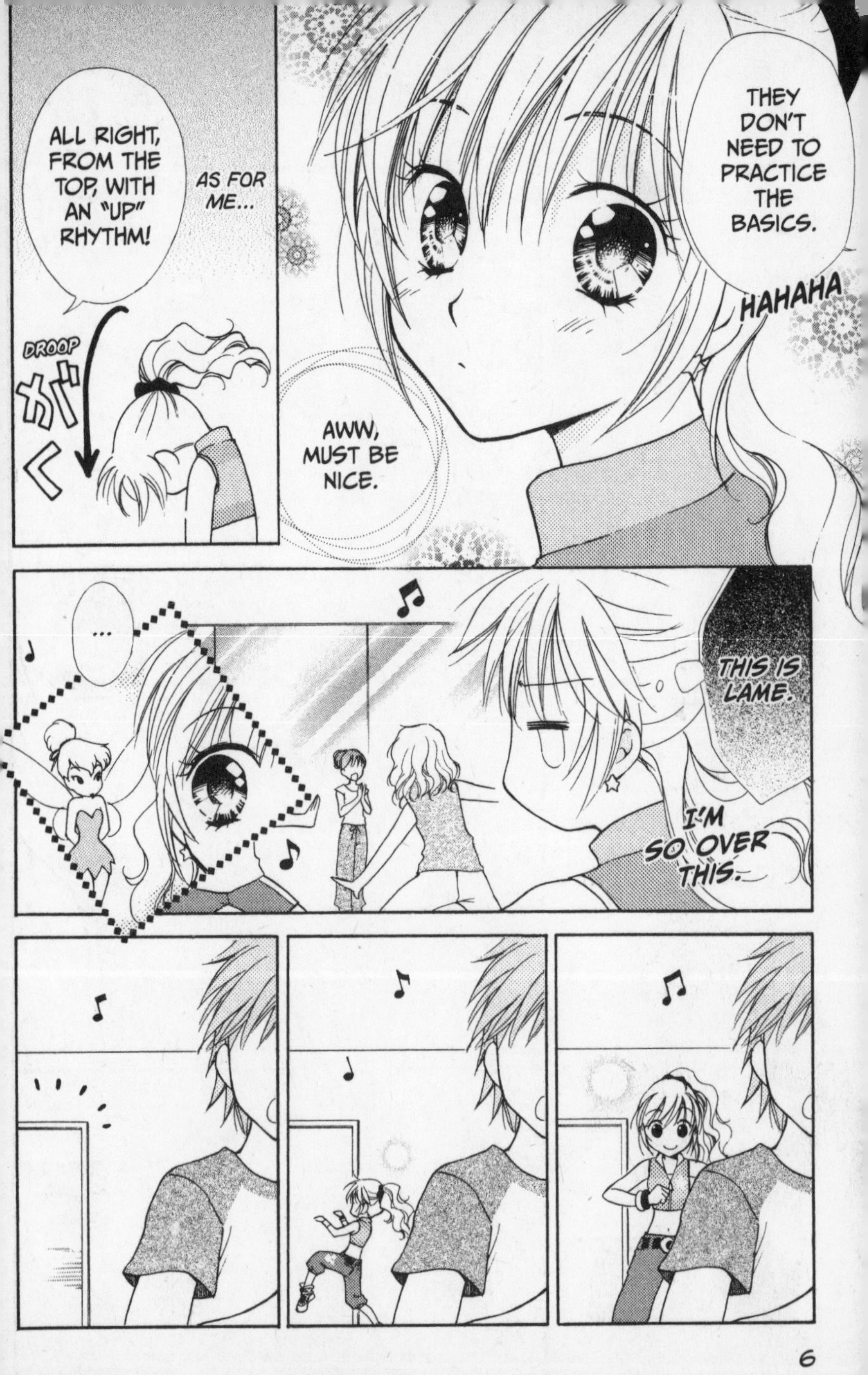
THEY DON'T NEED TO PRACTICE THE BASICS.
HAHAHA
AWW, MUST BE NICE.
AS FOR ME...
ALL RIGHT, FROM THE TOP, WITH AN "UP" RHYTHM!
DROOP
がく
THIS IS LAME.
I'M SO OVER THIS.
...

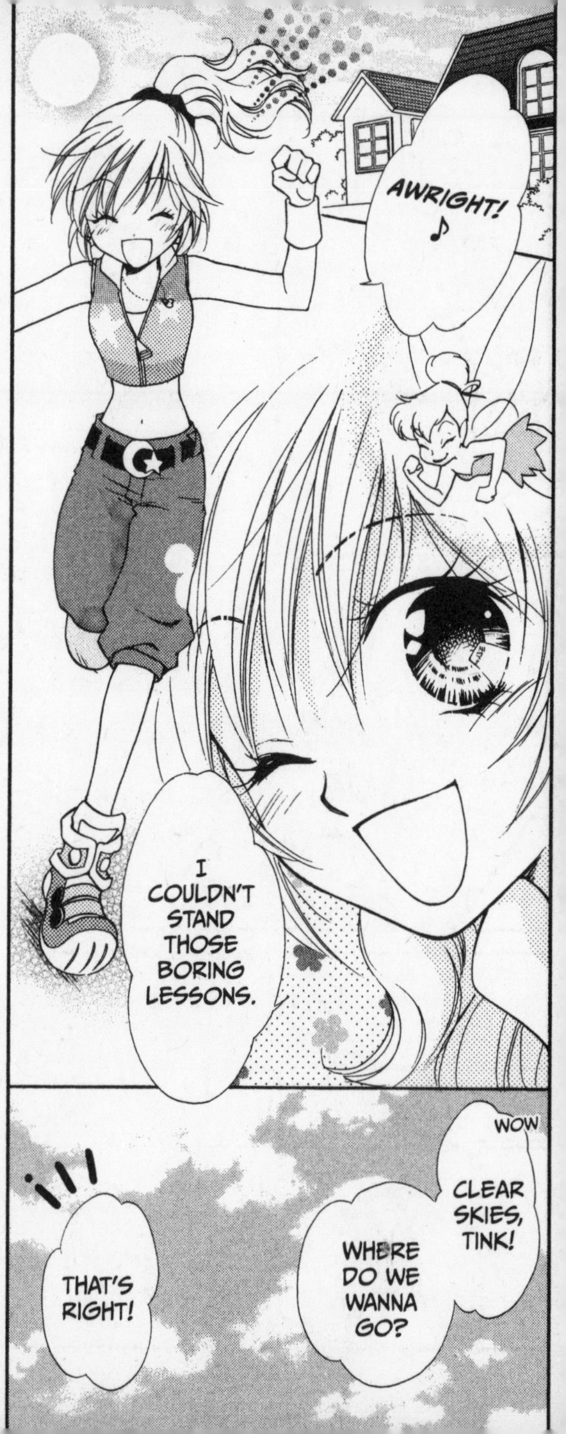
AWRIGHT! ♪
I COULDN'T STAND THOSE BORING LESSONS.
WOW
CLEAR SKIES, TINK!
WHERE DO WE WANNA GO?
THAT'S RIGHT!
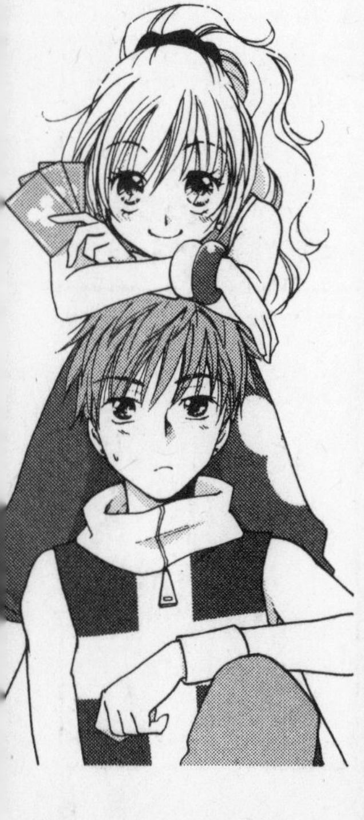

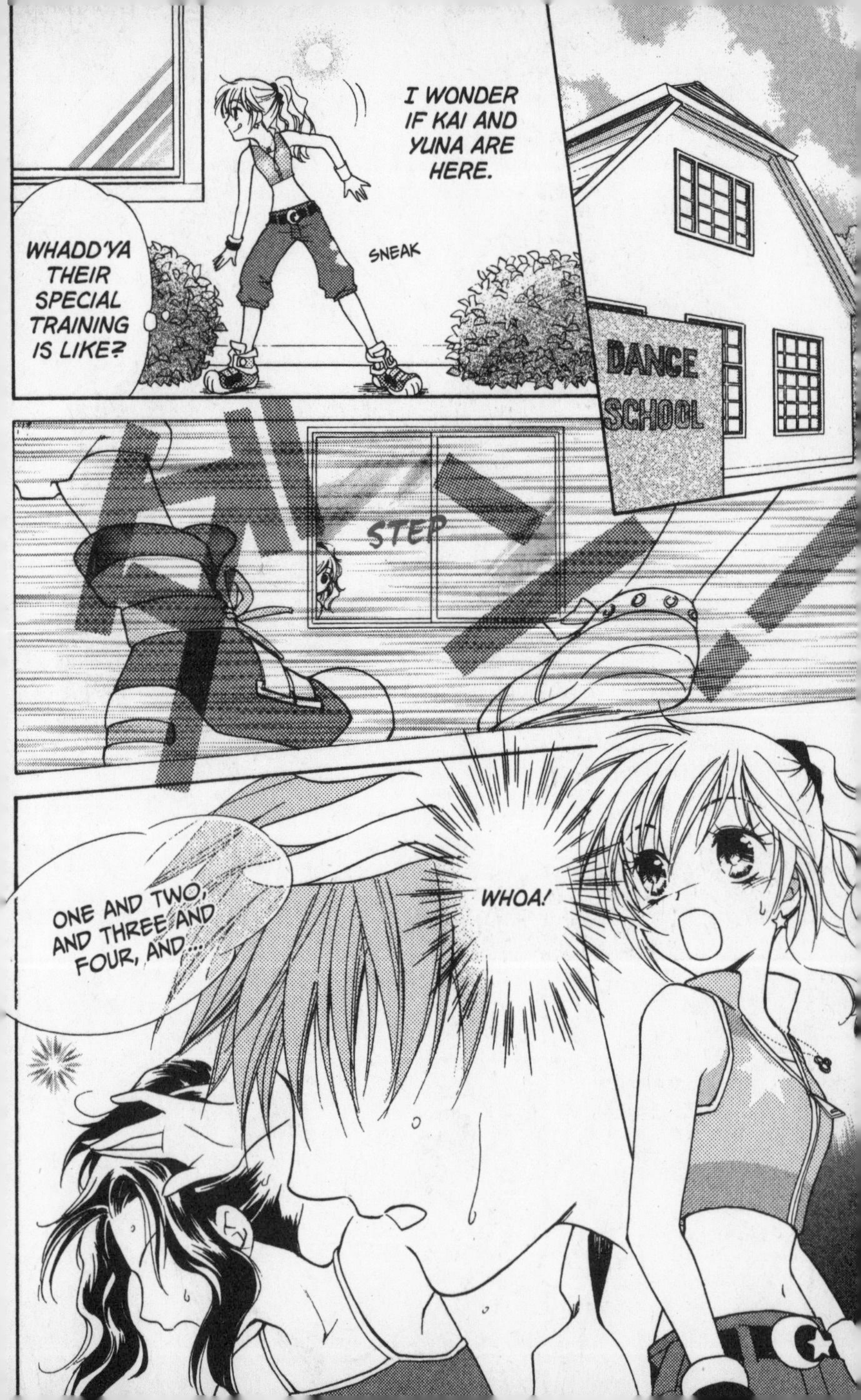

DANCE SCHOOL
I WONDER IF KAI AND YUNA ARE HERE.
SNEAK
WHADD'YA THEIR SPECIAL TRAINING IS LIKE?
STEP
WHOA!
ONE AND TWO, AND THREE AND FOUR, AND...

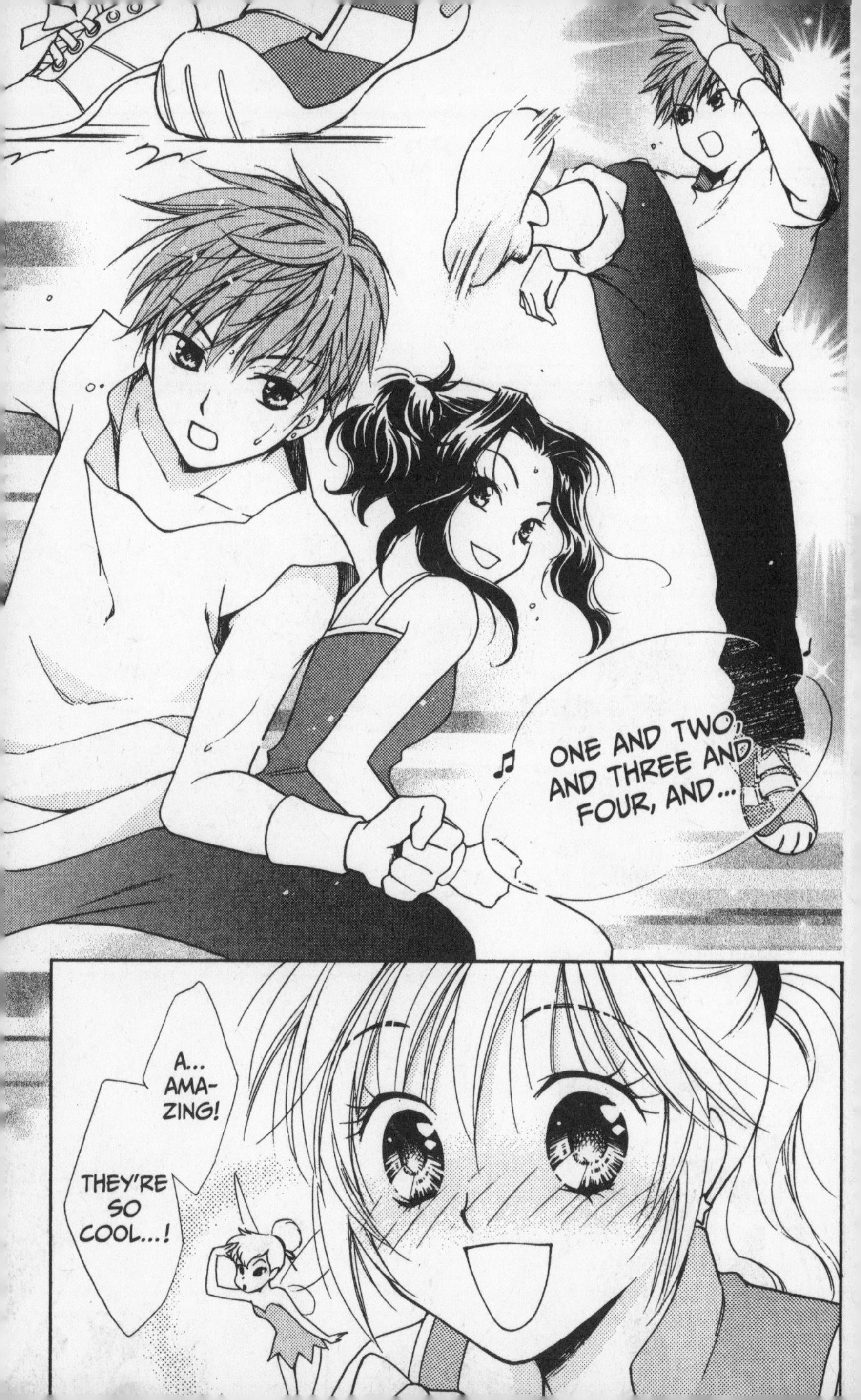
ONE AND TWO, AND THREE AND FOUR, AND...
A... AMA-ZING!
THEY'RE SO COOL...!

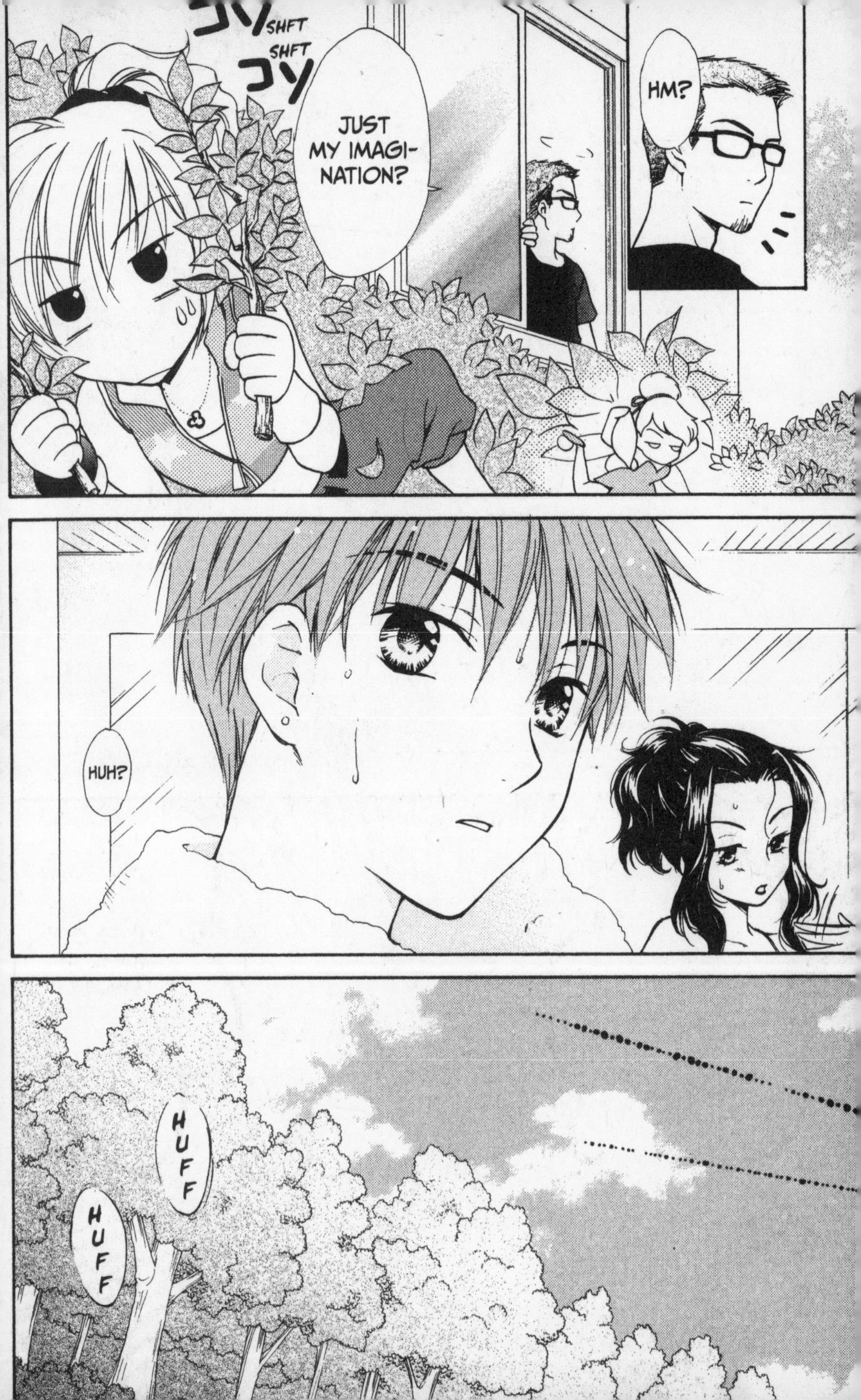
HM?
JUST MY IMAGI-NATION?
コソ SHFT
SHFT コソ
HUH?
HUFF
HUFF

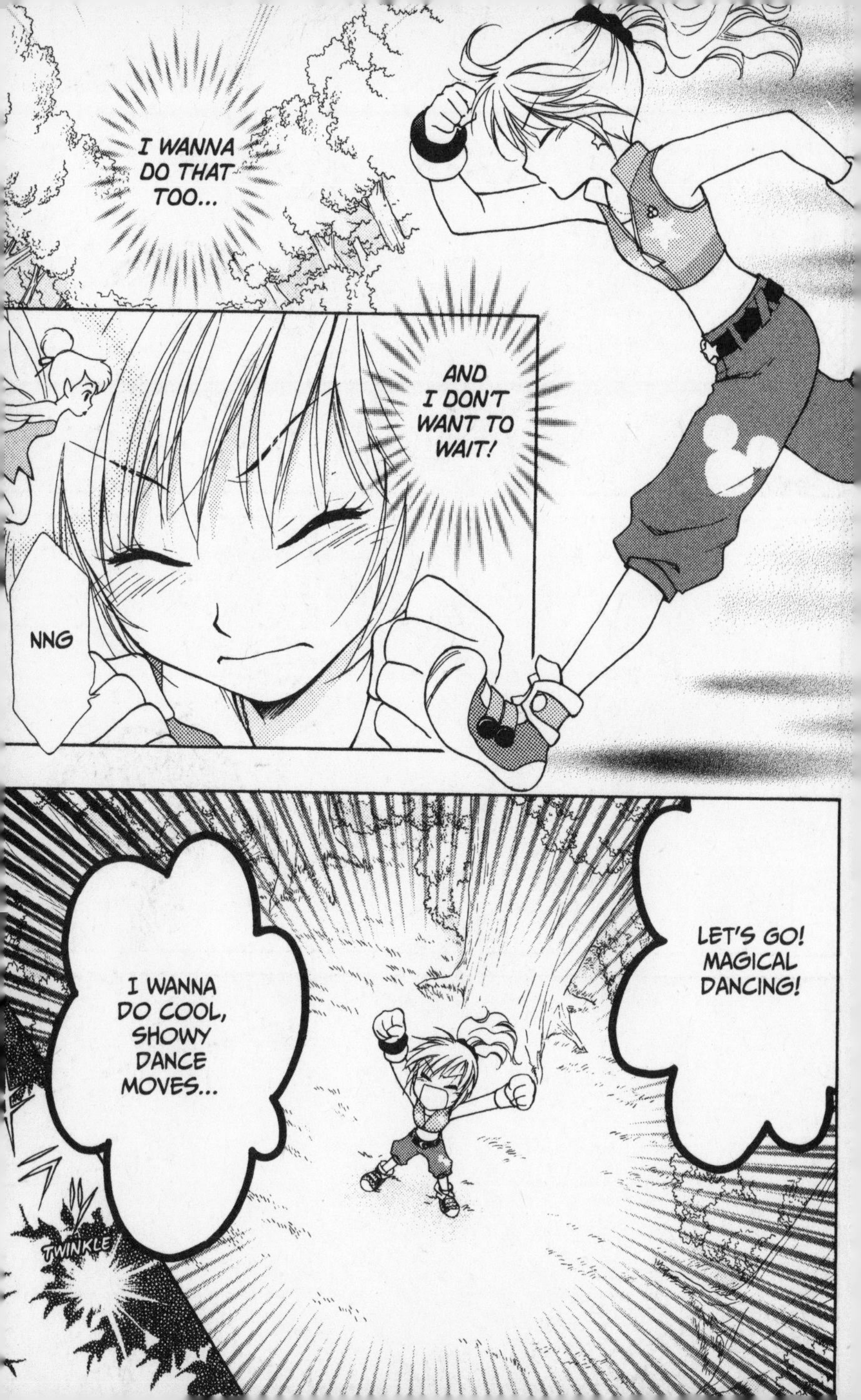
I WANNA DO THAT TOO...
AND I DON'T WANT TO WAIT!
NNG
LET'S GO! MAGICAL DANCING!
I WANNA DO COOL, SHOWY DANCE MOVES...
TWINKLE

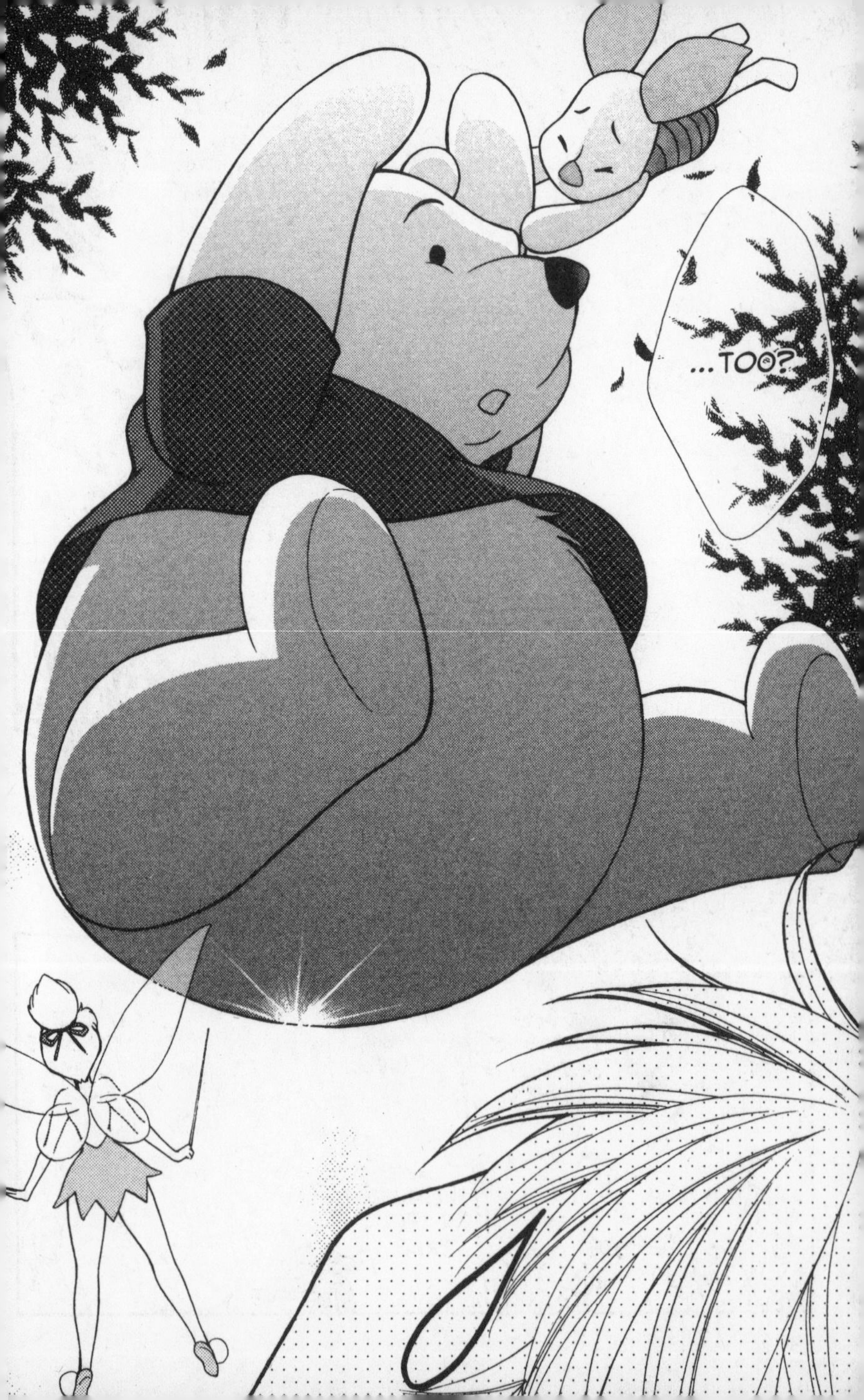
...TOO?

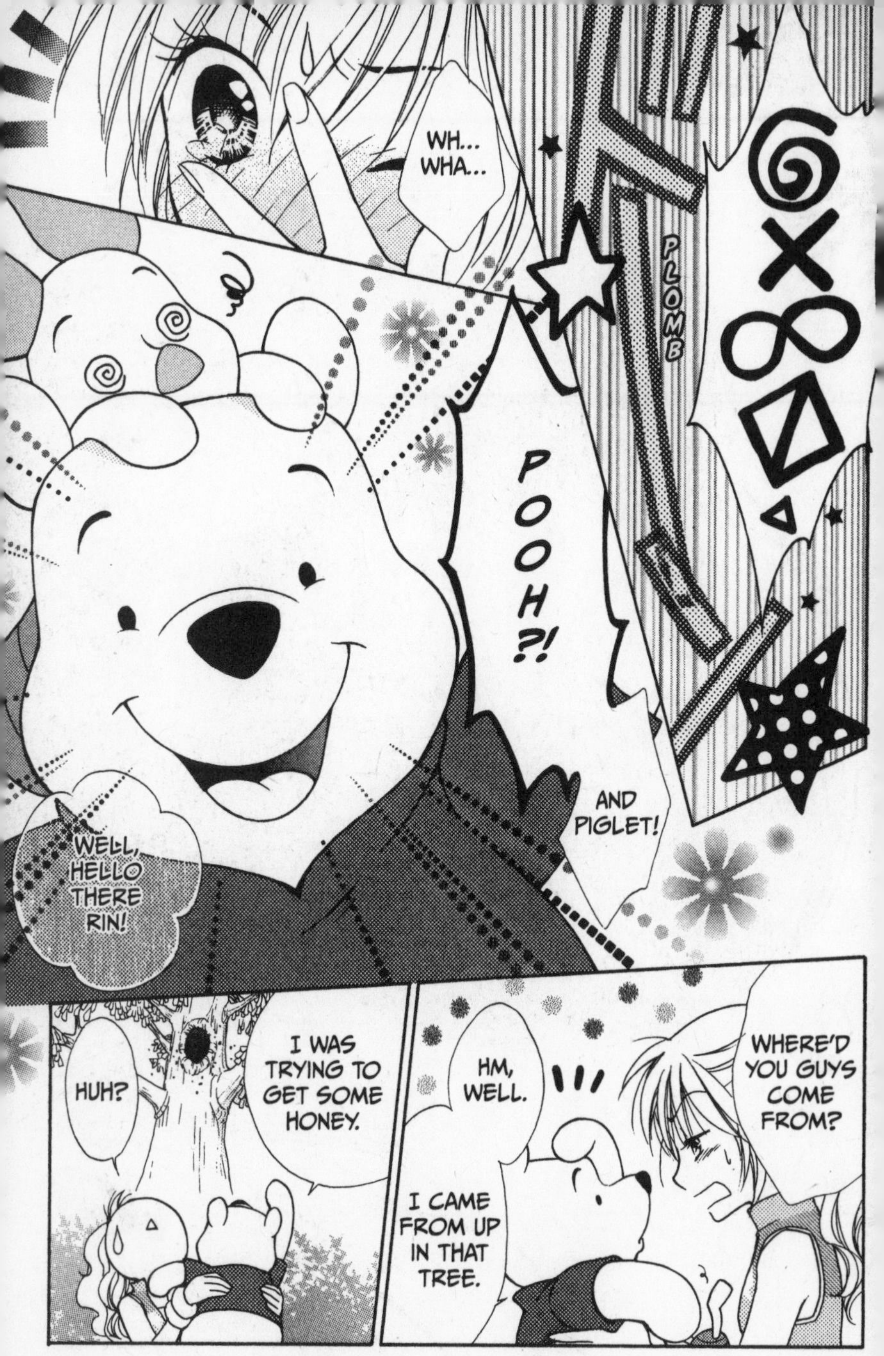
WH... WHA...
PLOMB
POOH?!
AND PIGLET!
WELL, HELLO THERE RIN!
WHERE'D YOU GUYS COME FROM?
HM, WELL.
I CAME FROM UP IN THAT TREE.
I WAS TRYING TO GET SOME HONEY.
HUH?

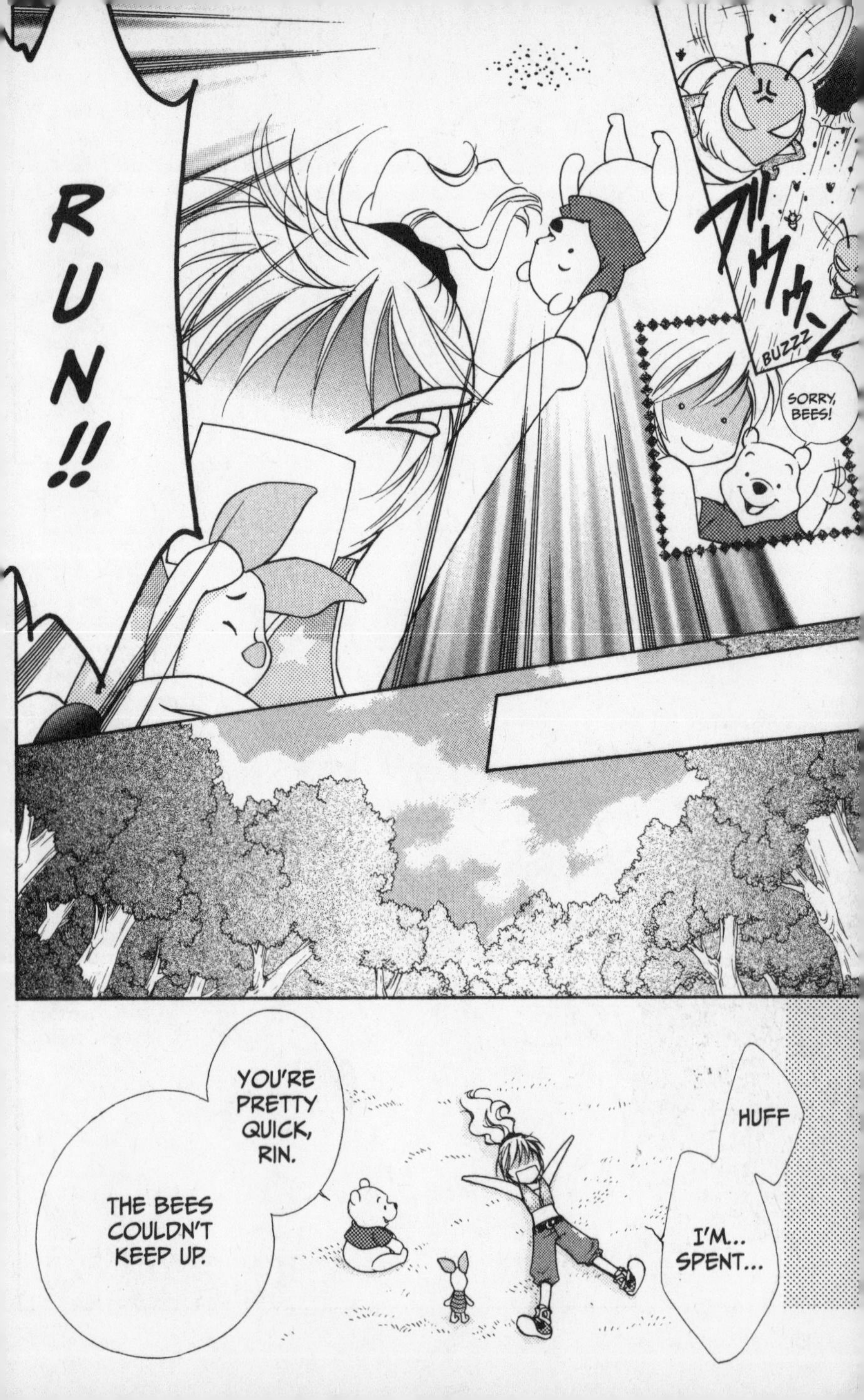
BUZZZ
SORRY, BEES!
RUN!!
HUFF
I'M... SPENT...
YOU'RE PRETTY QUICK, RIN.
THE BEES COULDN'T KEEP UP.

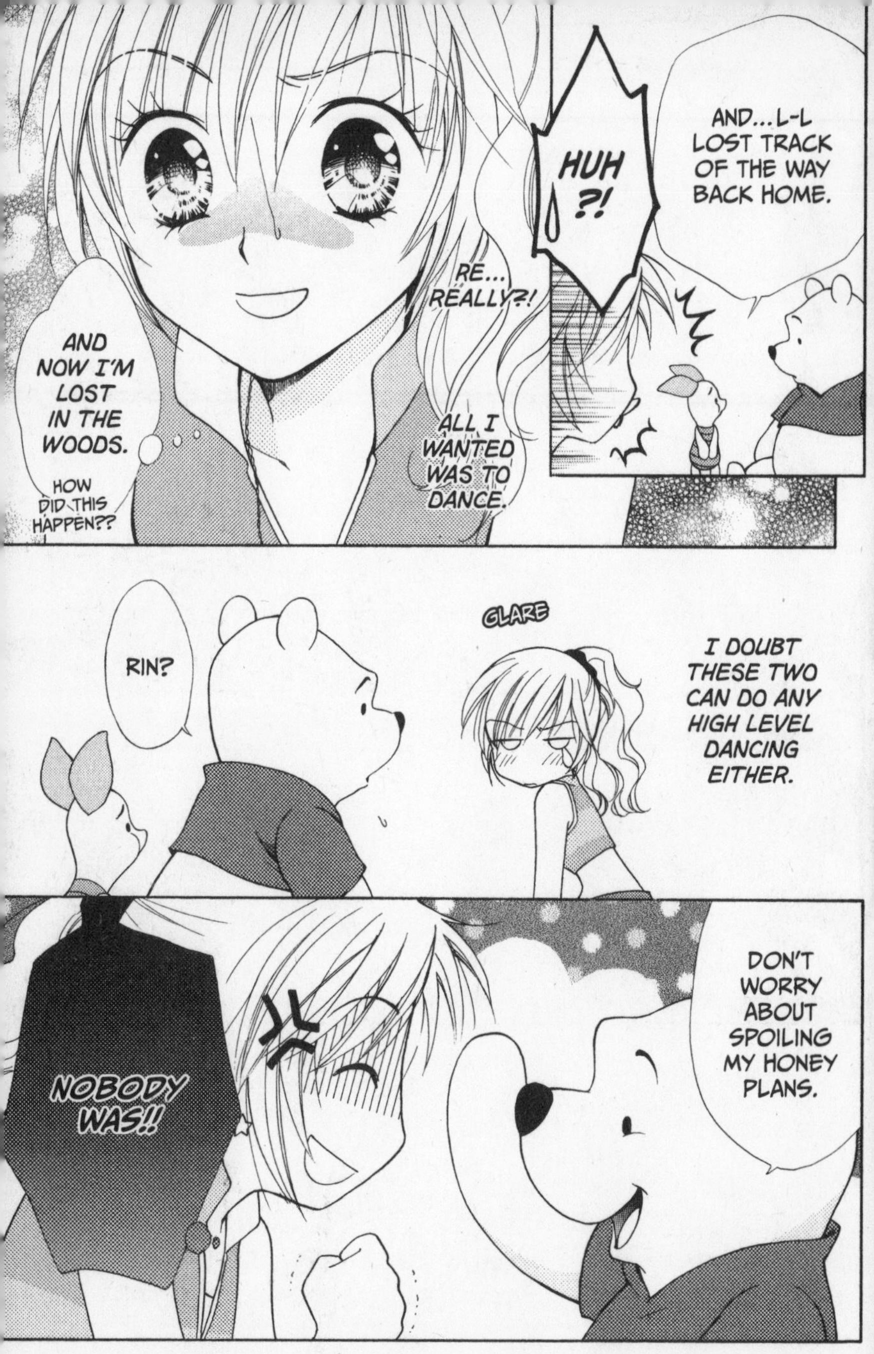
AND...L-L LOST TRACK OF THE WAY BACK HOME.
HUH ?!
RE... REALLY?!
ALL I WANTED WAS TO DANCE.
AND NOW I'M LOST IN THE WOODS.
HOW DID THIS HAPPEN??
I DOUBT THESE TWO CAN DO ANY HIGH LEVEL DANCING EITHER.
GLARE
RIN?
DON'T WORRY ABOUT SPOILING MY HONEY PLANS.
NOBODY WAS!!

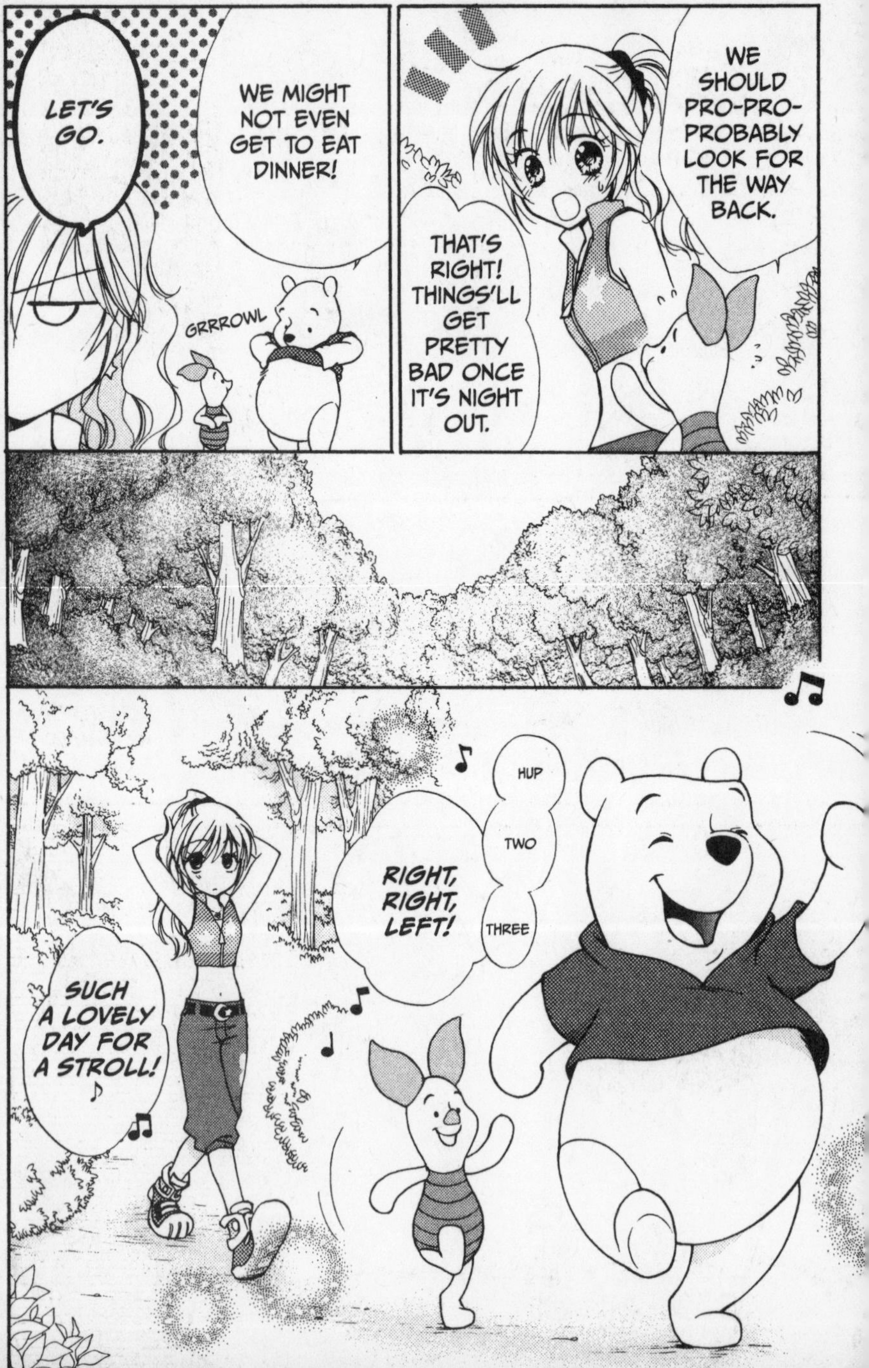
WE SHOULD PRO-PRO-PROBABLY LOOK FOR THE WAY BACK.
THAT'S RIGHT! THINGS'LL GET PRETTY BAD ONCE IT'S NIGHT OUT.
WE MIGHT NOT EVEN GET TO EAT DINNER!
LET'S GO.
GRRROWL
HUP
TWO
THREE
RIGHT, RIGHT, LEFT!
SUCH A LOVELY DAY FOR A STROLL! ♪

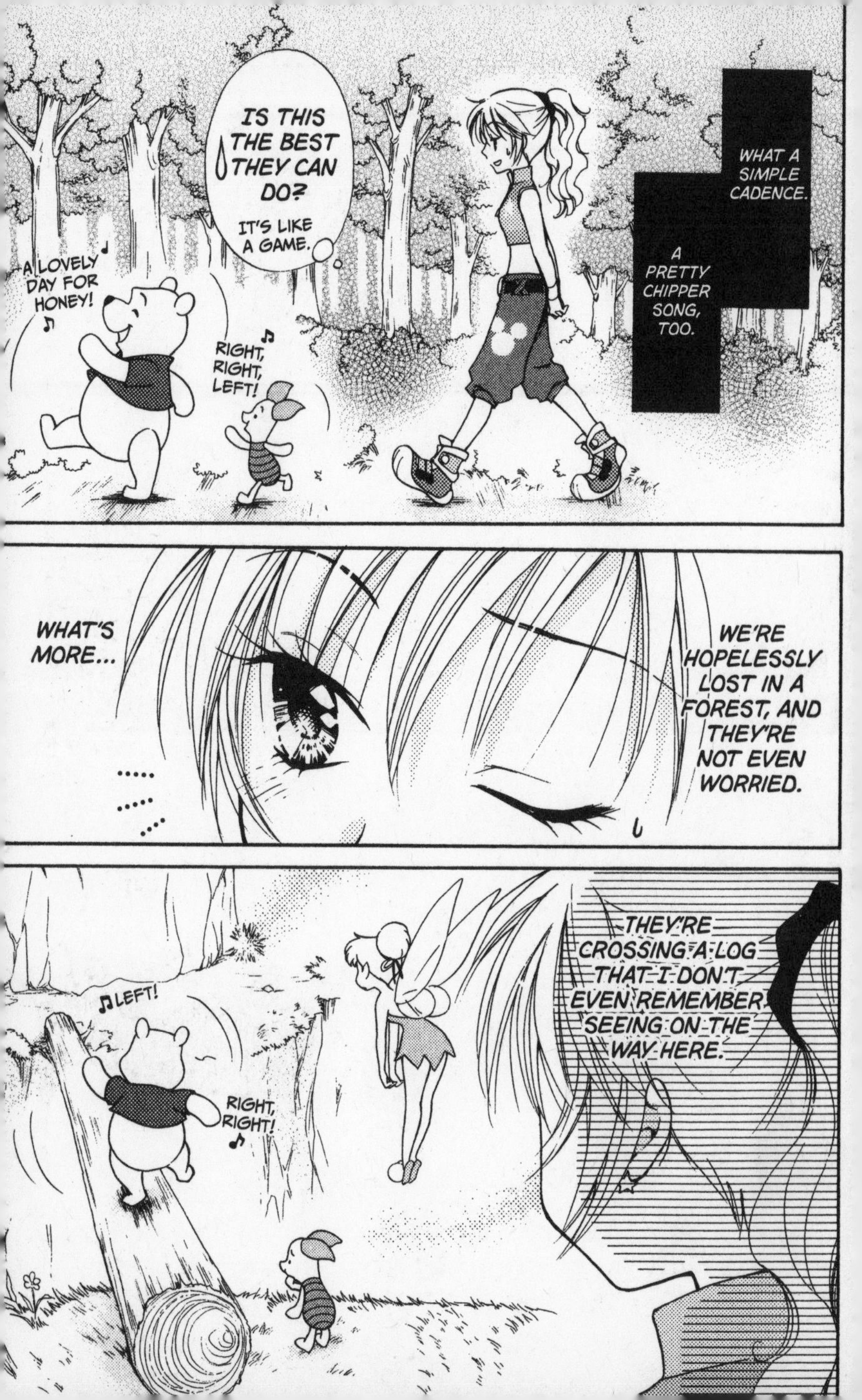
WHAT A SIMPLE CADENCE.
A PRETTY CHIPPER SONG, TOO.
IS THIS THE BEST THEY CAN DO?
IT'S LIKE A GAME.
A LOVELY DAY FOR HONEY! ♪
RIGHT, RIGHT, LEFT! ♪
WE'RE HOPELESSLY LOST IN A FOREST, AND THEY'RE NOT EVEN WORRIED.
WHAT'S MORE...
......
THEY'RE CROSSING A LOG THAT I DON'T EVEN REMEMBER SEEING ON THE WAY HERE.
RIGHT, RIGHT! ♪
♫LEFT!

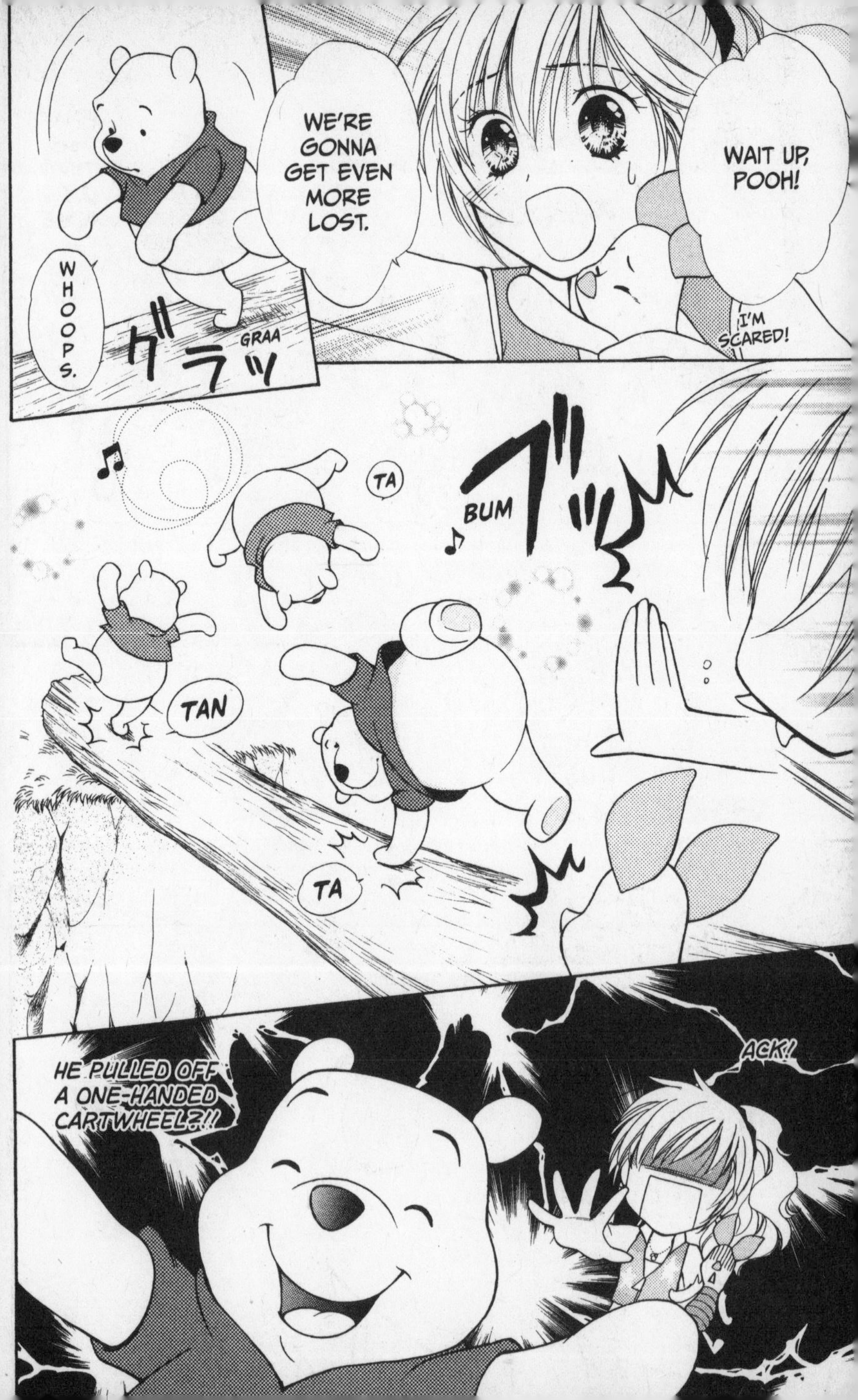
WAIT UP, POOH!
I'M SCARED!
WE'RE GONNA GET EVEN MORE LOST.
WHOOPS.
グラッ
GRAA
BUM
TA
TAN
TA
ACK!
HE PULLED OFF A ONE-HANDED CARTWHEEL?!!

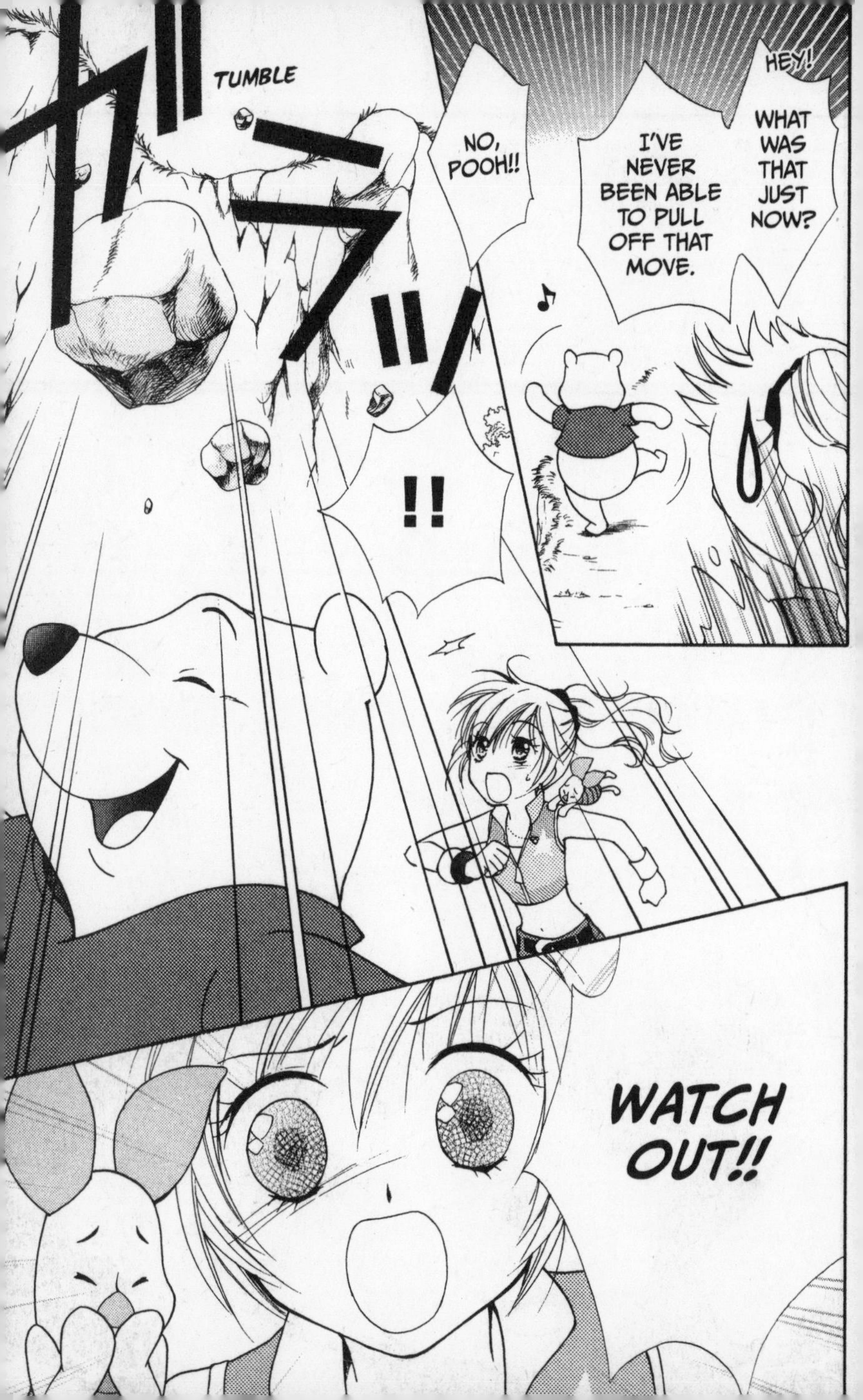
HEY!
WHAT WAS THAT JUST NOW?
I'VE NEVER BEEN ABLE TO PULL OFF THAT MOVE.
TUMBLE
NO, POOH!!
!!
WATCH OUT!!

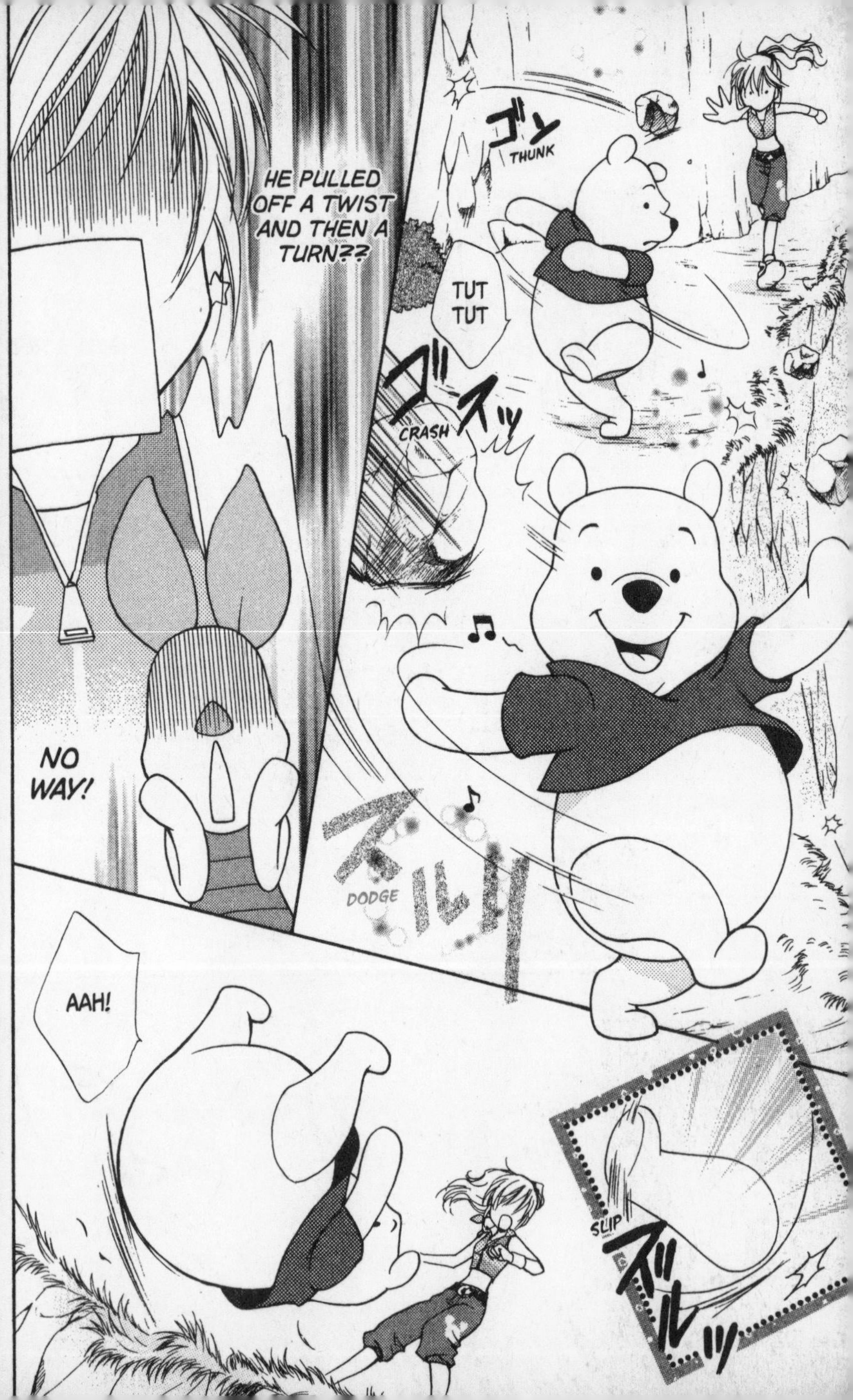

ゴン
THUNK
TUT TUT
ゴスッ
CRASH
スルッ
DODGE
HE PULLED OFF A TWIST AND THEN A TURN??
NO WAY!
AAH!
ズルッ
SLIP

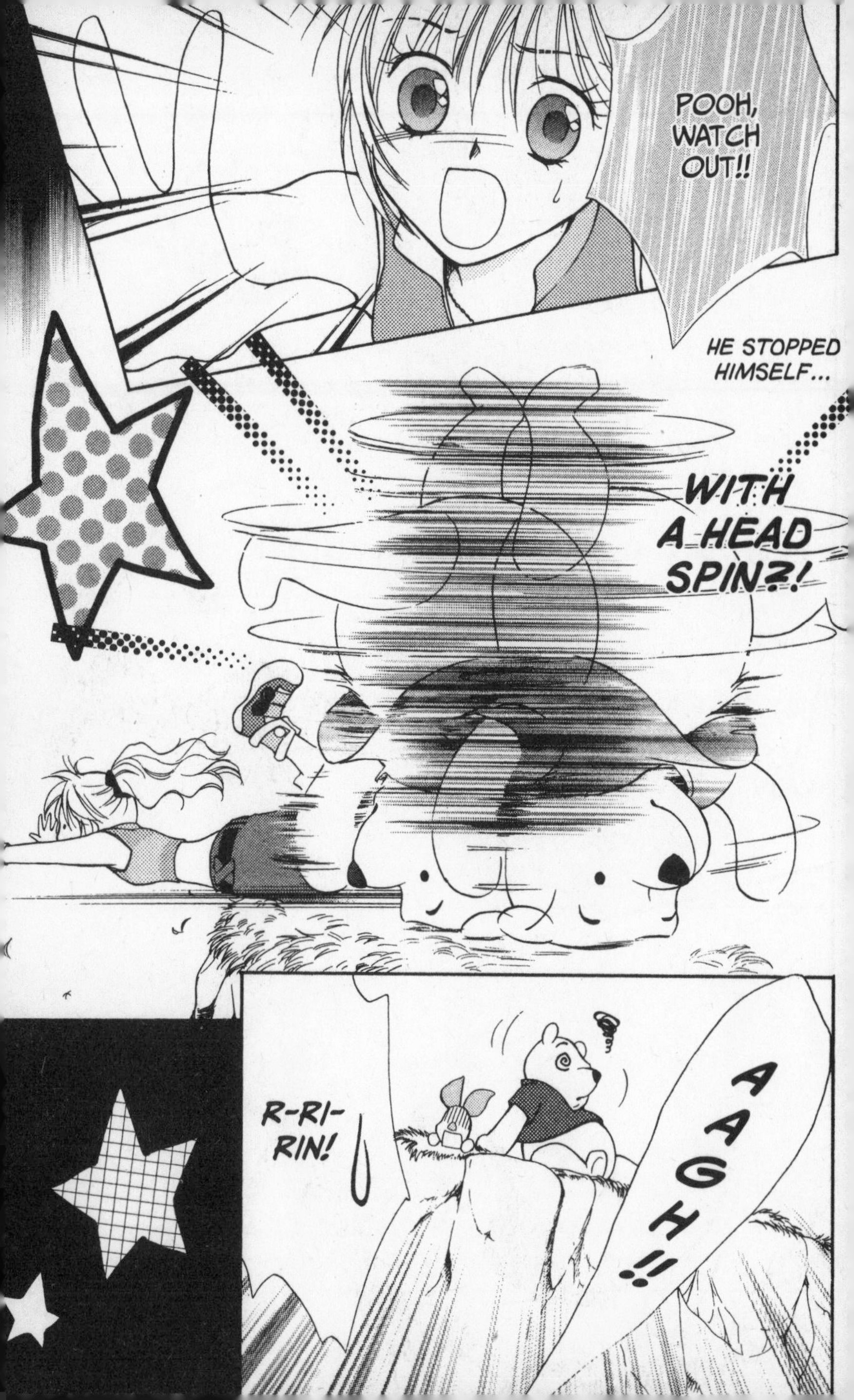
POOH, WATCH OUT!!
HE STOPPED HIMSELF...
WITH A HEAD SPIN?!
AAGH!!
R-RI-RIN!

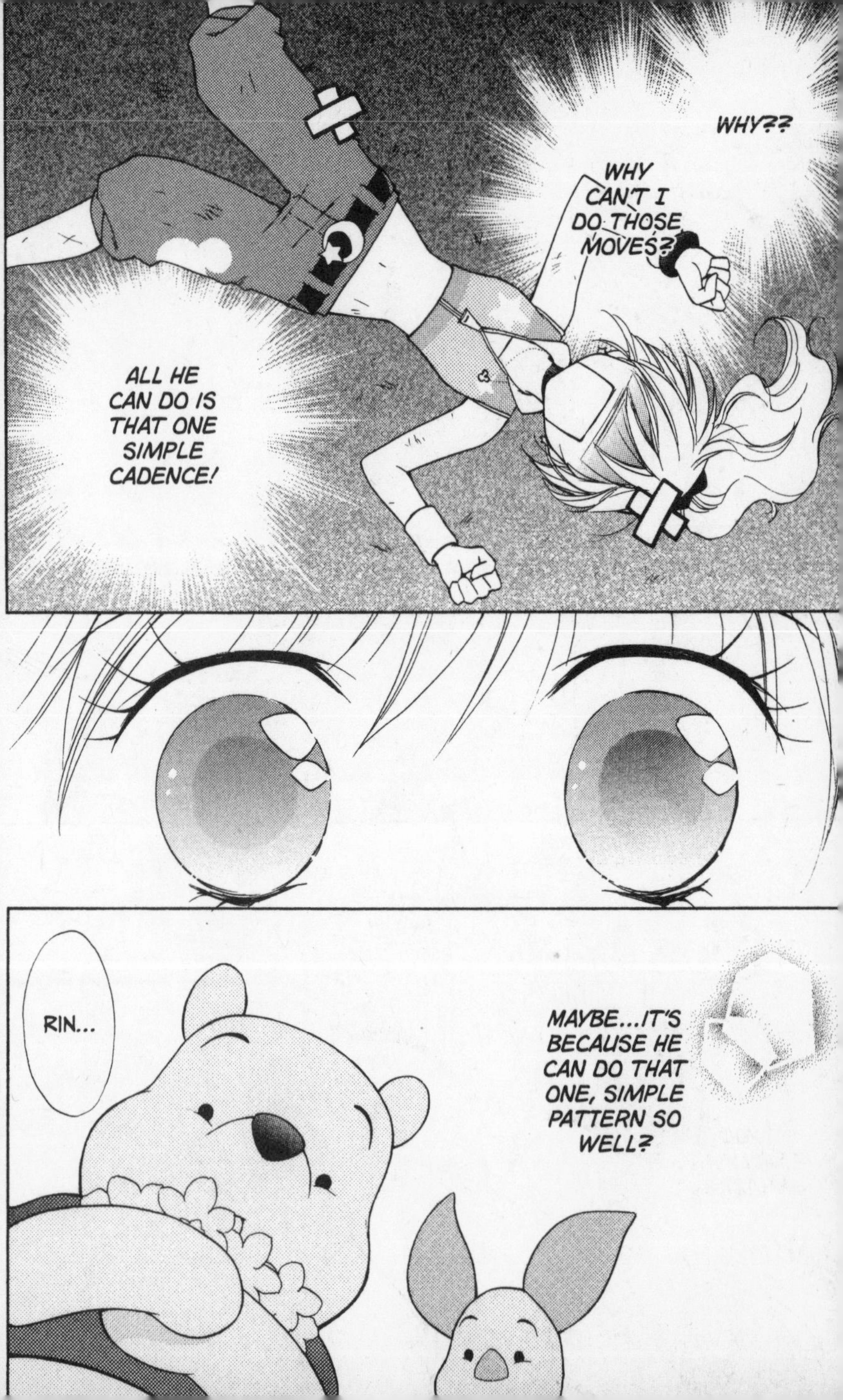
WHY??
WHY CAN'T I DO THOSE MOVES?
ALL HE CAN DO IS THAT ONE SIMPLE CADENCE!
MAYBE...IT'S BECAUSE HE CAN DO THAT ONE, SIMPLE PATTERN SO WELL?
RIN...

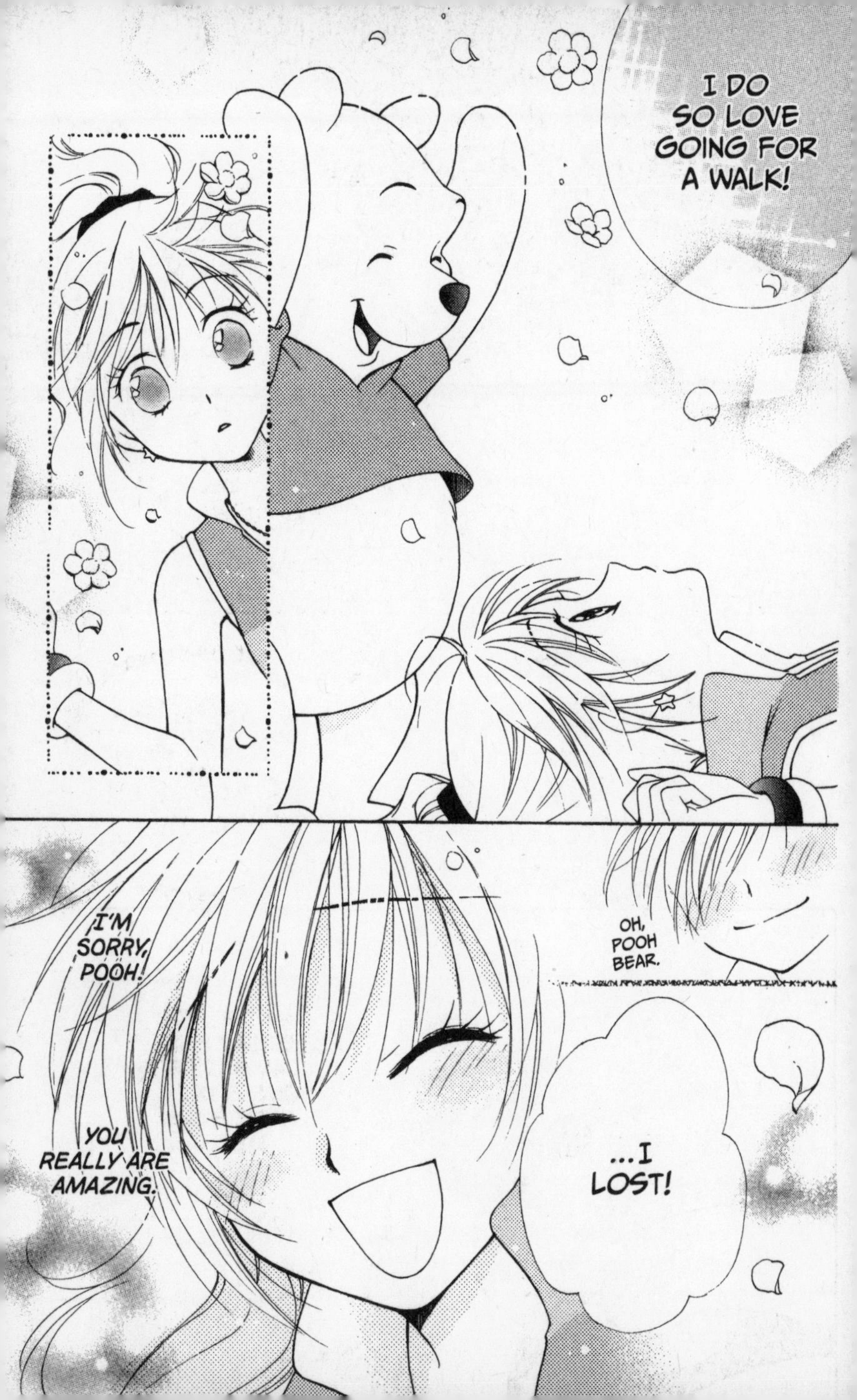
I DO SO LOVE GOING FOR A WALK!
OH, POOH BEAR.
...I LOST!
I'M SORRY, POOH!
YOU REALLY ARE AMAZING.

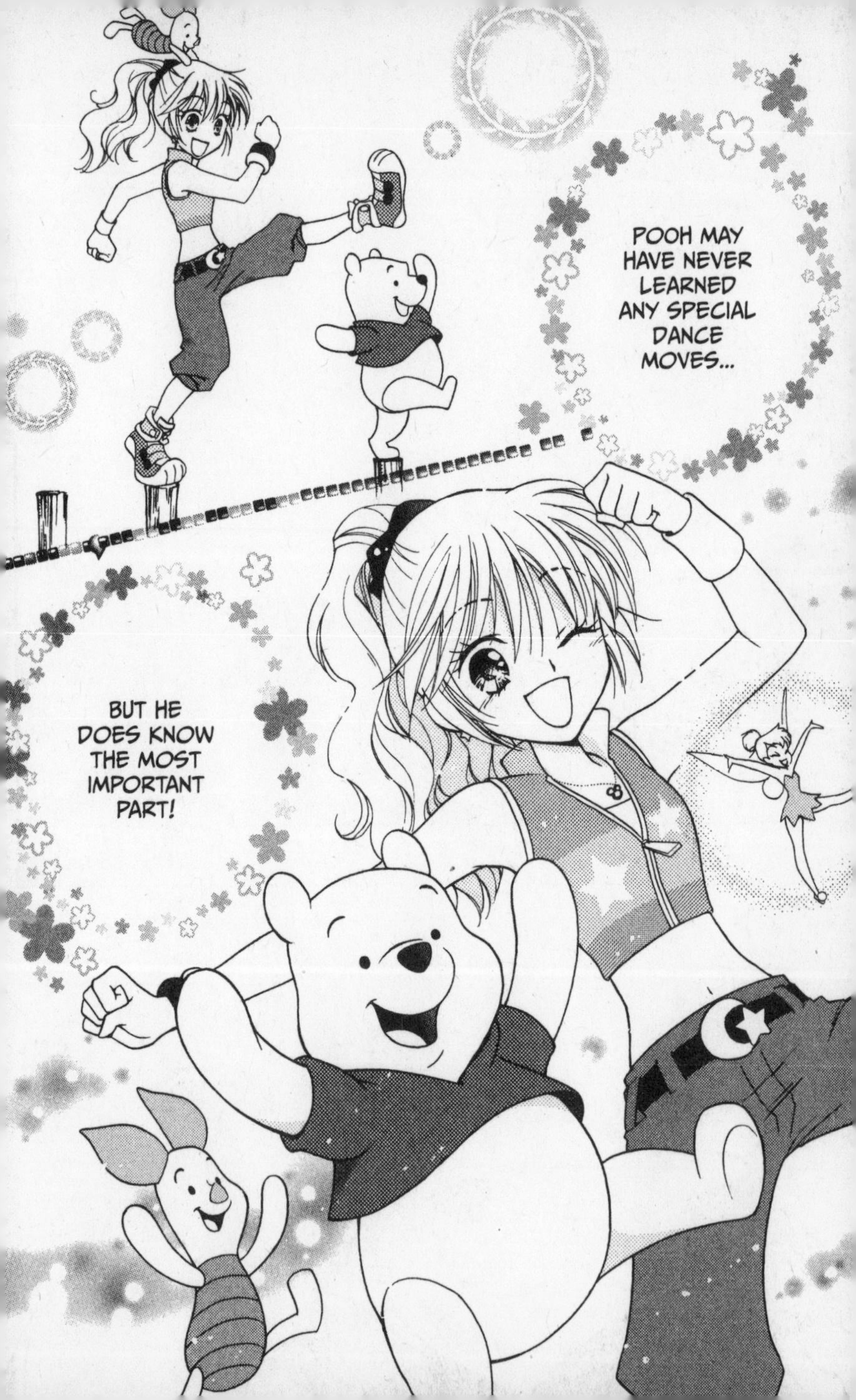
POOH MAY HAVE NEVER LEARNED ANY SPECIAL DANCE MOVES...
BUT HE DOES KNOW THE MOST IMPORTANT PART!

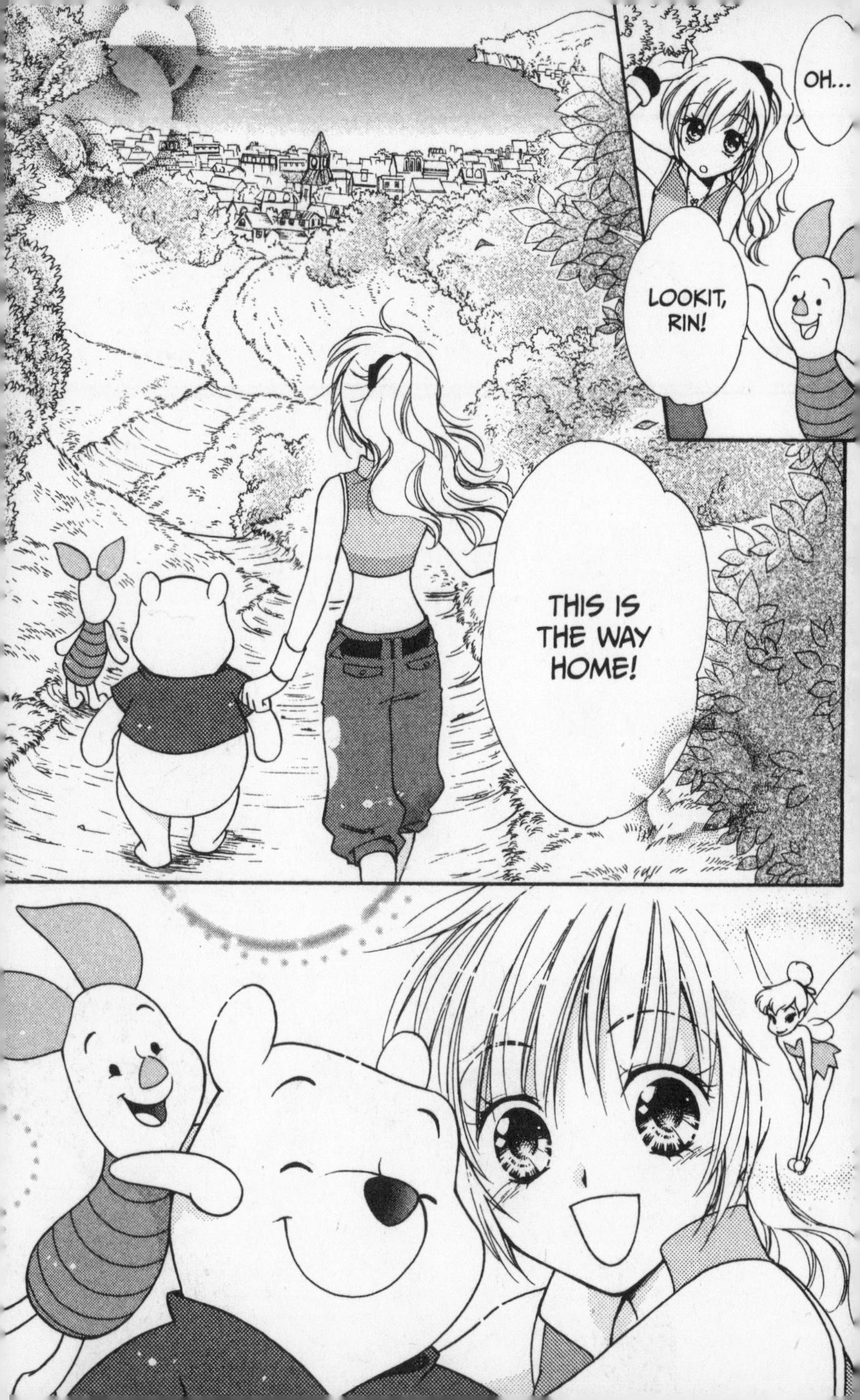
OH...
LOOKIT, RIN!
THIS IS THE WAY HOME!

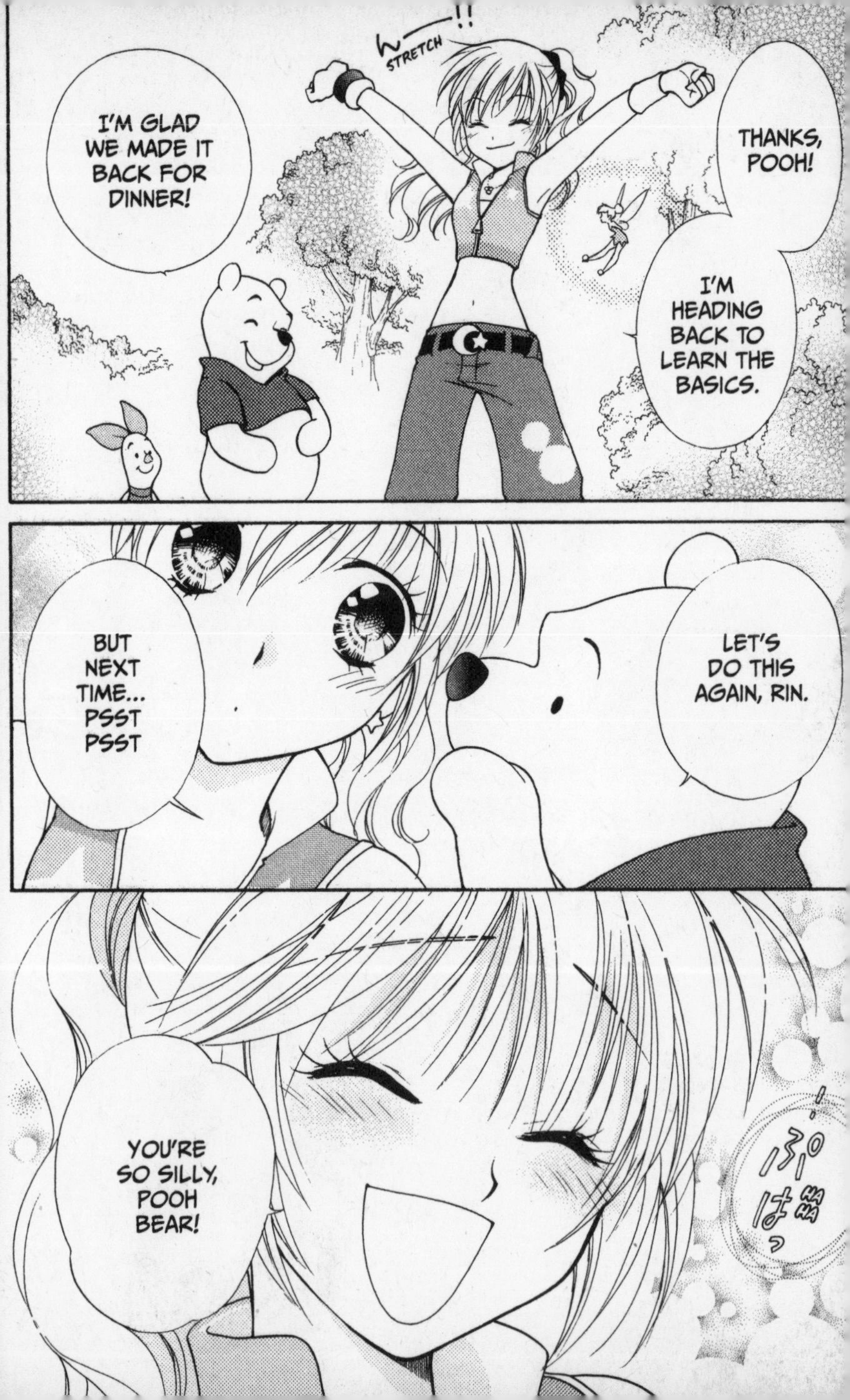
ん——!!
STRETCH
THANKS, POOH!
I'M HEADING BACK TO LEARN THE BASICS.
I'M GLAD WE MADE IT BACK FOR DINNER!
LET'S DO THIS AGAIN, RIN.
BUT NEXT TIME... PSST PSST
ぷはっ
HA HA
YOU'RE SO SILLY, POOH BEAR!

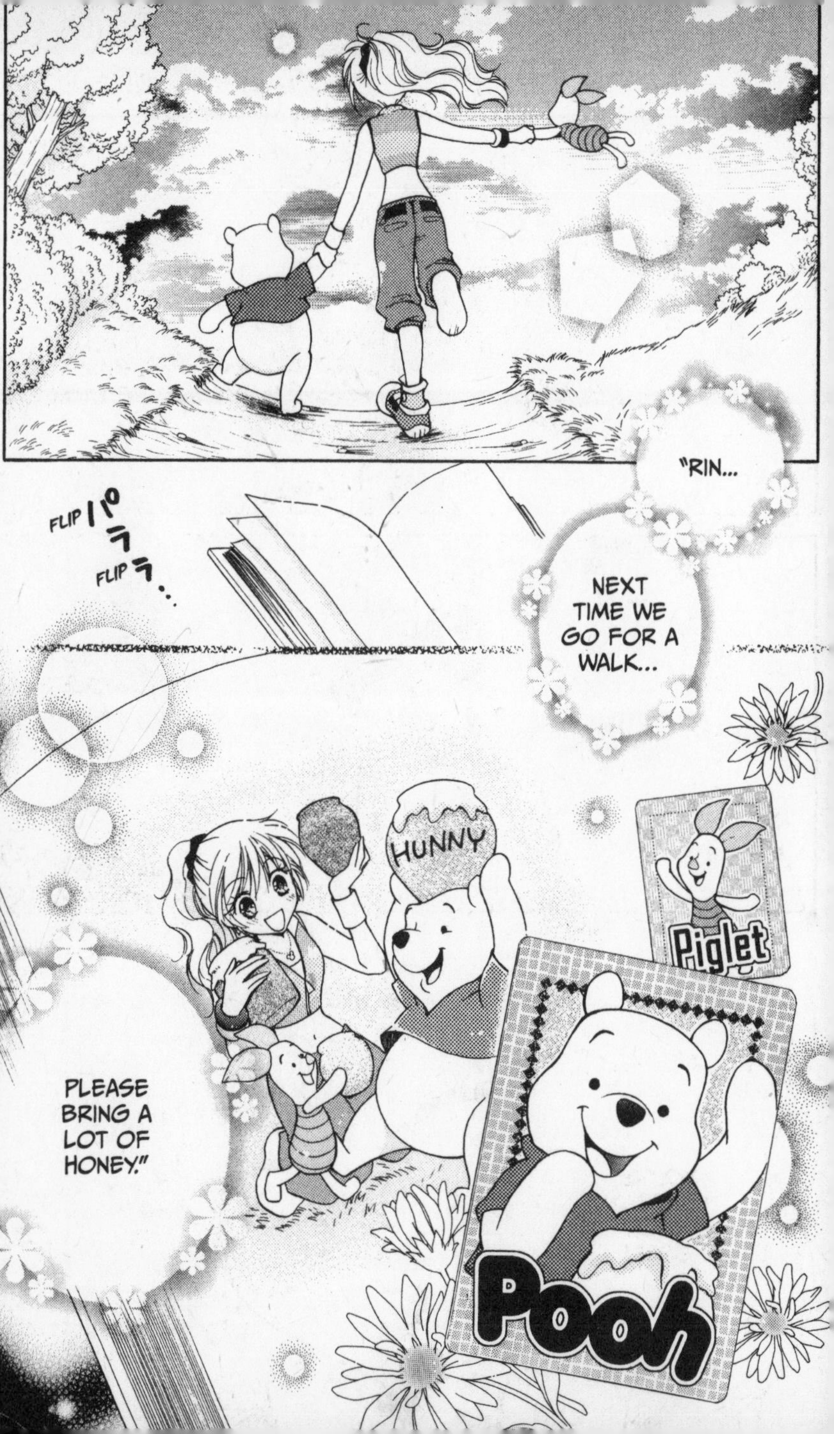
"RIN...
NEXT TIME WE GO FOR A WALK...
FLIP パラ FLIP ラ...
HUNNY
Piglet
Pooh
PLEASE BRING A LOT OF HONEY."

SIDE STORY ★ COMIC (1)

YEEAH! WHAT A BEAUTIFUL DAY.
AND TODAY...
I'M GONNA DANCE WITH POOH!
MAGICAL DANCE!!
HUNNY
I CAN'T DANCE ON AN EMPTY STOMACH.
LET'S EAT A LITTLE SNACK FIRST.
AAH, I CAN'T DANCE ON A FULL STOMACH.
WHA?!

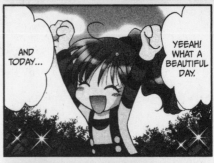

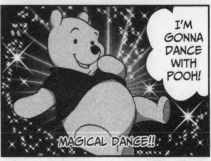

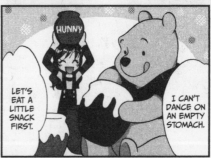

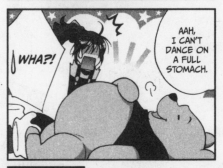

CONTINUED ON P. 52

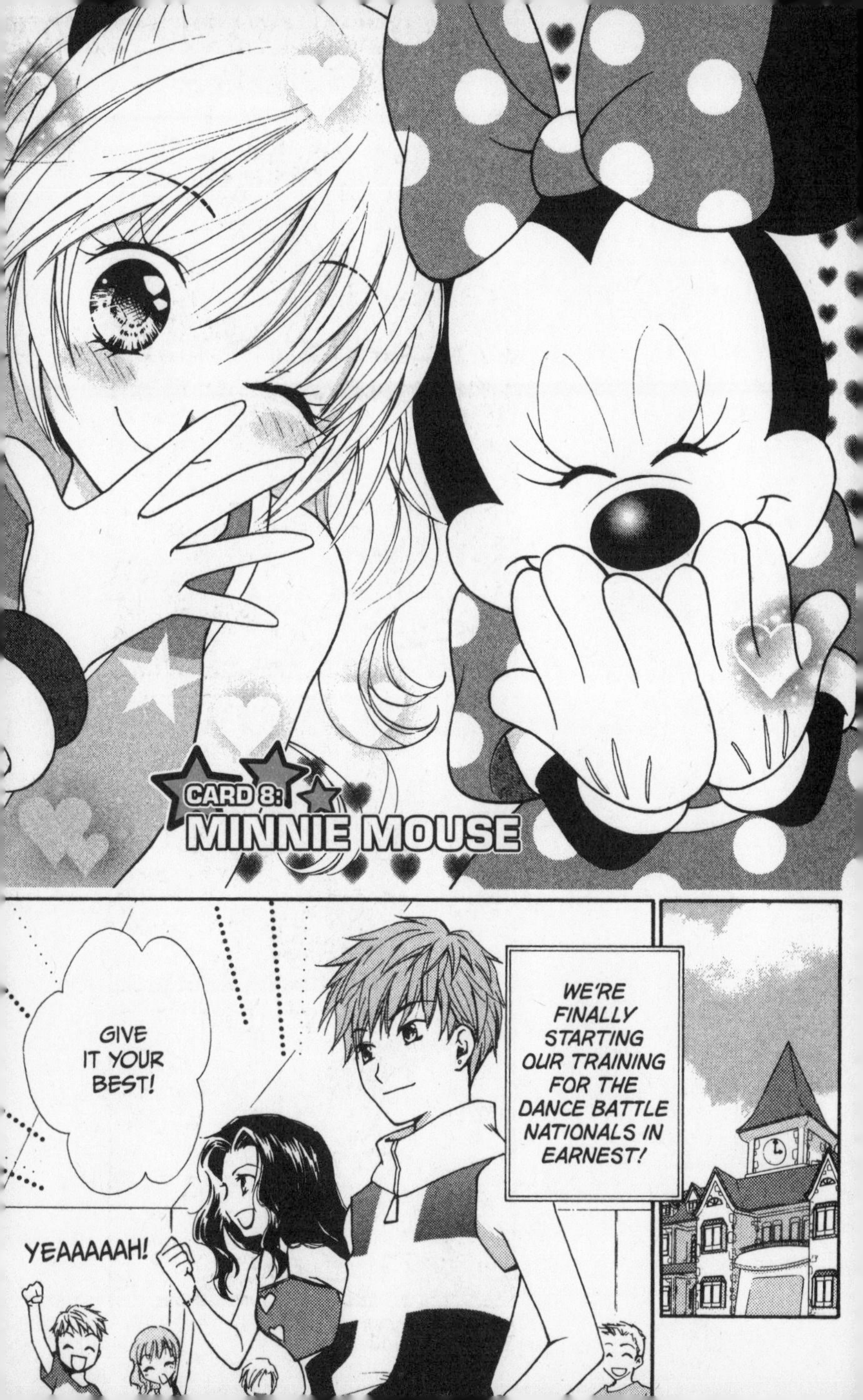
CARD 8:
MINNIE MOUSE
WE'RE FINALLY STARTING OUR TRAINING FOR THE DANCE BATTLE NATIONALS IN EARNEST!
GIVE IT YOUR BEST!
YEAAAAAH!

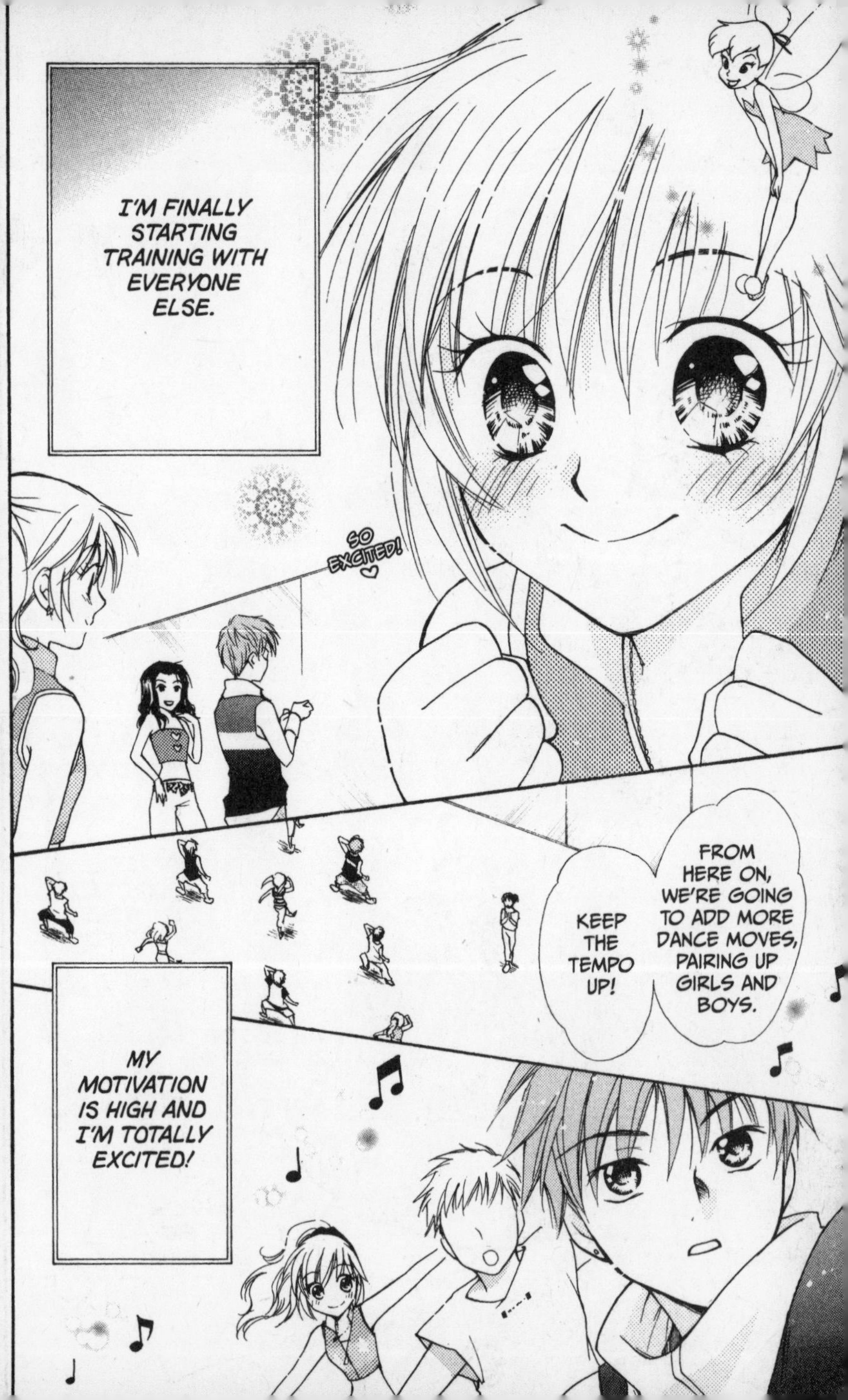
I'M FINALLY STARTING TRAINING WITH EVERYONE ELSE.
SO EXCITED!
FROM HERE ON, WE'RE GOING TO ADD MORE DANCE MOVES, PAIRING UP GIRLS AND BOYS.
KEEP THE TEMPO UP!
MY MOTIVATION IS HIGH AND I'M TOTALLY EXCITED!

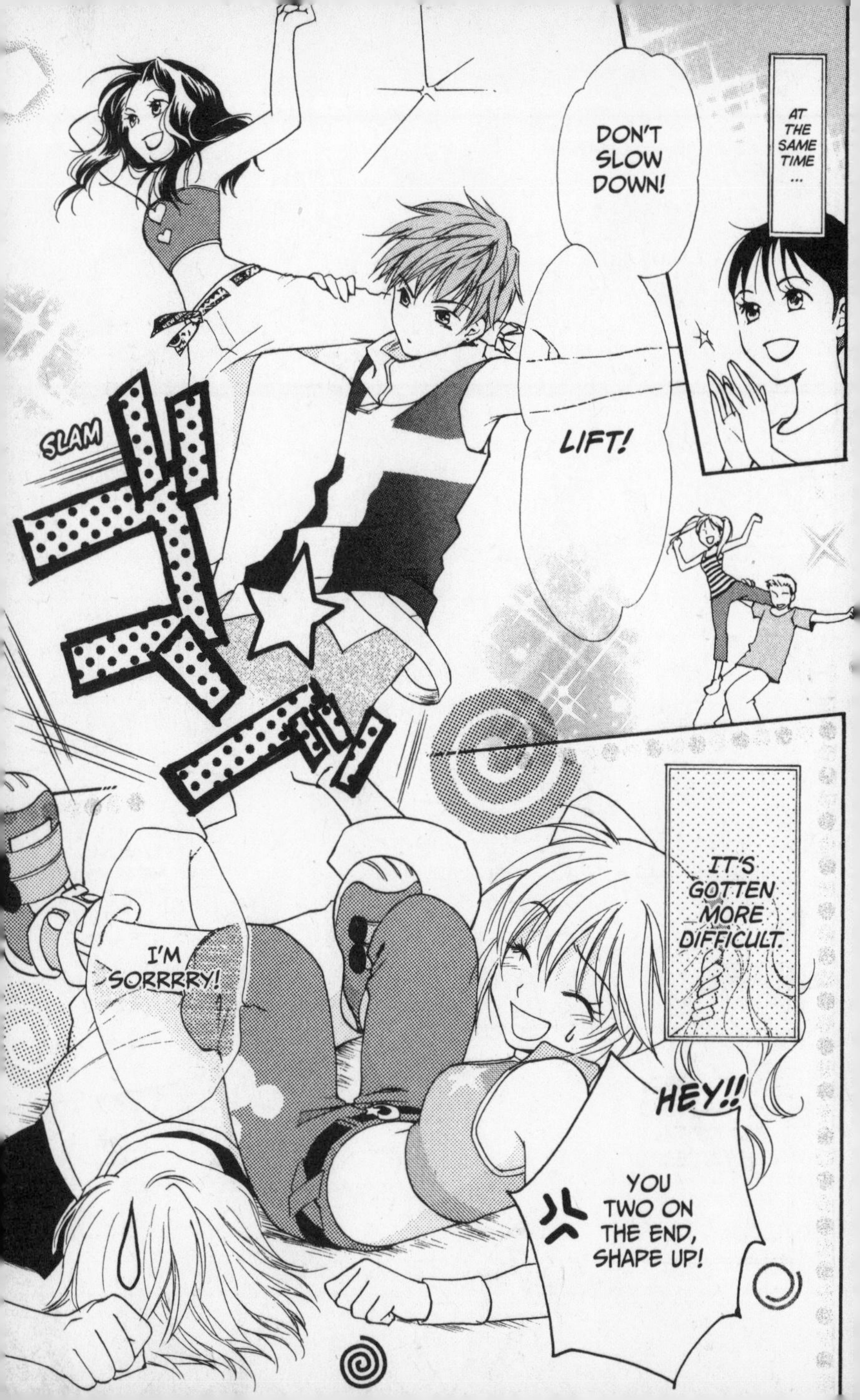
AT THE SAME TIME ...
DON'T SLOW DOWN!
LIFT!
SLAM
IT'S GOTTEN MORE DIFFICULT.
HEY!!
YOU TWO ON THE END, SHAPE UP!
I'M SORRRRY!

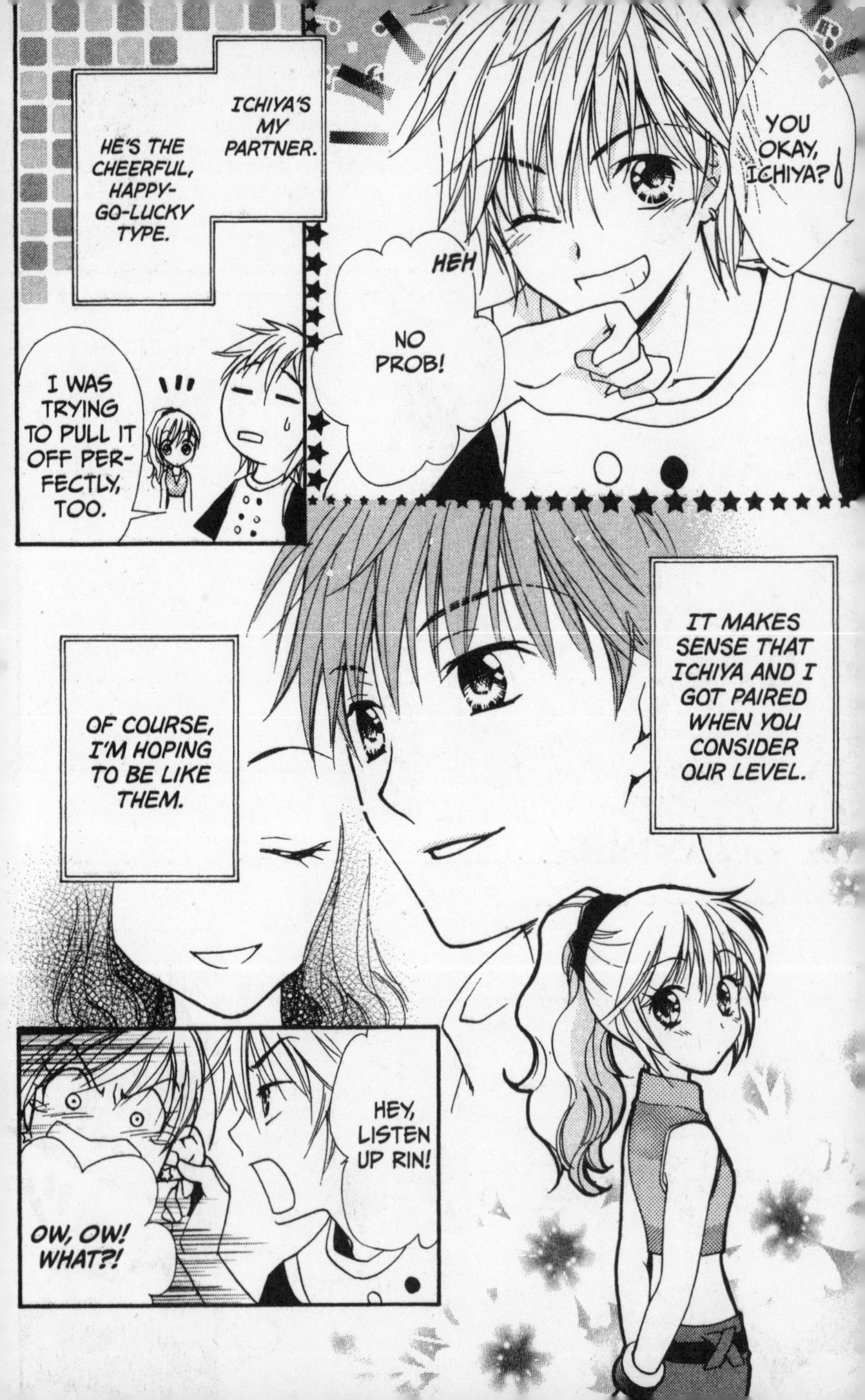
YOU OKAY, ICHIYA?
HEH
NO PROB!
ICHIYA'S MY PARTNER.
HE'S THE CHEERFUL, HAPPY-GO-LUCKY TYPE.
I WAS TRYING TO PULL IT OFF PERFECTLY, TOO.
IT MAKES SENSE THAT ICHIYA AND I GOT PAIRED WHEN YOU CONSIDER OUR LEVEL.
OF COURSE, I'M HOPING TO BE LIKE THEM.
HEY, LISTEN UP RIN!
OW, OW! WHAT?!

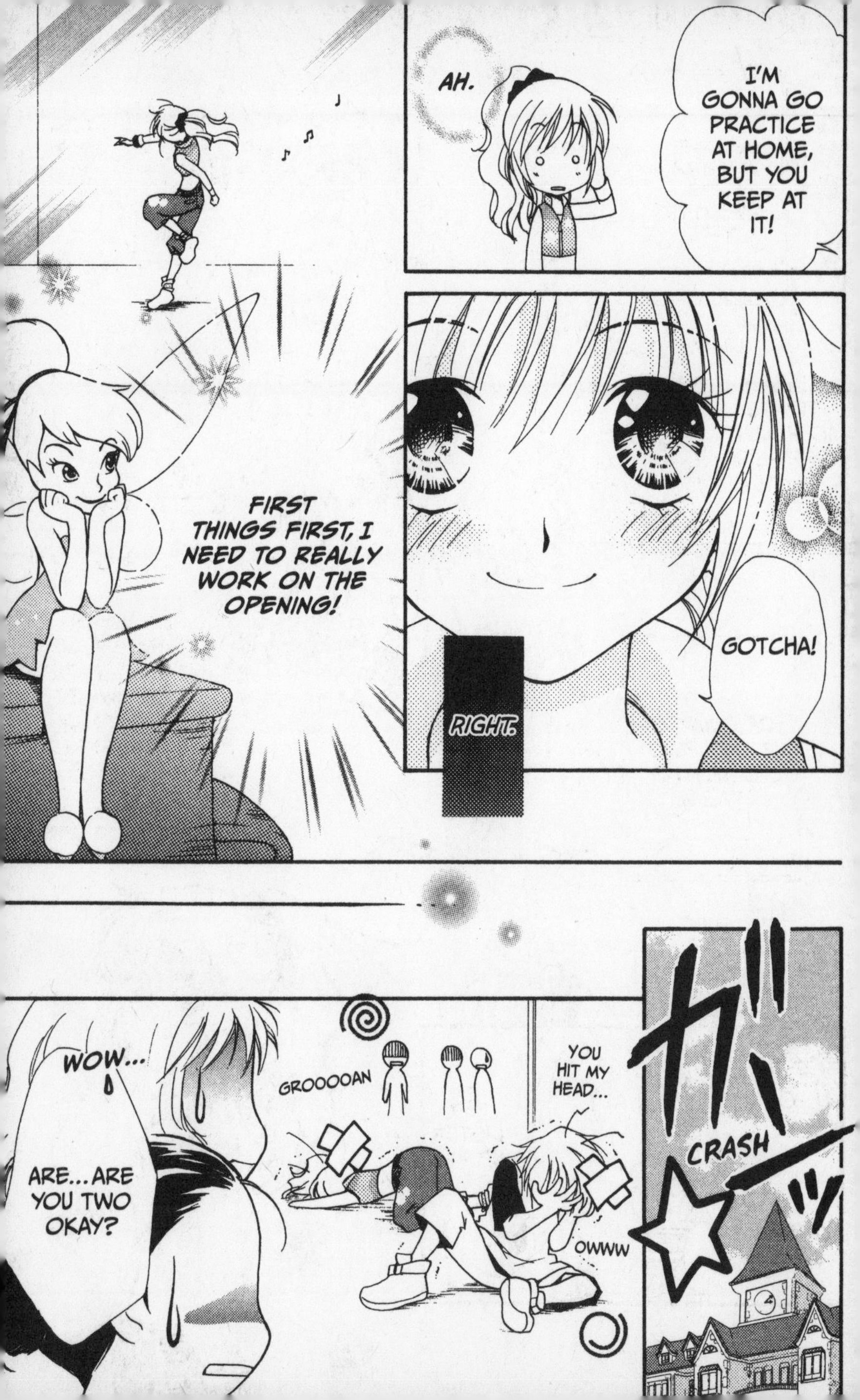
I'M GONNA GO PRACTICE AT HOME, BUT YOU KEEP AT IT!
AH.
GOTCHA!
RIGHT.
FIRST THINGS FIRST, I NEED TO REALLY WORK ON THE OPENING!
ガッ
CRASH
YOU HIT MY HEAD...
OWWW
GROOOOAN
WOW...
ARE...ARE YOU TWO OKAY?

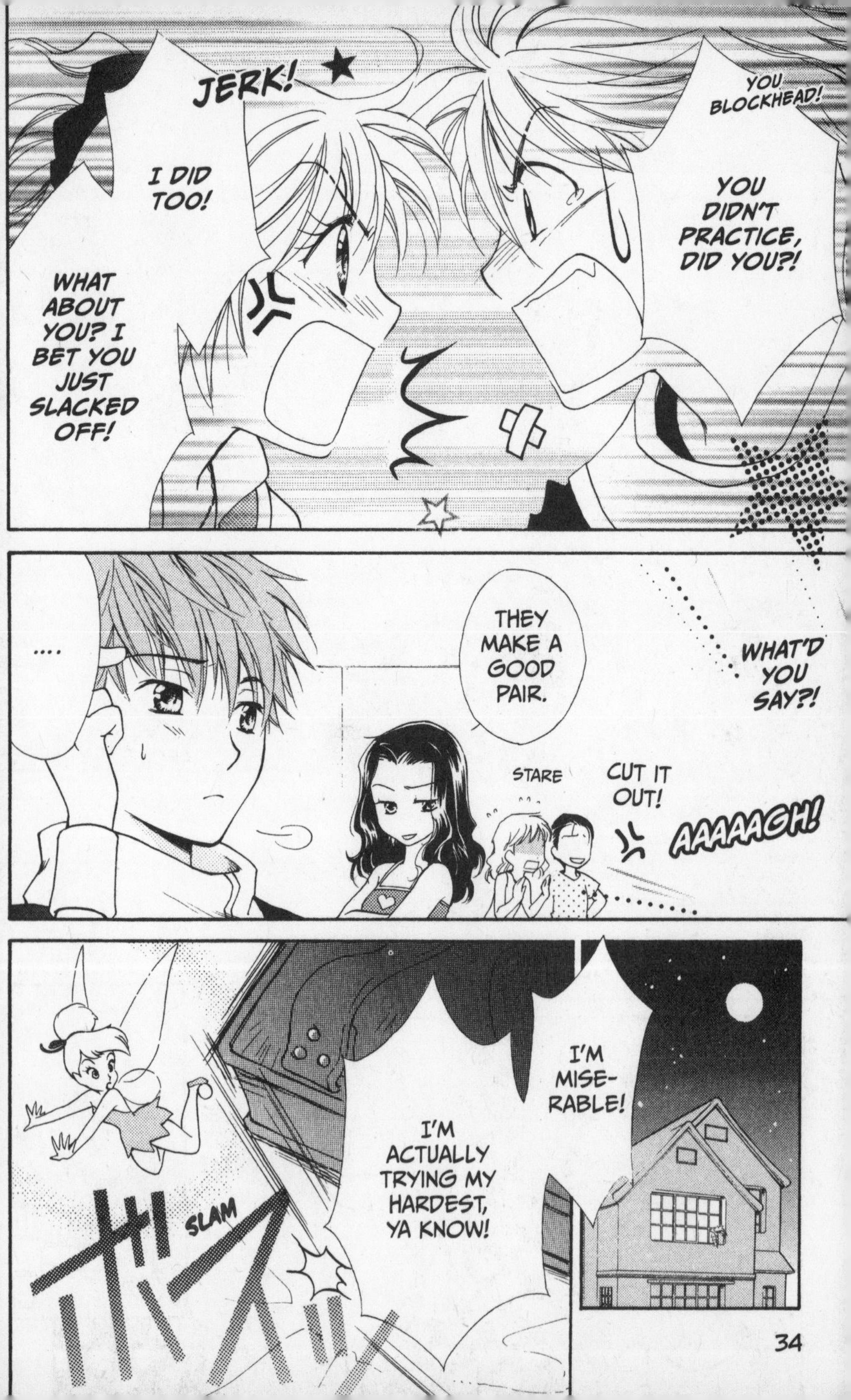
YOU BLOCKHEAD!
YOU DIDN'T PRACTICE, DID YOU?!
JERK!
I DID TOO!
WHAT ABOUT YOU? I BET YOU JUST SLACKED OFF!
WHAT'D YOU SAY?!
AAAAAGH!
CUT IT OUT!
STARE
THEY MAKE A GOOD PAIR.
....
I'M MISE-RABLE!
I'M ACTUALLY TRYING MY HARDEST, YA KNOW!
SLAM

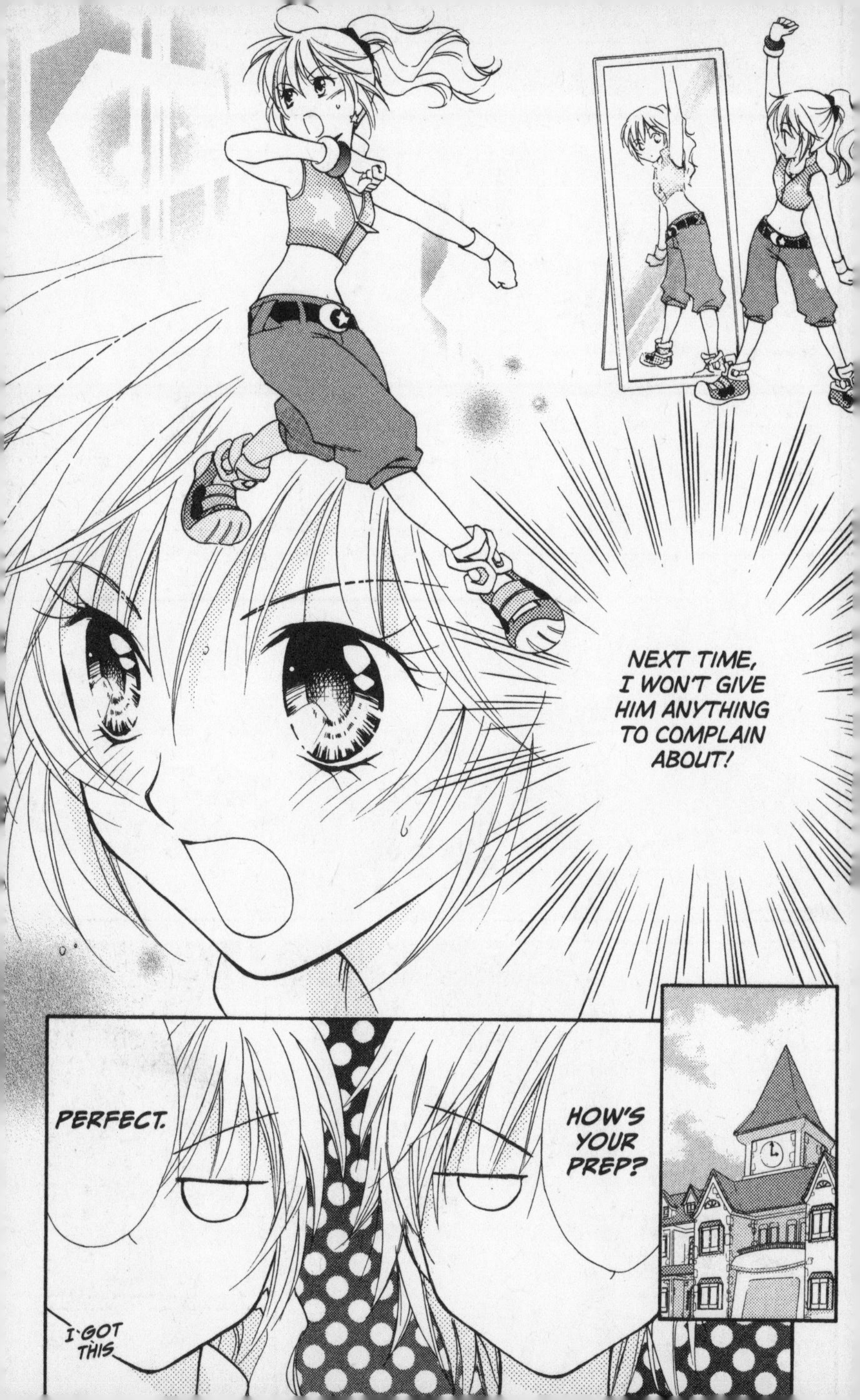
NEXT TIME, I WON'T GIVE HIM ANYTHING TO COMPLAIN ABOUT!
HOW'S YOUR PREP?
PERFECT.
I GOT THIS

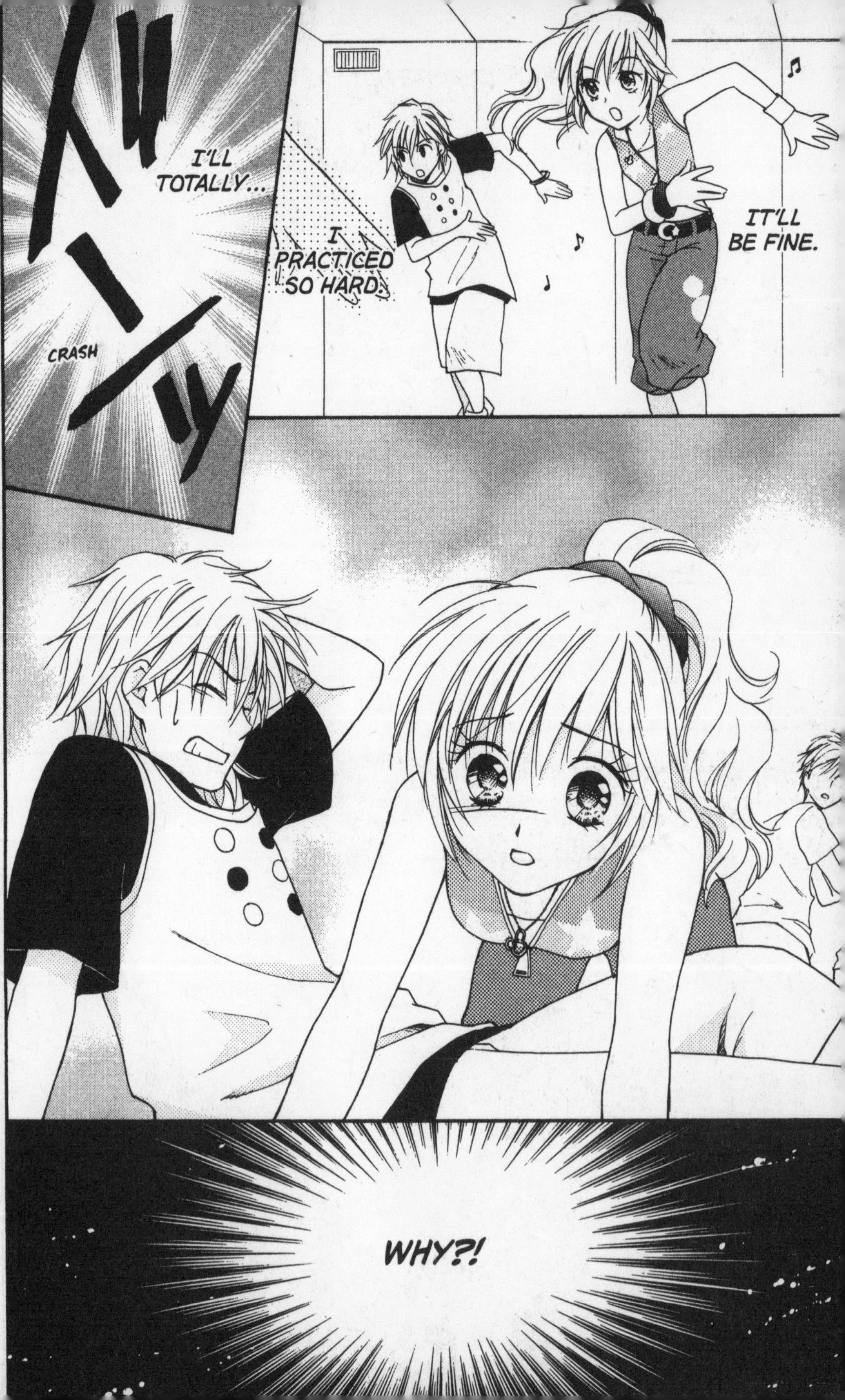
IT'LL BE FINE.
I PRACTICED SO HARD.
I'LL TOTALLY...
CRASH
WHY?!

READ THIS WAY

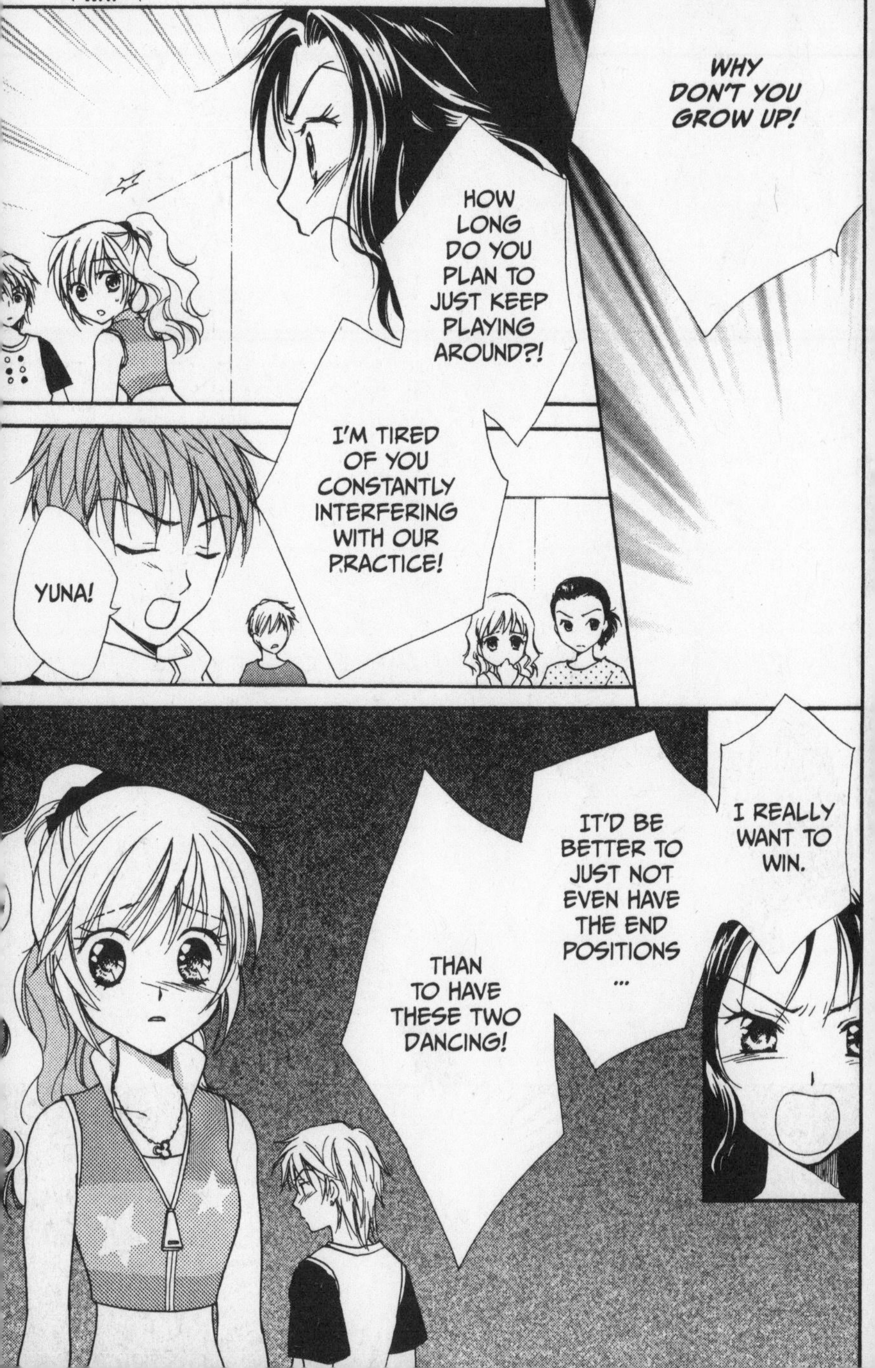
WHY DON'T YOU GROW UP!
HOW LONG DO YOU PLAN TO JUST KEEP PLAYING AROUND?!
I'M TIRED OF YOU CONSTANTLY INTERFERING WITH OUR PRACTICE!
YUNA!
I REALLY WANT TO WIN.
IT'D BE BETTER TO JUST NOT EVEN HAVE THE END POSITIONS ...
THAN TO HAVE THESE TWO DANCING!

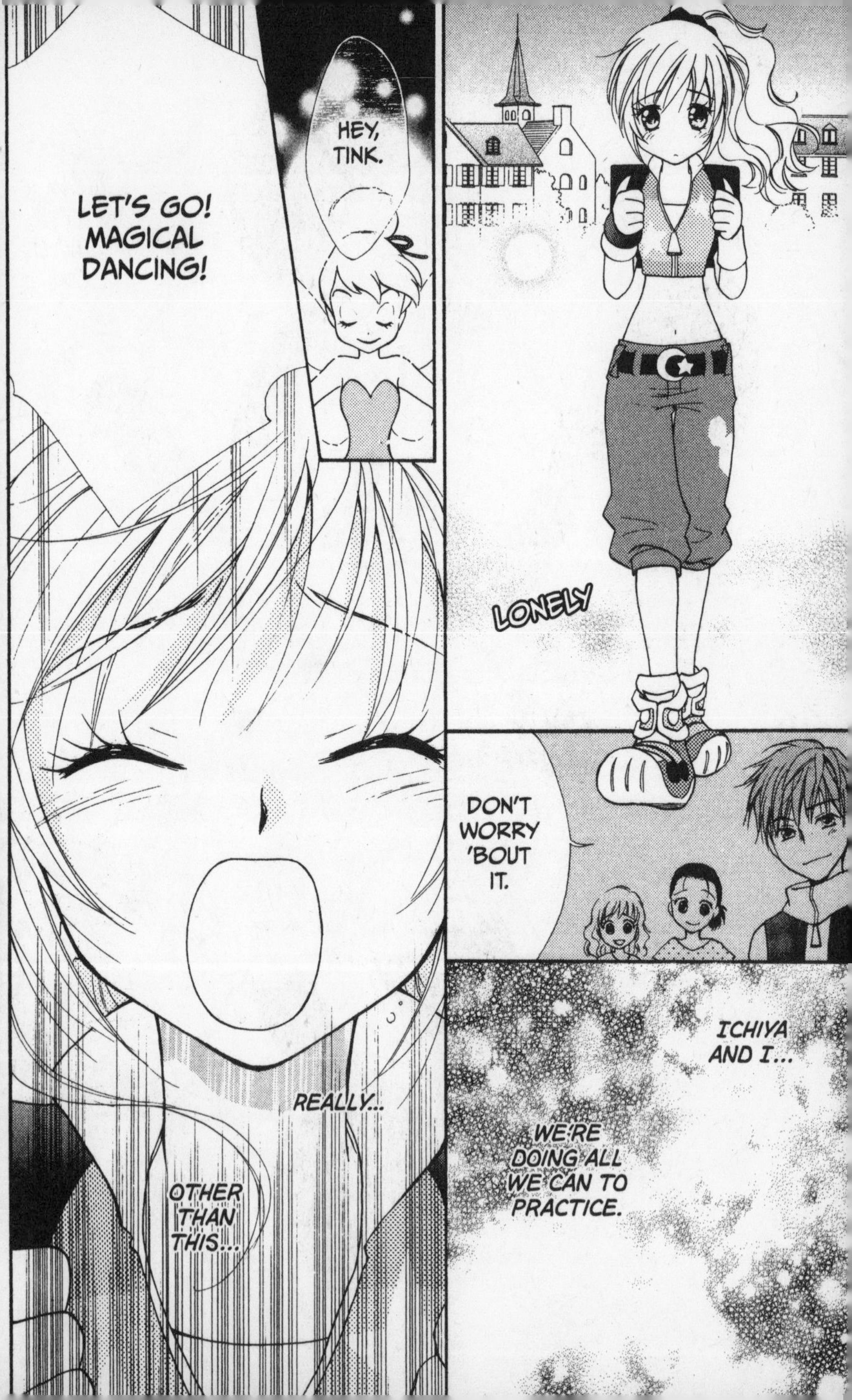
LONELY
DON'T WORRY 'BOUT IT.
ICHIYA AND I...
WE'RE DOING ALL WE CAN TO PRACTICE.
HEY, TINK.
LET'S GO! MAGICAL DANCING!
REALLY...
OTHER THAN THIS...

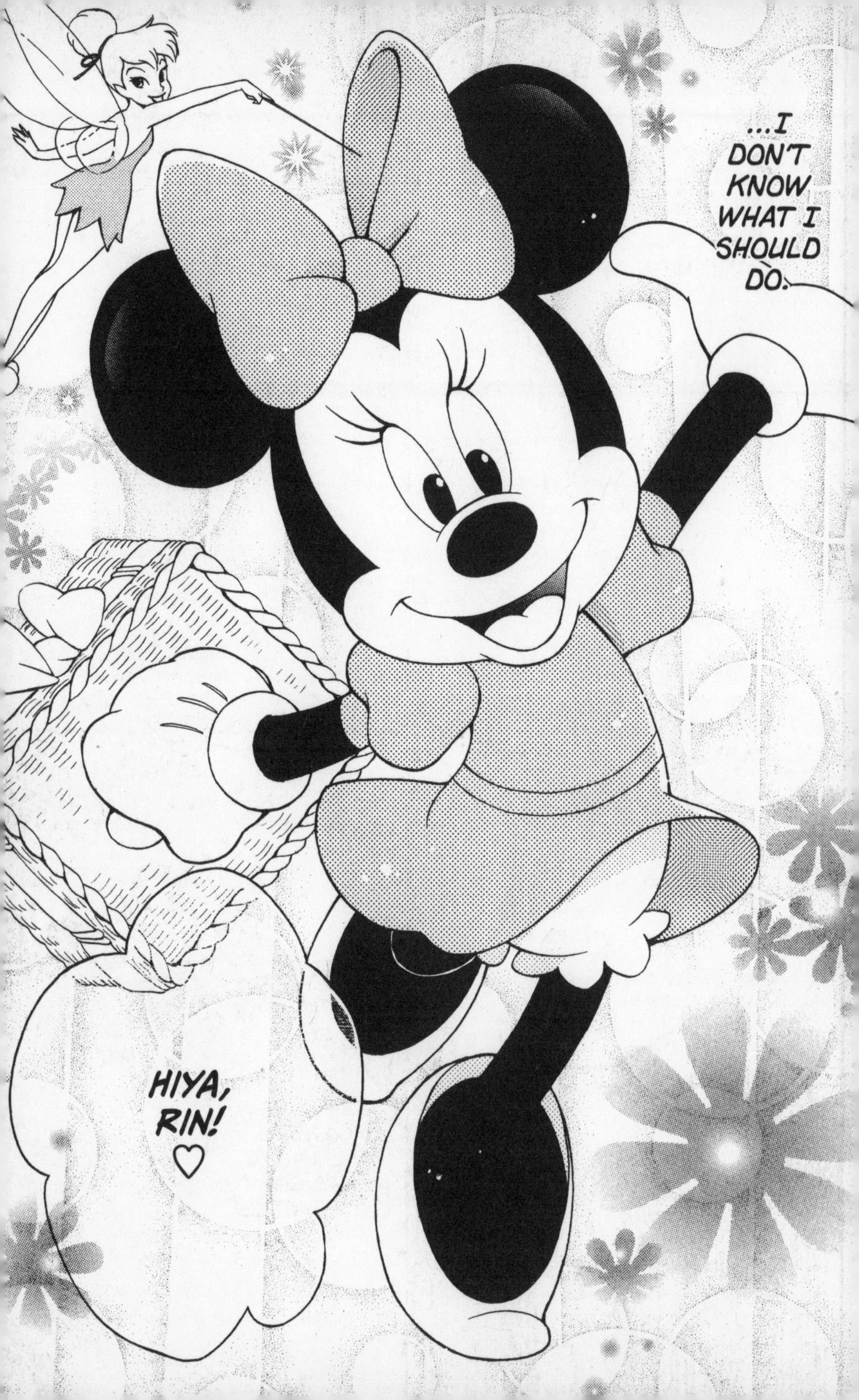
...I DON'T KNOW WHAT I SHOULD DO.
HIYA, RIN! ♡

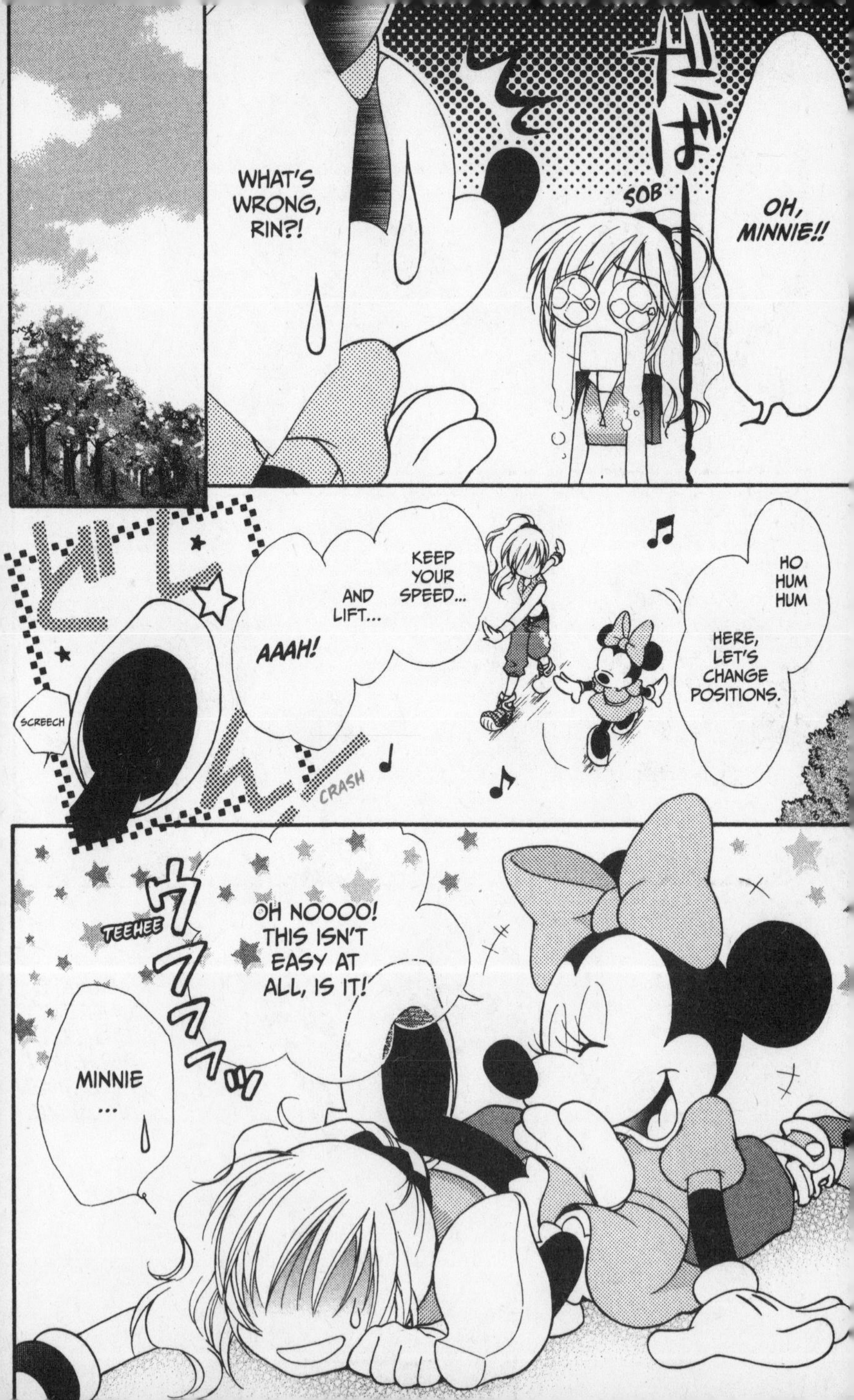
OH, MINNIE!!
SOB
WHAT'S WRONG, RIN?!
HO HUM HUM
HERE, LET'S CHANGE POSITIONS.
KEEP YOUR SPEED...
AND LIFT...
AAAH!
SCREECH
CRASH
OH NOOOO! THIS ISN'T EASY AT ALL, IS IT!
TEEHEE
MINNIE ...

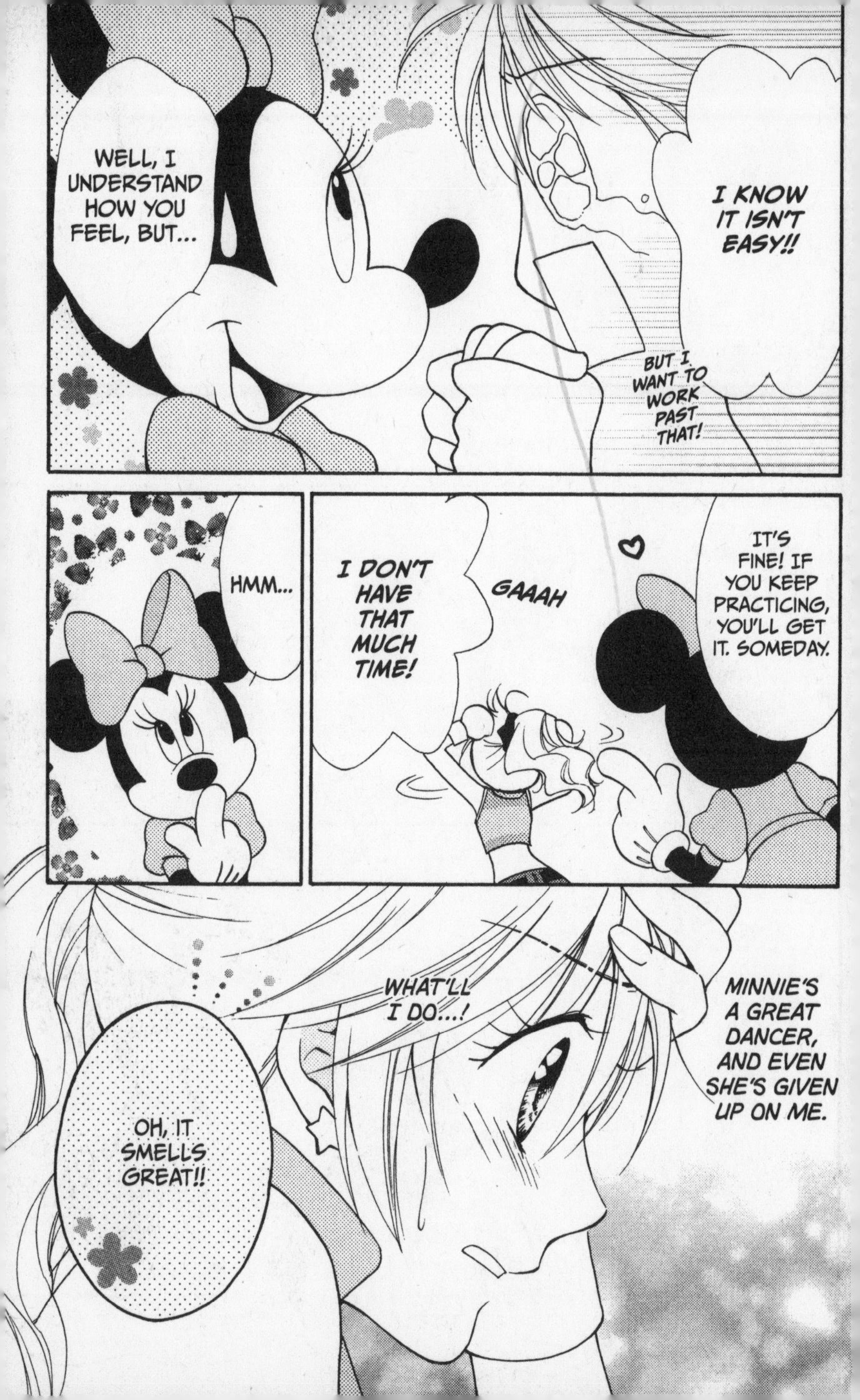
I KNOW IT ISN'T EASY!!
BUT I WANT TO WORK PAST THAT!
WELL, I UNDERSTAND HOW YOU FEEL, BUT...
IT'S FINE! IF YOU KEEP PRACTICING, YOU'LL GET IT. SOMEDAY.
GAAAH
I DON'T HAVE THAT MUCH TIME!
HMM...
MINNIE'S A GREAT DANCER, AND EVEN SHE'S GIVEN UP ON ME.
WHAT'LL I DO...!
OH, IT SMELLS GREAT!!

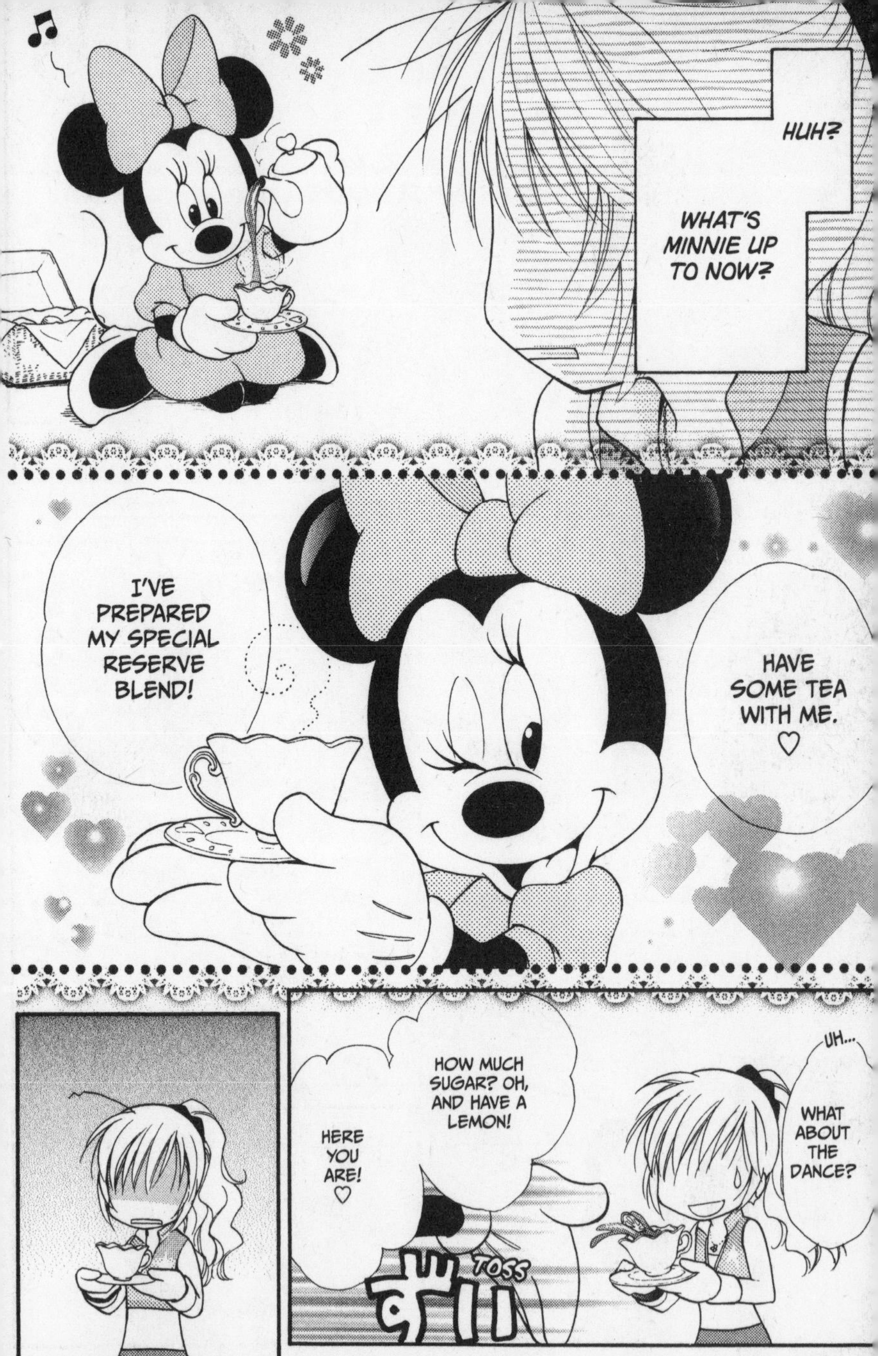
HUH?
WHAT'S MINNIE UP TO NOW?
HAVE SOME TEA WITH ME. ♡
I'VE PREPARED MY SPECIAL RESERVE BLEND!
UH...
WHAT ABOUT THE DANCE?
HOW MUCH SUGAR? OH, AND HAVE A LEMON!
HERE YOU ARE! ♡
TOSS

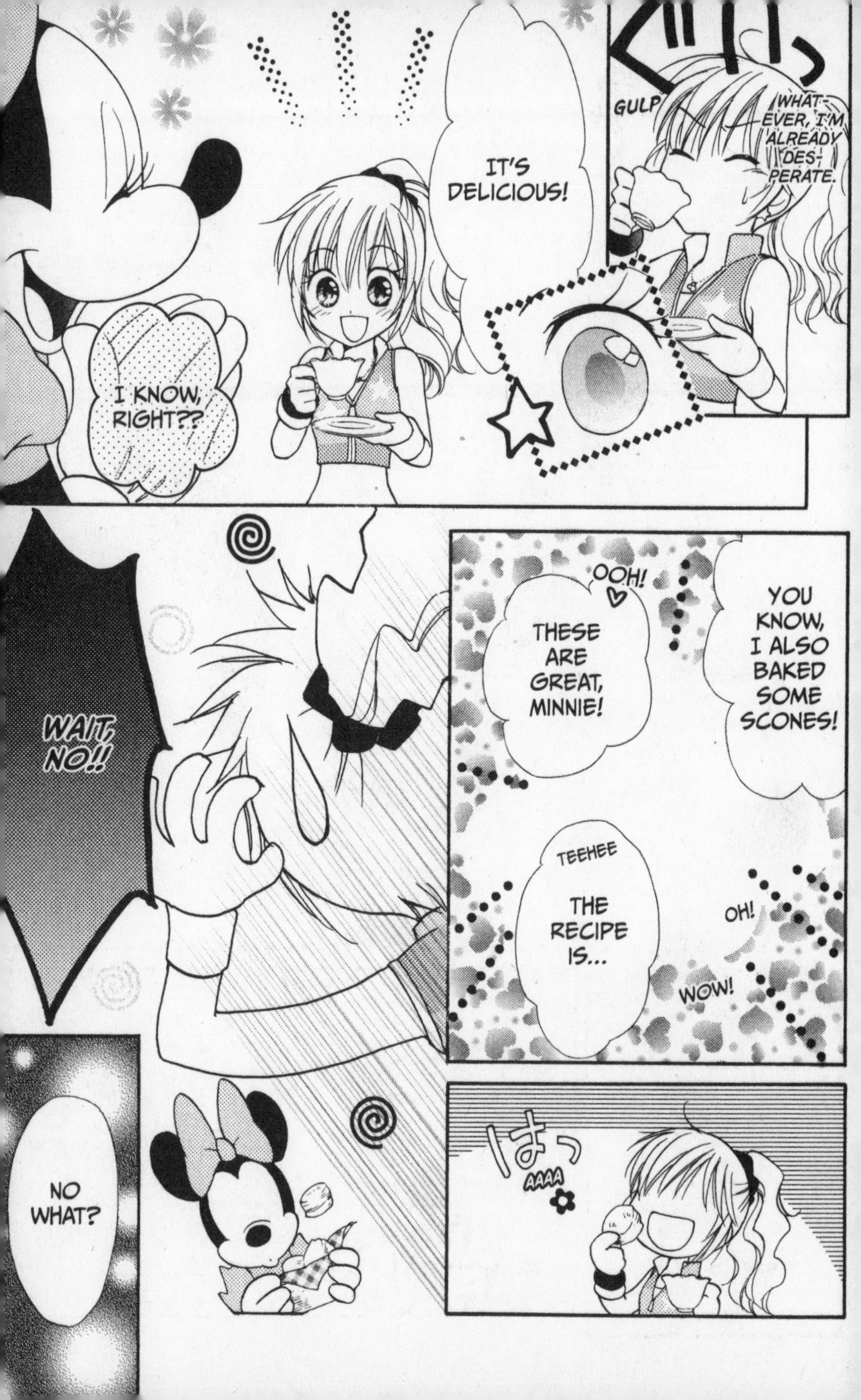
ぐいっ
GULP
WHAT-EVER, I'M ALREADY DES-PERATE.
IT'S DELICIOUS!
I KNOW, RIGHT??
YOU KNOW, I ALSO BAKED SOME SCONES!
OOH! ♡
THESE ARE GREAT, MINNIE!
OH!
TEEHEE
THE RECIPE IS...
WOW!
はっ
AAAA
WAIT, NO!!
NO WHAT?

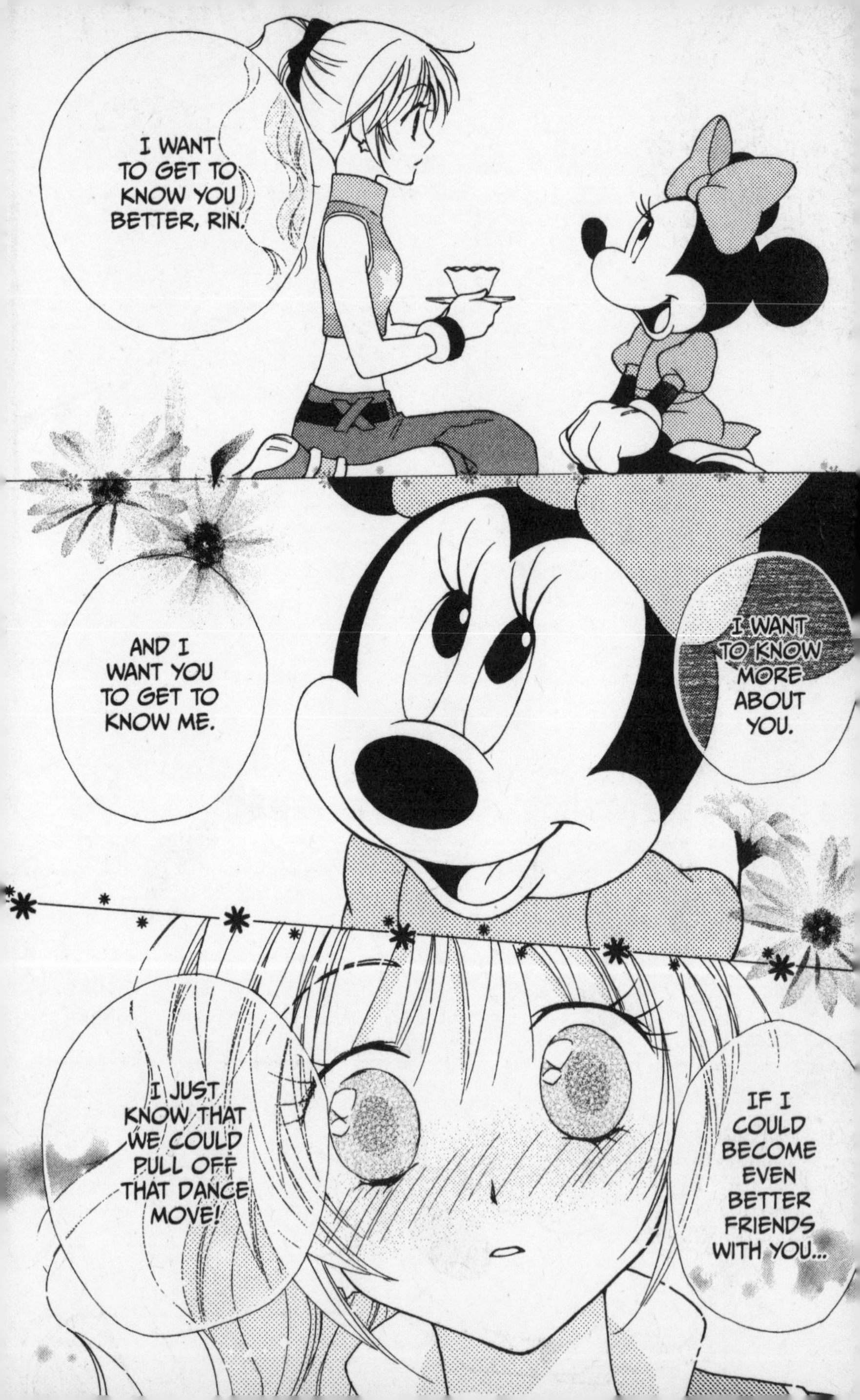
I WANT TO GET TO KNOW YOU BETTER, RIN.
I WANT TO KNOW MORE ABOUT YOU.
AND I WANT YOU TO GET TO KNOW ME.
IF I COULD BECOME EVEN BETTER FRIENDS WITH YOU...
I JUST KNOW THAT WE COULD PULL OFF THAT DANCE MOVE!

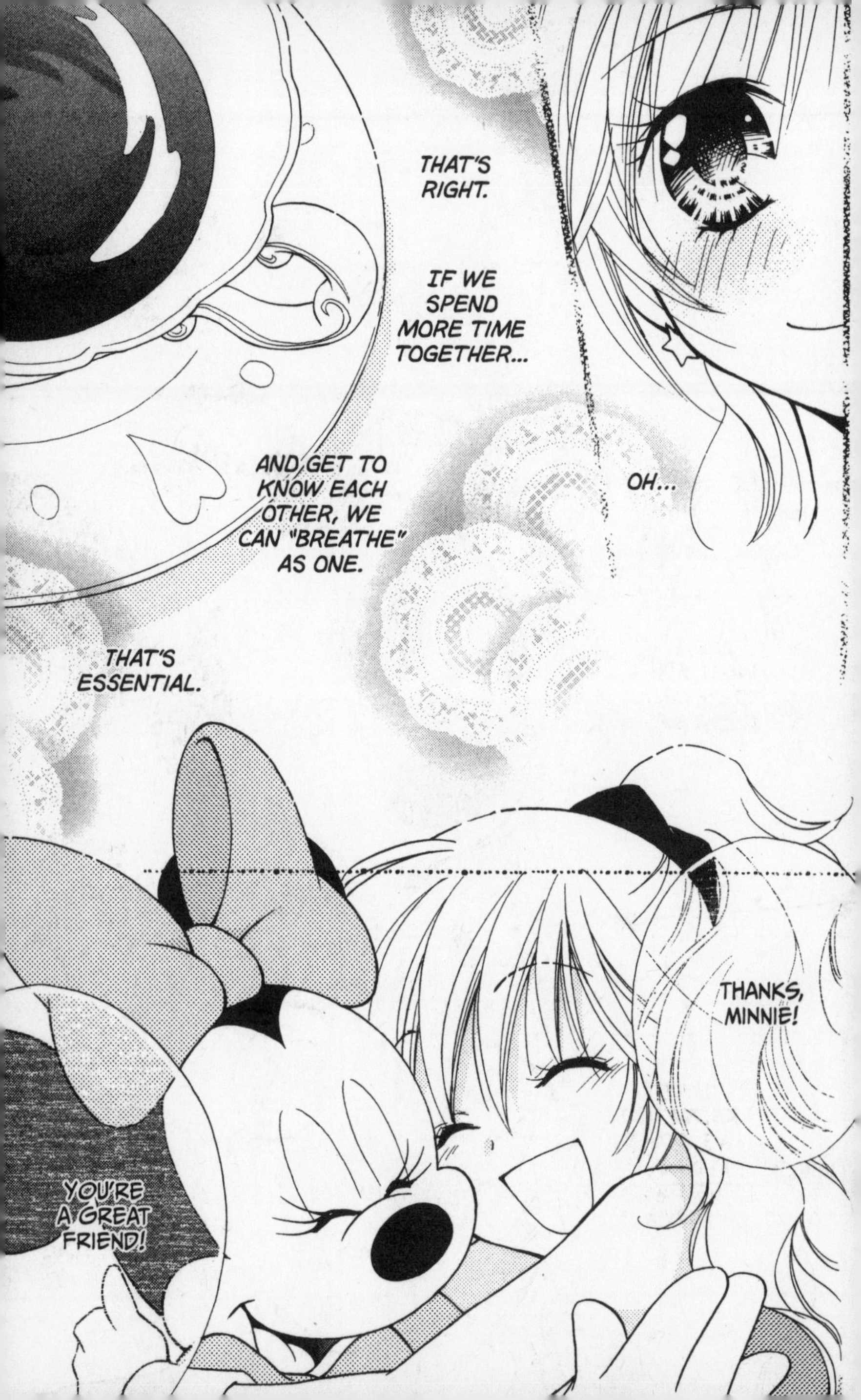
THAT'S RIGHT.
IF WE SPEND MORE TIME TOGETHER...
OH...
AND GET TO KNOW EACH OTHER, WE CAN "BREATHE" AS ONE.
THAT'S ESSENTIAL.
THANKS, MINNIE!
YOU'RE A GREAT FRIEND!

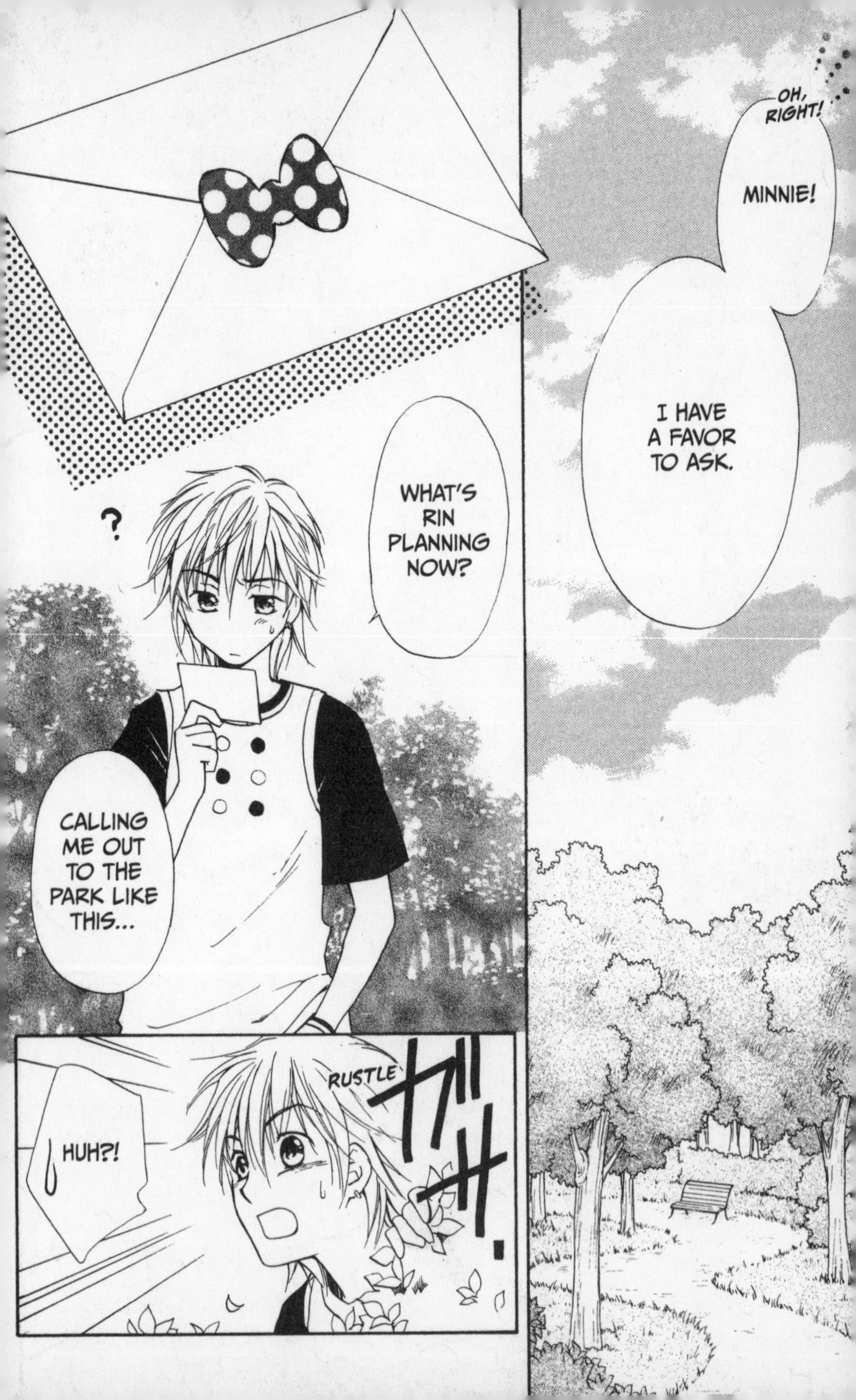
OH, RIGHT!
MINNIE!
I HAVE A FAVOR TO ASK.
WHAT'S RIN PLANNING NOW?
?
CALLING ME OUT TO THE PARK LIKE THIS...
RUSTLE
HUH?!

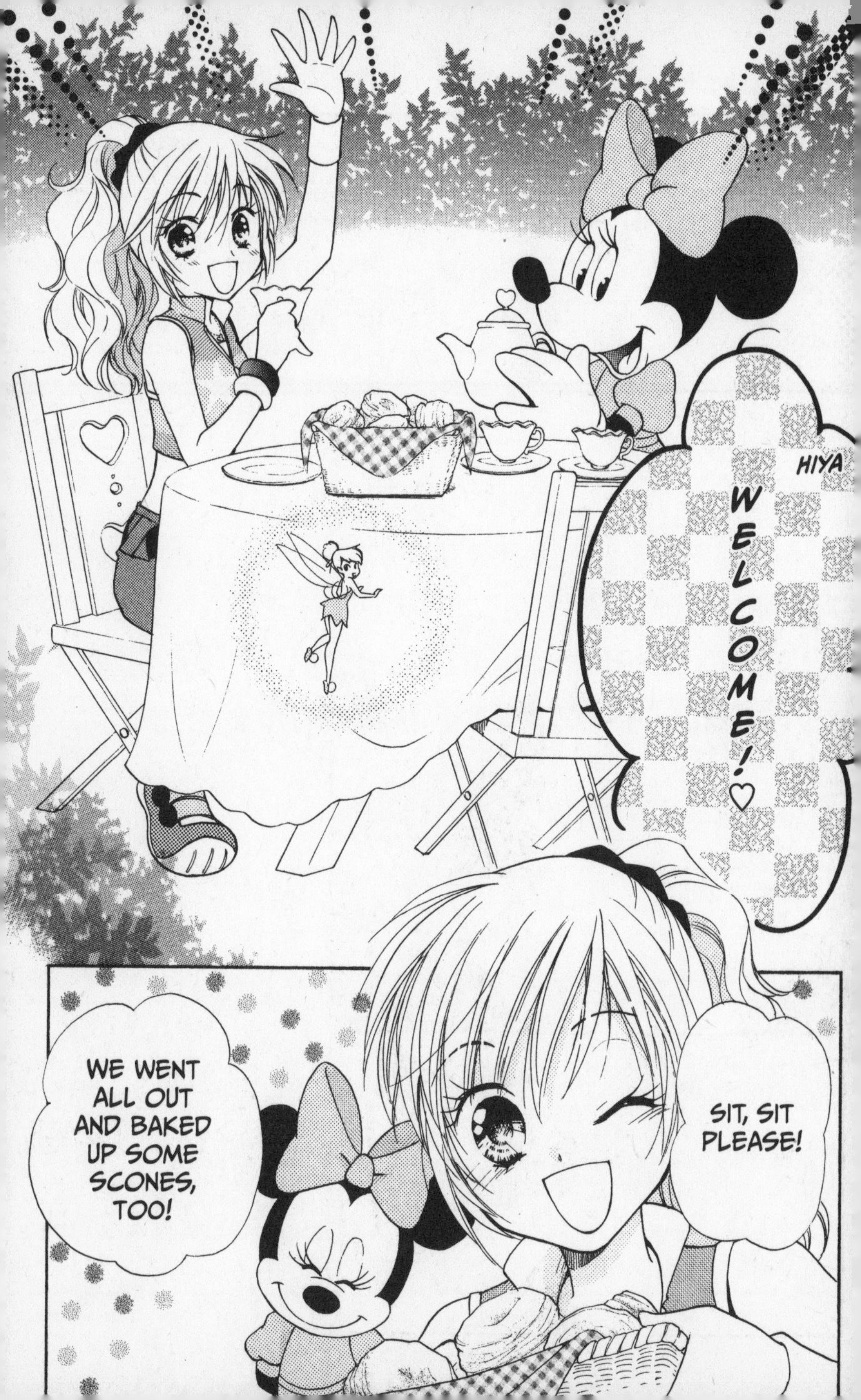
HIYA
WELCOME!♥
SIT, SIT PLEASE!
WE WENT ALL OUT AND BAKED UP SOME SCONES, TOO!

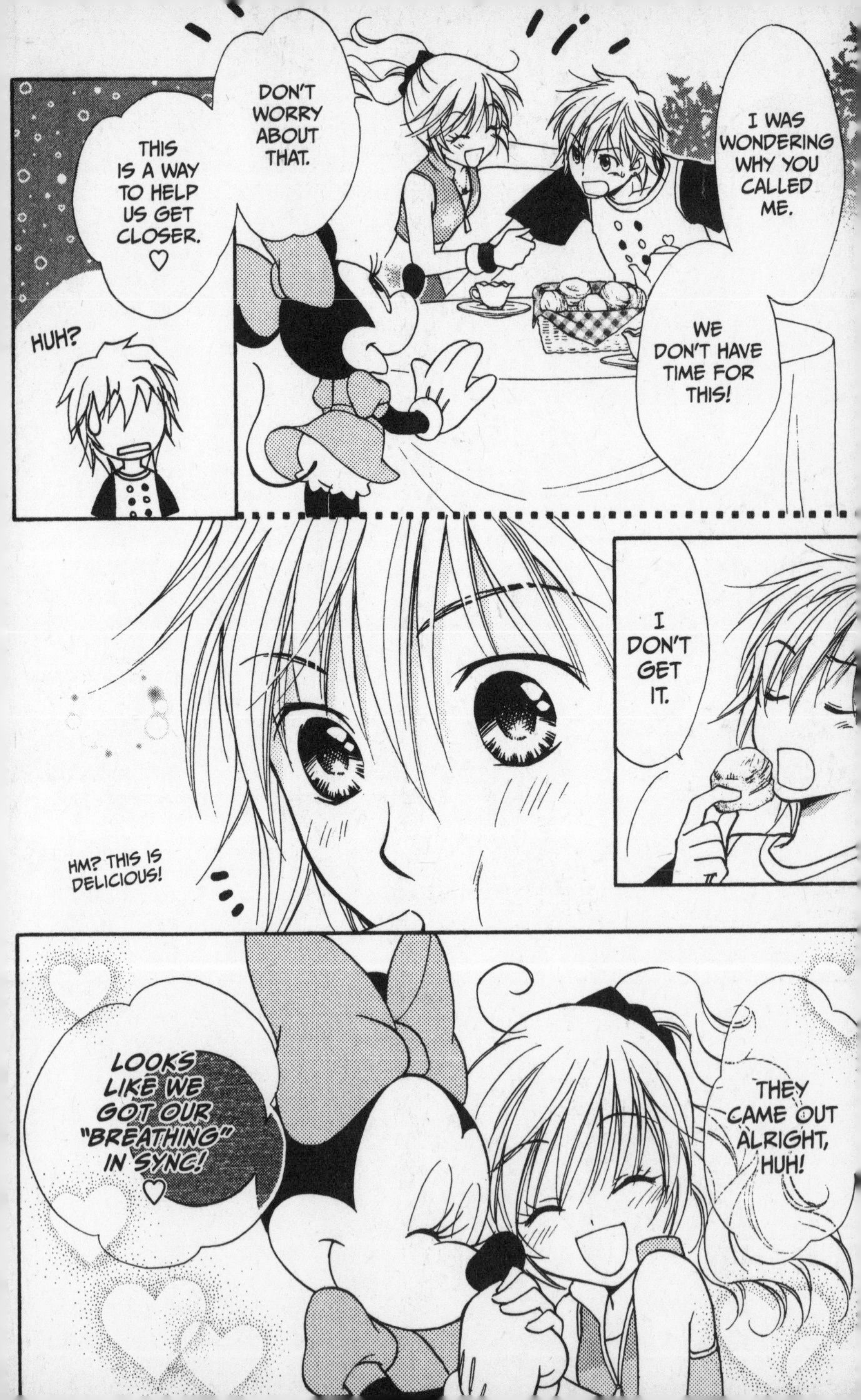
I WAS WONDERING WHY YOU CALLED ME.
WE DON'T HAVE TIME FOR THIS!
DON'T WORRY ABOUT THAT.
THIS IS A WAY TO HELP US GET CLOSER. ♡
HUH?
I DON'T GET IT.
HM? THIS IS DELICIOUS!
THEY CAME OUT ALRIGHT, HUH!
LOOKS LIKE WE GOT OUR "BREATHING" IN SYNC! ♡

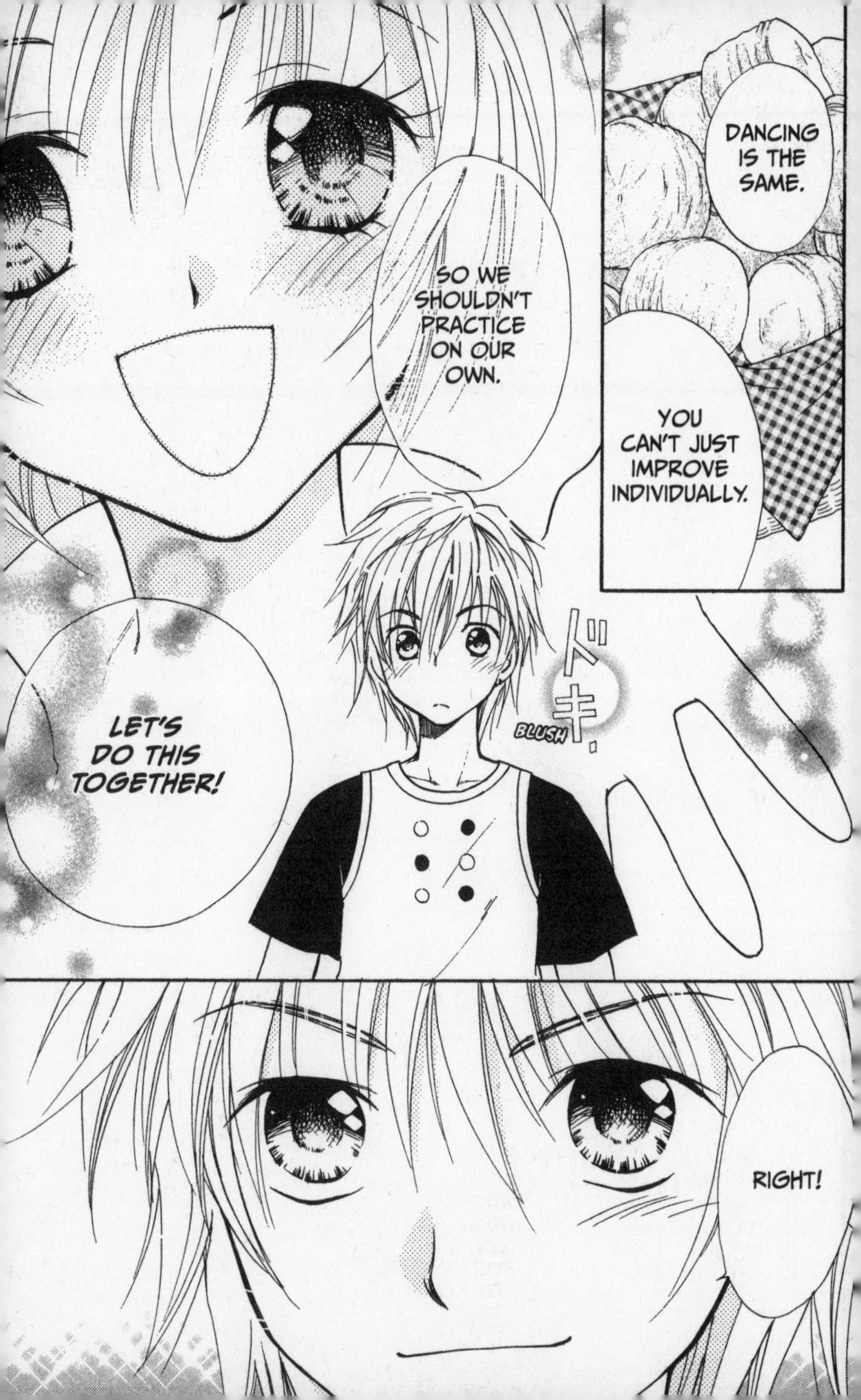
DANCING IS THE SAME.
YOU CAN'T JUST IMPROVE INDIVIDUALLY.
SO WE SHOULDN'T PRACTICE ON OUR OWN.
ドキ
BLUSH
LET'S DO THIS TOGETHER!
RIGHT!

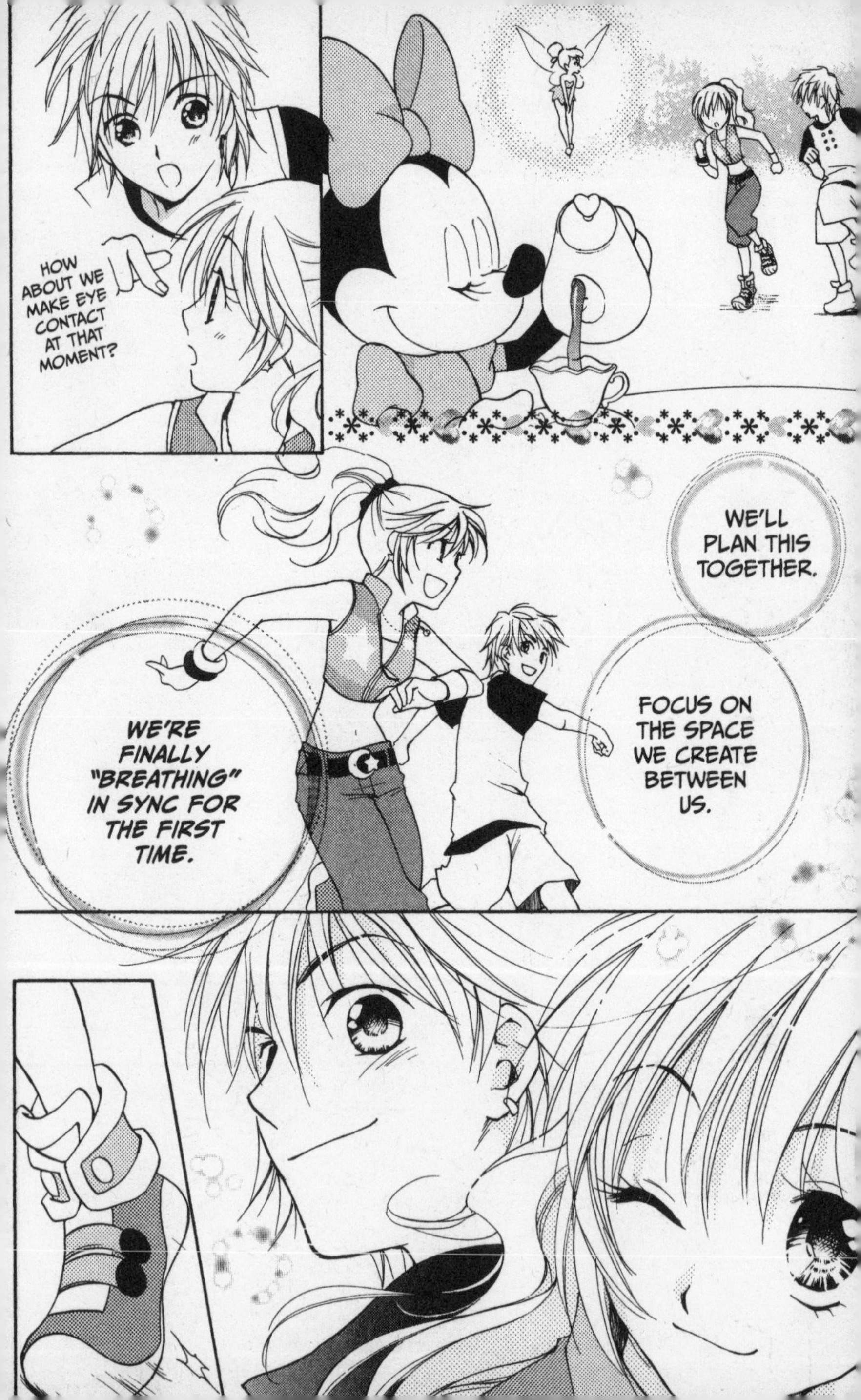
HOW ABOUT WE MAKE EYE CONTACT AT THAT MOMENT?
WE'LL PLAN THIS TOGETHER.
FOCUS ON THE SPACE WE CREATE BETWEEN US.
WE'RE FINALLY "BREATHING" IN SYNC FOR THE FIRST TIME.

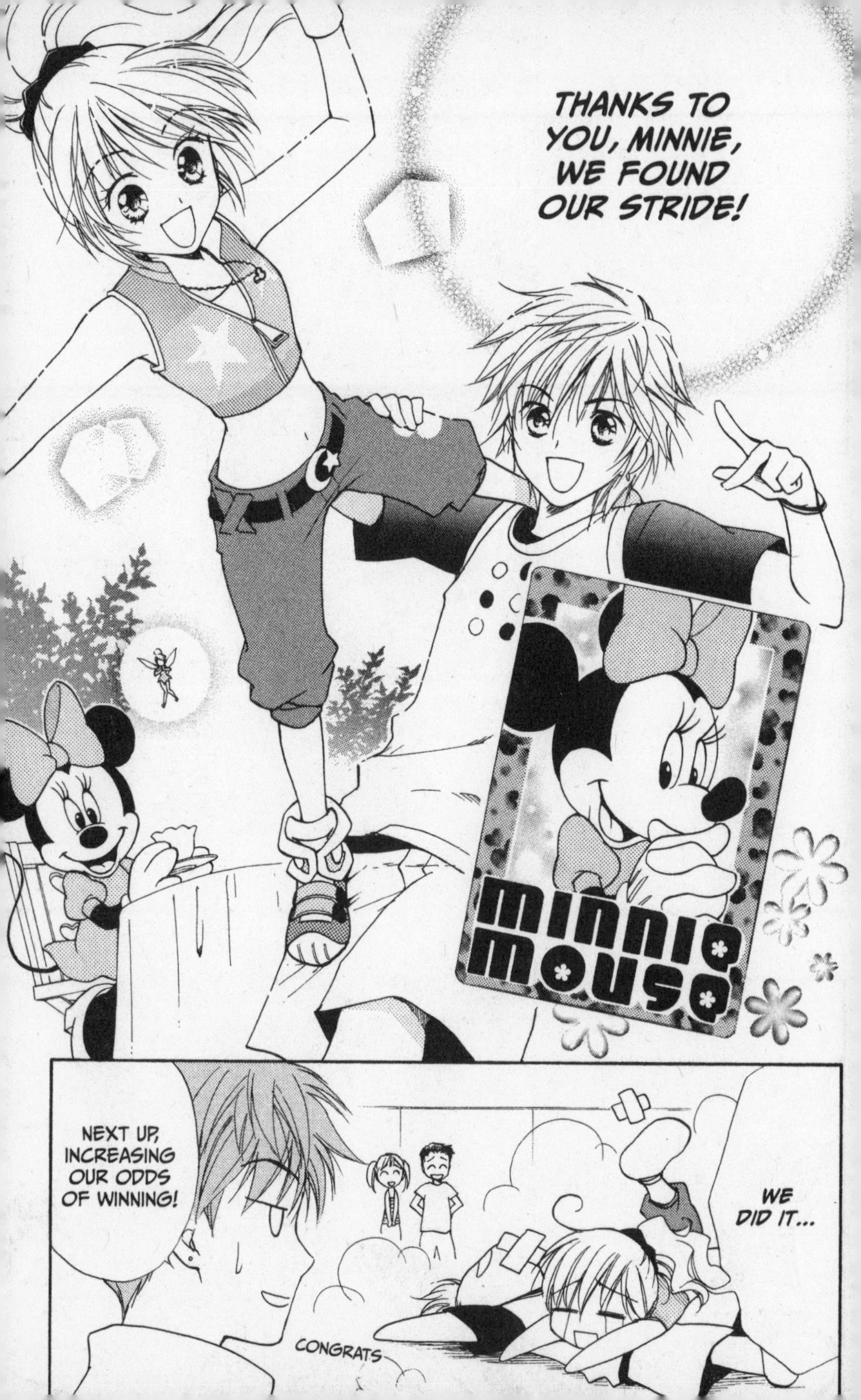
THANKS TO YOU, MINNIE, WE FOUND OUR STRIDE!
MINNIE MOUSE
WE DID IT...
CONGRATS
NEXT UP, INCREASING OUR ODDS OF WINNING!

YOU'RE GOING TO EAT ALL THAT BEFORE DANCING?
SHOCK
OH, MINNIE!
MAGICAL DANCE!!
WE'RE GONNA DANCE AND BURN SOME CALORIES!
WOW
YOU'RE PRETTY DEDICATED.
TIME FOR A BREAK?
I MADE A CAKE! ♡
EEK
OH, LET'S! ♡♡
BACK TO PANEL 1 AND REPEAT.

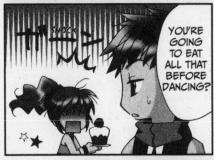

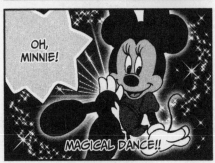

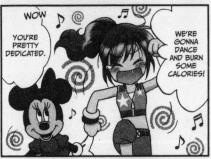

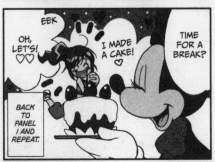

CONTINUED ON P. 120

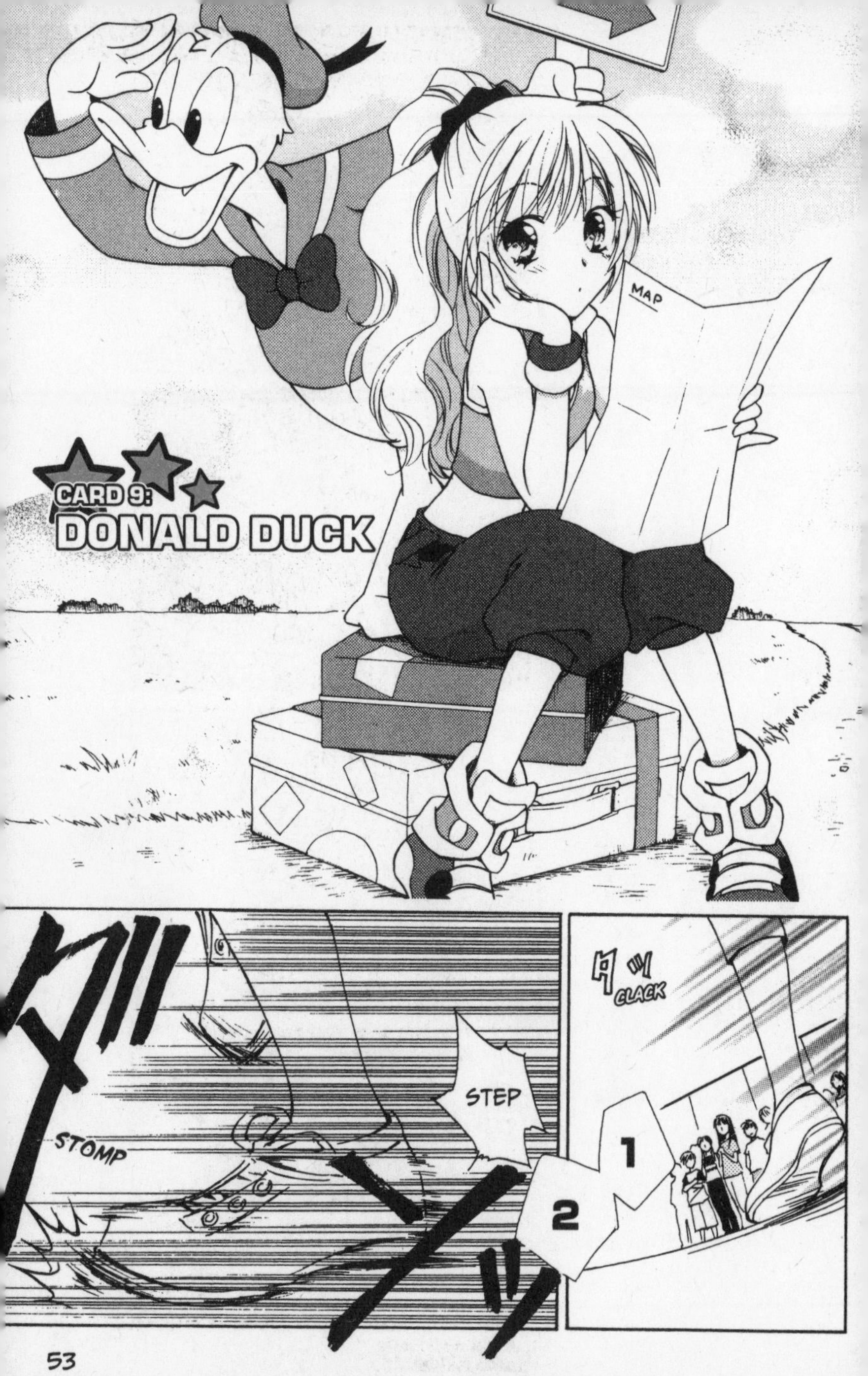
MAP
CARD 9:
DONALD DUCK
CLACK
1
2
STEP
STOMP

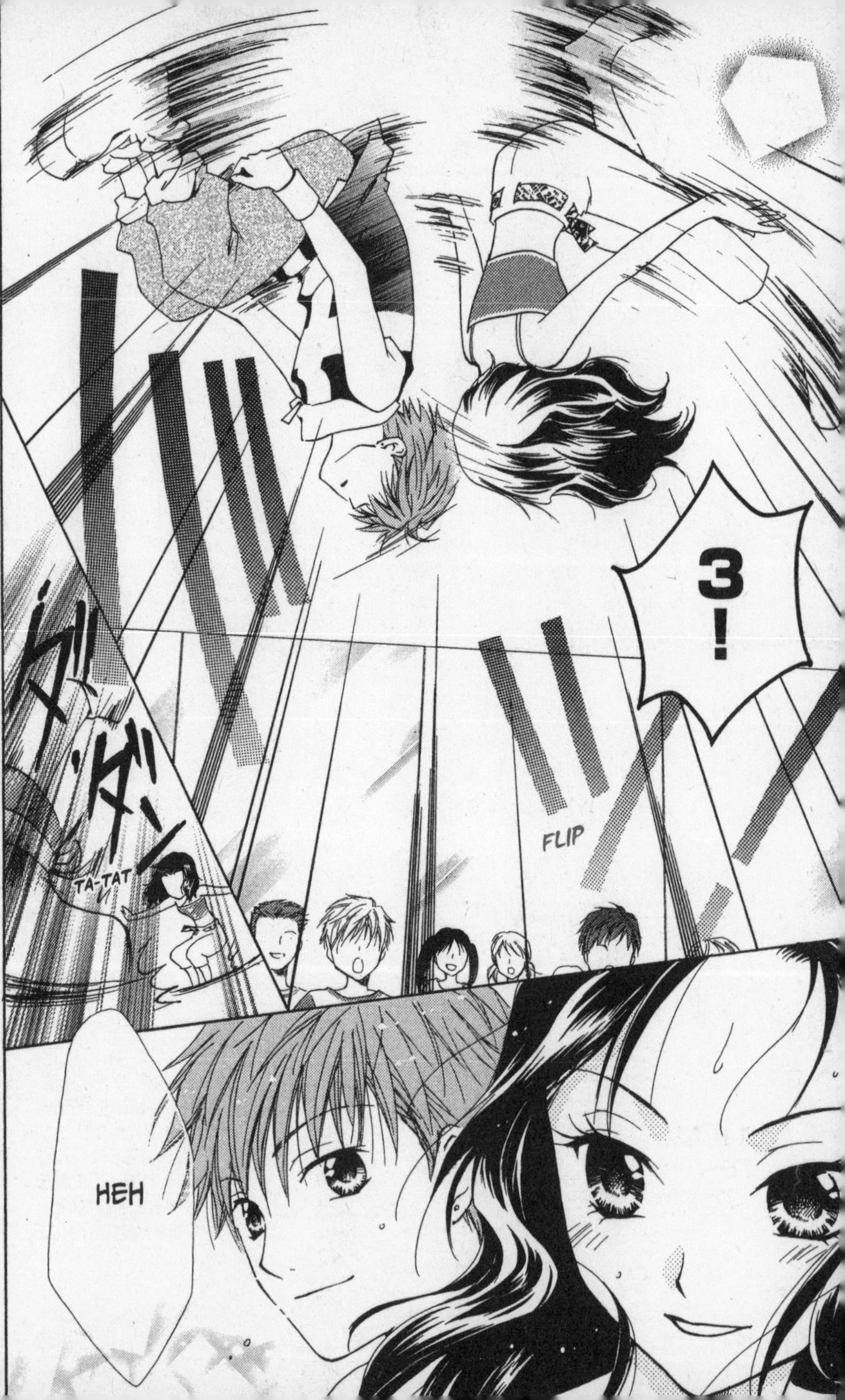
3!
FLIP
TA-TAT
HEH

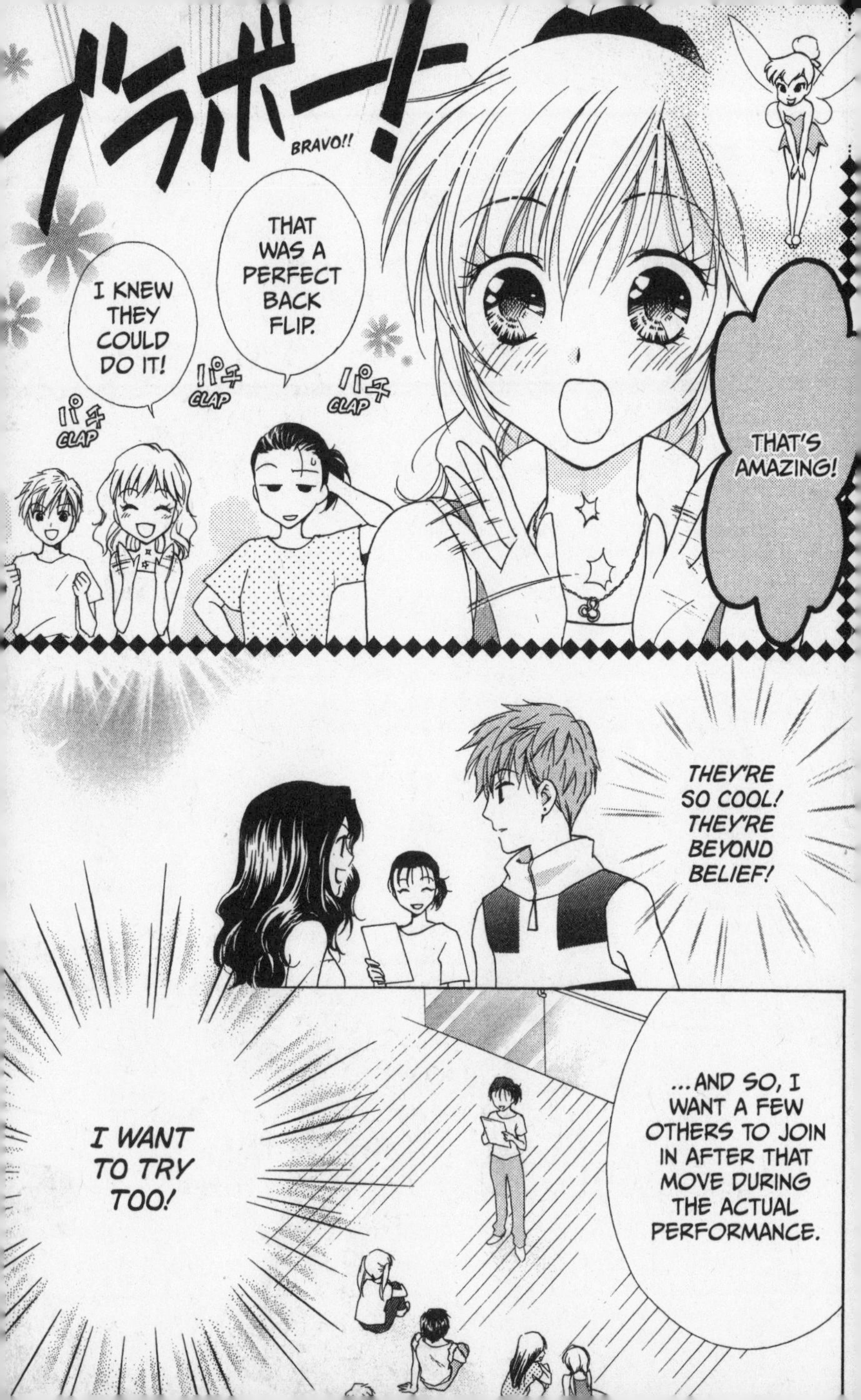
ブラボー!
BRAVO!!
THAT'S AMAZING!
THAT WAS A PERFECT BACK FLIP.
パチ CLAP
パチ CLAP
I KNEW THEY COULD DO IT!
パチ CLAP
THEY'RE SO COOL! THEY'RE BEYOND BELIEF!
...AND SO, I WANT A FEW OTHERS TO JOIN IN AFTER THAT MOVE DURING THE ACTUAL PERFORMANCE.
I WANT TO TRY TOO!

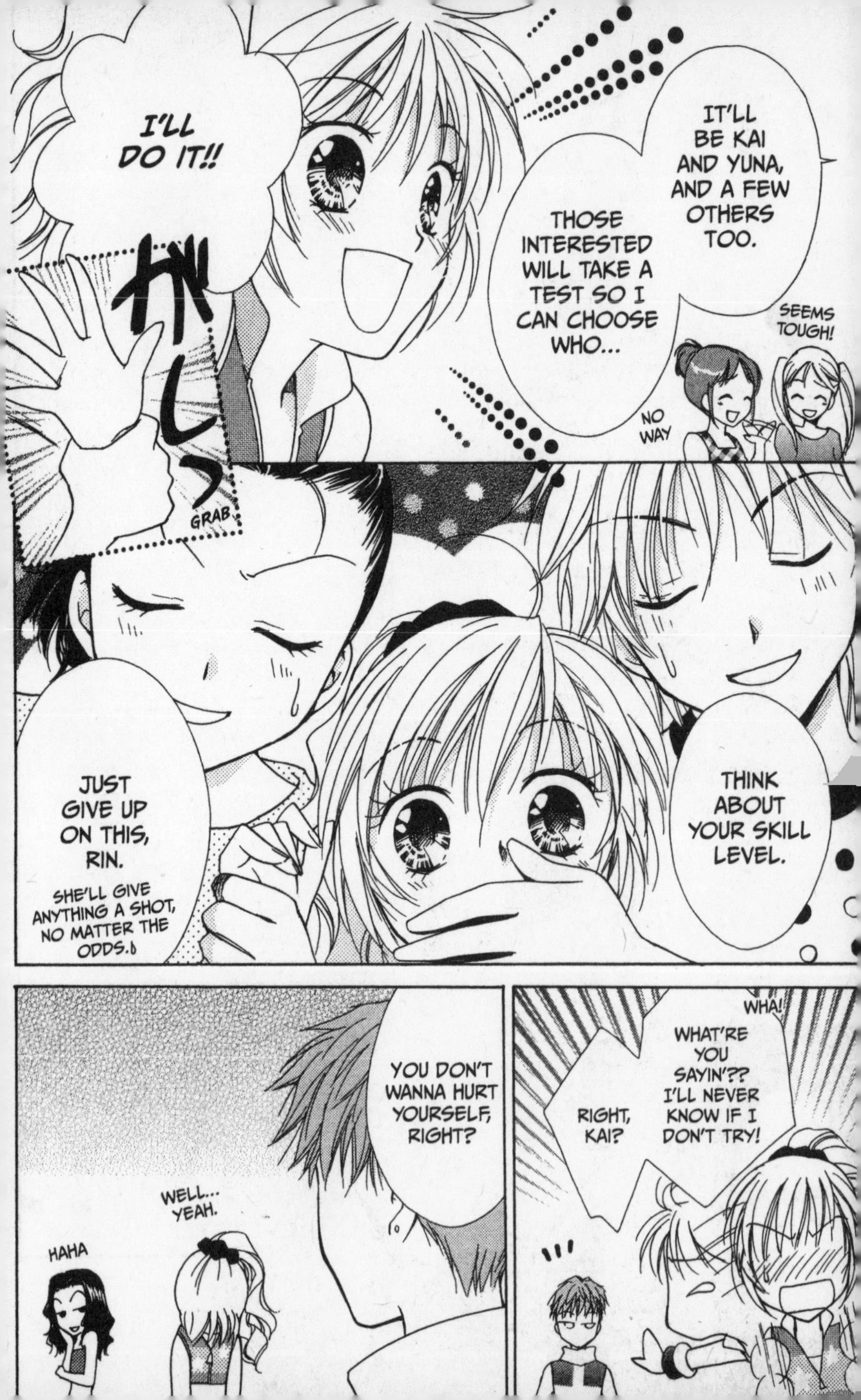
IT'LL BE KAI AND YUNA, AND A FEW OTHERS TOO.
SEEMS TOUGH!
NO WAY
THOSE INTERESTED WILL TAKE A TEST SO I CAN CHOOSE WHO...
I'LL DO IT!!
がしっ
GRAB
THINK ABOUT YOUR SKILL LEVEL.
JUST GIVE UP ON THIS, RIN.
SHE'LL GIVE ANYTHING A SHOT, NO MATTER THE ODDS.
WHA!
WHAT'RE YOU SAYIN'?? I'LL NEVER KNOW IF I DON'T TRY!
RIGHT, KAI?
YOU DON'T WANNA HURT YOURSELF, RIGHT?
WELL... YEAH.
HAHA

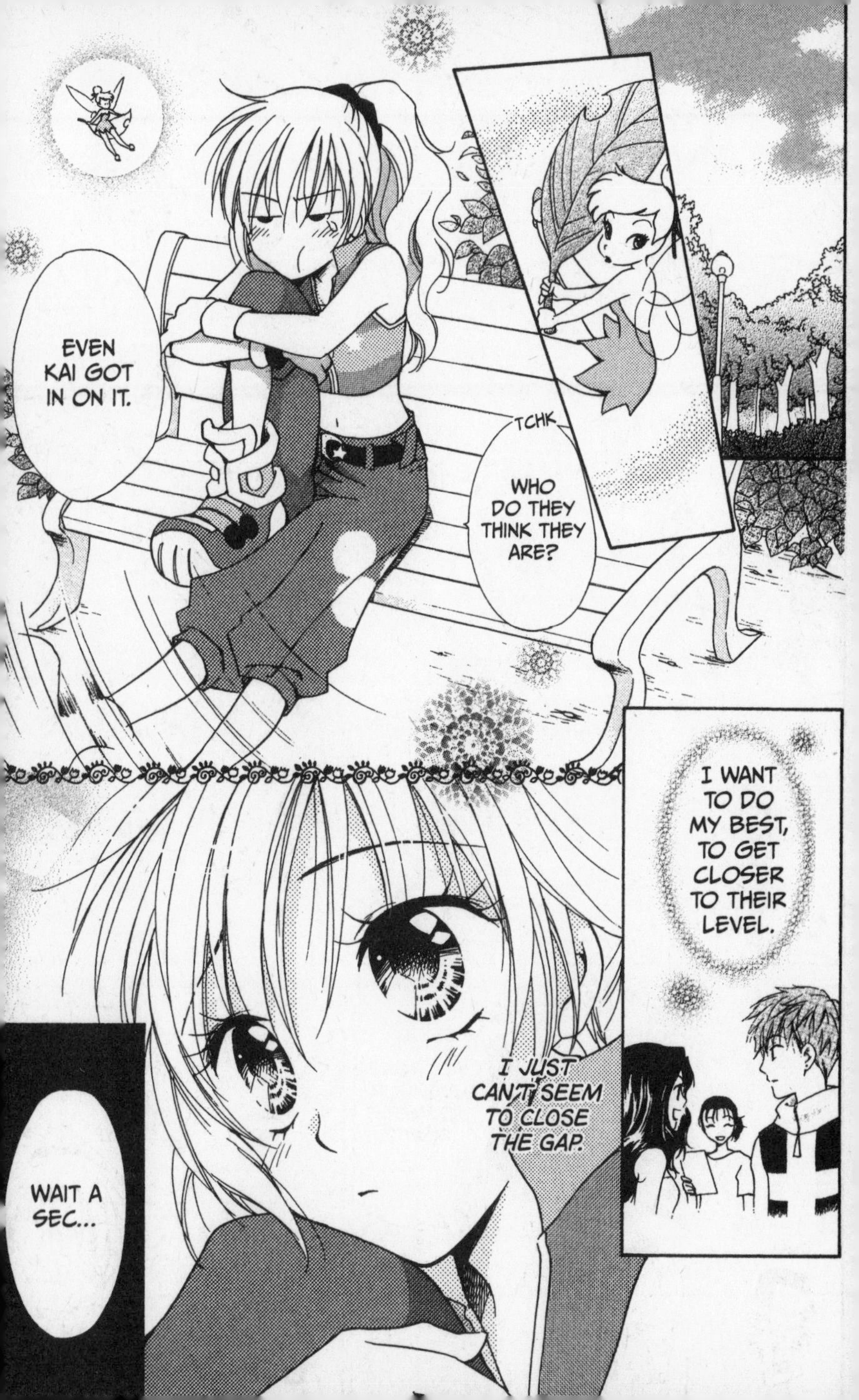
TCHK
WHO DO THEY THINK THEY ARE?
EVEN KAI GOT IN ON IT.
I WANT TO DO MY BEST, TO GET CLOSER TO THEIR LEVEL.
I JUST CAN'T SEEM TO CLOSE THE GAP.
WAIT A SEC...

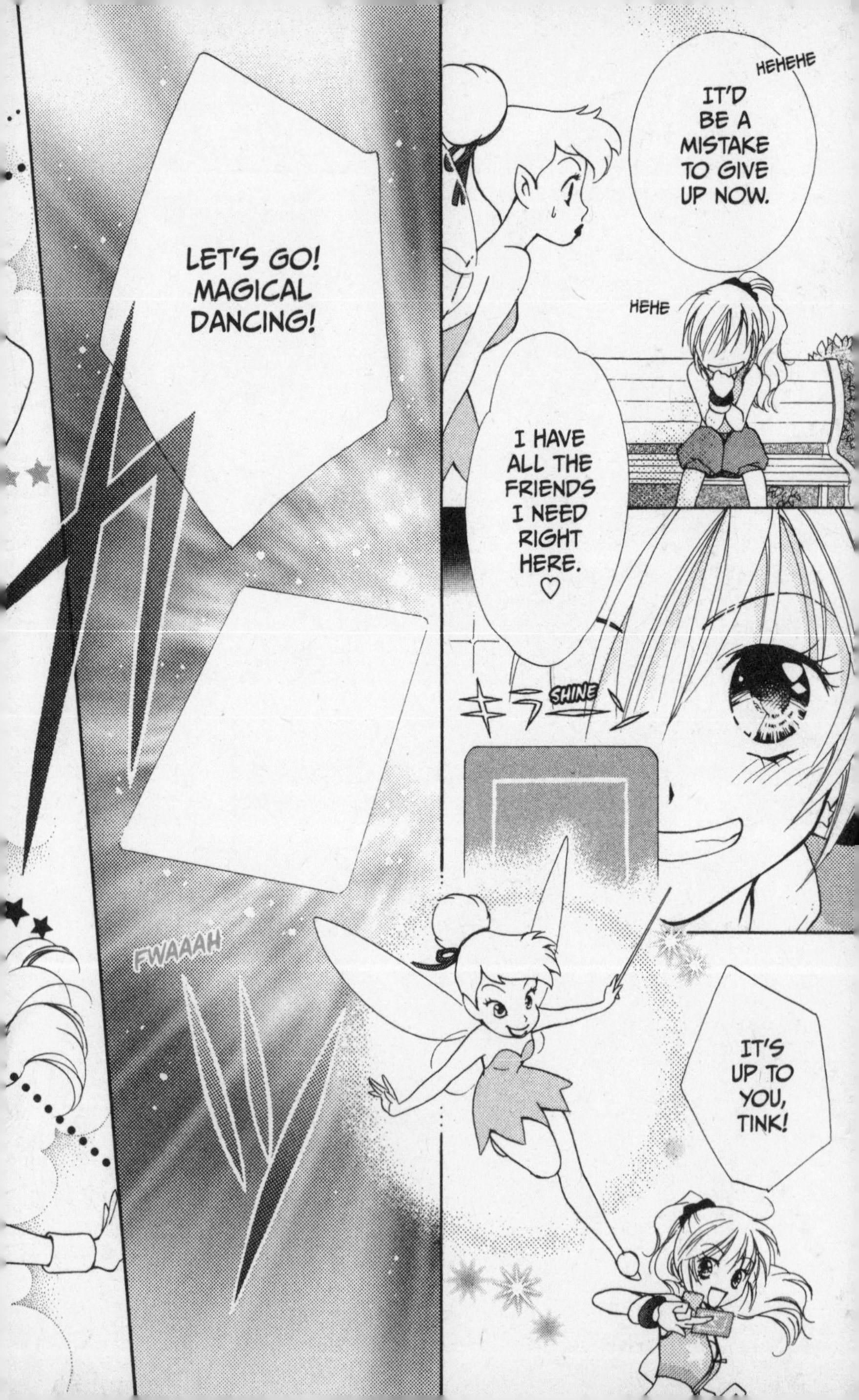
HEHEHE
IT'D BE A MISTAKE TO GIVE UP NOW.
HEHE
I HAVE ALL THE FRIENDS I NEED RIGHT HERE. ♡
SHINE
IT'S UP TO YOU, TINK!
LET'S GO! MAGICAL DANCING!
FWAAAH

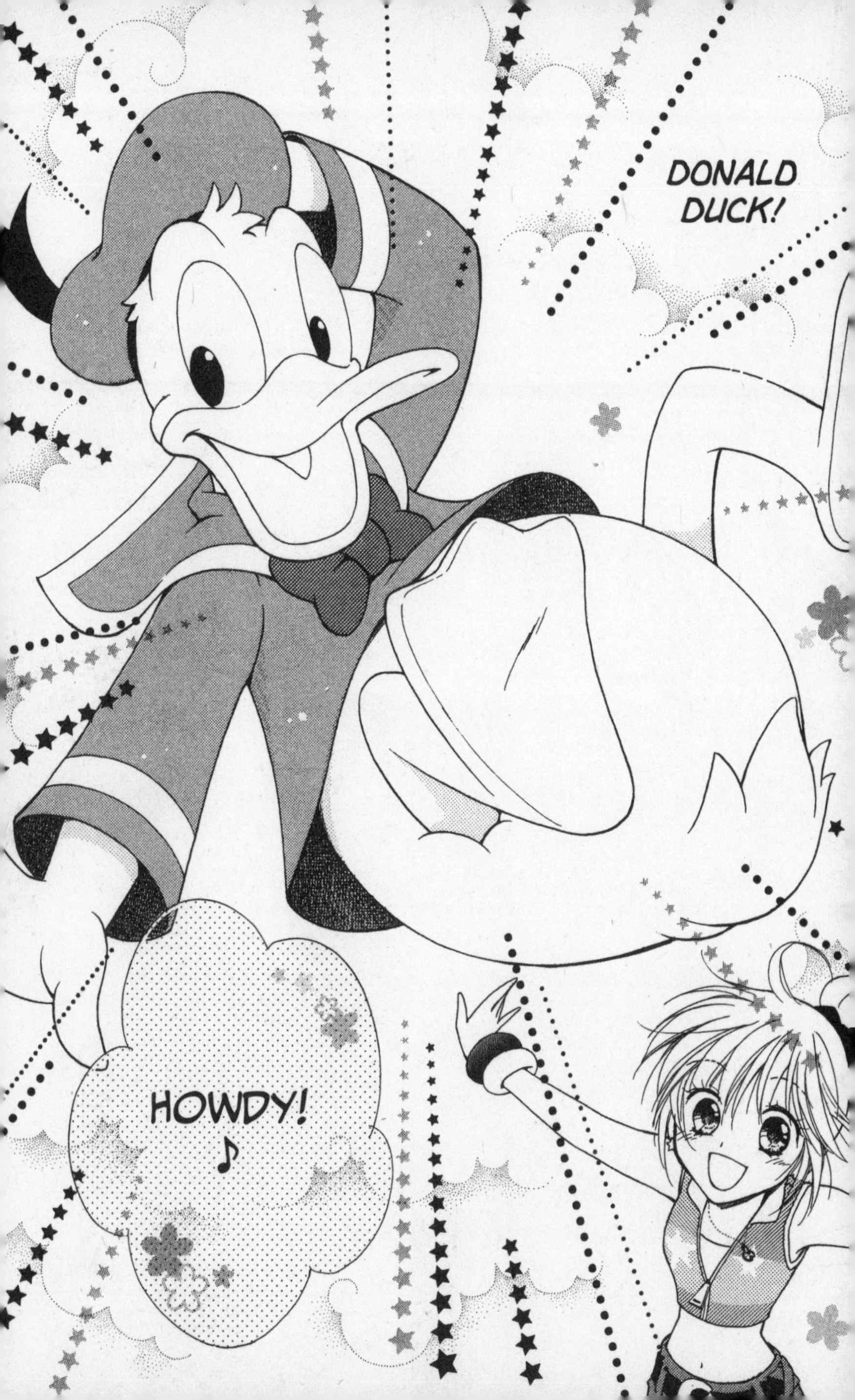
DONALD DUCK!
HOWDY! ♪

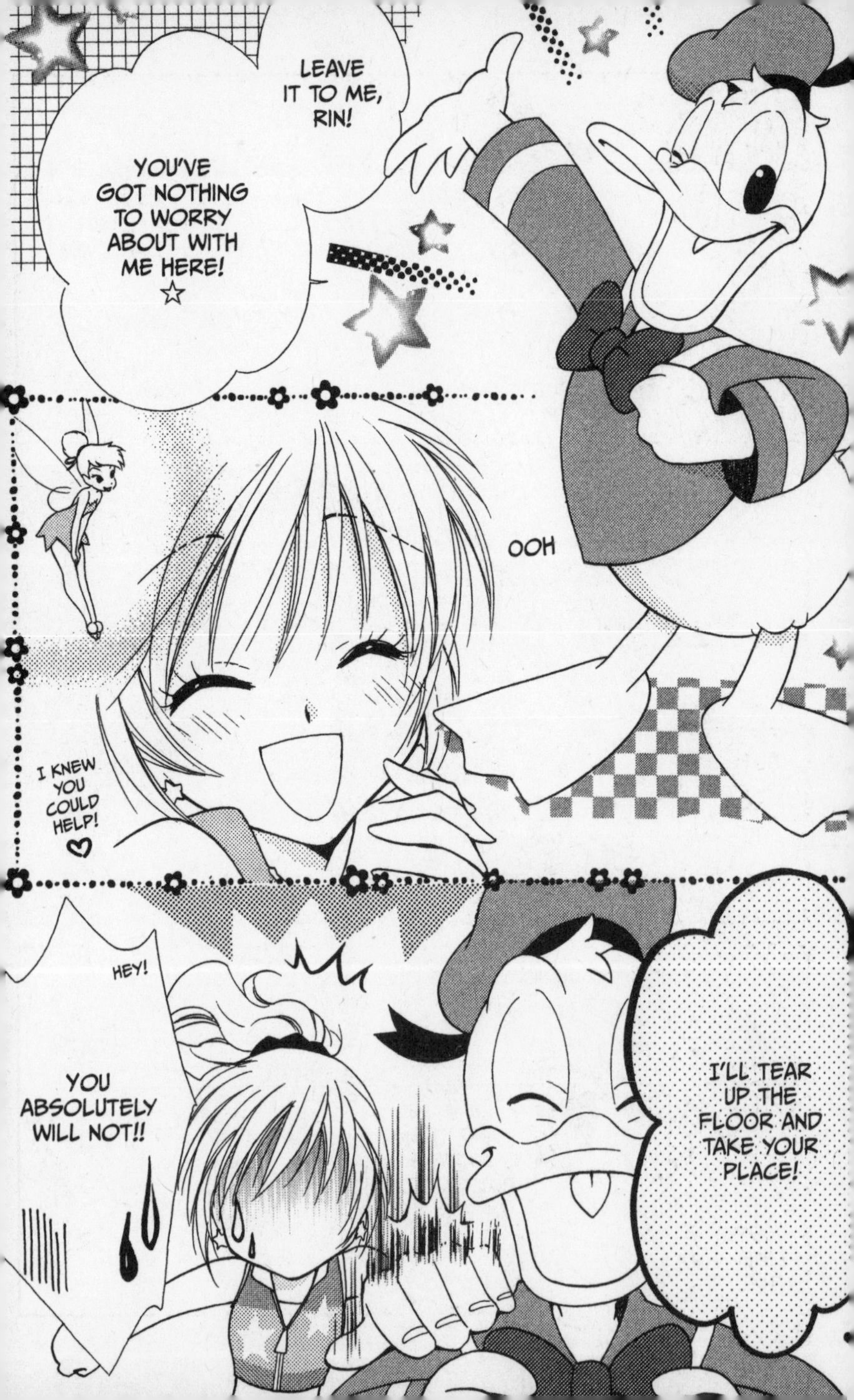
LEAVE IT TO ME, RIN!
YOU'VE GOT NOTHING TO WORRY ABOUT WITH ME HERE! ☆
OOH
I KNEW YOU COULD HELP! ♡
I'LL TEAR UP THE FLOOR AND TAKE YOUR PLACE!
HEY!
YOU ABSOLUTELY WILL NOT!!

READ THIS WAY

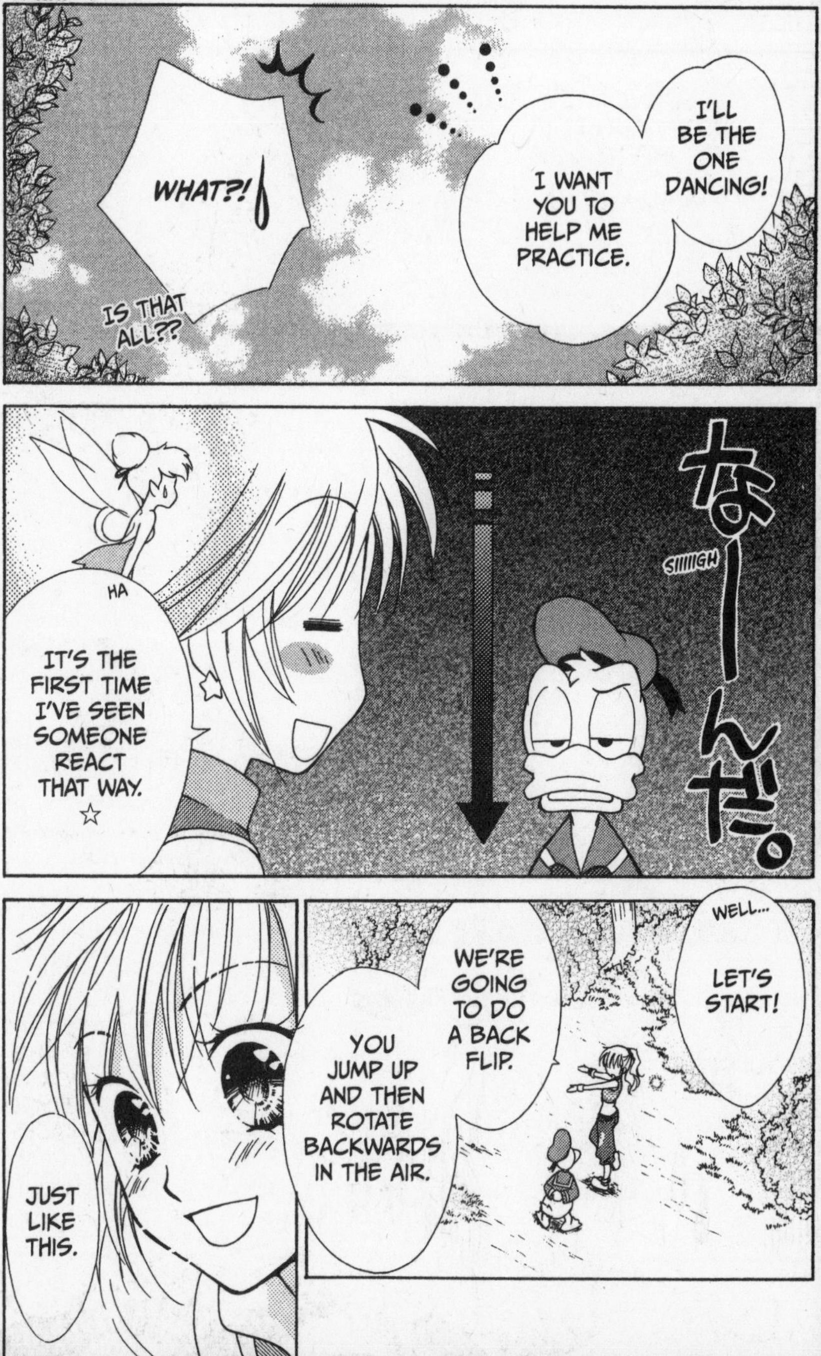
I'LL BE THE ONE DANCING!
I WANT YOU TO HELP ME PRACTICE.
WHAT?!
IS THAT ALL??
なーんだ。
SIIIIGH
HA
IT'S THE FIRST TIME I'VE SEEN SOMEONE REACT THAT WAY. ☆
WELL...
LET'S START!
WE'RE GOING TO DO A BACK FLIP.
YOU JUMP UP AND THEN ROTATE BACKWARDS IN THE AIR.
JUST LIKE THIS.

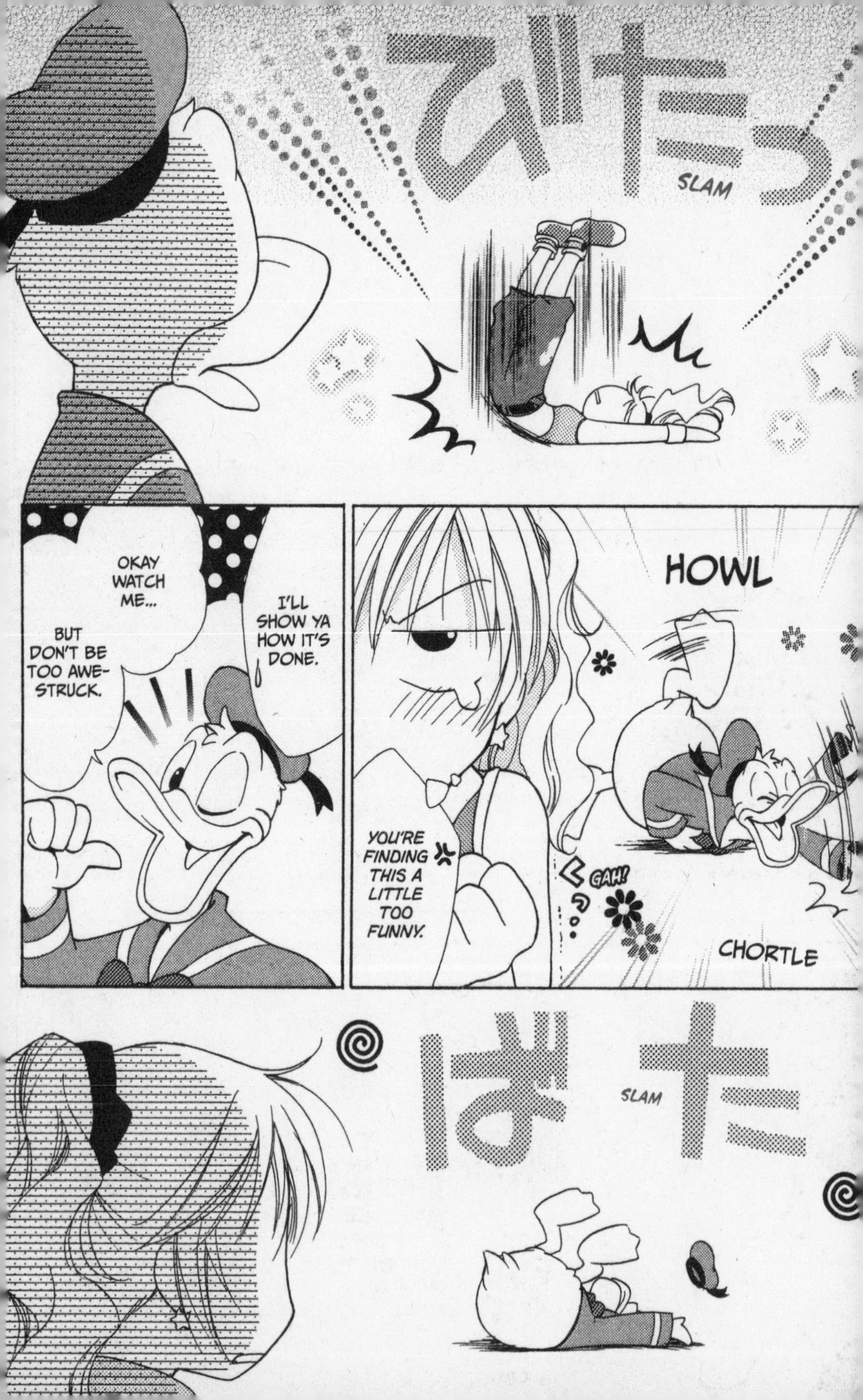
SLAM
HOWL
CHORTLE
YOU'RE FINDING THIS A LITTLE TOO FUNNY.
GAH!
I'LL SHOW YA HOW IT'S DONE.
OKAY WATCH ME...
BUT DON'T BE TOO AWE-STRUCK.
SLAM

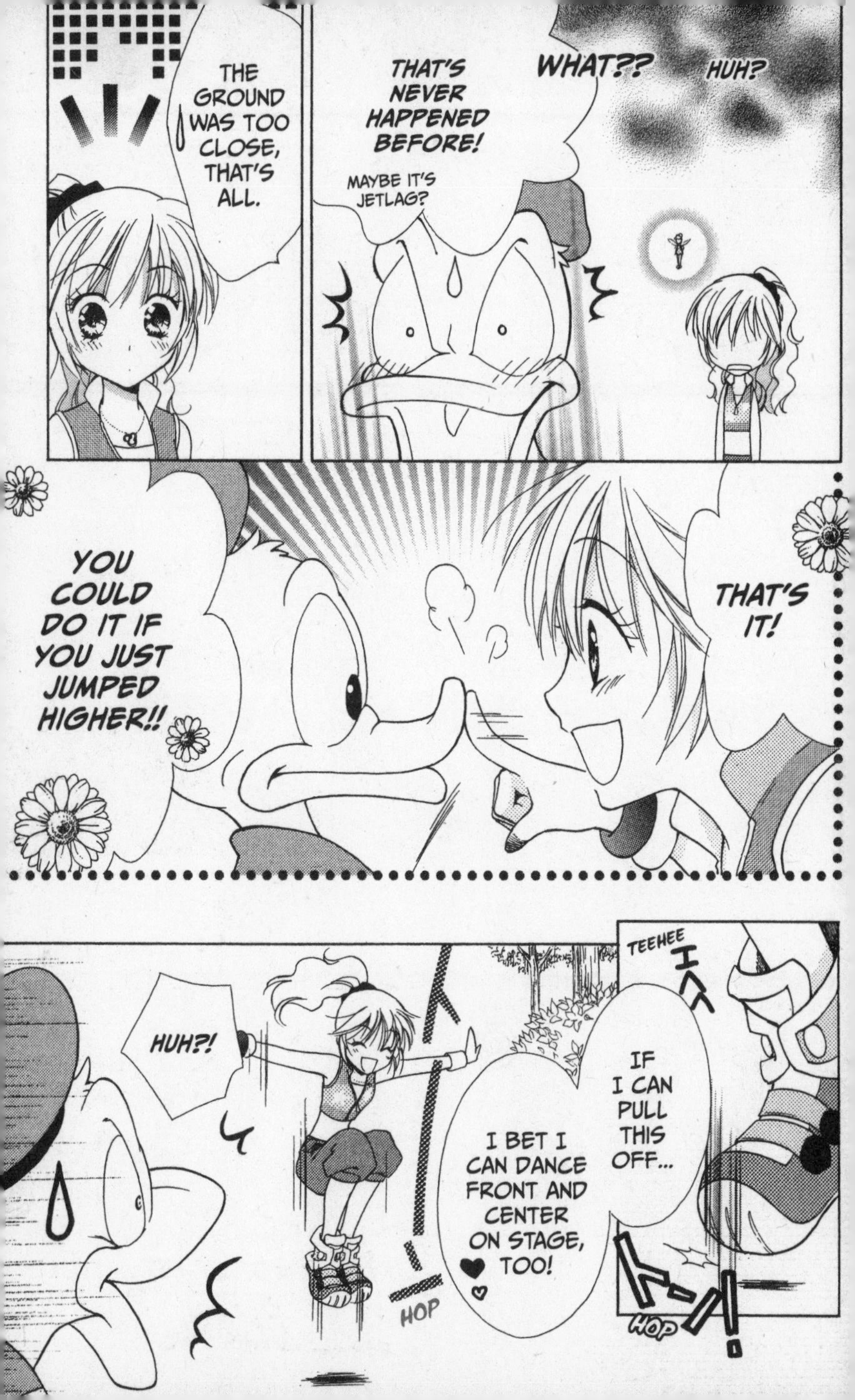
HUH?
WHAT??
THAT'S NEVER HAPPENED BEFORE!
MAYBE IT'S JETLAG?
THE GROUND WAS TOO CLOSE, THAT'S ALL.
THAT'S IT!
YOU COULD DO IT IF YOU JUST JUMPED HIGHER!!
TEEHEE
IF I CAN PULL THIS OFF...
HOP
I BET I CAN DANCE FRONT AND CENTER ON STAGE, TOO!
HOP
HUH?!

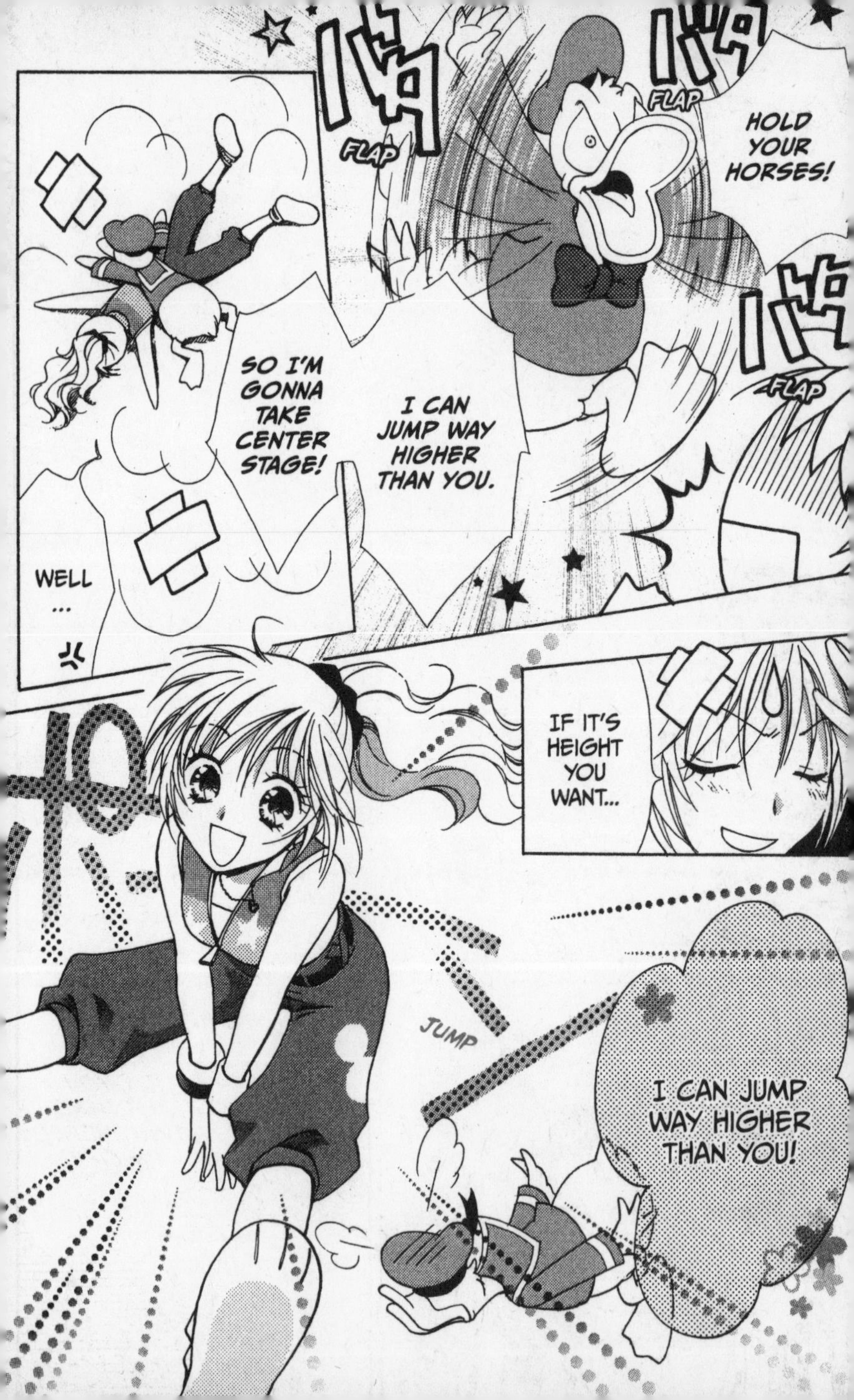
FLAP
FLAP
HOLD YOUR HORSES!
FLAP
I CAN JUMP WAY HIGHER THAN YOU.
SO I'M GONNA TAKE CENTER STAGE!
WELL ...
IF IT'S HEIGHT YOU WANT...
JUMP
I CAN JUMP WAY HIGHER THAN YOU!

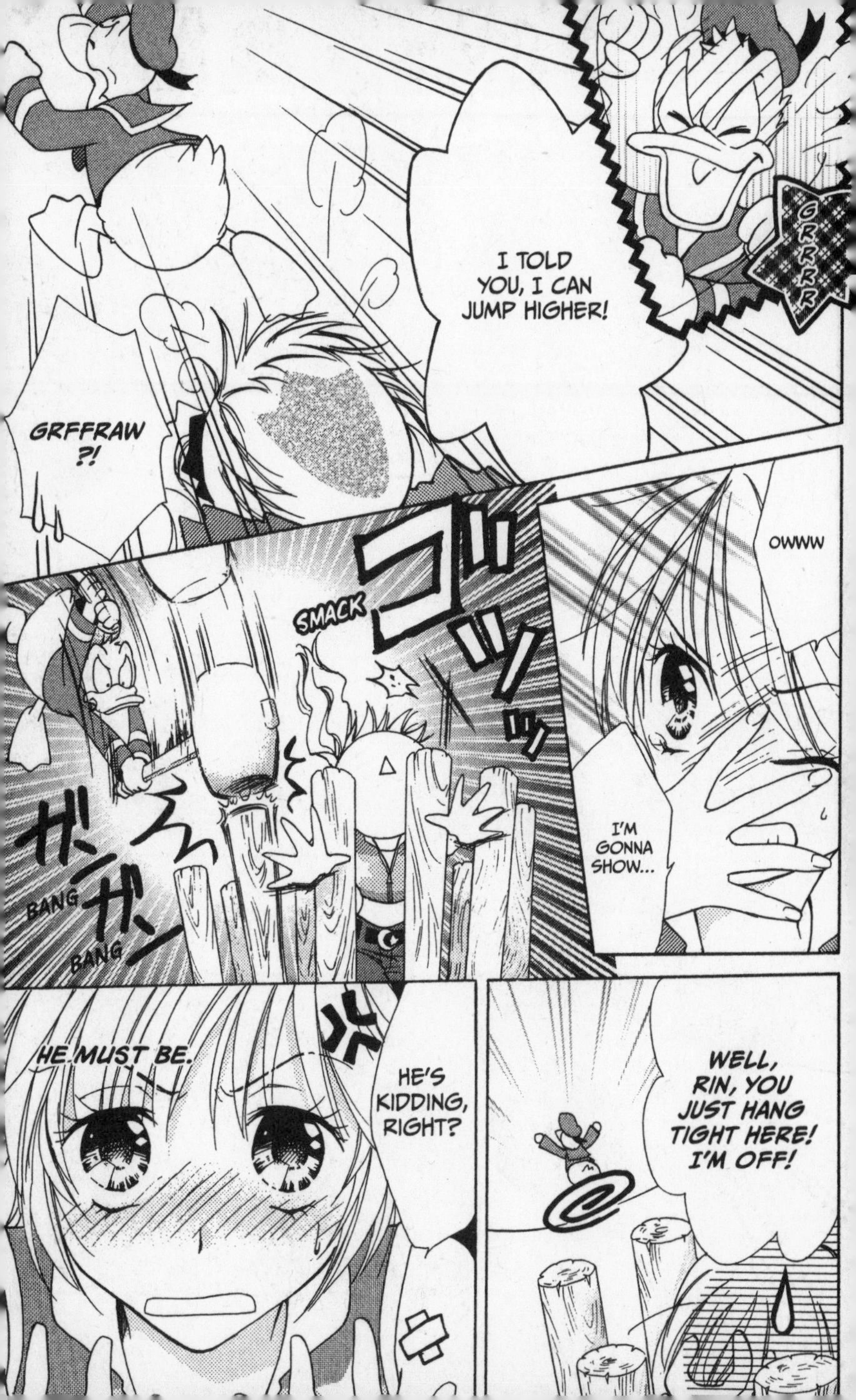
GRRRR
I TOLD YOU, I CAN JUMP HIGHER!
GRFFRAW ?!
OWWW
I'M GONNA SHOW...
SMACK
BANG
BANG
WELL, RIN, YOU JUST HANG TIGHT HERE! I'M OFF!
HE'S KIDDING, RIGHT?
HE MUST BE.

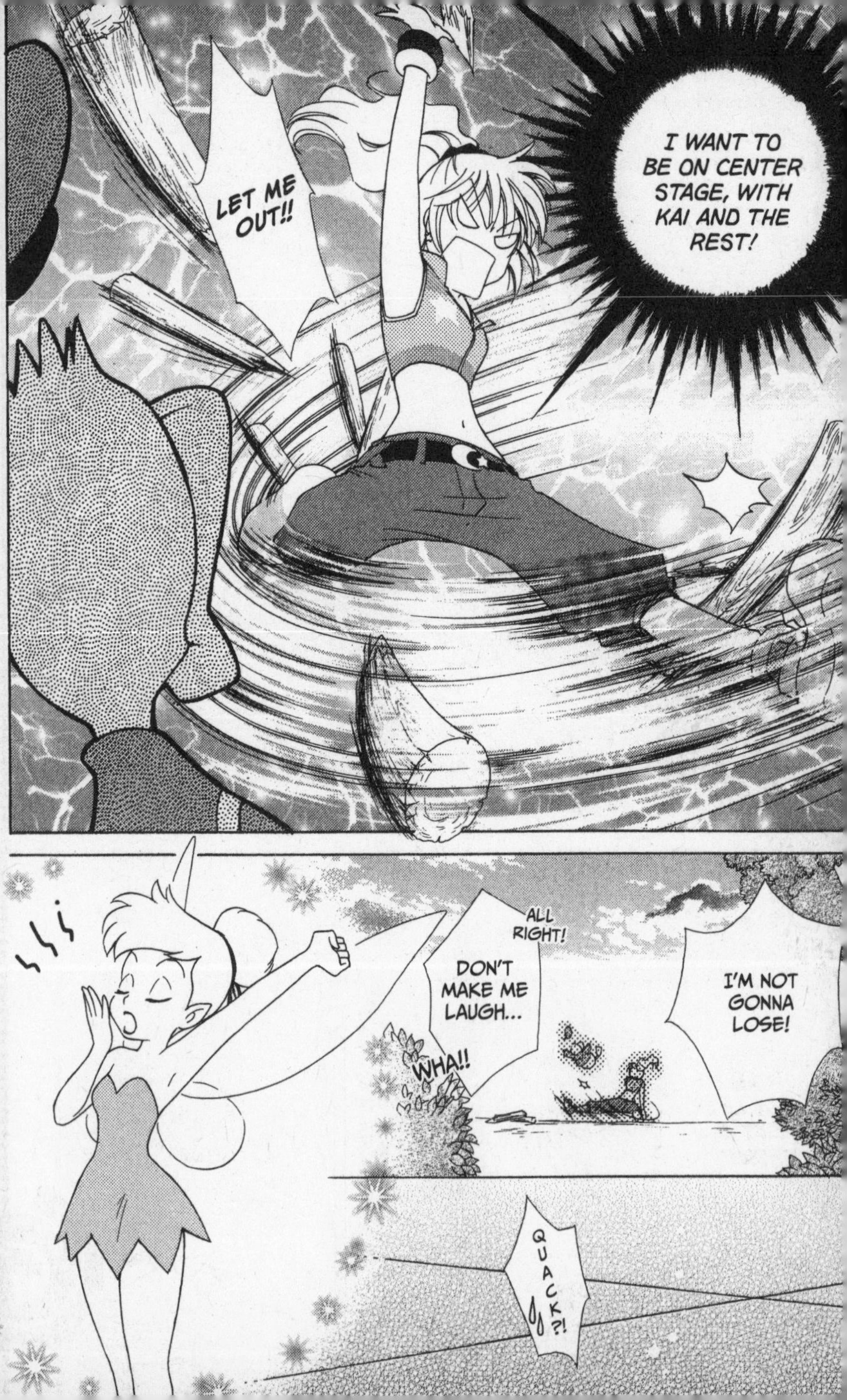
I WANT TO BE ON CENTER STAGE, WITH KAI AND THE REST!
LET ME OUT!!
I'M NOT GONNA LOSE!
ALL RIGHT!
DON'T MAKE ME LAUGH...
WHA!!
QUACK?!

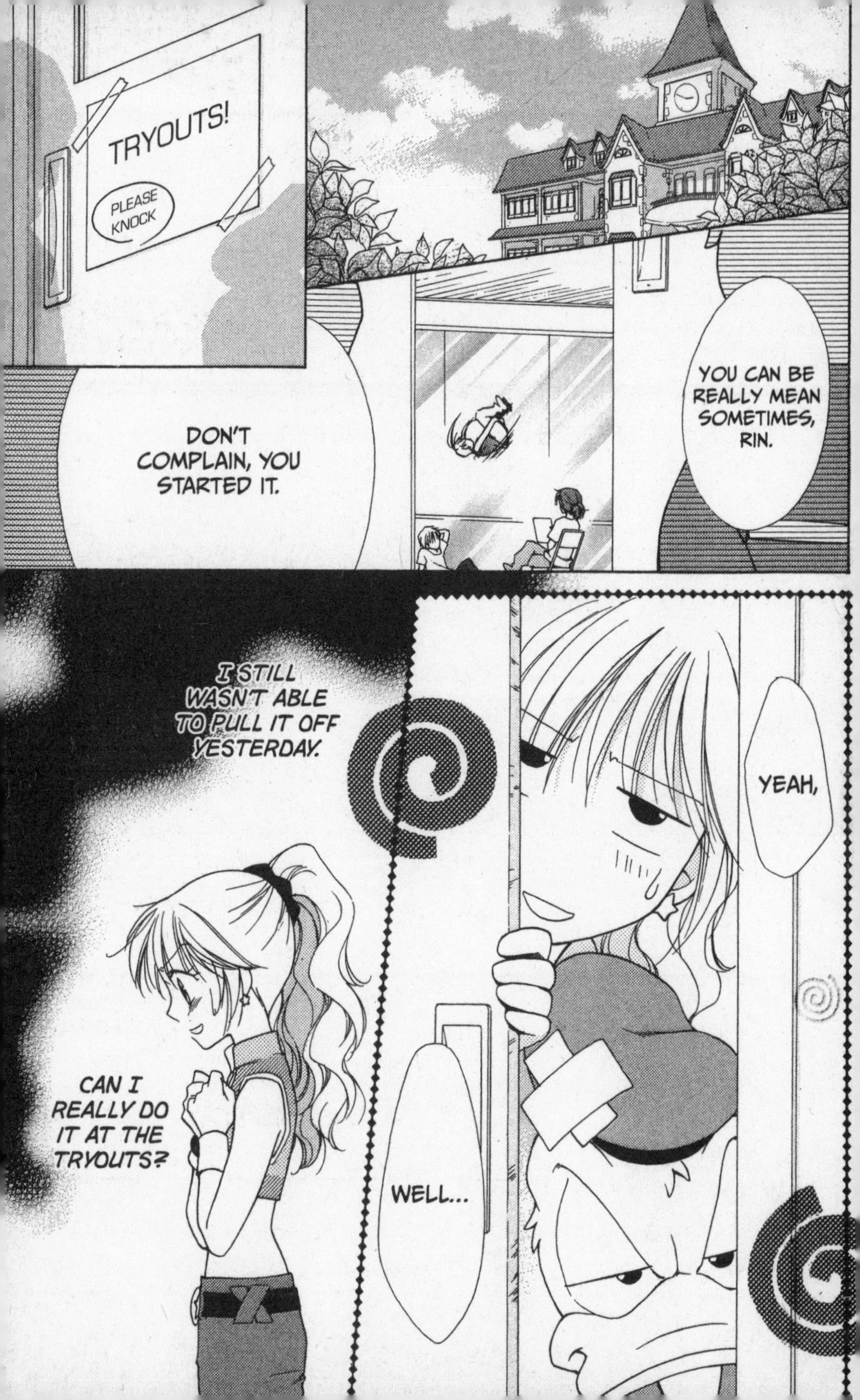
TRYOUTS!
PLEASE KNOCK
YOU CAN BE REALLY MEAN SOMETIMES, RIN.
DON'T COMPLAIN, YOU STARTED IT.
YEAH,
WELL...
I STILL WASN'T ABLE TO PULL IT OFF YESTERDAY.
CAN I REALLY DO IT AT THE TRYOUTS?

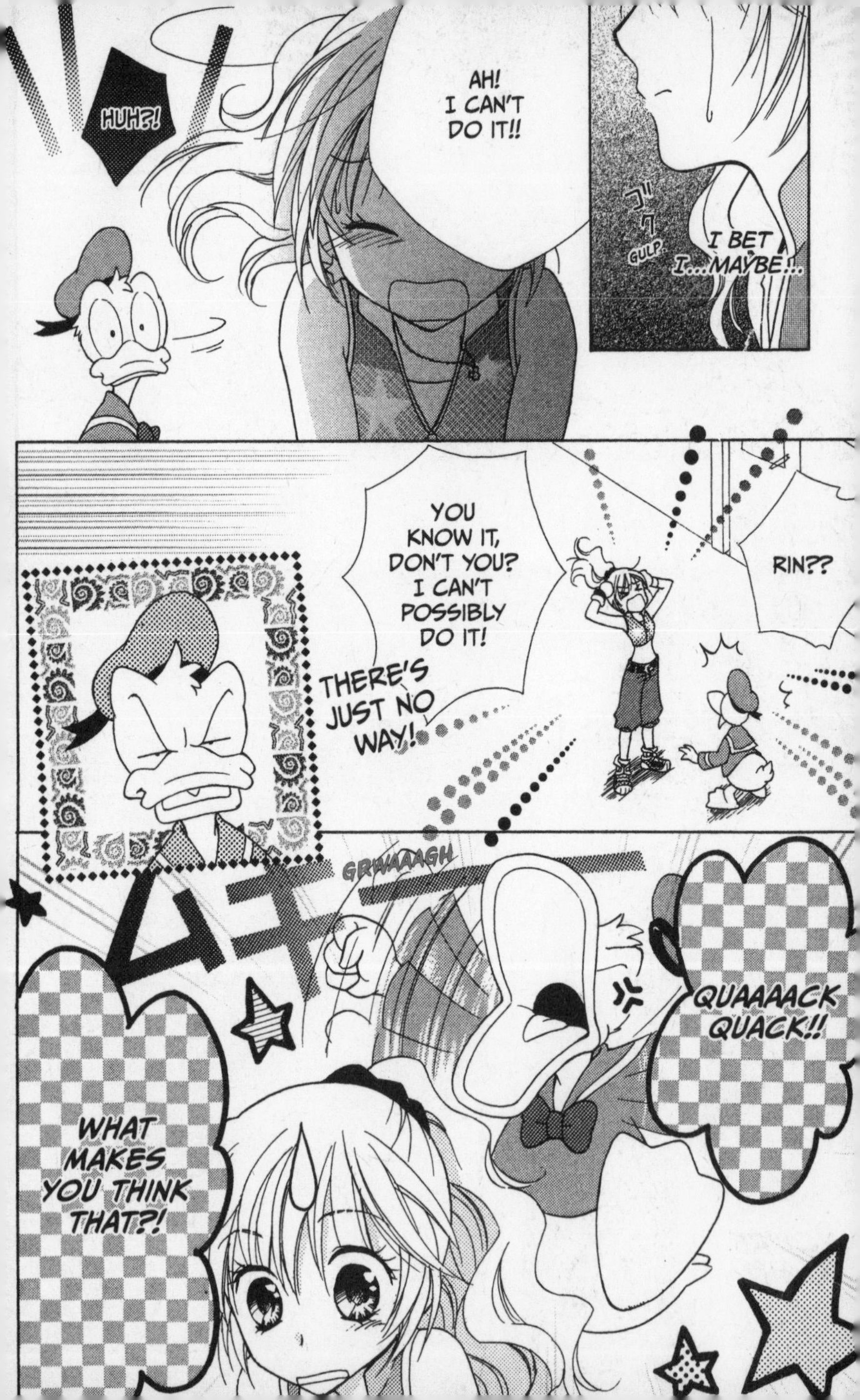
ゴク
GULP
I BET I...MAYBE...
AH! I CAN'T DO IT!!
HUH?!
RIN??
YOU KNOW IT, DON'T YOU? I CAN'T POSSIBLY DO IT!
THERE'S JUST NO WAY!
GRWAAAGH
QUAAAACK QUACK!!
WHAT MAKES YOU THINK THAT?!

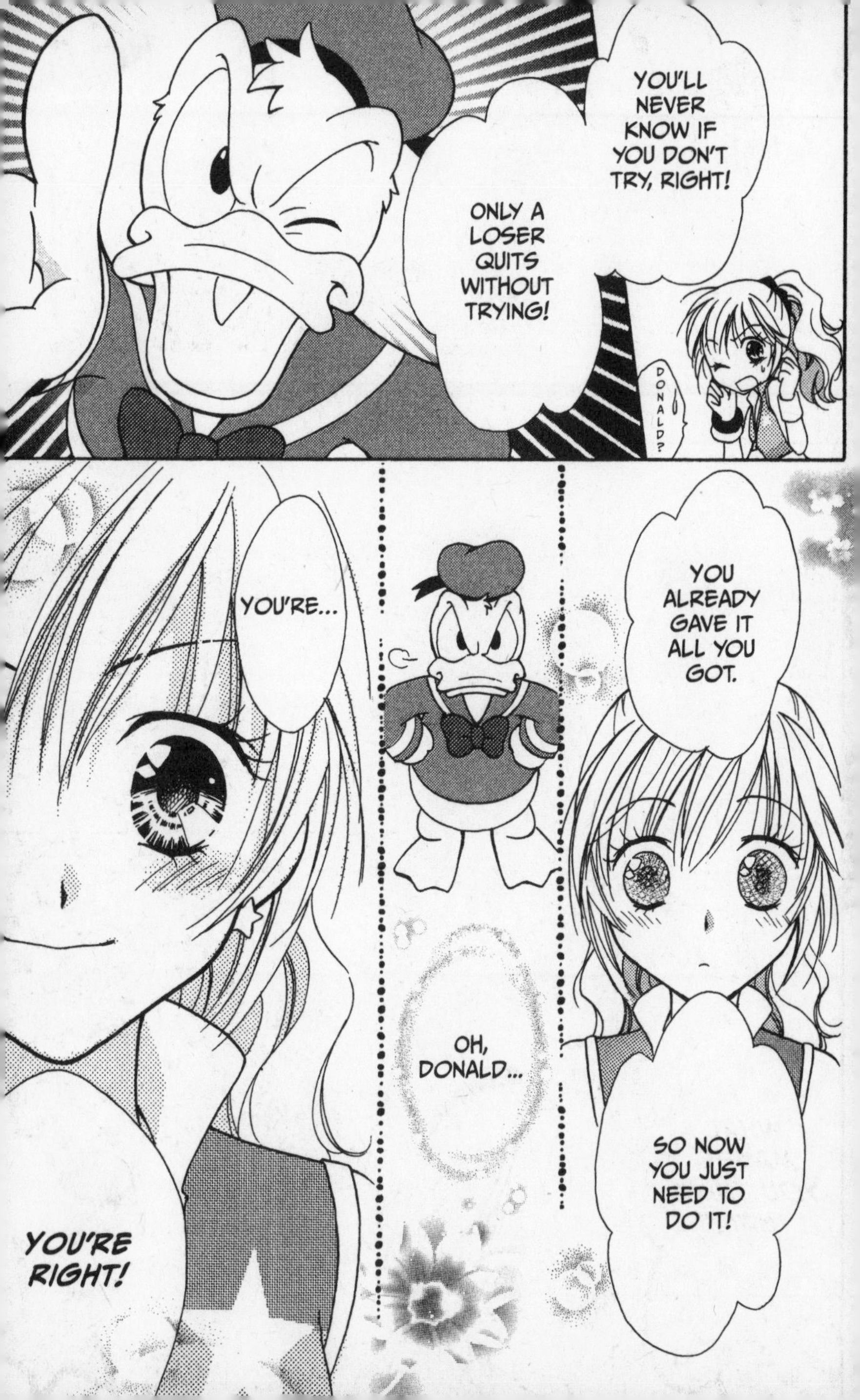
YOU'LL NEVER KNOW IF YOU DON'T TRY, RIGHT!
ONLY A LOSER QUITS WITHOUT TRYING!
DONALD?
YOU ALREADY GAVE IT ALL YOU GOT.
SO NOW YOU JUST NEED TO DO IT!
OH, DONALD...
YOU'RE...
YOU'RE RIGHT!

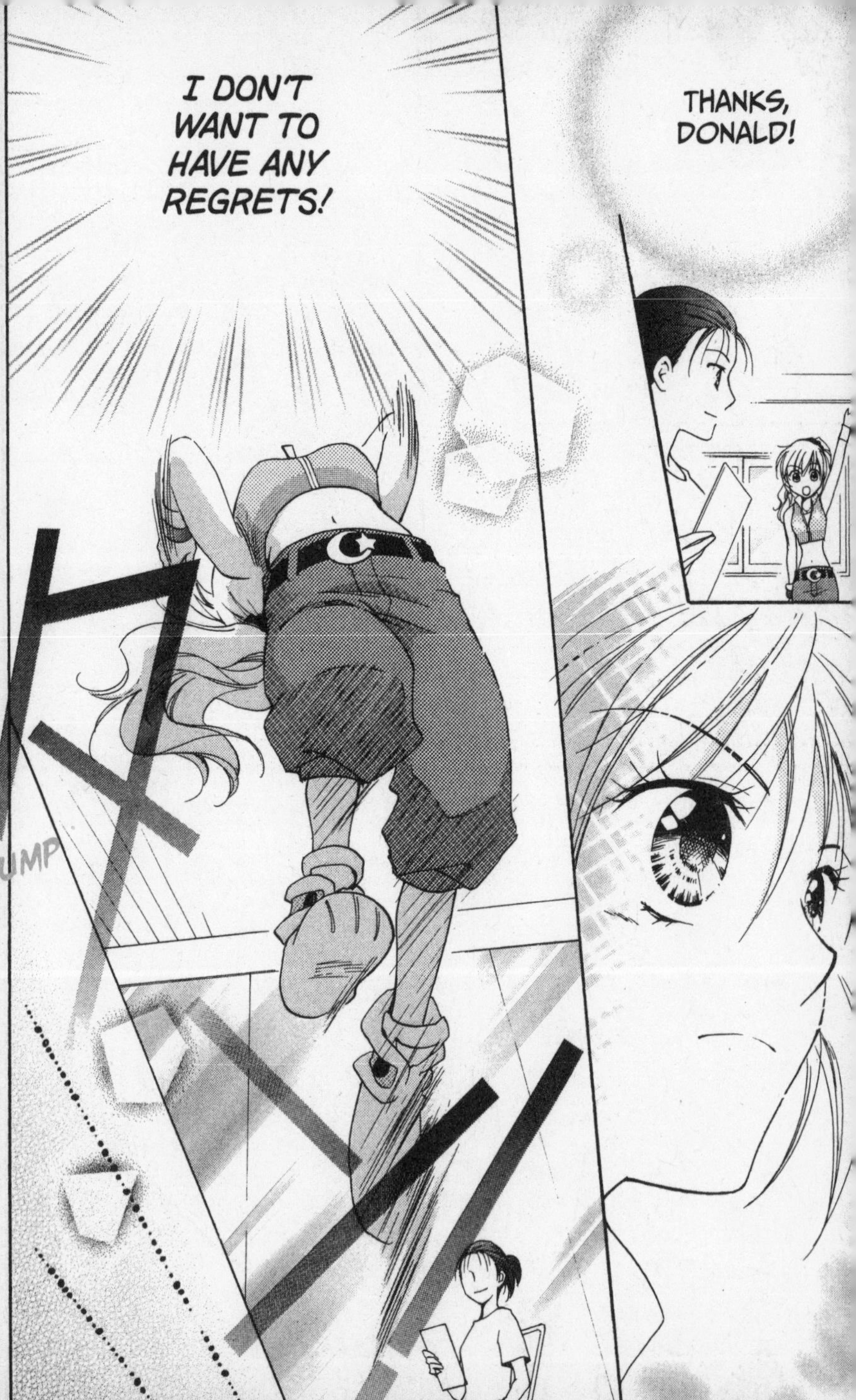
THANKS, DONALD!
I DON'T WANT TO HAVE ANY REGRETS!
UMP

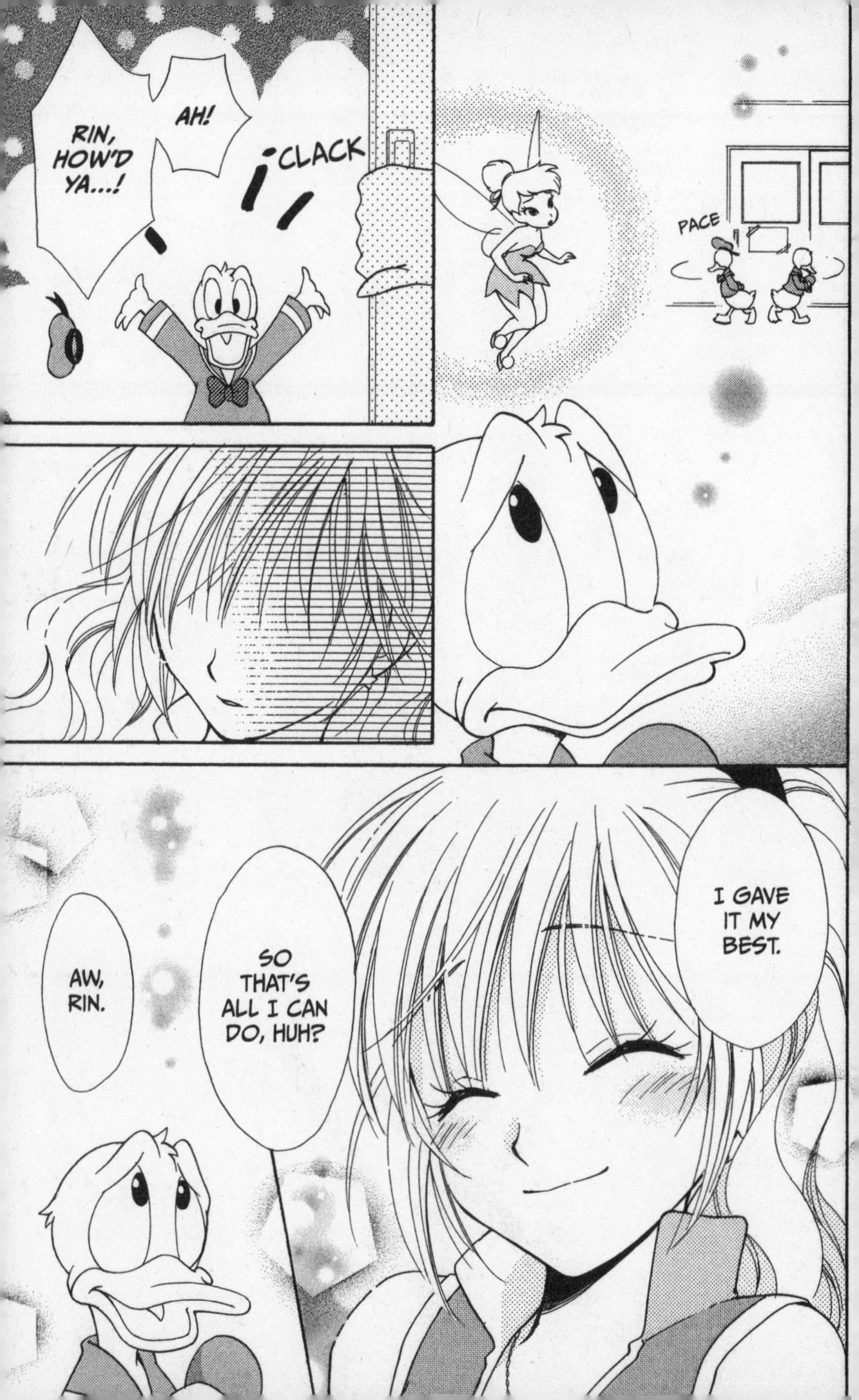
PACE
CLACK
AH!
RIN, HOW'D YA...!
I GAVE IT MY BEST.
SO THAT'S ALL I CAN DO, HUH?
AW, RIN.

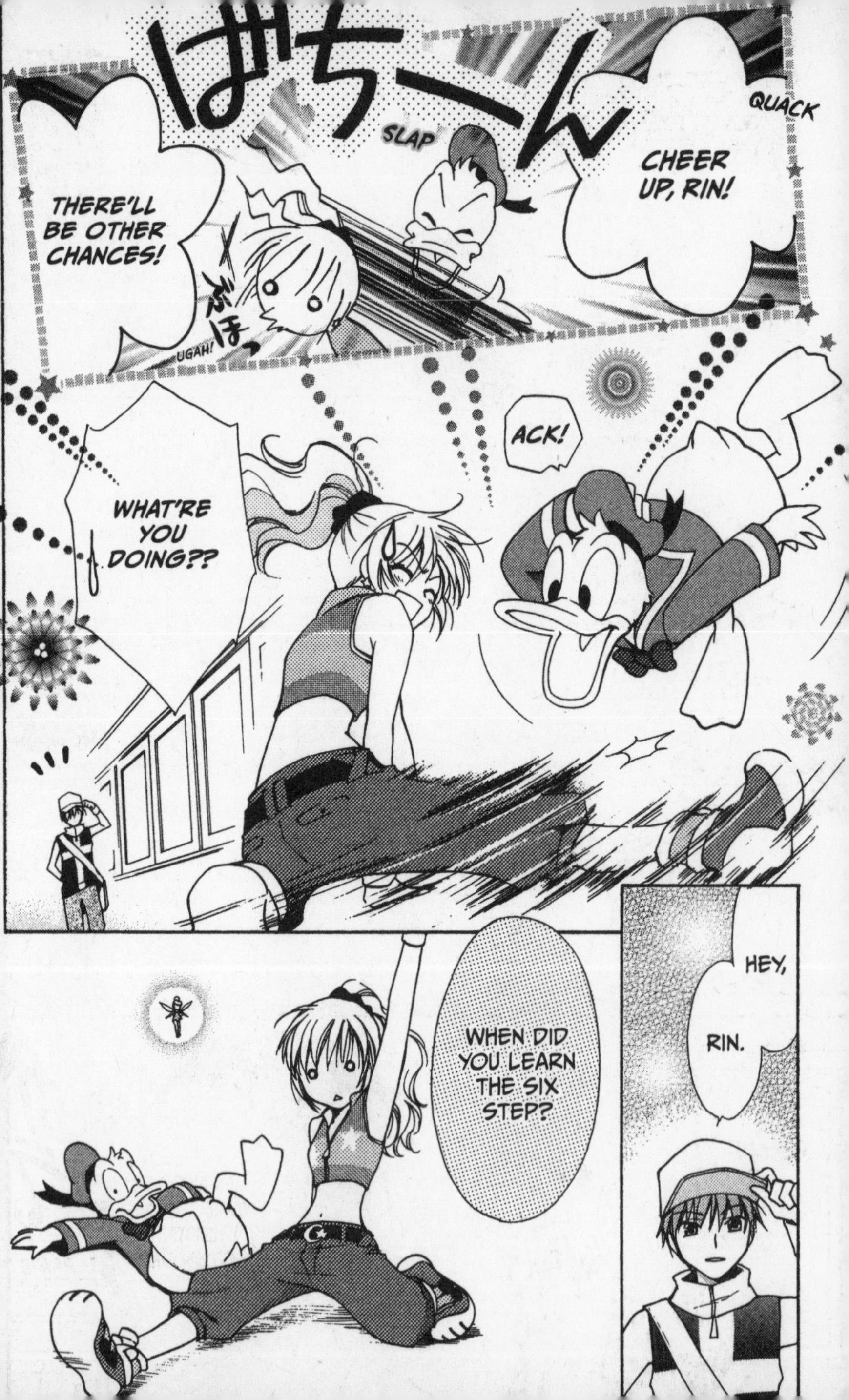
QUACK
CHEER UP, RIN!
SLAP
ぱちーん
THERE'LL BE OTHER CHANCES!
ぶほっ
UGAH!
ACK!
WHAT'RE YOU DOING??
HEY, RIN.
WHEN DID YOU LEARN THE SIX STEP?

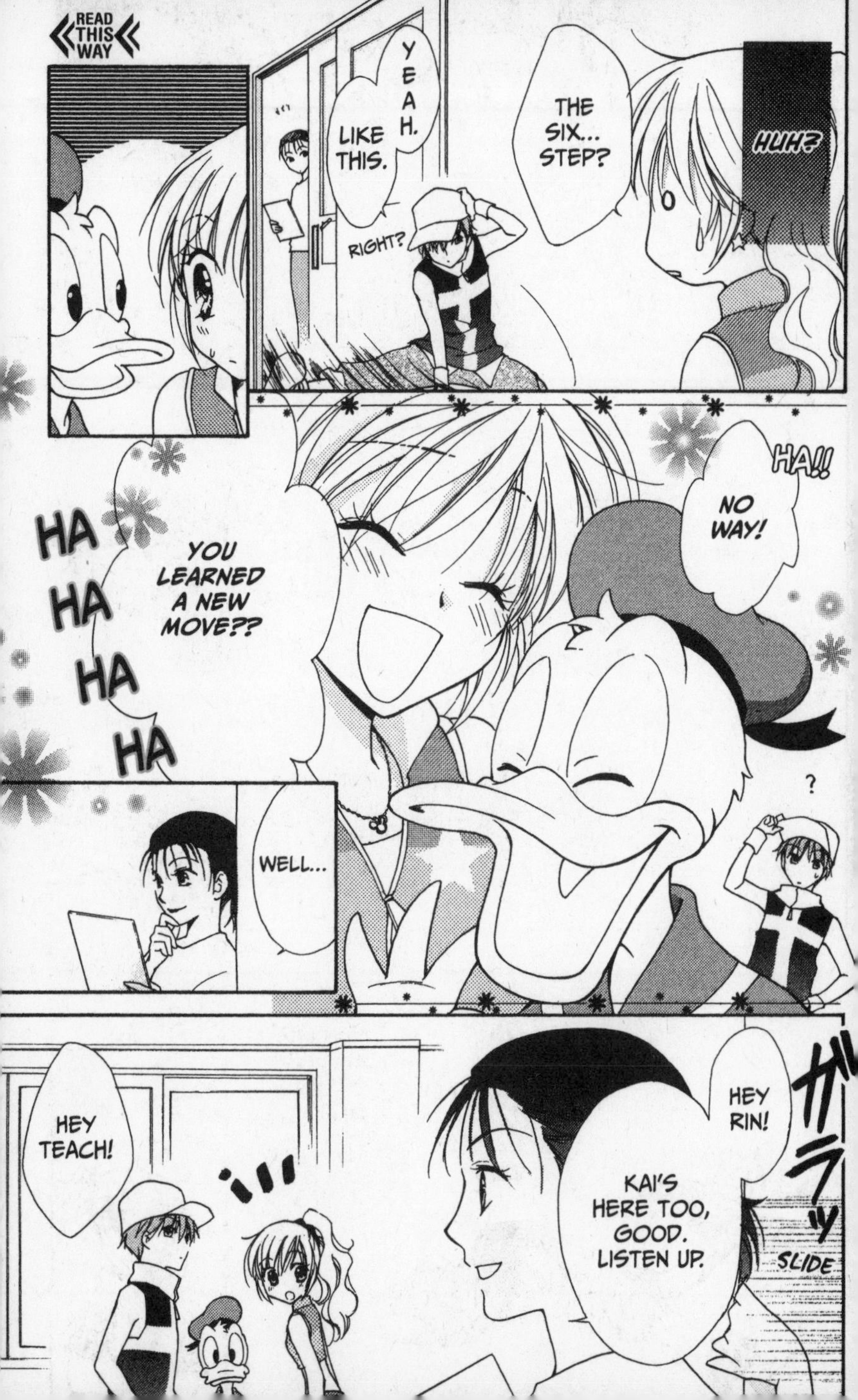
READ THIS WAY
HUH?
THE SIX... STEP?
YEAH.
LIKE THIS.
RIGHT?
HA!!
NO WAY!
YOU LEARNED A NEW MOVE??
HA HA HA HA
?
WELL...
ガラッ
SLIDE
HEY RIN!
KAI'S HERE TOO, GOOD. LISTEN UP.
HEY TEACH!

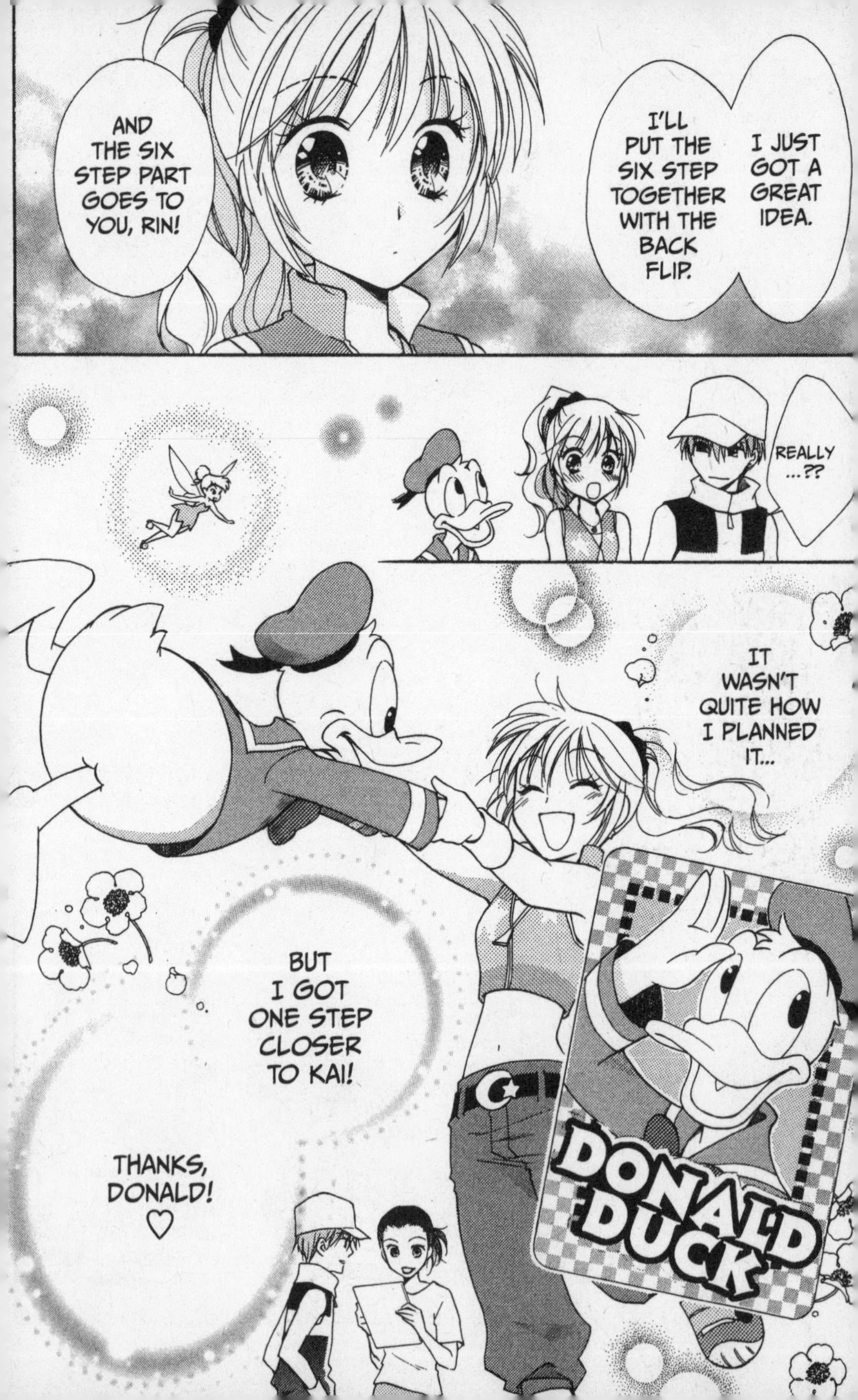
I JUST GOT A GREAT IDEA.
I'LL PUT THE SIX STEP TOGETHER WITH THE BACK FLIP.
AND THE SIX STEP PART GOES TO YOU, RIN!
REALLY ...??
IT WASN'T QUITE HOW I PLANNED IT...
BUT I GOT ONE STEP CLOSER TO KAI!
THANKS, DONALD! ♡
DONALD DUCK

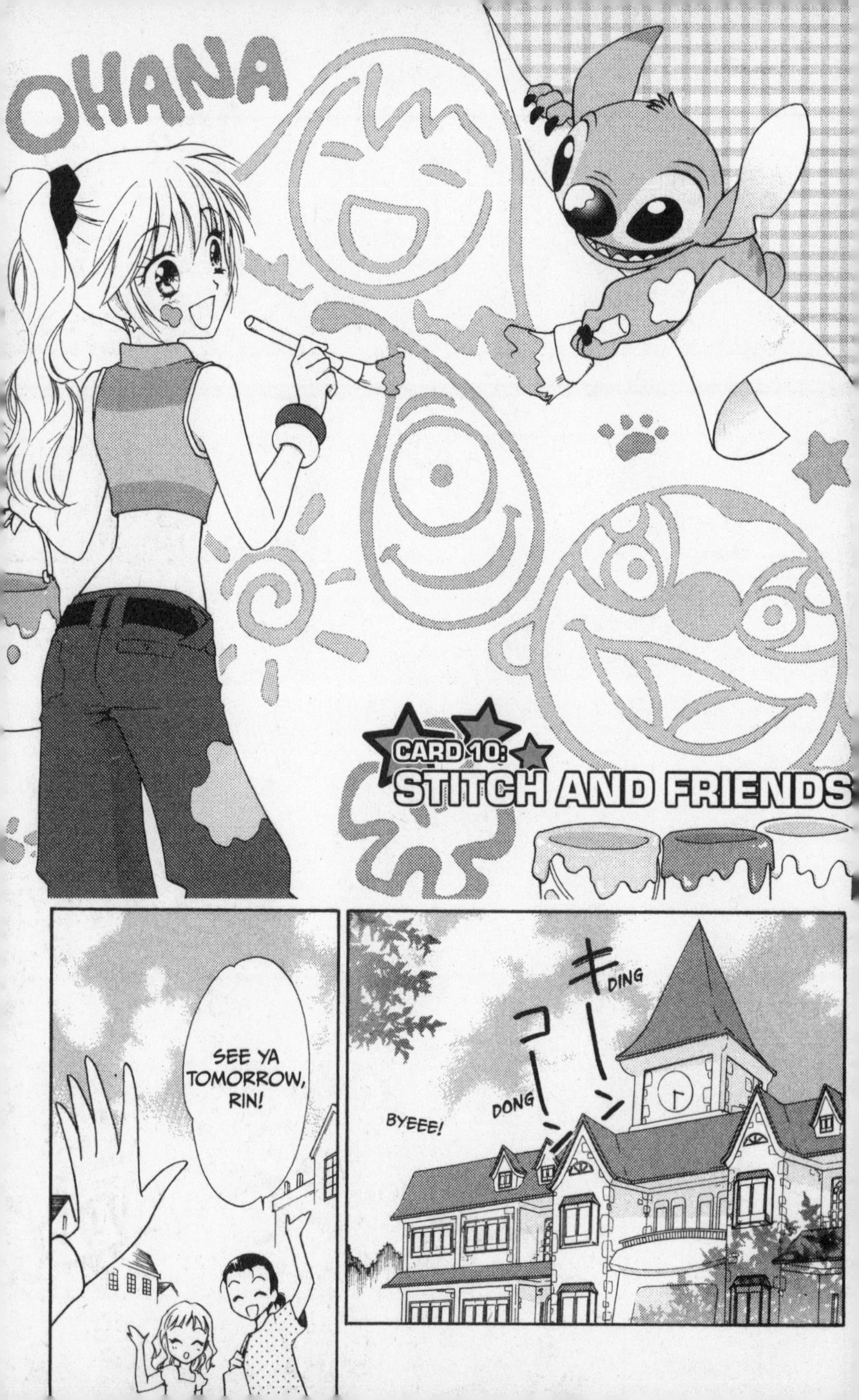
OHANA
CARD 10:
STITCH AND FRIENDS
キーン
DING
コーン
DONG
BYEEE!
SEE YA TOMORROW, RIN!

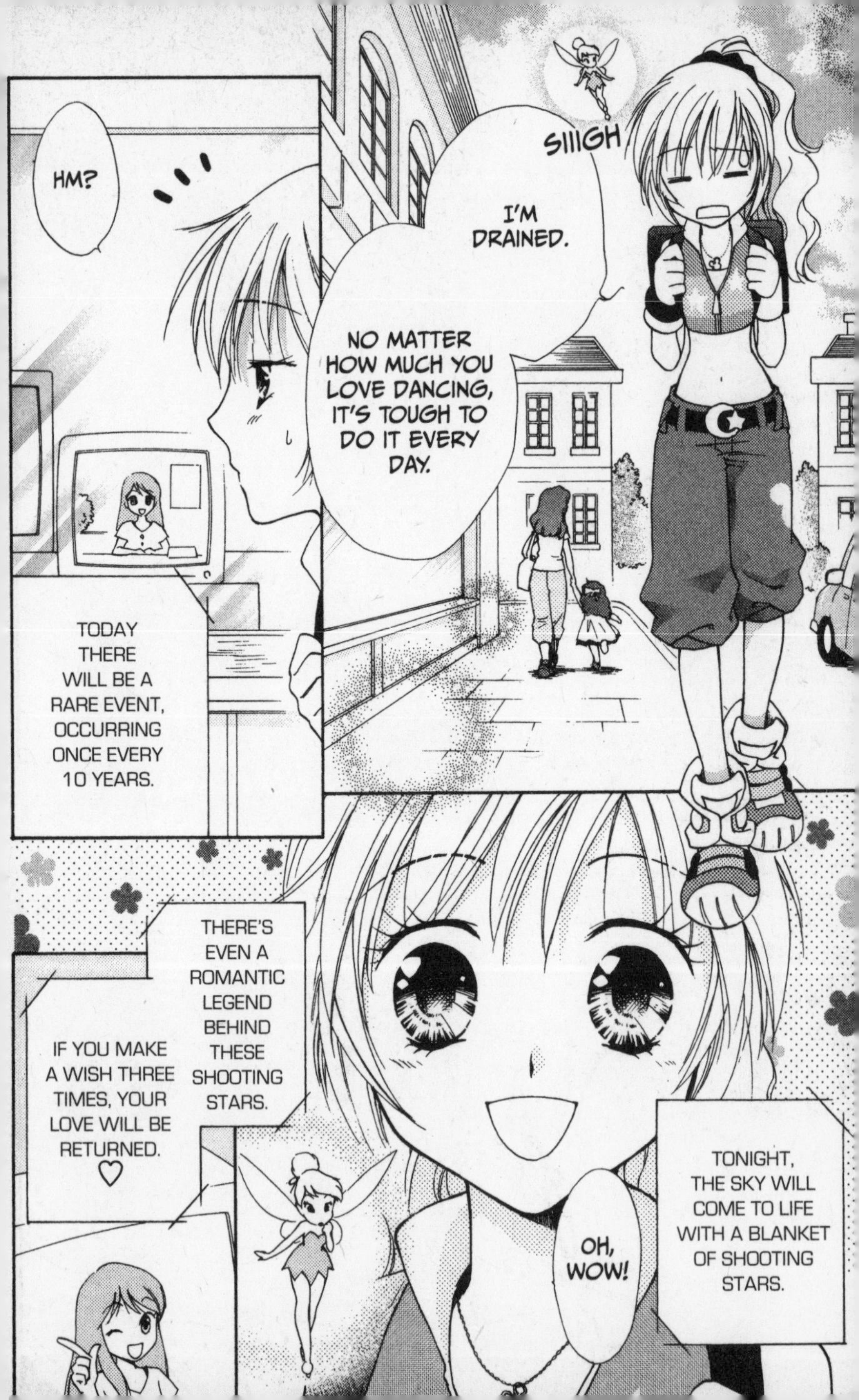
SIIIGH
I'M DRAINED.
NO MATTER HOW MUCH YOU LOVE DANCING, IT'S TOUGH TO DO IT EVERY DAY.
HM?
TODAY THERE WILL BE A RARE EVENT, OCCURRING ONCE EVERY 10 YEARS.
TONIGHT, THE SKY WILL COME TO LIFE WITH A BLANKET OF SHOOTING STARS.
OH, WOW!
THERE'S EVEN A ROMANTIC LEGEND BEHIND THESE SHOOTING STARS.
IF YOU MAKE A WISH THREE TIMES, YOUR LOVE WILL BE RETURNED. ♡

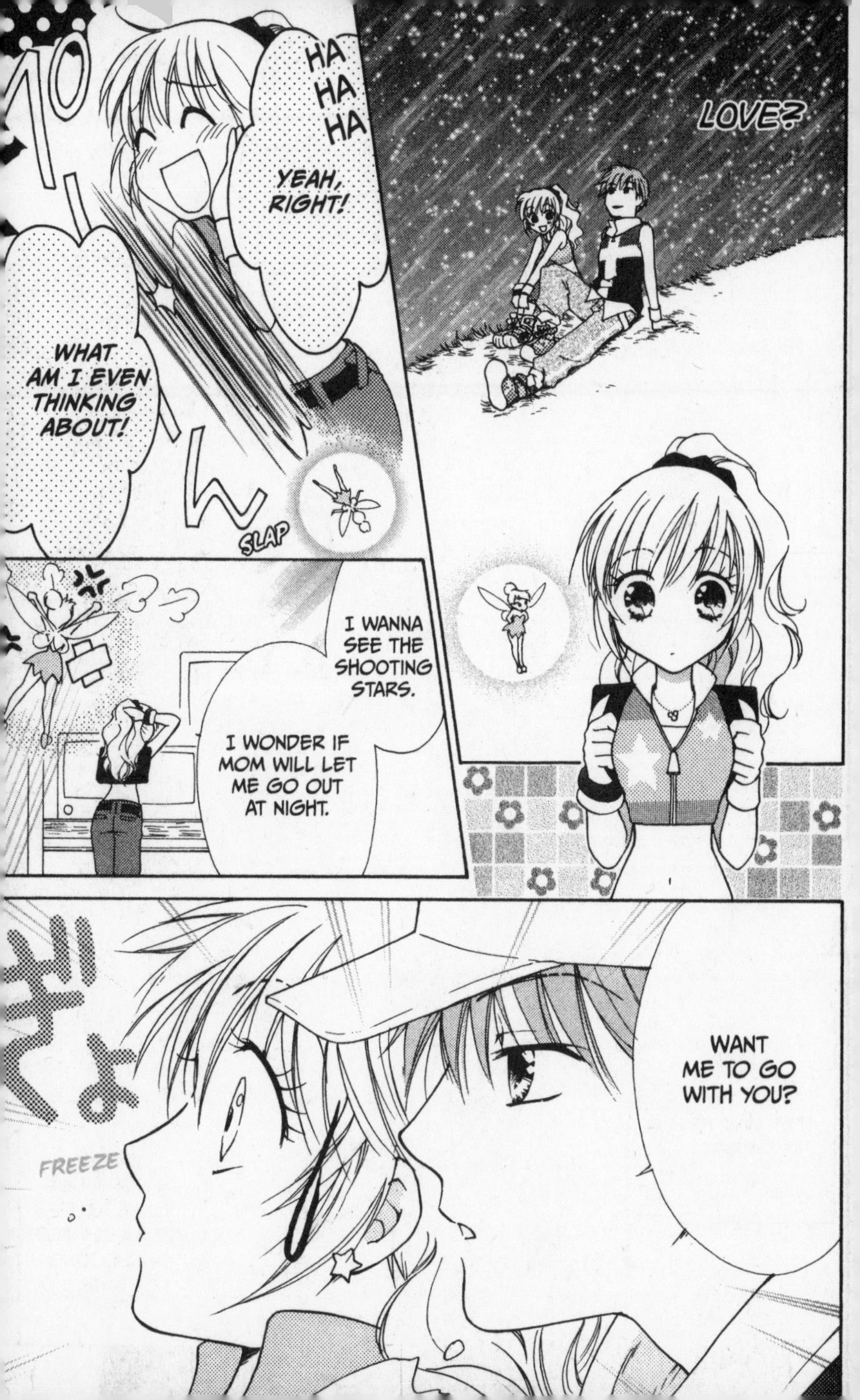
LOVE?
HA HA HA
YEAH, RIGHT!
WHAT AM I EVEN THINKING ABOUT!
SLAP
I WANNA SEE THE SHOOTING STARS.
I WONDER IF MOM WILL LET ME GO OUT AT NIGHT.
WANT ME TO GO WITH YOU?
FREEZE

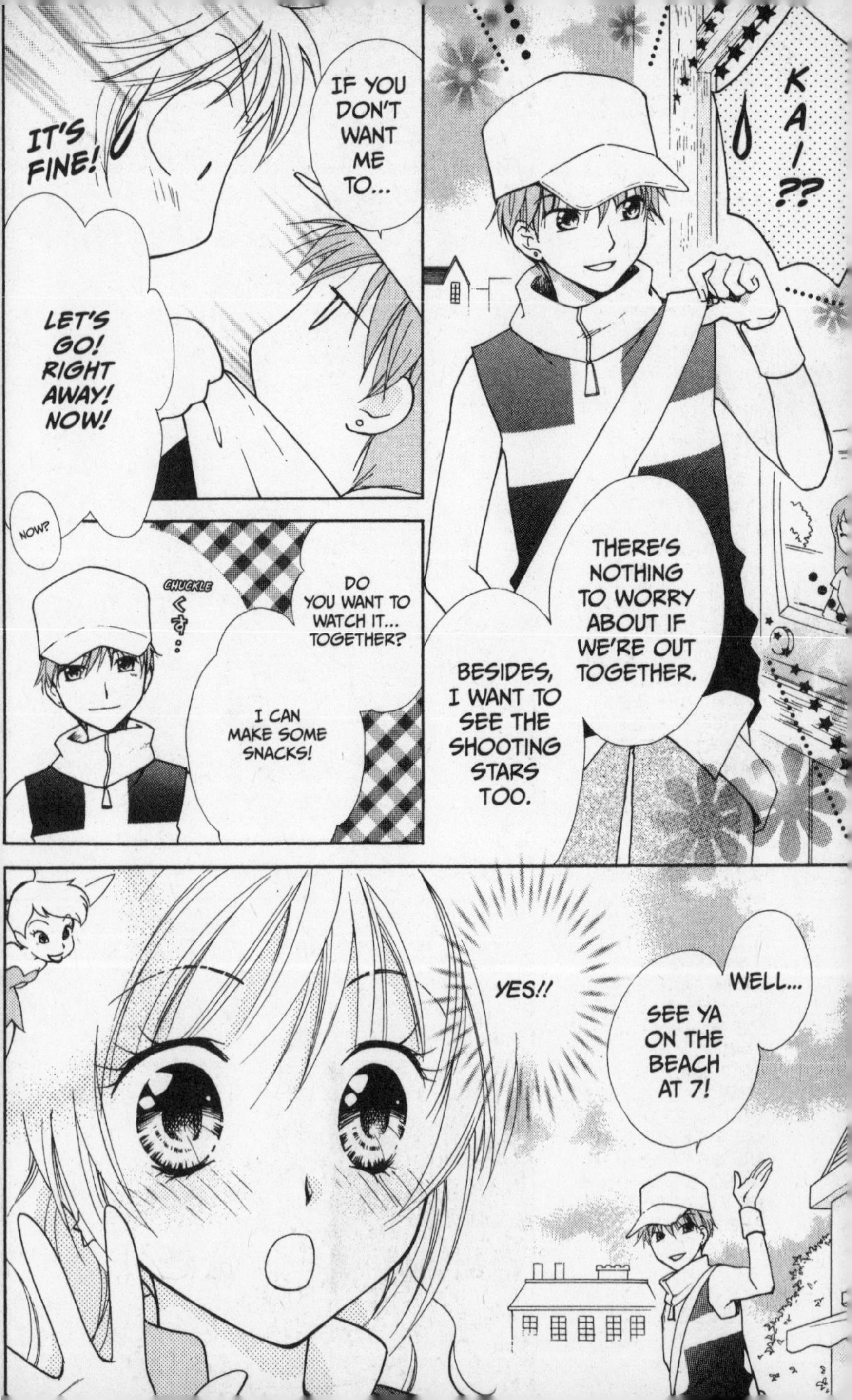
KAI??
THERE'S NOTHING TO WORRY ABOUT IF WE'RE OUT TOGETHER.
BESIDES, I WANT TO SEE THE SHOOTING STARS TOO.
IF YOU DON'T WANT ME TO...
IT'S FINE!
LET'S GO! RIGHT AWAY! NOW!
DO YOU WANT TO WATCH IT... TOGETHER?
NOW?
CHUCKLE
くす
I CAN MAKE SOME SNACKS!
WELL...
SEE YA ON THE BEACH AT 7!
YES!!

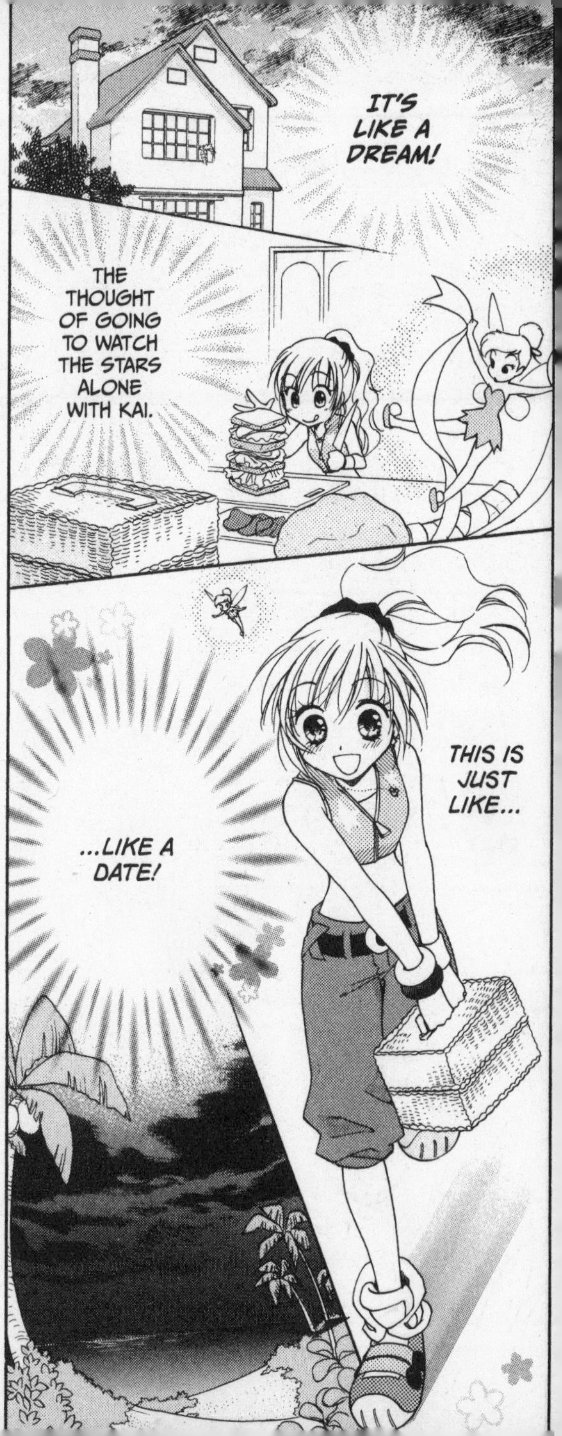
IT'S LIKE A DREAM!
THE THOUGHT OF GOING TO WATCH THE STARS ALONE WITH KAI.
THIS IS JUST LIKE...
...LIKE A DATE!

READ THIS WAY

HELLO! NAO KODAKA HERE, BRINGING YOU VOLUME 2 OF "DISNEY'S MAGICAL DANCE!!" OVER THIS PAST YEAR OR SO SINCE RIN FIRST MET TINK, SHE'S DANCED WITH A LOT OF DIFFERENT DISNEY CHARACTERS. 21 CHARACTERS IN ALL!! EACH TIME BEFORE I DRAW A CHARACTER, I DO MY RESEARCH BY WATCHING DVDS AND LOOKING AT REFERENCE MATERIALS, BUT I SOMETIMES FORGET WHAT I'M TRYING TO DO AND JUST WATCH THE MOVIES. (LAUGH) I GET A FEELING MY RESEARCH HAS BROUGHT ABOUT A BIT OF DISNEY MANIAC INSIDE ME. HAS YOUR FAVORITE CHARACTER SHOWN UP? RIN USED TO BE AN ABSOLUTELY AWFUL DANCER, BUT THROUGH ALL HER NEW FRIENDS, EACH SHOWING UP TO COME TO HER AID, EVEN SHE HAS BEEN ABLE TO GET CLOSER AND CLOSER TO MAKING HER DREAM COME TRUE. ALL YOU KIDS OUT THERE WHO KEEP ON FIGHTING AND DON'T GIVE UP, I'M SURE TINK IS ON HER WAY! DEFINITELY. SHE'S HEADING TO YOU NOW. ☆

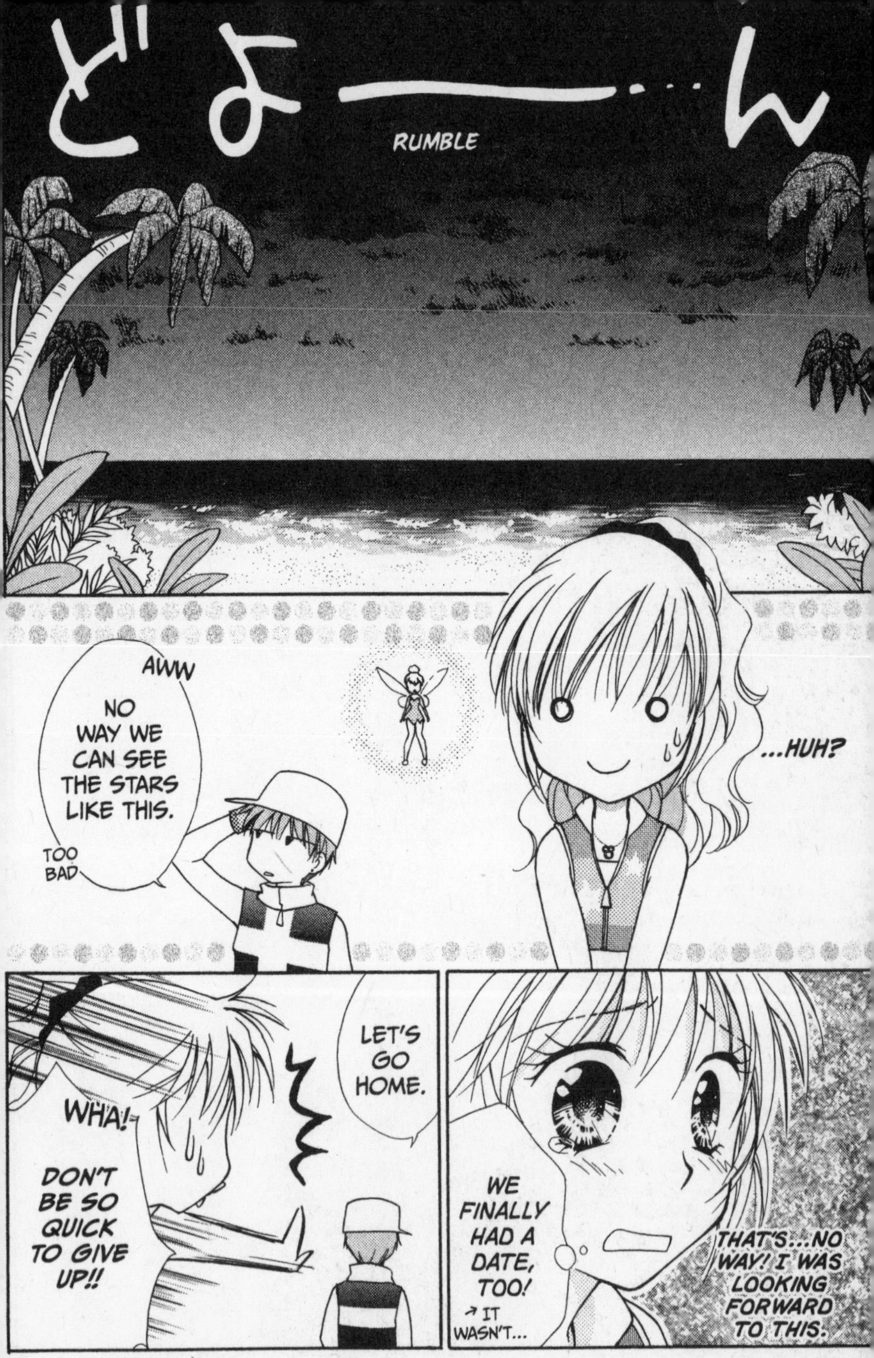
どよーー…ん
RUMBLE
AWW
NO WAY WE CAN SEE THE STARS LIKE THIS.
TOO BAD
...HUH?
THAT'S...NO WAY! I WAS LOOKING FORWARD TO THIS.
WE FINALLY HAD A DATE, TOO!
IT WASN'T...
LET'S GO HOME.
WHA!
DON'T BE SO QUICK TO GIVE UP!!

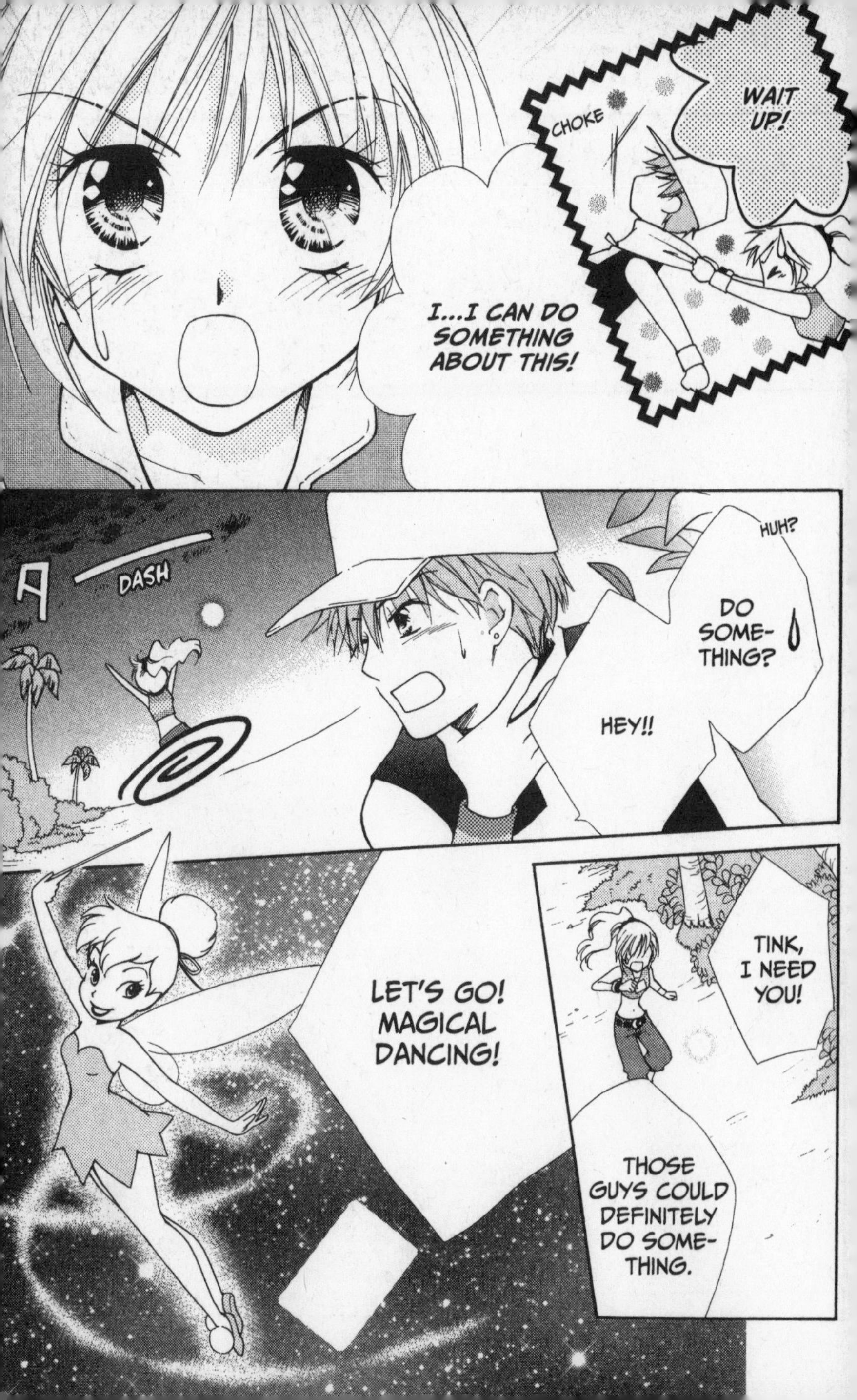
WAIT UP!
CHOKE
I...I CAN DO SOMETHING ABOUT THIS!
HUH?
DO SOME-THING?
HEY!!
DASH
TINK, I NEED YOU!
THOSE GUYS COULD DEFINITELY DO SOME-THING.
LET'S GO! MAGICAL DANCING!

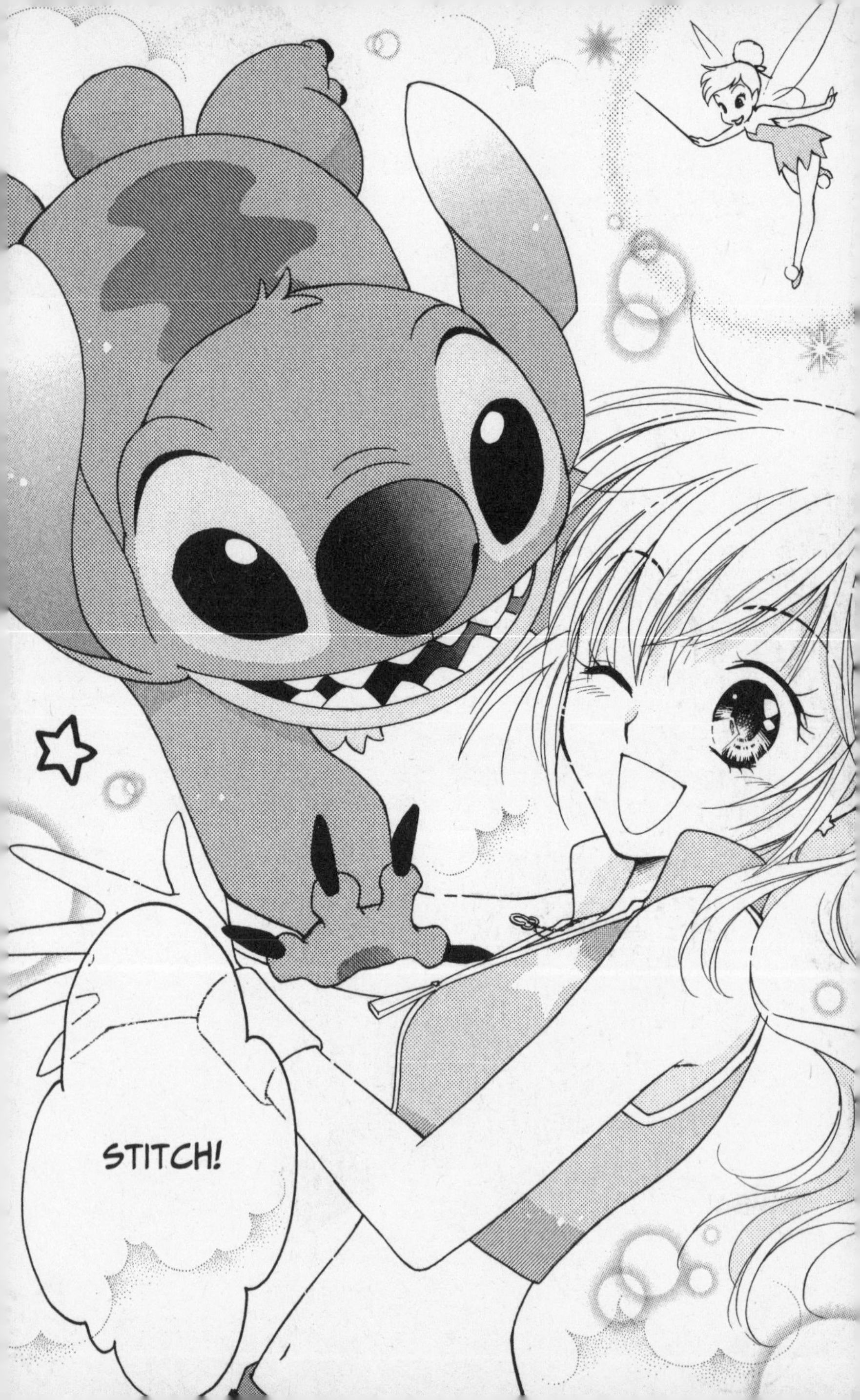
STITCH!

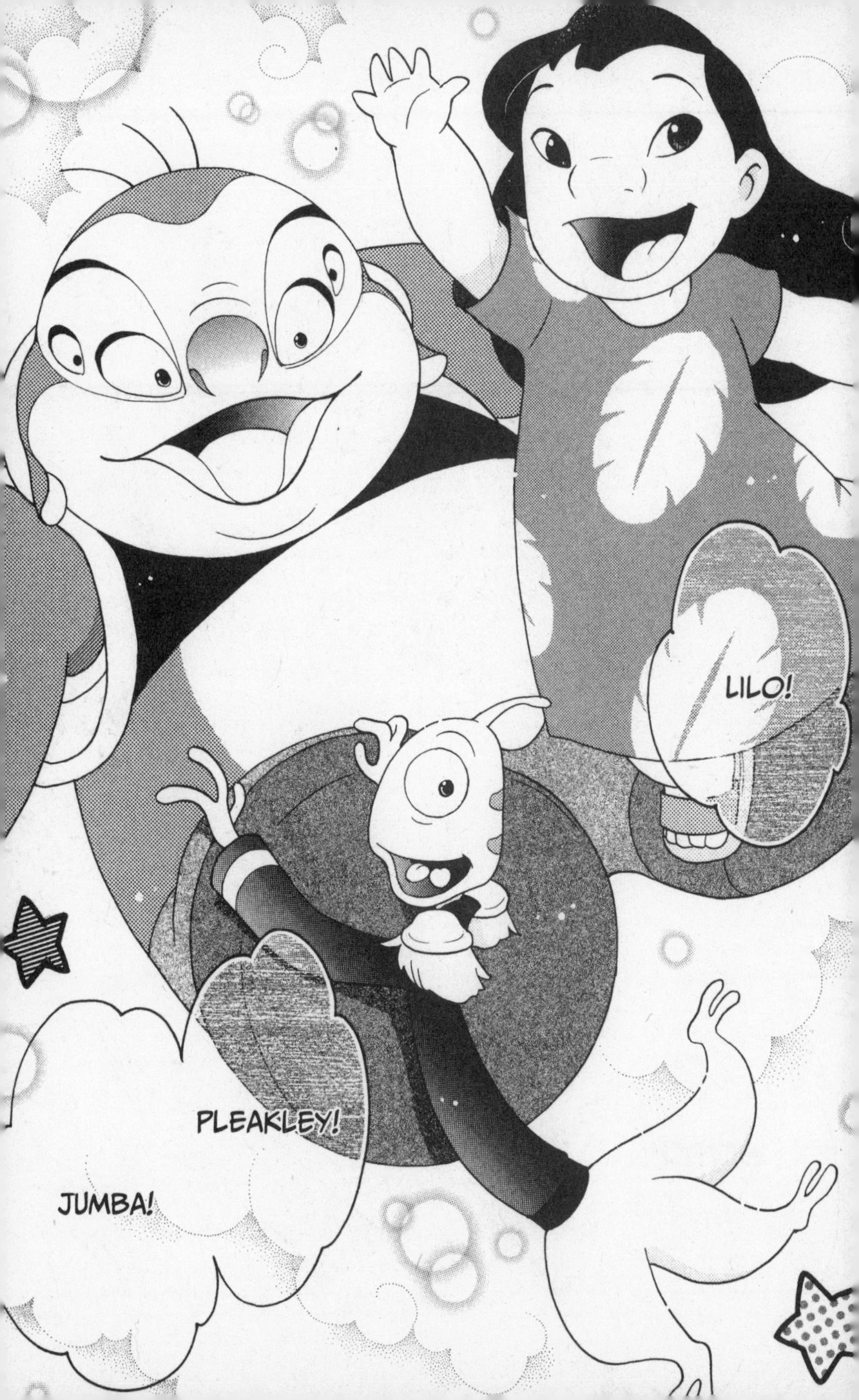
LILO!
PLEAKLEY!
JUMBA!

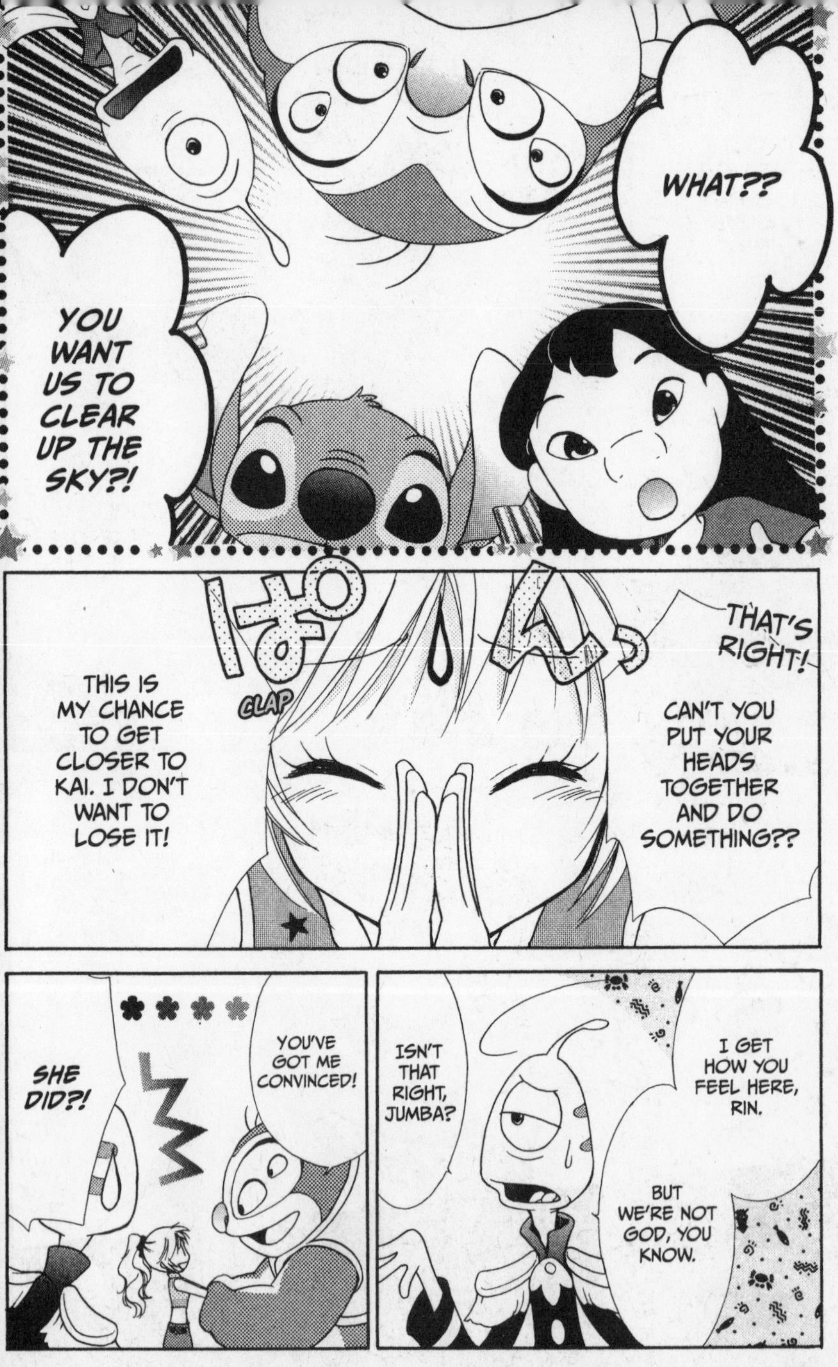
WHAT??
YOU WANT US TO CLEAR UP THE SKY?!
ぽんっ
THAT'S RIGHT!
CAN'T YOU PUT YOUR HEADS TOGETHER AND DO SOMETHING??
CLAP
THIS IS MY CHANCE TO GET CLOSER TO KAI. I DON'T WANT TO LOSE IT!
I GET HOW YOU FEEL HERE, RIN.
BUT WE'RE NOT GOD, YOU KNOW.
ISN'T THAT RIGHT, JUMBA?
YOU'VE GOT ME CONVINCED!
SHE DID?!

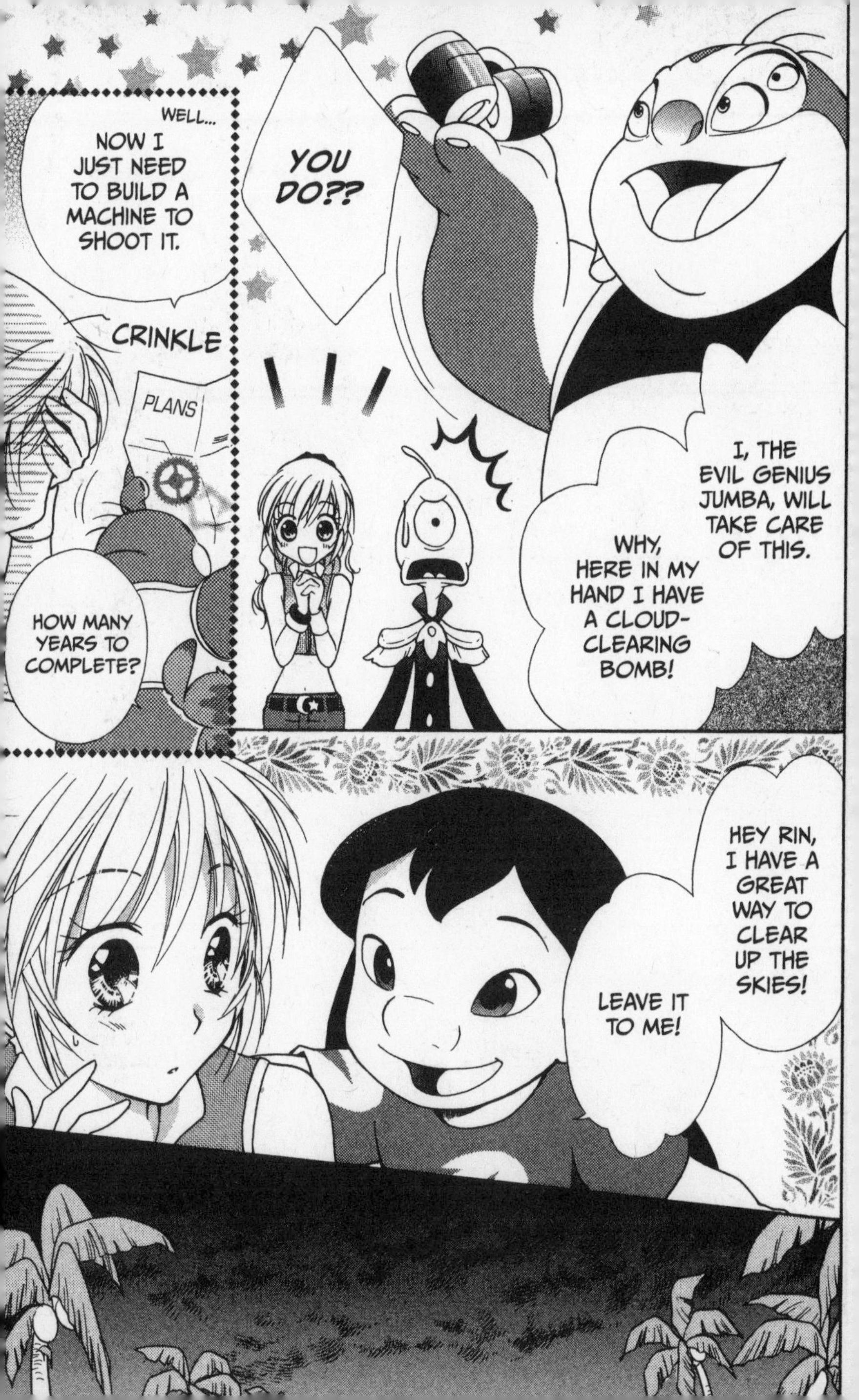
I, THE EVIL GENIUS JUMBA, WILL TAKE CARE OF THIS.
WHY, HERE IN MY HAND I HAVE A CLOUD-CLEARING BOMB!
YOU DO??
WELL...
NOW I JUST NEED TO BUILD A MACHINE TO SHOOT IT.
CRINKLE
PLANS
HOW MANY YEARS TO COMPLETE?
HEY RIN, I HAVE A GREAT WAY TO CLEAR UP THE SKIES!
LEAVE IT TO ME!

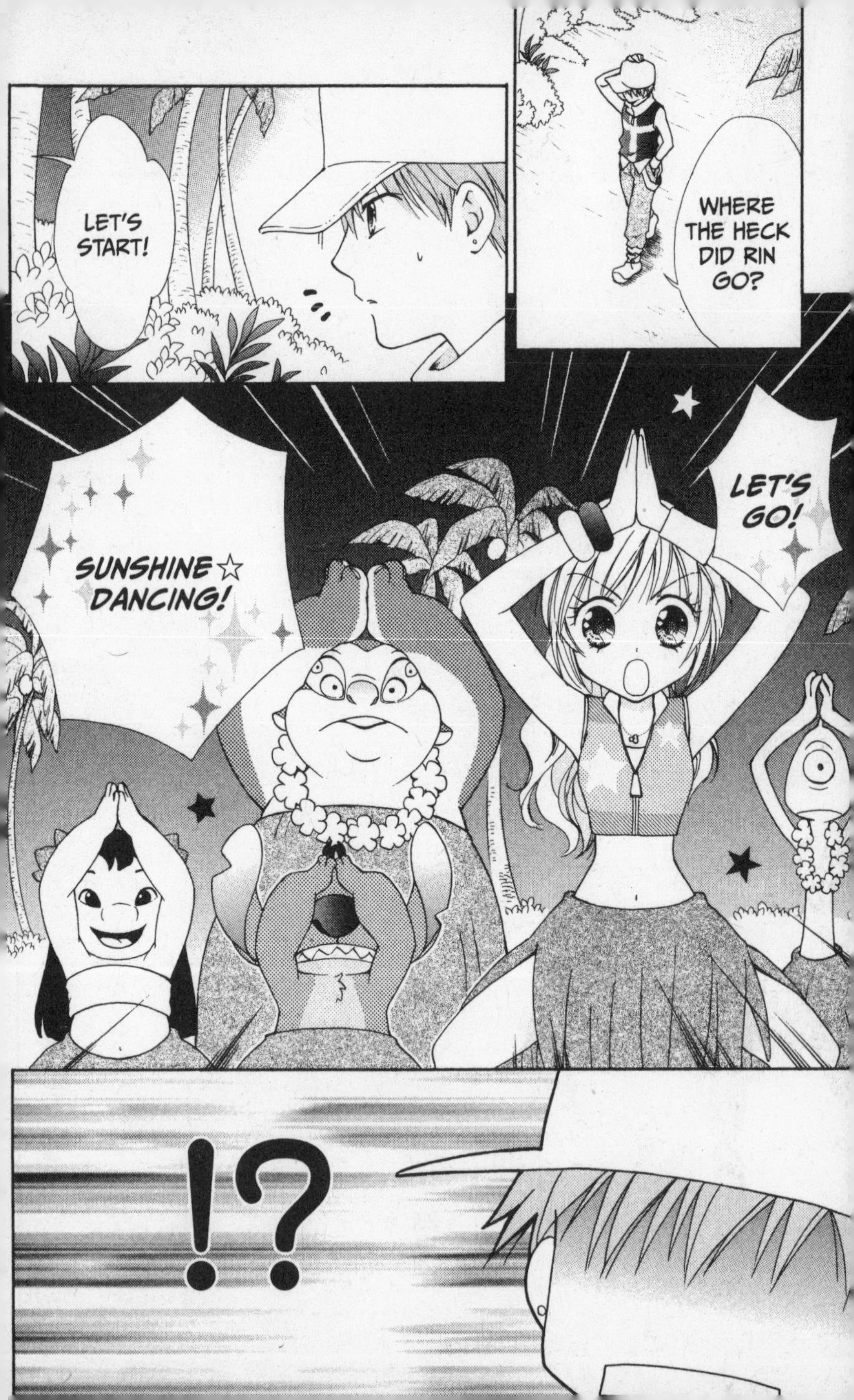
WHERE THE HECK DID RIN GO?
LET'S START!
LET'S GO!
SUNSHINE☆ DANCING!
!?

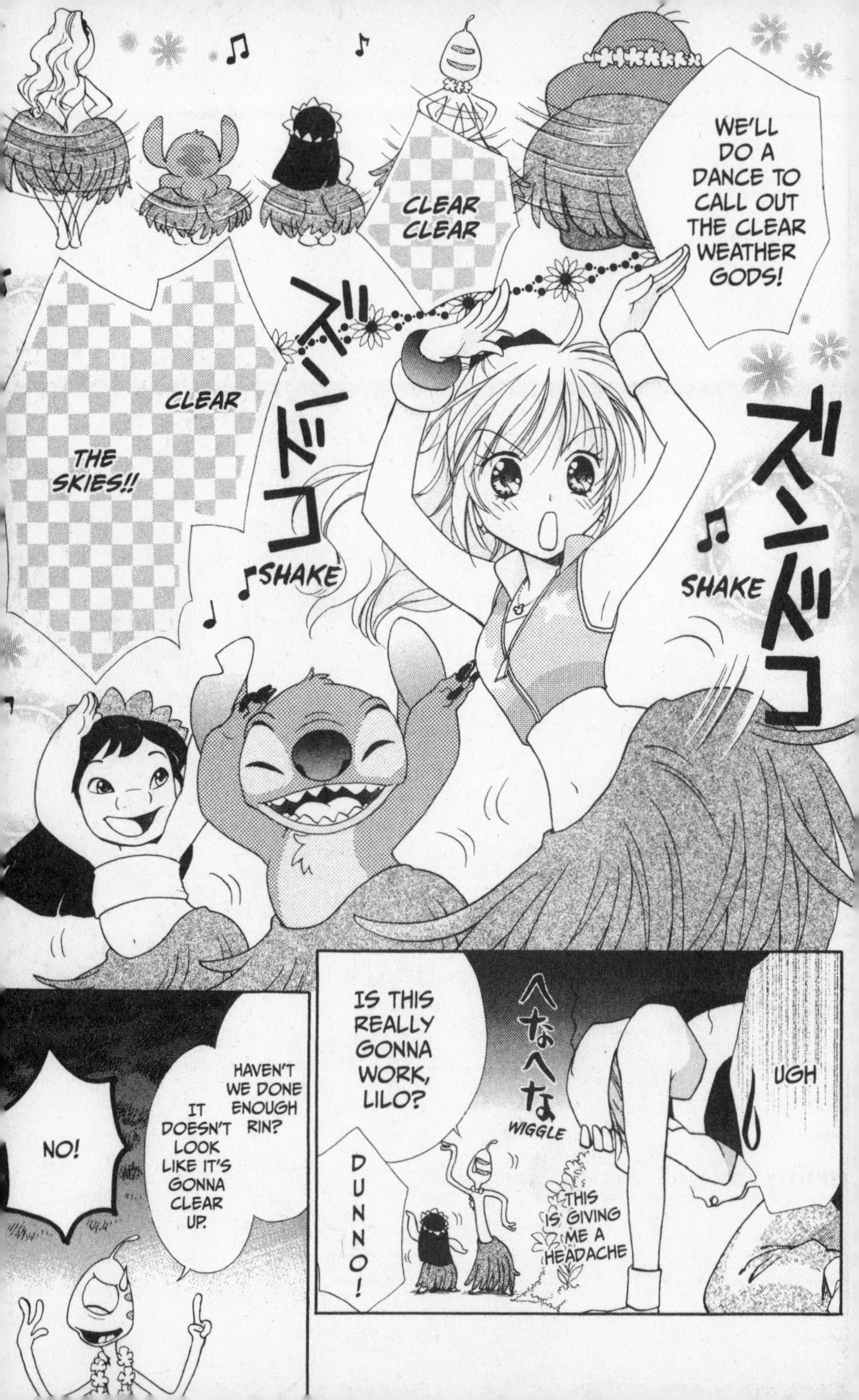

WE'LL DO A DANCE TO CALL OUT THE CLEAR WEATHER GODS!
ズ～ンドコ
SHAKE
CLEAR CLEAR
ズ～ンドコ
SHAKE
CLEAR
THE SKIES!!
UGH
IS THIS REALLY GONNA WORK, LILO?
へなへな
WIGGLE
THIS IS GIVING ME A HEADACHE
DUNNO!
HAVEN'T WE DONE ENOUGH RIN?
IT DOESN'T LOOK LIKE IT'S GONNA CLEAR UP.
NO!

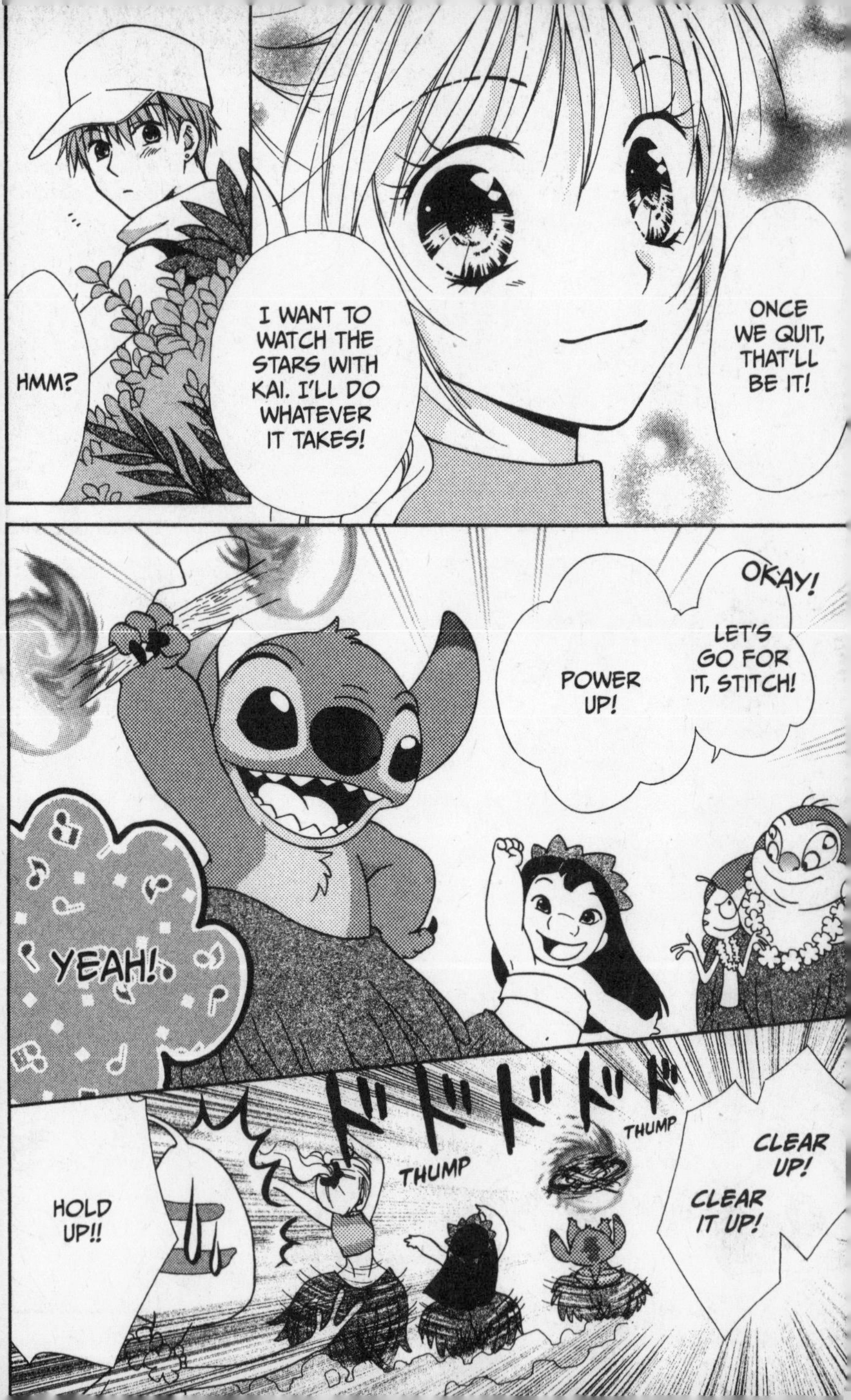
ONCE WE QUIT, THAT'LL BE IT!
I WANT TO WATCH THE STARS WITH KAI. I'LL DO WHATEVER IT TAKES!
HMM?
OKAY!
LET'S GO FOR IT, STITCH!
POWER UP!
YEAH!
CLEAR UP!
CLEAR IT UP!
THUMP
ドドドドドド
THUMP
HOLD UP!!

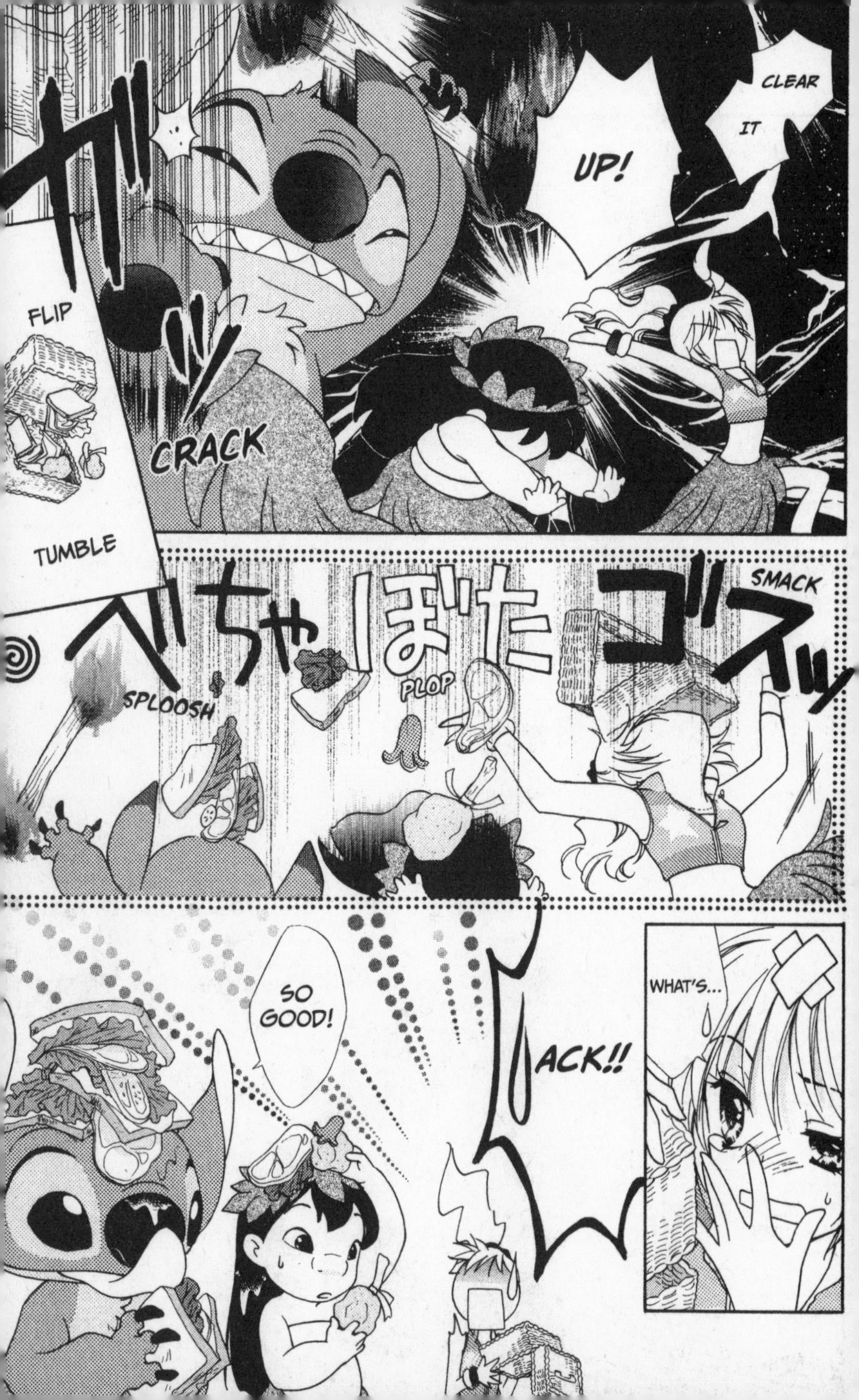
CLEAR IT UP!
CRACK
FLIP
TUMBLE
SMACK
ゴスッ
ぼた
PLOP
べちゃ
SPLOOSH
WHAT'S...
ACK!!
SO GOOD!

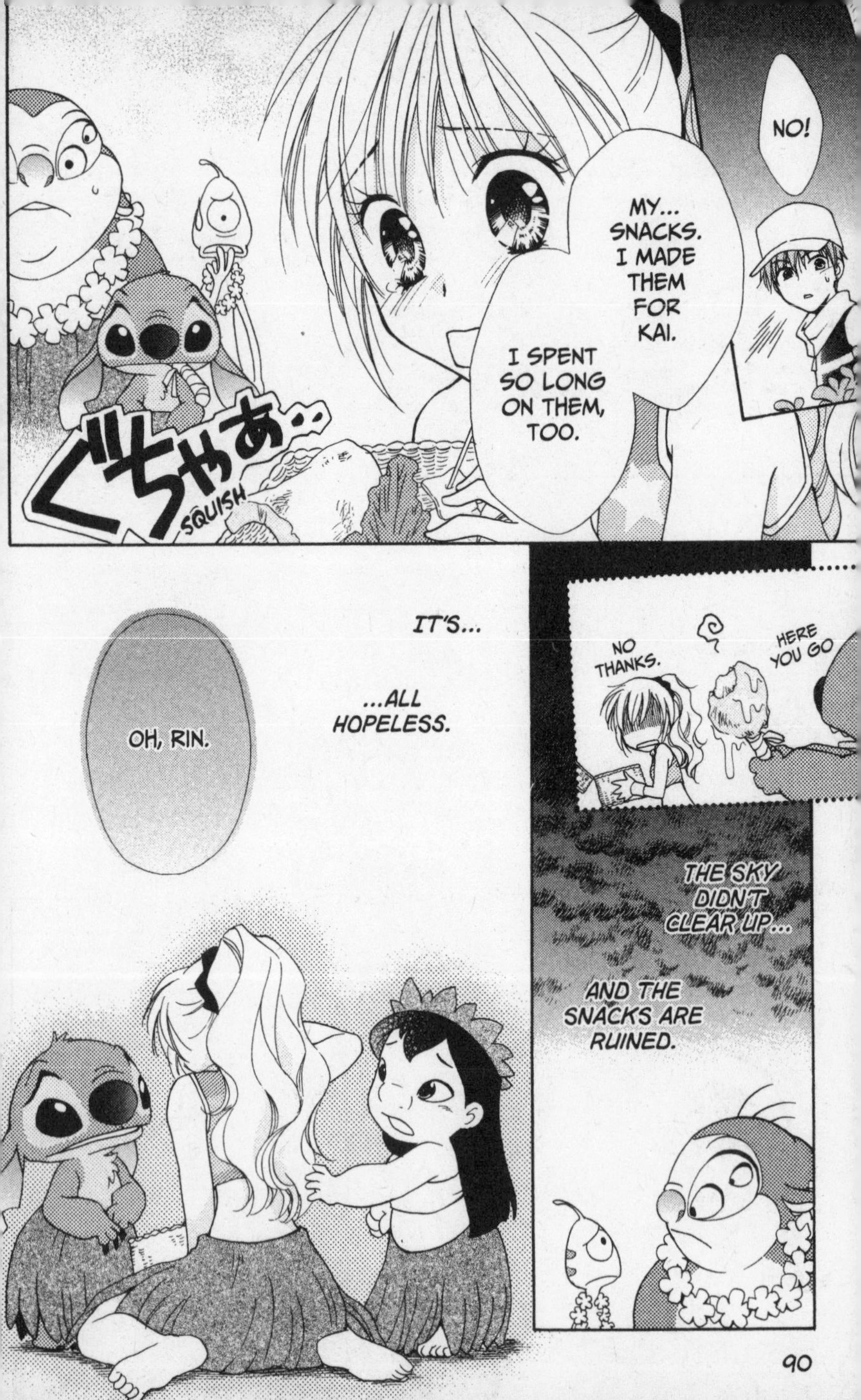
NO!
MY... SNACKS. I MADE THEM FOR KAI.
I SPENT SO LONG ON THEM, TOO.
ぐちゃあ..
SQUISH
HERE YOU GO
NO THANKS.
THE SKY DIDN'T CLEAR UP...
AND THE SNACKS ARE RUINED.
IT'S...
...ALL HOPELESS.
OH, RIN.

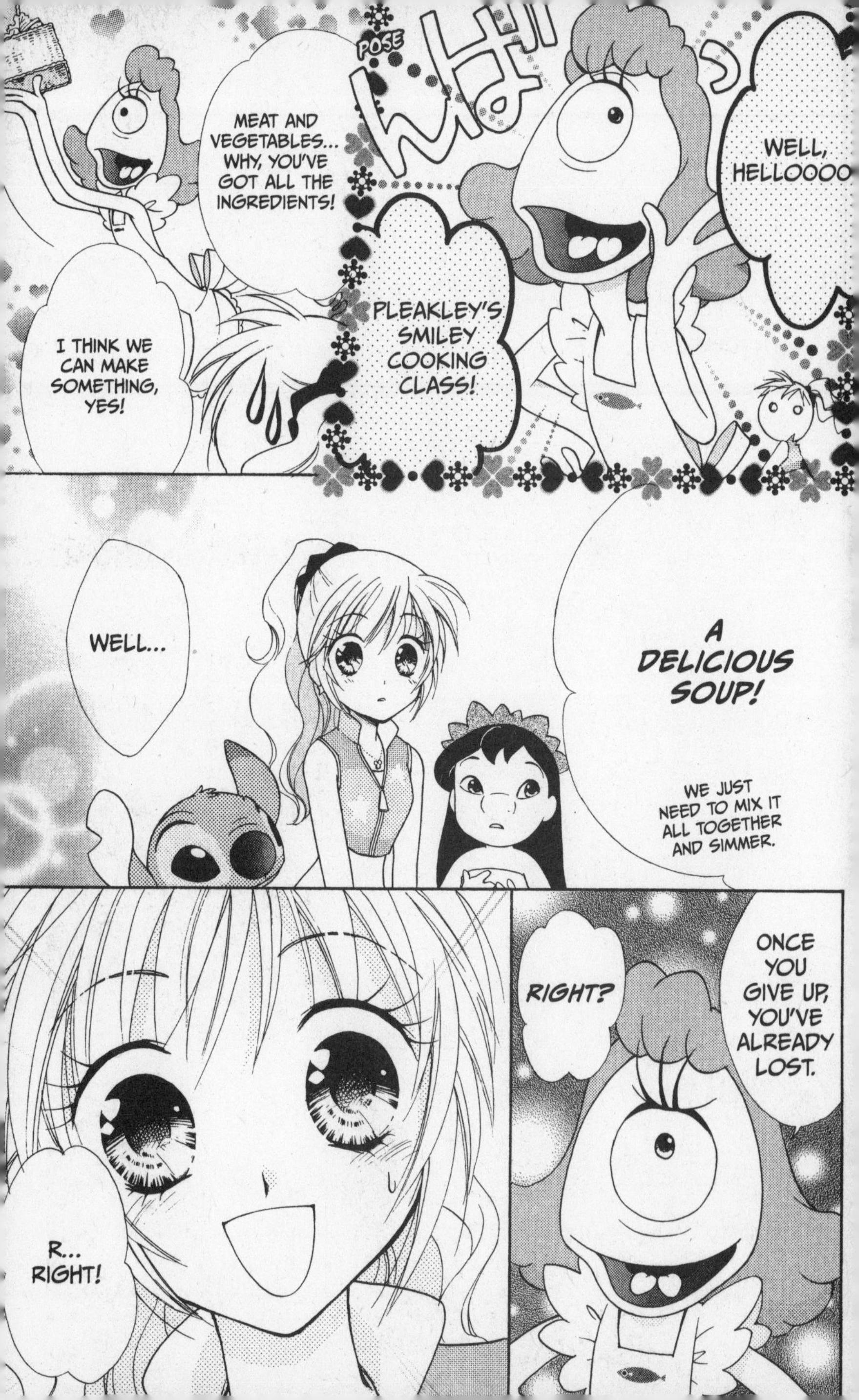
POSE
んばっ
WELL, HELLOOOO
PLEAKLEY'S SMILEY COOKING CLASS!
MEAT AND VEGETABLES... WHY, YOU'VE GOT ALL THE INGREDIENTS!
I THINK WE CAN MAKE SOMETHING, YES!
A DELICIOUS SOUP!
WE JUST NEED TO MIX IT ALL TOGETHER AND SIMMER.
WELL...
ONCE YOU GIVE UP, YOU'VE ALREADY LOST.
RIGHT?
R... RIGHT!

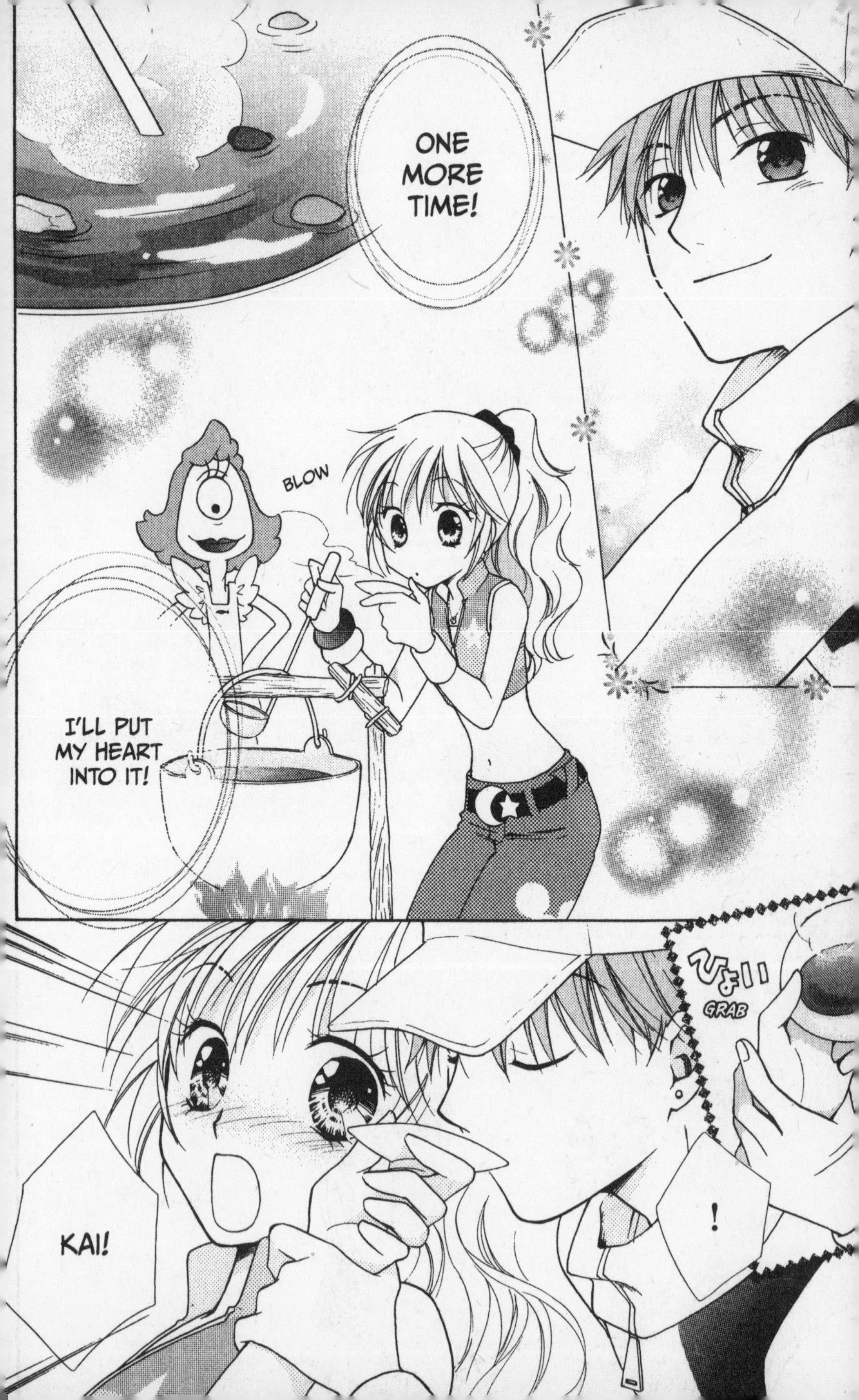
ONE MORE TIME!
BLOW
I'LL PUT MY HEART INTO IT!
ひょい
GRAB
!
KAI!

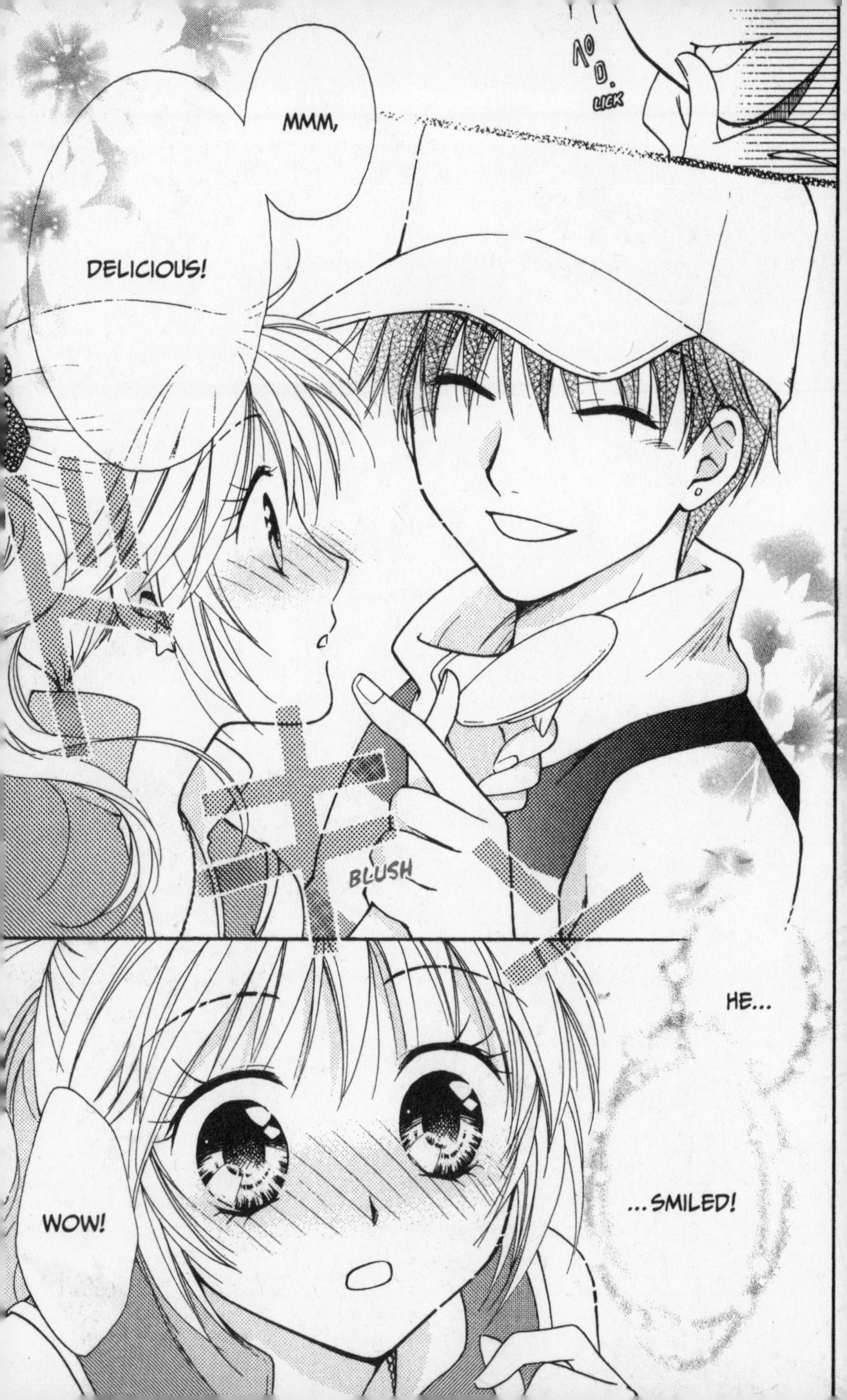
LICK
MMM, DELICIOUS!
BLUSH
HE...
...SMILED!
WOW!

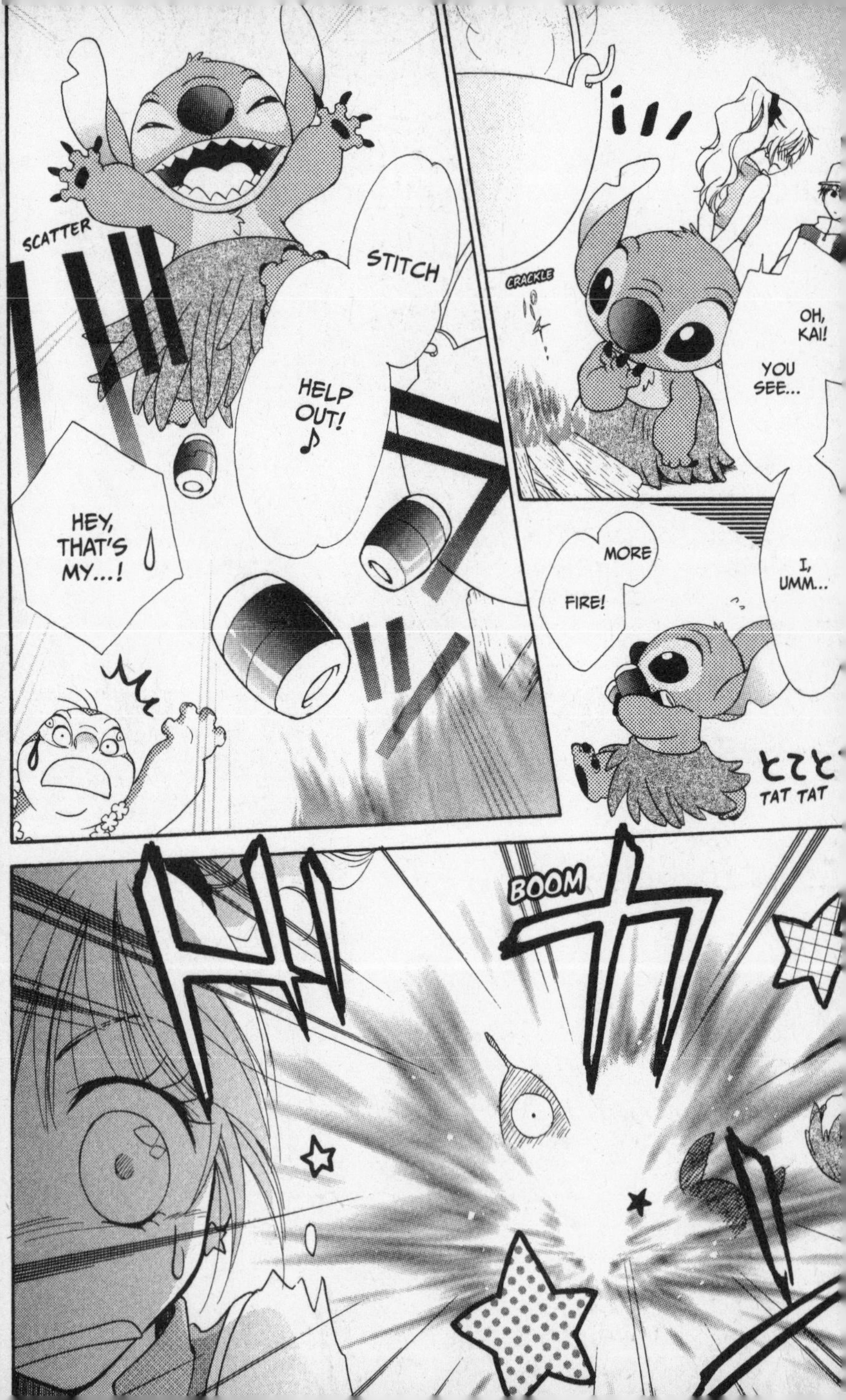
OH, KAI!
YOU SEE...
CRACKLE
I, UMM...
MORE FIRE!
とてと
TAT TAT
STITCH
HELP OUT! ♪
SCATTER
HEY, THAT'S MY...!
BOOM

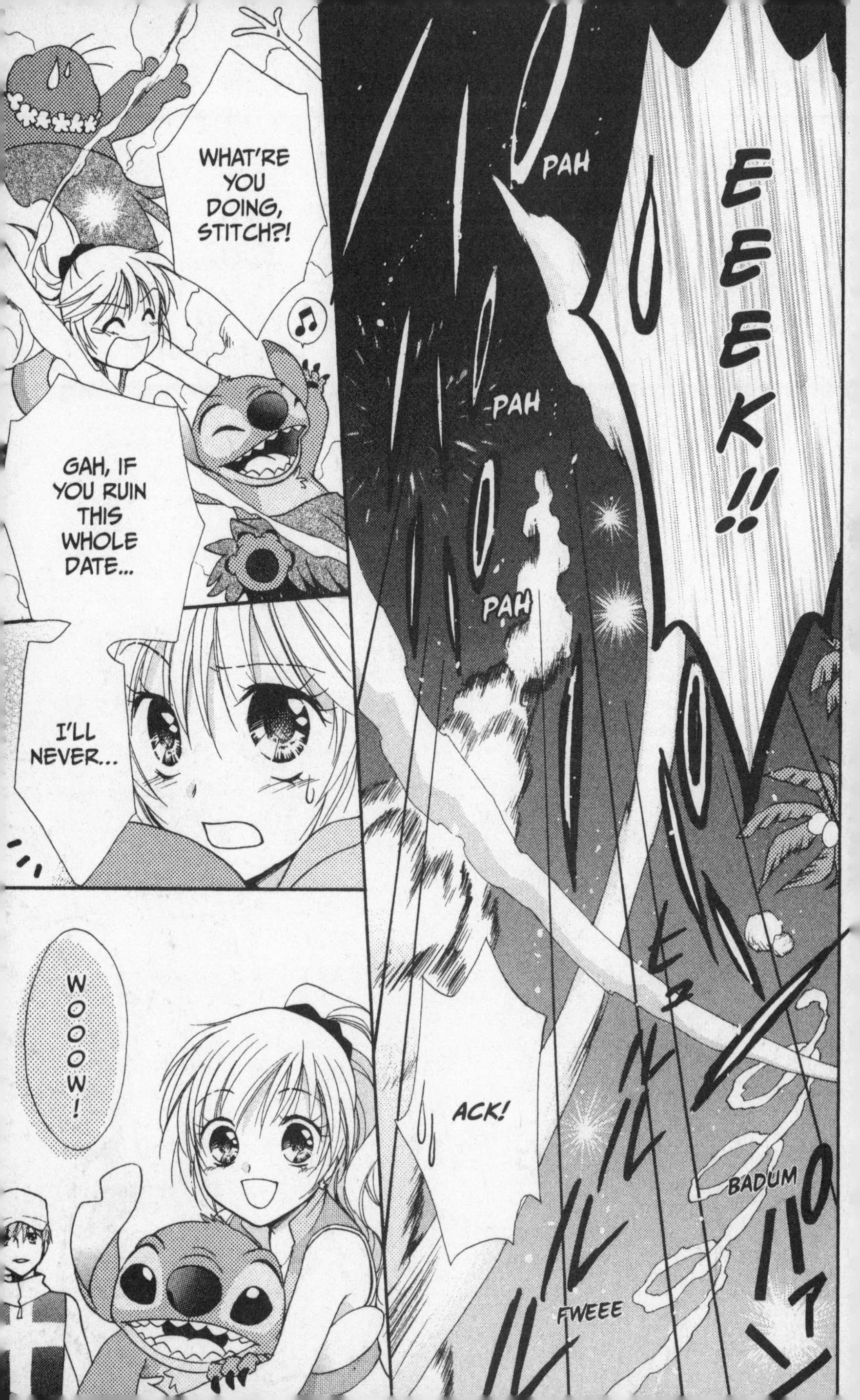
EEEK!!
PAH
PAH
PAH
ACK!
BADUM
FWEEE
WHAT'RE YOU DOING, STITCH?!
♪
GAH, IF YOU RUIN THIS WHOLE DATE...
I'LL NEVER...
WOOOOW!

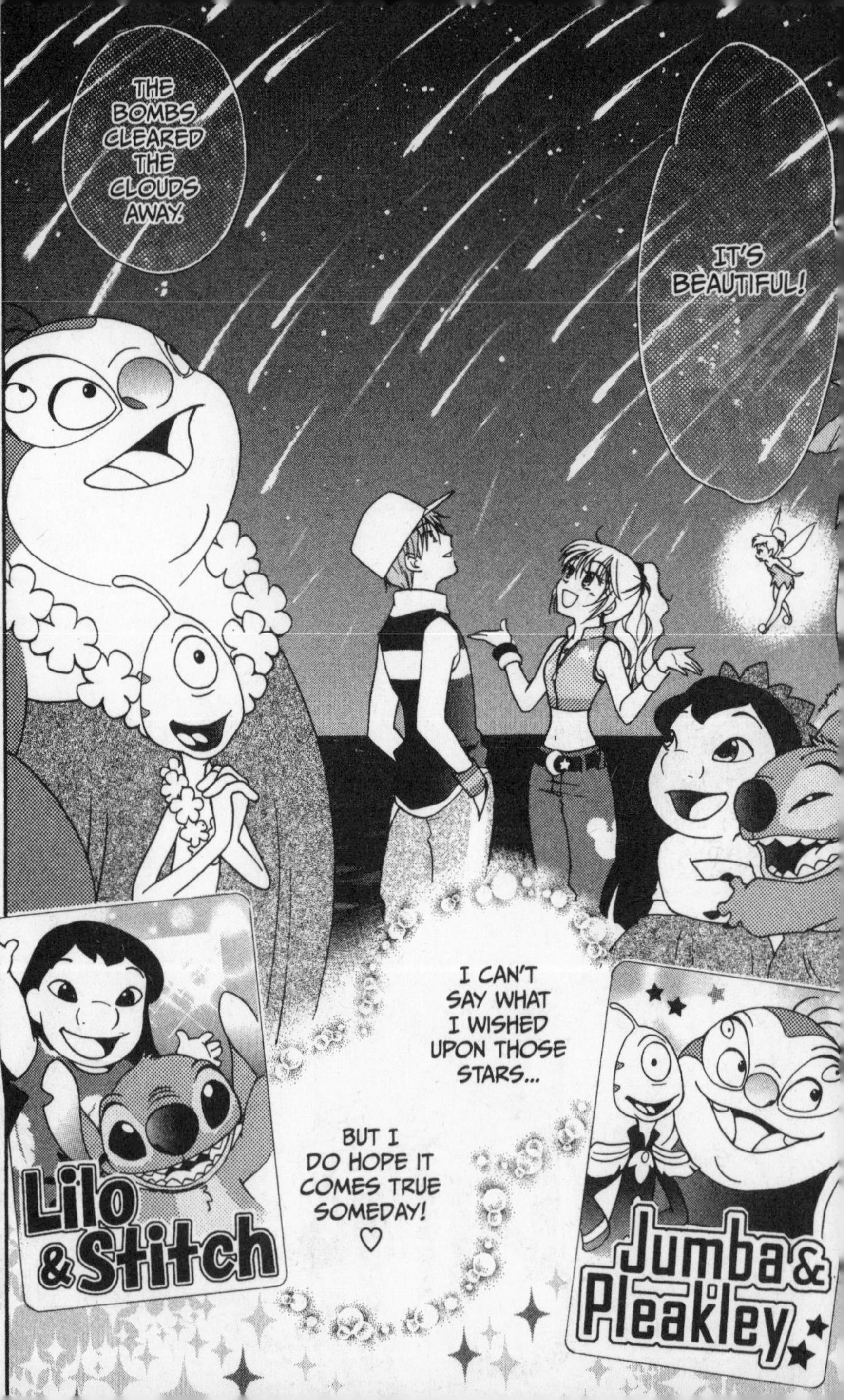
IT'S BEAUTIFUL!
THE BOMBS CLEARED THE CLOUDS AWAY.
I CAN'T SAY WHAT I WISHED UPON THOSE STARS...
BUT I DO HOPE IT COMES TRUE SOMEDAY! ♡
Jumba & Pleakley
Lilo & Stitch

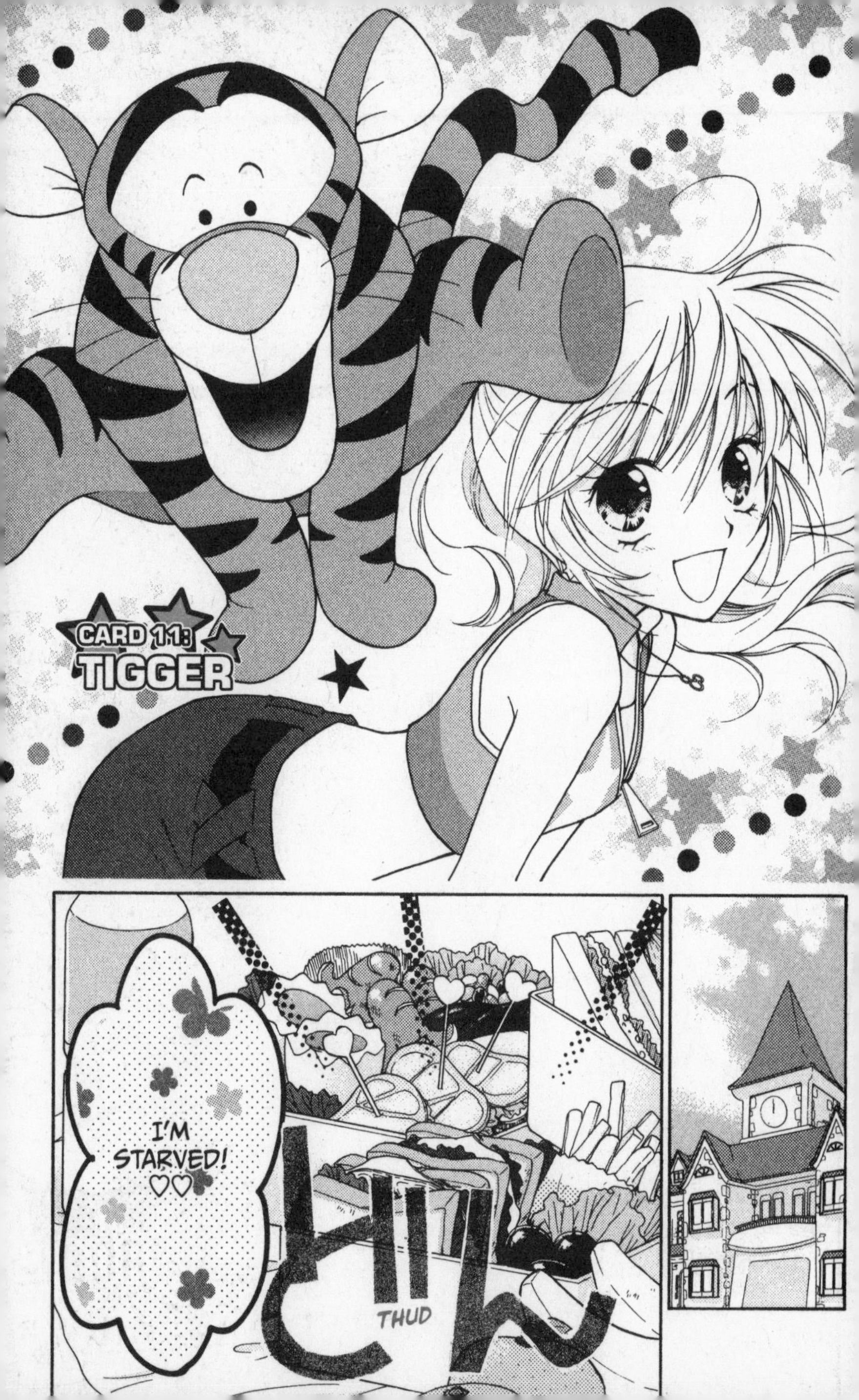
CARD 11:
TIGGER
I'M STARVED! ♡♡
THUD

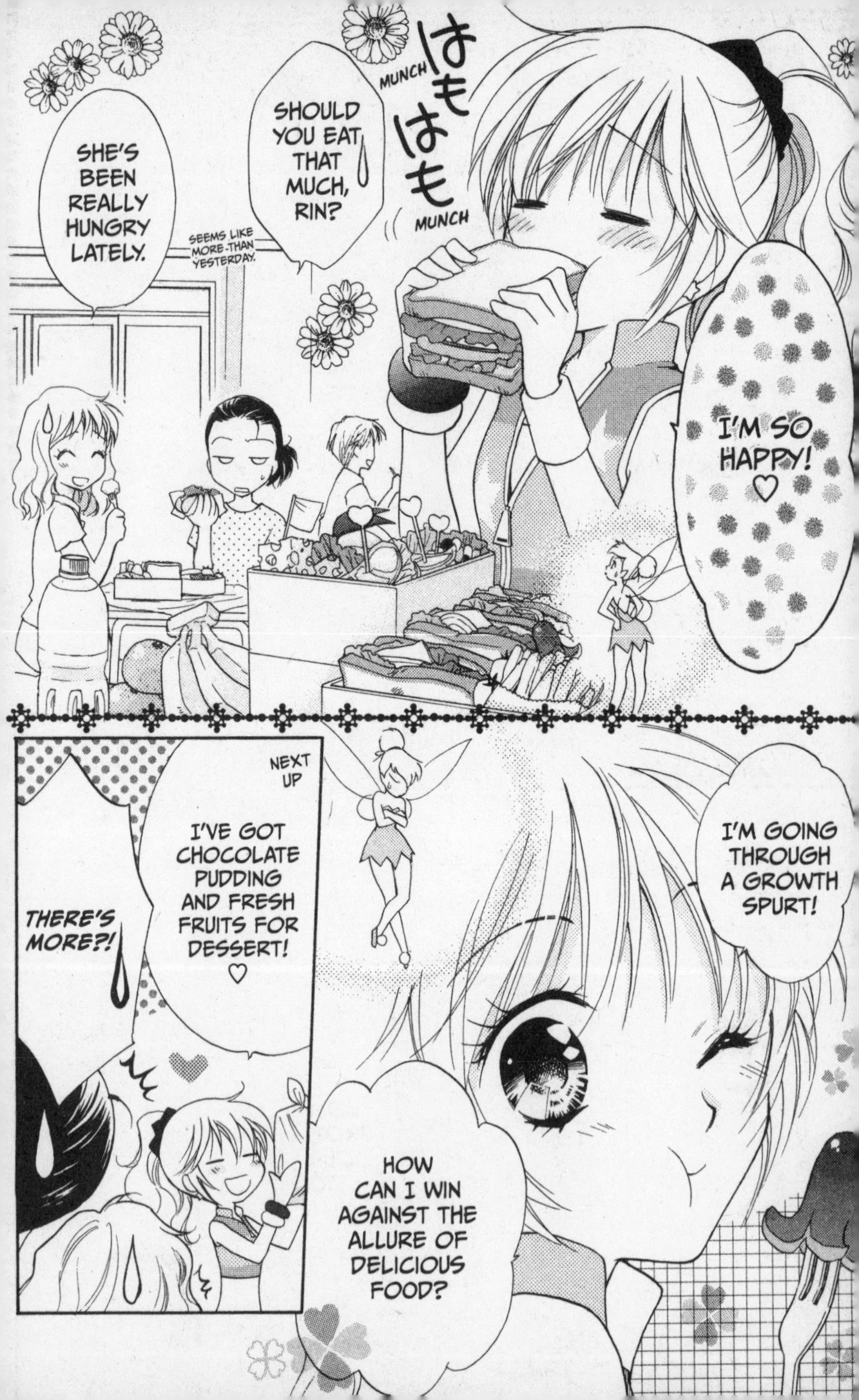
I'M SO HAPPY! ♡
はもはも
MUNCH
MUNCH
SHOULD YOU EAT THAT MUCH, RIN?
SEEMS LIKE MORE THAN YESTERDAY.
SHE'S BEEN REALLY HUNGRY LATELY.
I'M GOING THROUGH A GROWTH SPURT!
HOW CAN I WIN AGAINST THE ALLURE OF DELICIOUS FOOD?
NEXT UP
I'VE GOT CHOCOLATE PUDDING AND FRESH FRUITS FOR DESSERT! ♡
THERE'S MORE?!

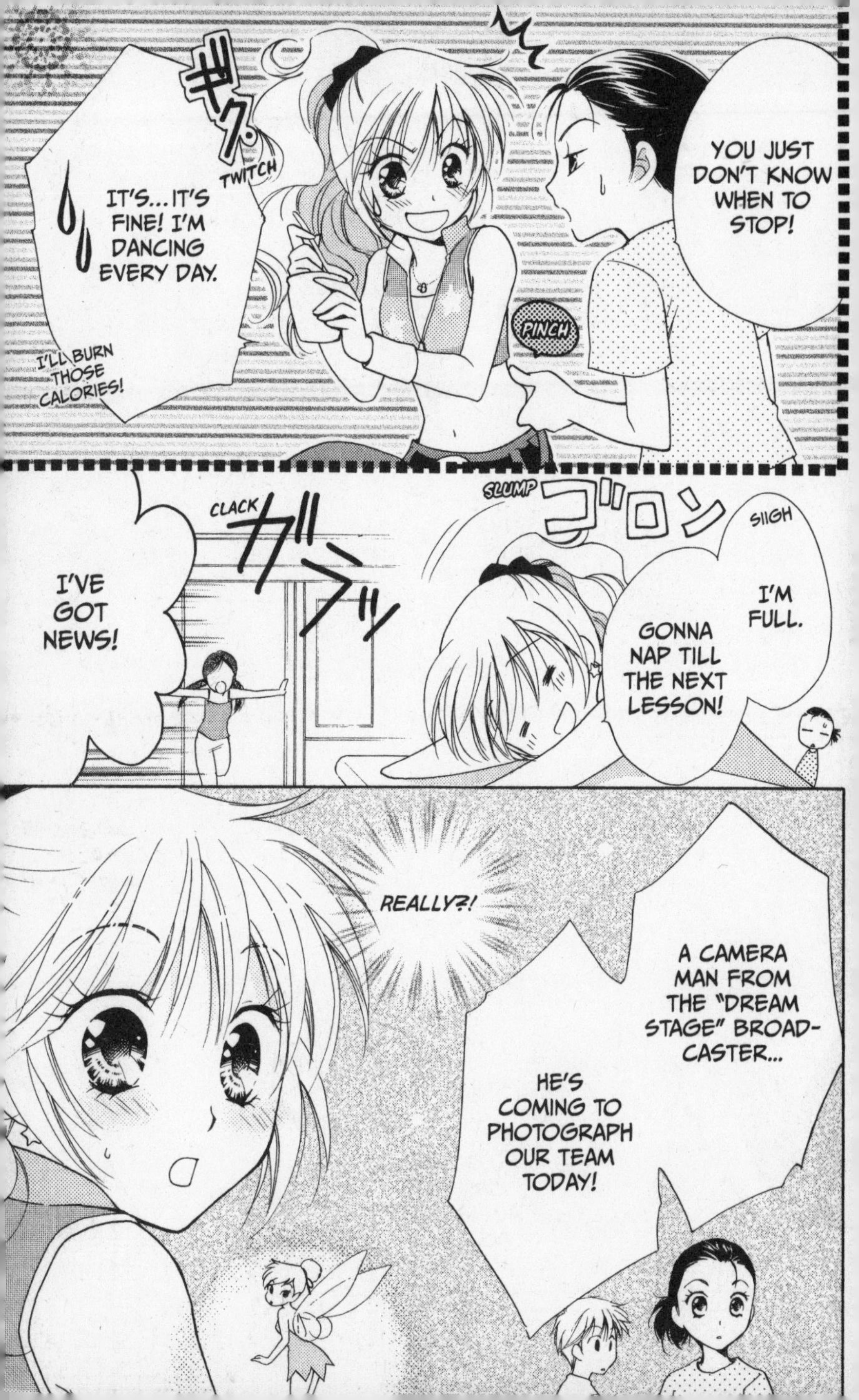
YOU JUST DON'T KNOW WHEN TO STOP!
PINCH
ギク
TWITCH
IT'S... IT'S FINE! I'M DANCING EVERY DAY.
I'LL BURN THOSE CALORIES!
SLUMP
ゴロン
SIIGH
I'M FULL.
GONNA NAP TILL THE NEXT LESSON!
CLACK
ガラッ
I'VE GOT NEWS!
A CAMERA MAN FROM THE "DREAM STAGE" BROAD-CASTER...
HE'S COMING TO PHOTOGRAPH OUR TEAM TODAY!
REALLY?!

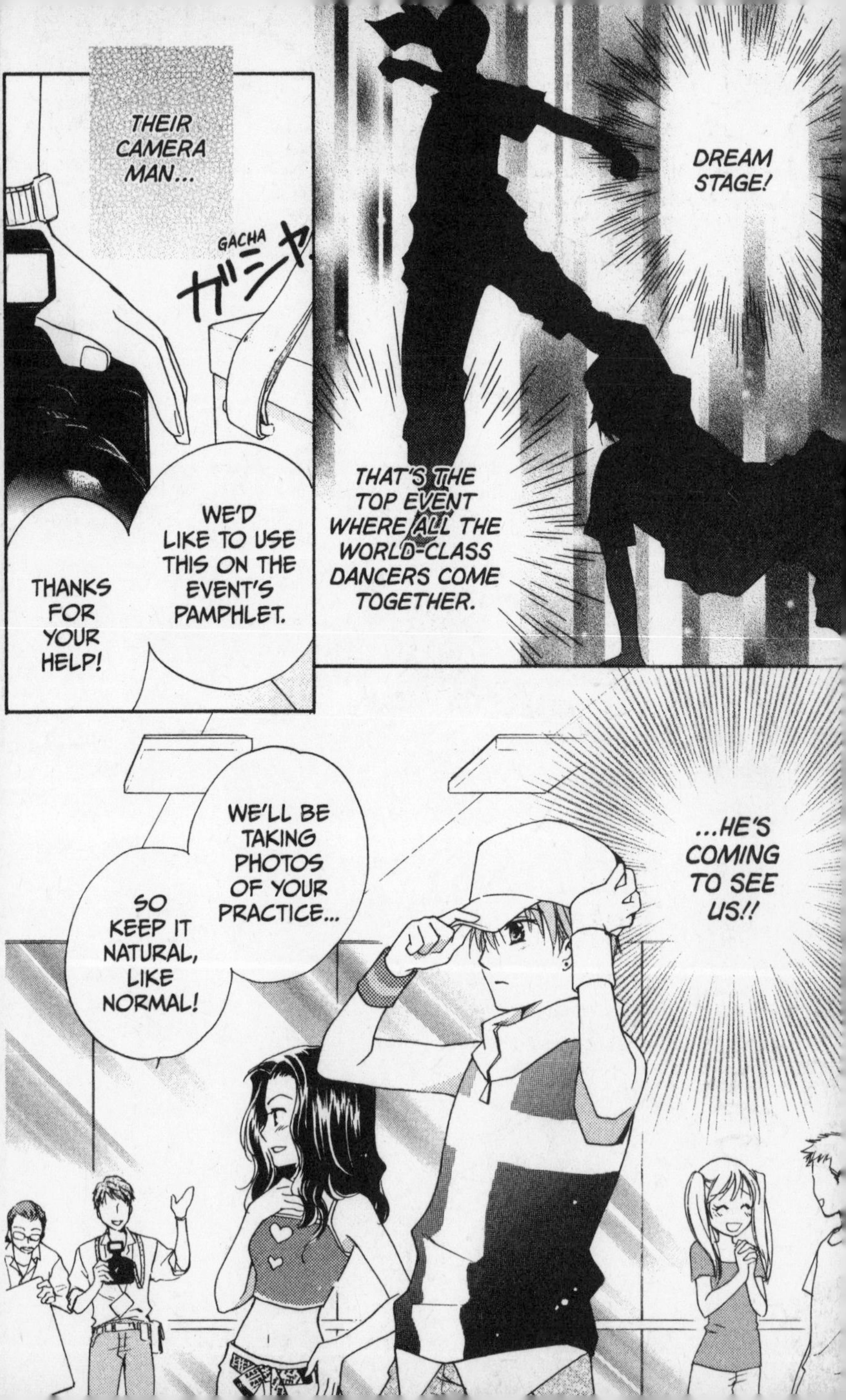
DREAM STAGE!
THAT'S THE TOP EVENT WHERE ALL THE WORLD-CLASS DANCERS COME TOGETHER.
THEIR CAMERA MAN...
GACHA
WE'D LIKE TO USE THIS ON THE EVENT'S PAMPHLET.
THANKS FOR YOUR HELP!
...HE'S COMING TO SEE US!!
WE'LL BE TAKING PHOTOS OF YOUR PRACTICE...
SO KEEP IT NATURAL, LIKE NORMAL!

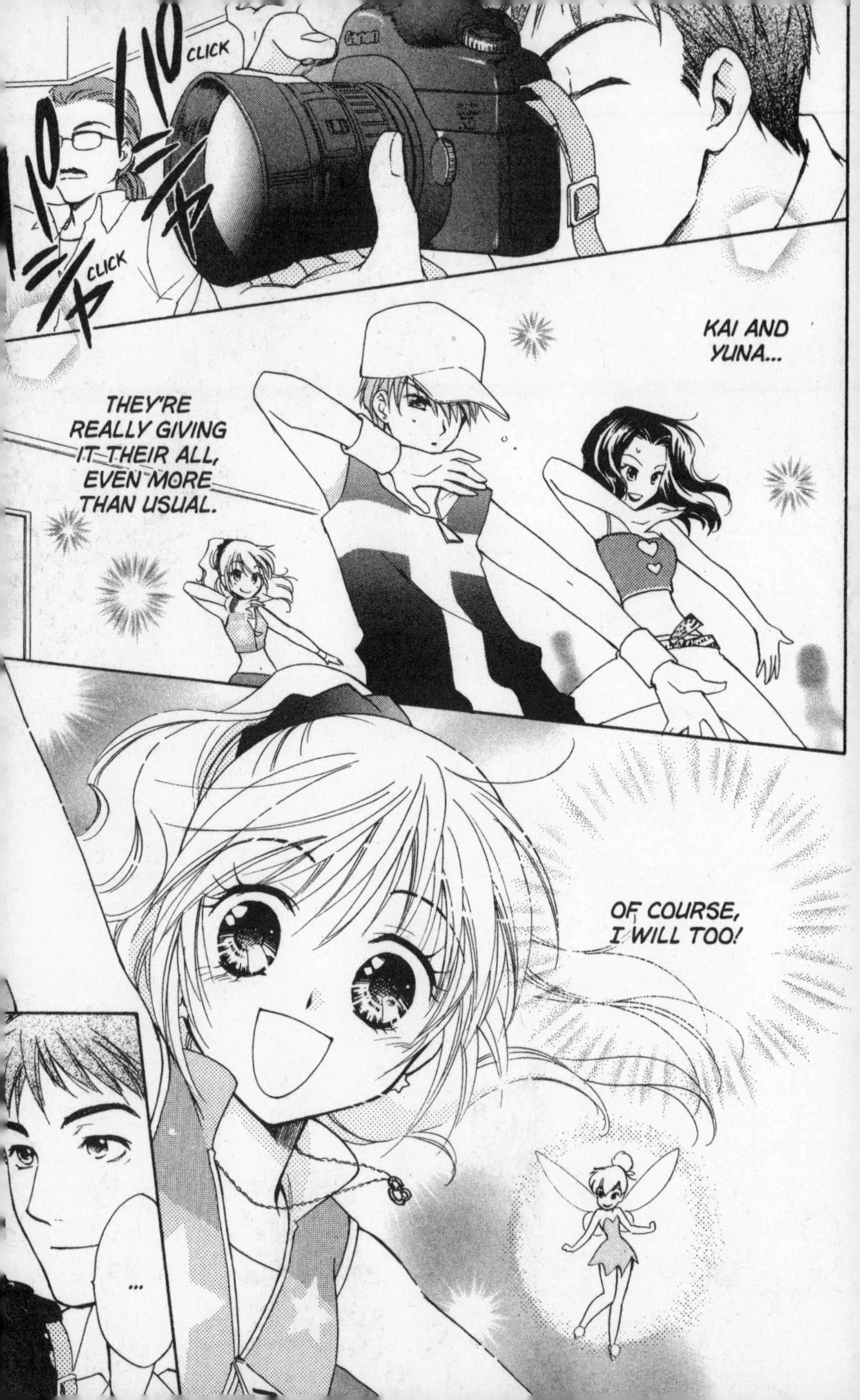
CLICK
CLICK
KAI AND YUNA...
THEY'RE REALLY GIVING IT THEIR ALL, EVEN MORE THAN USUAL.
OF COURSE, I WILL TOO!
...

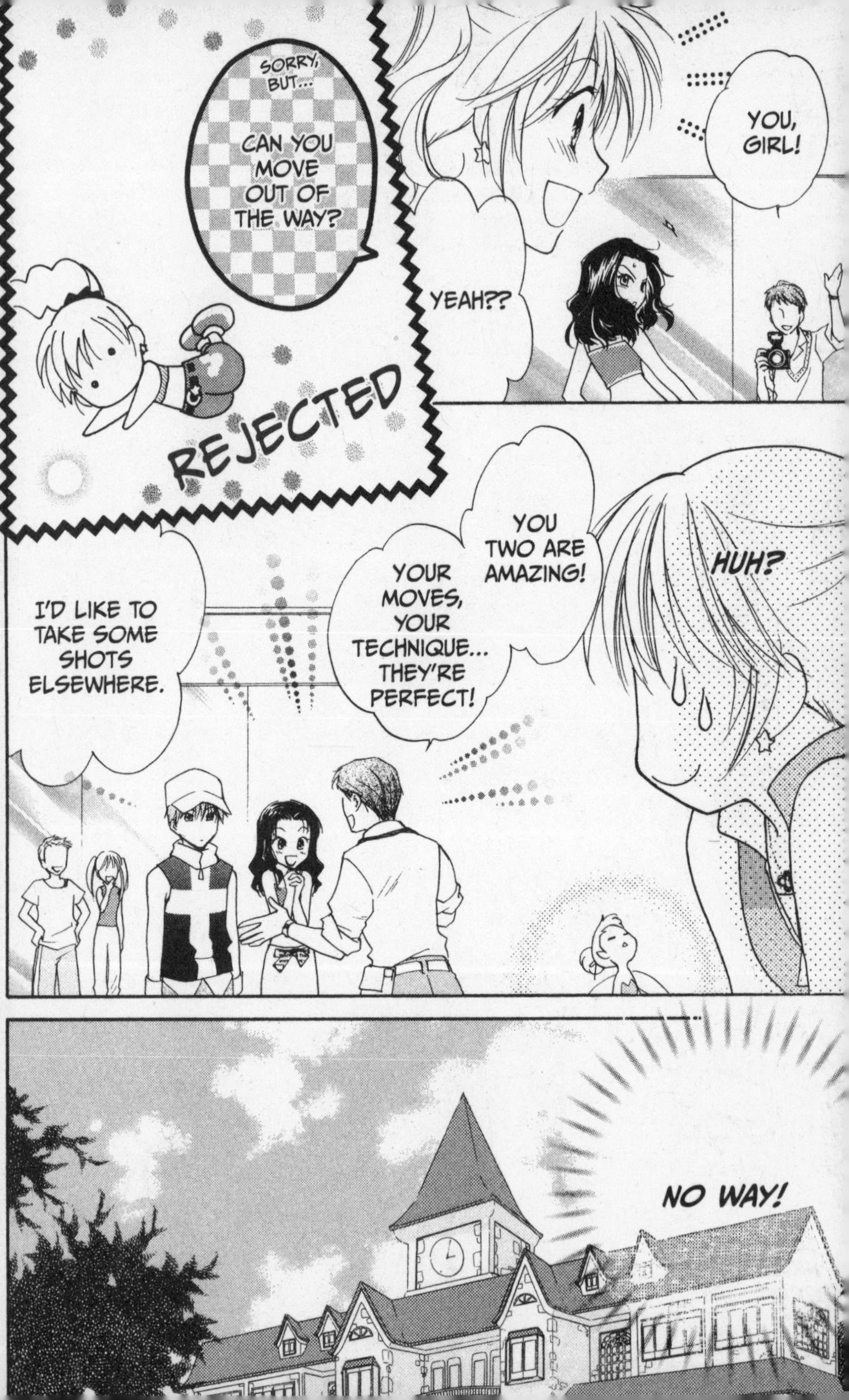
YOU, GIRL!
YEAH??
SORRY, BUT...
CAN YOU MOVE OUT OF THE WAY?
REJECTED
HUH?
YOU TWO ARE AMAZING!
YOUR MOVES, YOUR TECHNIQUE... THEY'RE PERFECT!
I'D LIKE TO TAKE SOME SHOTS ELSEWHERE.
NO WAY!

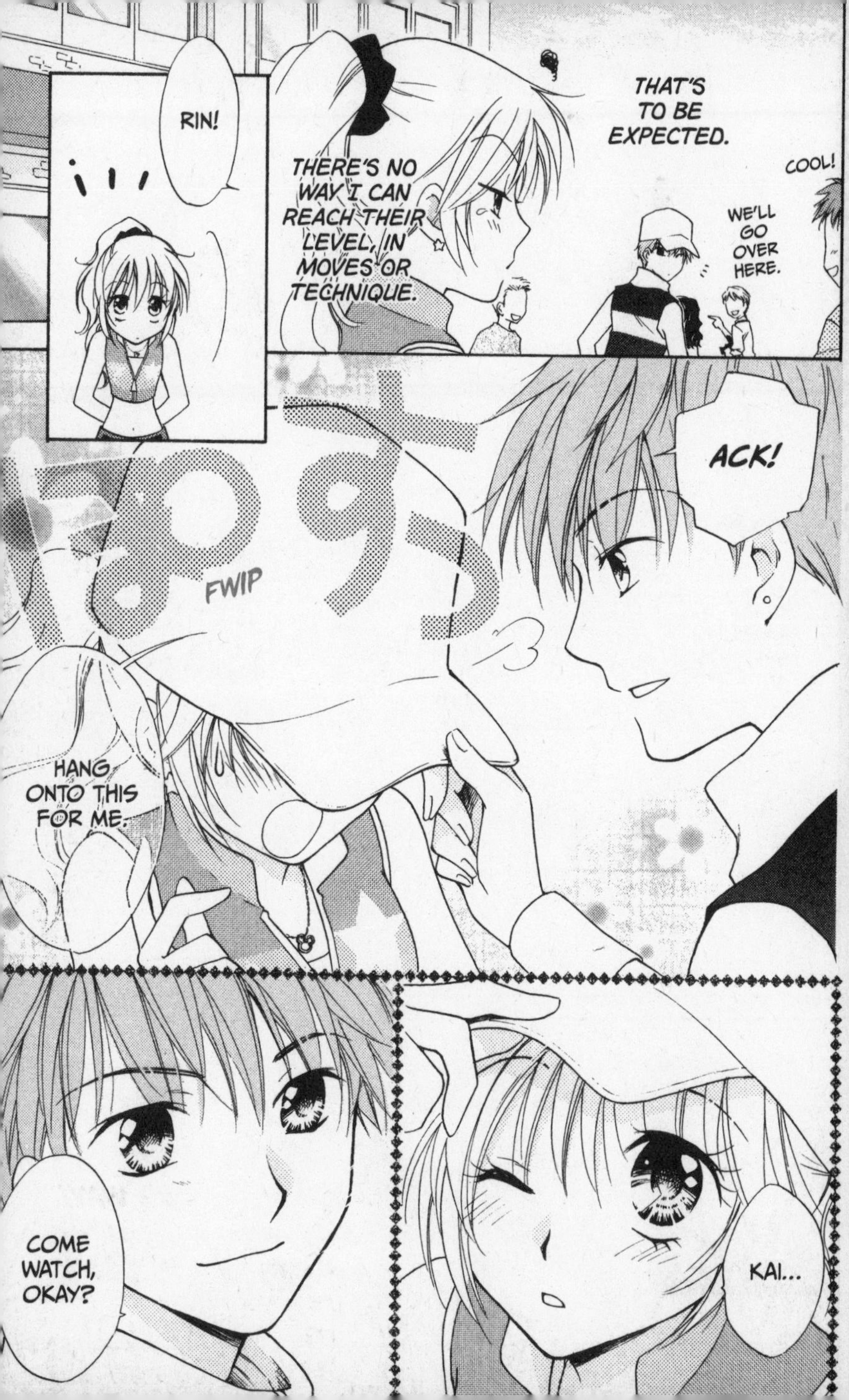
THAT'S TO BE EXPECTED.
COOL!
WE'LL GO OVER HERE.
THERE'S NO WAY I CAN REACH THEIR LEVEL, IN MOVES OR TECHNIQUE.
RIN!
ACK!
FWIP
HANG ONTO THIS FOR ME.
KAI...
COME WATCH, OKAY?

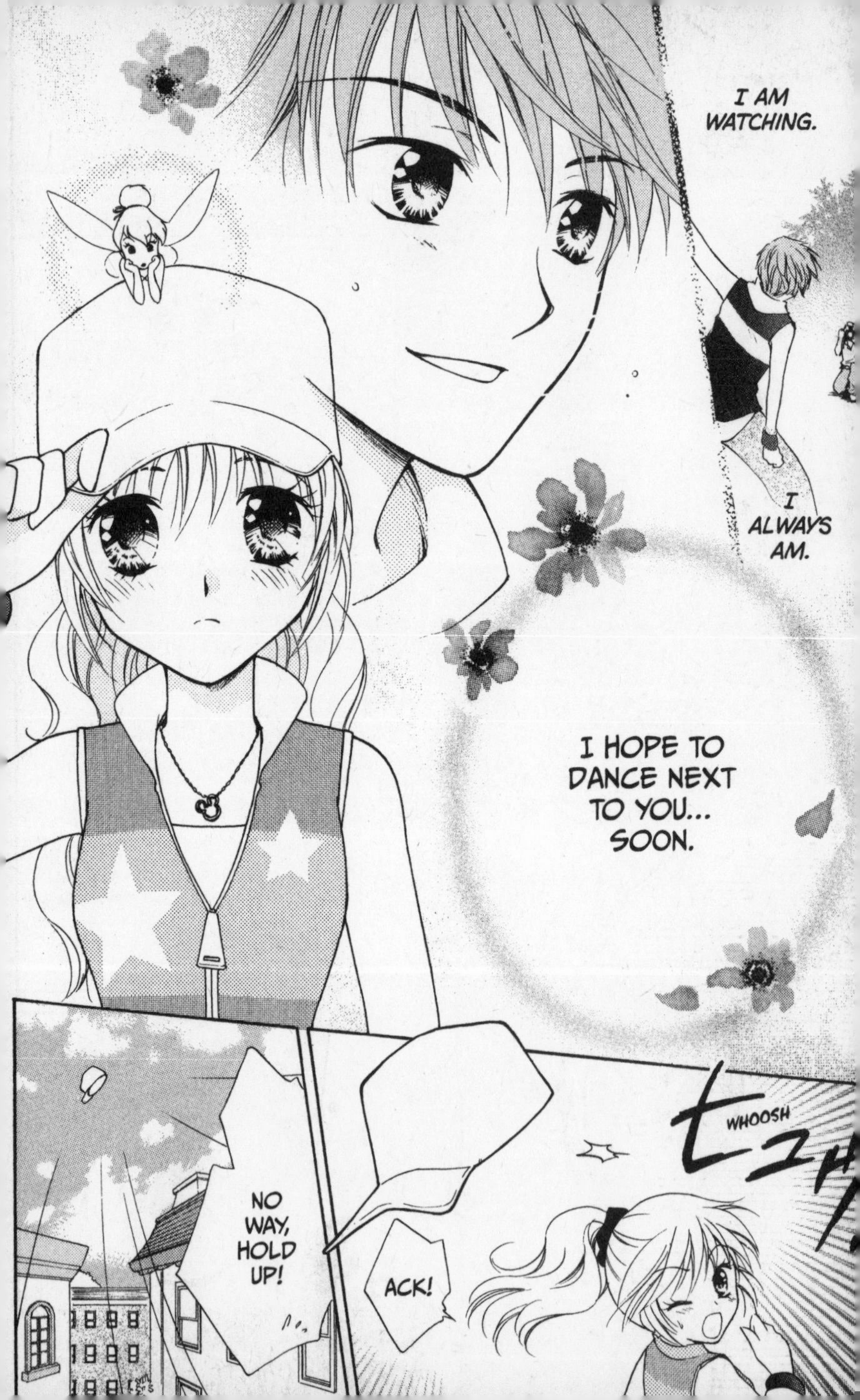
I AM WATCHING.
I ALWAYS AM.
I HOPE TO DANCE NEXT TO YOU... SOON.
WHOOSH
ACK!
NO WAY, HOLD UP!

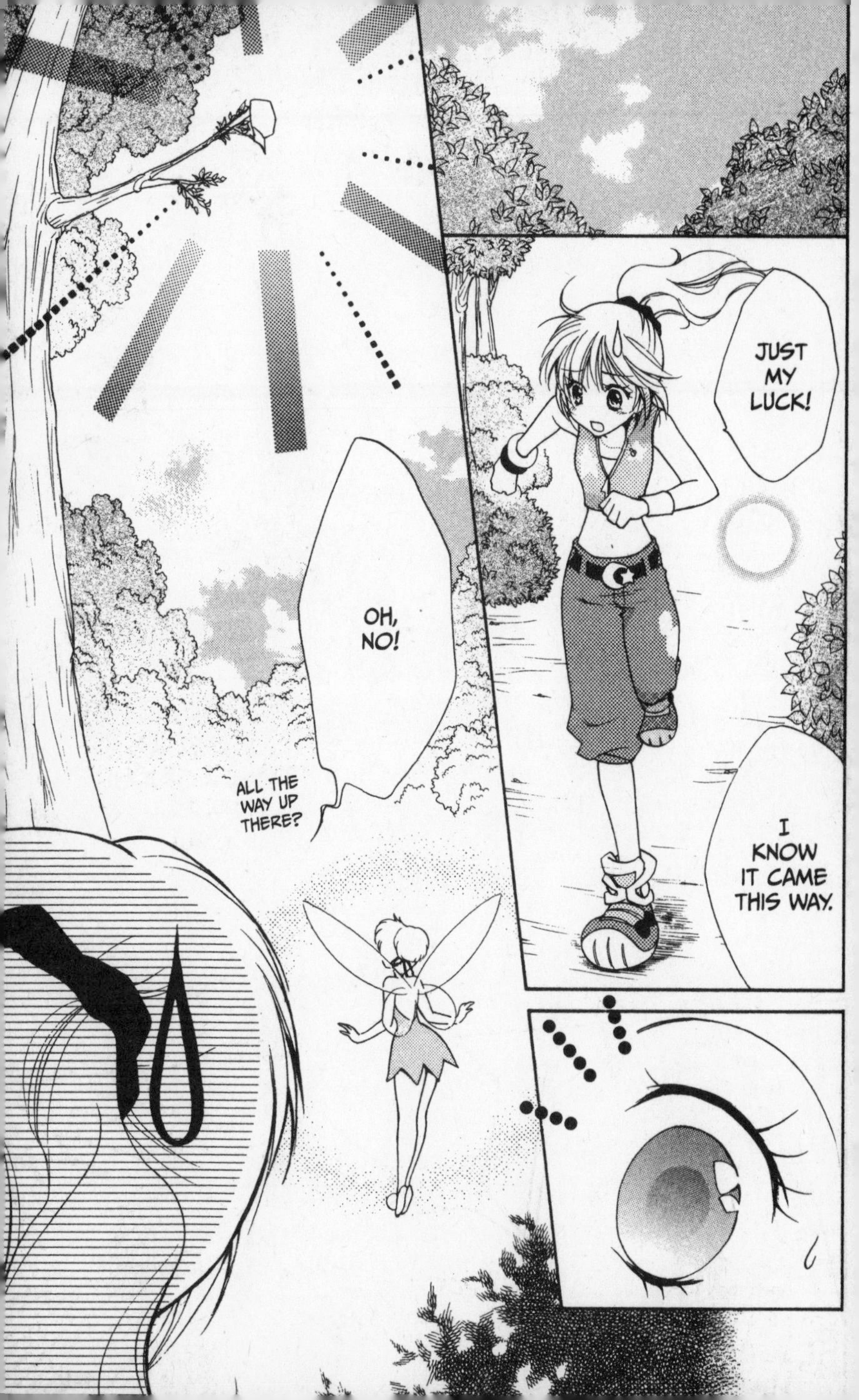
JUST MY LUCK!
I KNOW IT CAME THIS WAY.
OH, NO!
ALL THE WAY UP THERE?

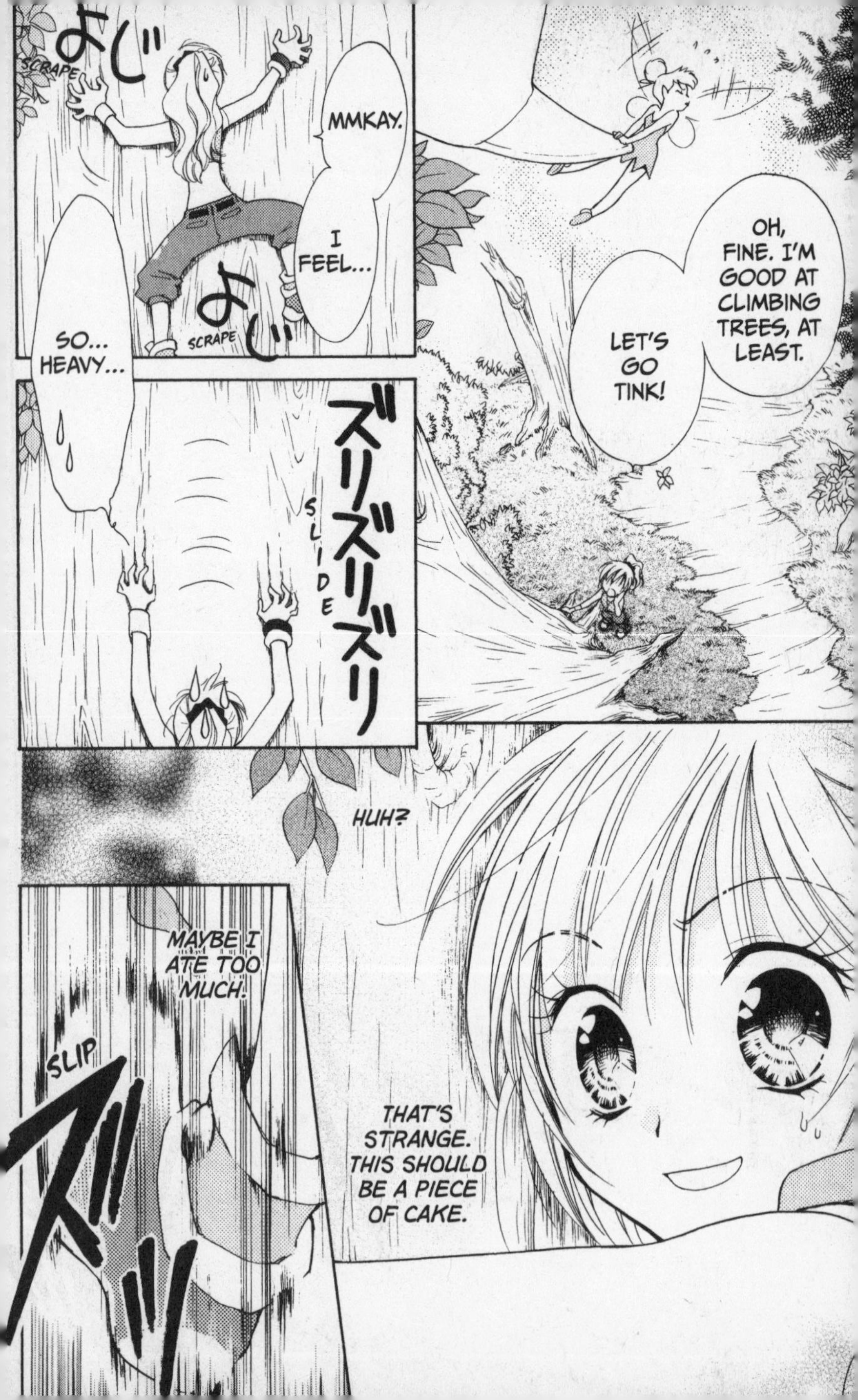
OH, FINE. I'M GOOD AT CLIMBING TREES, AT LEAST.
LET'S GO TINK!
よじ
SCRAPE
MMKAY.
I FEEL...
よじ
SCRAPE
SO... HEAVY...
ズリズリズリ
SLIDE
HUH?
THAT'S STRANGE. THIS SHOULD BE A PIECE OF CAKE.
MAYBE I ATE TOO MUCH.
SLIP
ズ

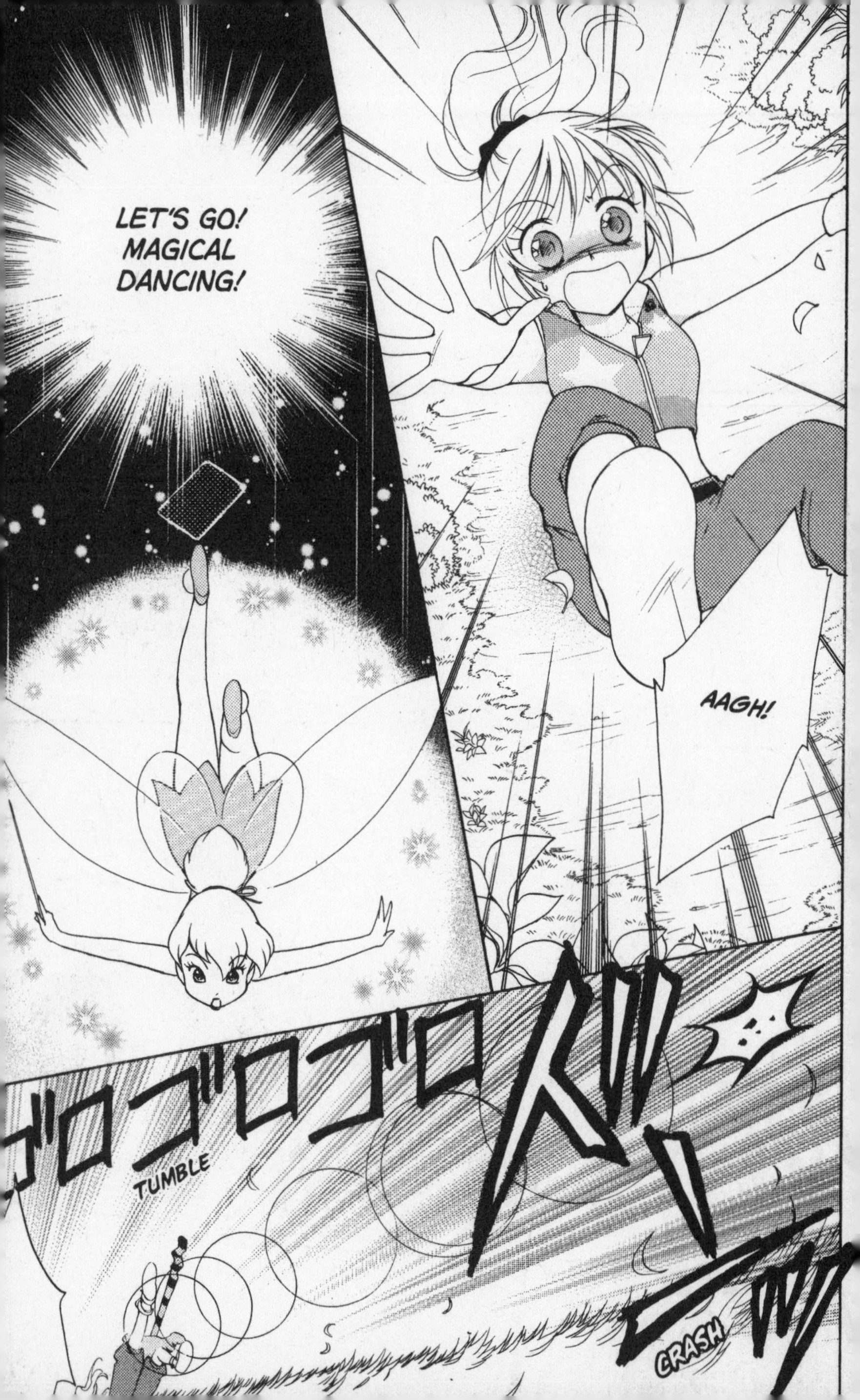
AAGH!
LET'S GO! MAGICAL DANCING!
CRASH
TUMBLE

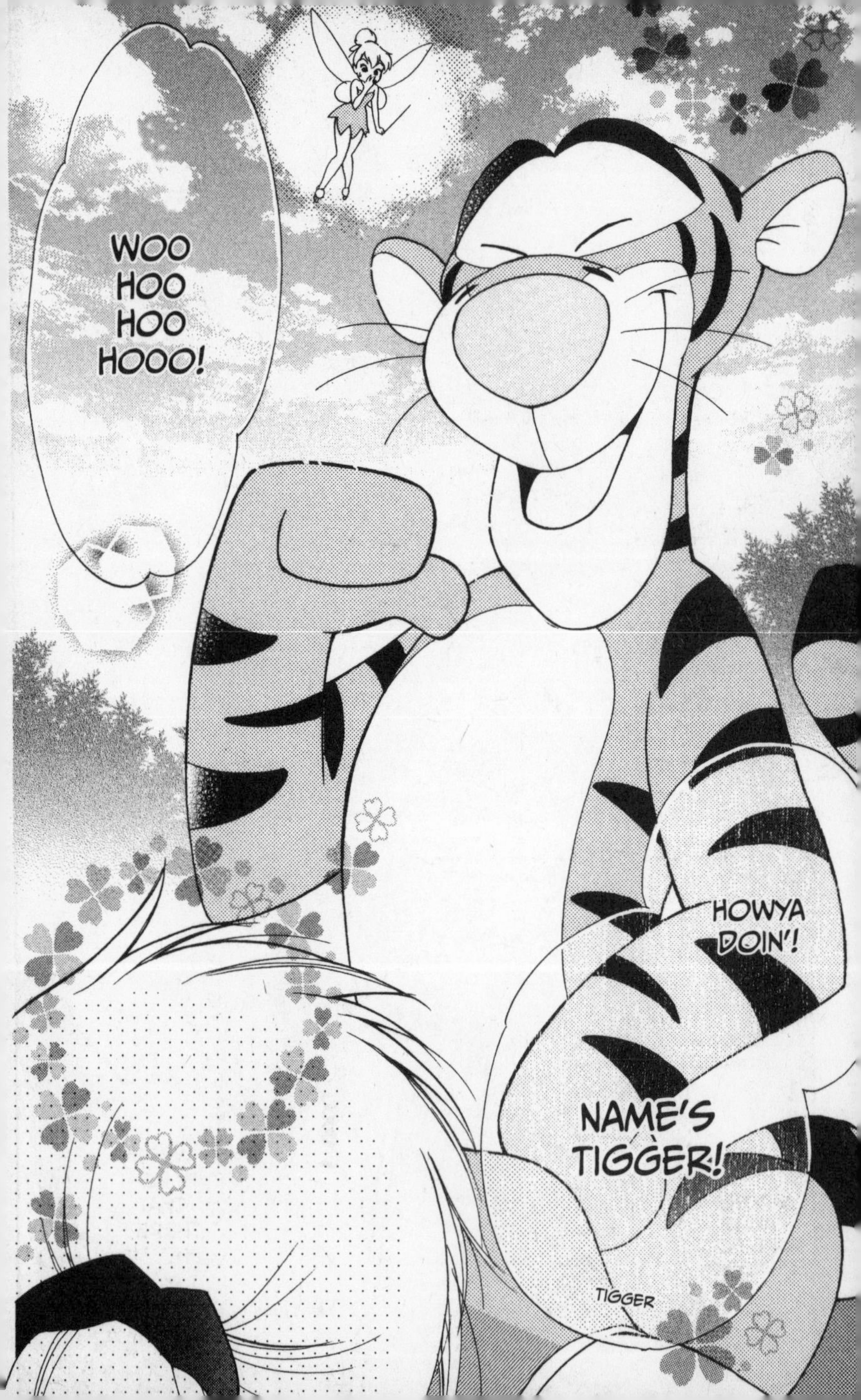
WOO HOO HOO HOOO!
HOWYA DOIN'!
NAME'S TIGGER!
TIGGER

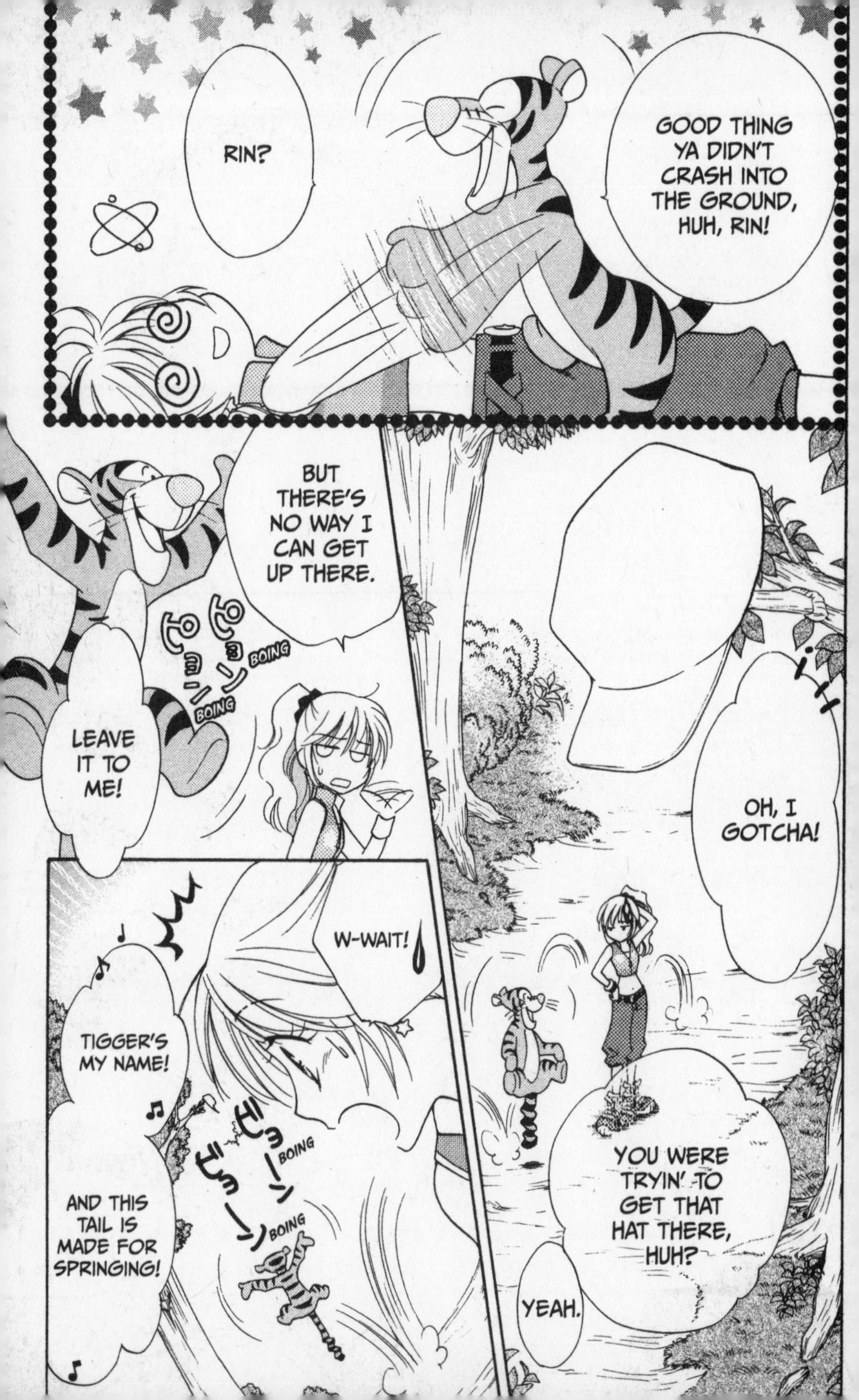
GOOD THING YA DIDN'T CRASH INTO THE GROUND, HUH, RIN!
RIN?
OH, I GOTCHA!
YOU WERE TRYIN' TO GET THAT HAT THERE, HUH?
YEAH.
BUT THERE'S NO WAY I CAN GET UP THERE.
BOING
BOING
LEAVE IT TO ME!
W-WAIT!
TIGGER'S MY NAME!
BOING
BOING
AND THIS TAIL IS MADE FOR SPRINGING!

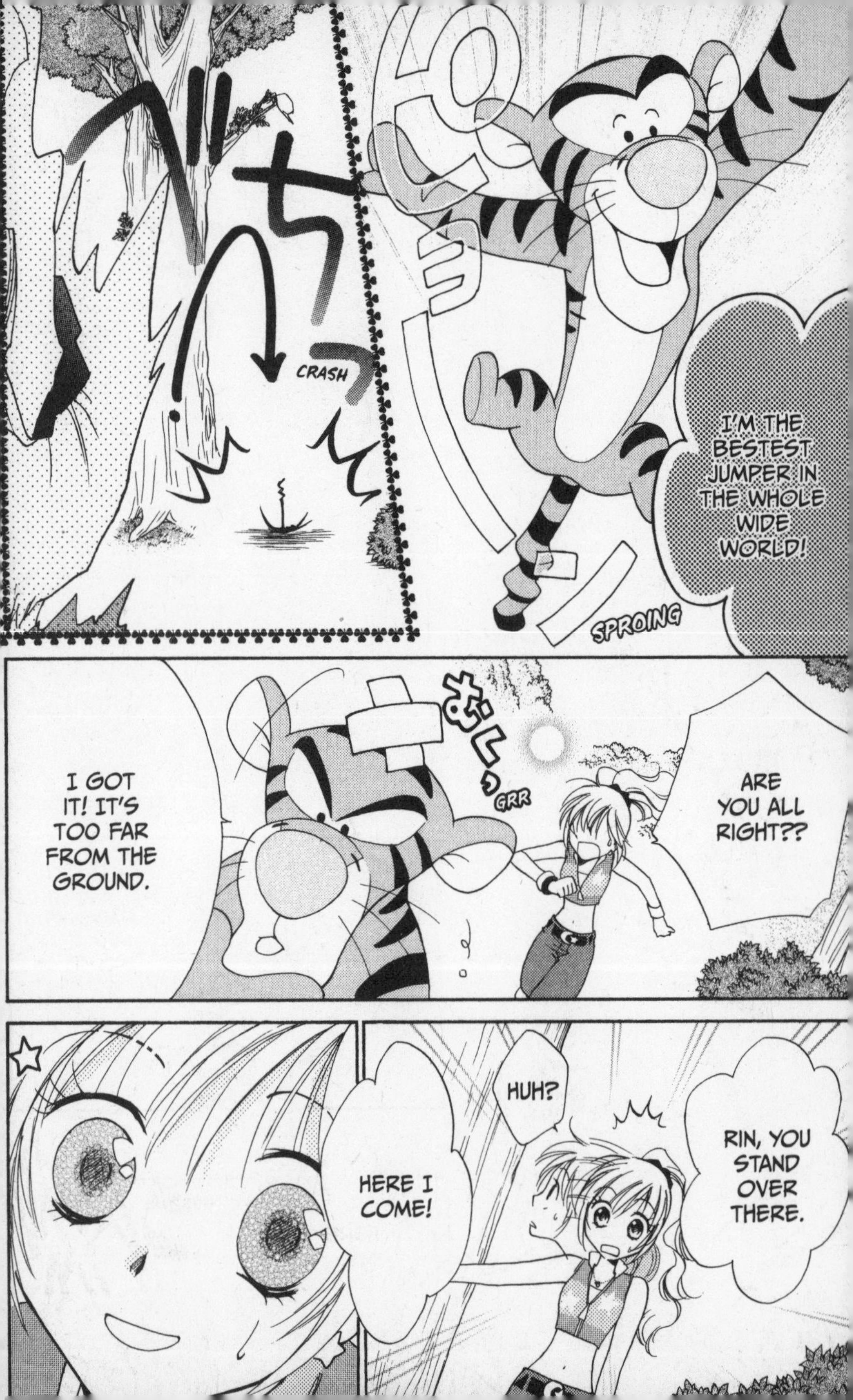

I'M THE BESTEST JUMPER IN THE WHOLE WIDE WORLD!
SPROING
CRASH
ARE YOU ALL RIGHT??
GRR
I GOT IT! IT'S TOO FAR FROM THE GROUND.
RIN, YOU STAND OVER THERE.
HUH?
HERE I COME!

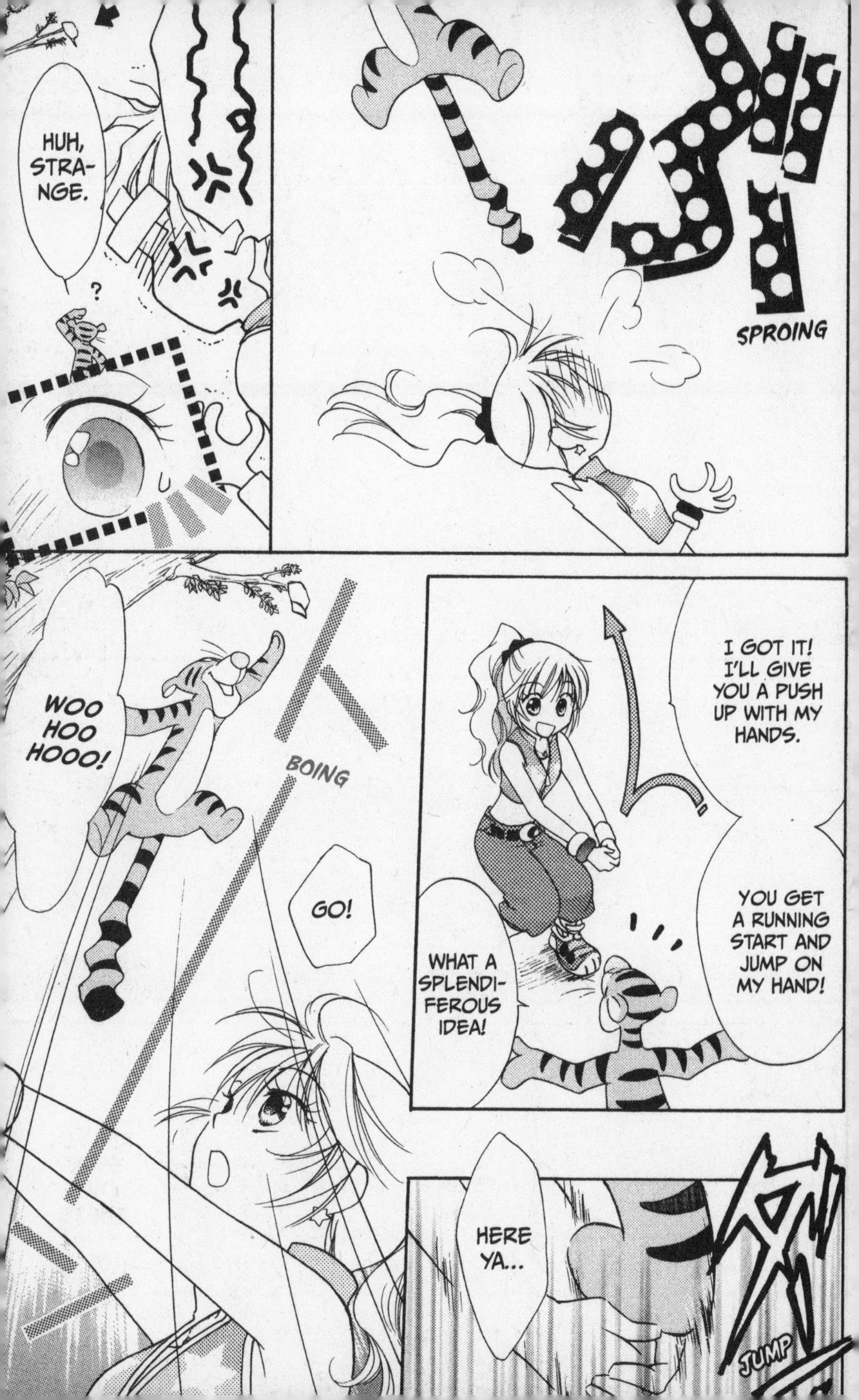
SPROING
HUH, STRA-NGE.
?
I GOT IT! I'LL GIVE YOU A PUSH UP WITH MY HANDS.
YOU GET A RUNNING START AND JUMP ON MY HAND!
WHAT A SPLENDI-FEROUS IDEA!
HERE YA...
JUMP
GO!
BOING
WOO HOO HOOO!

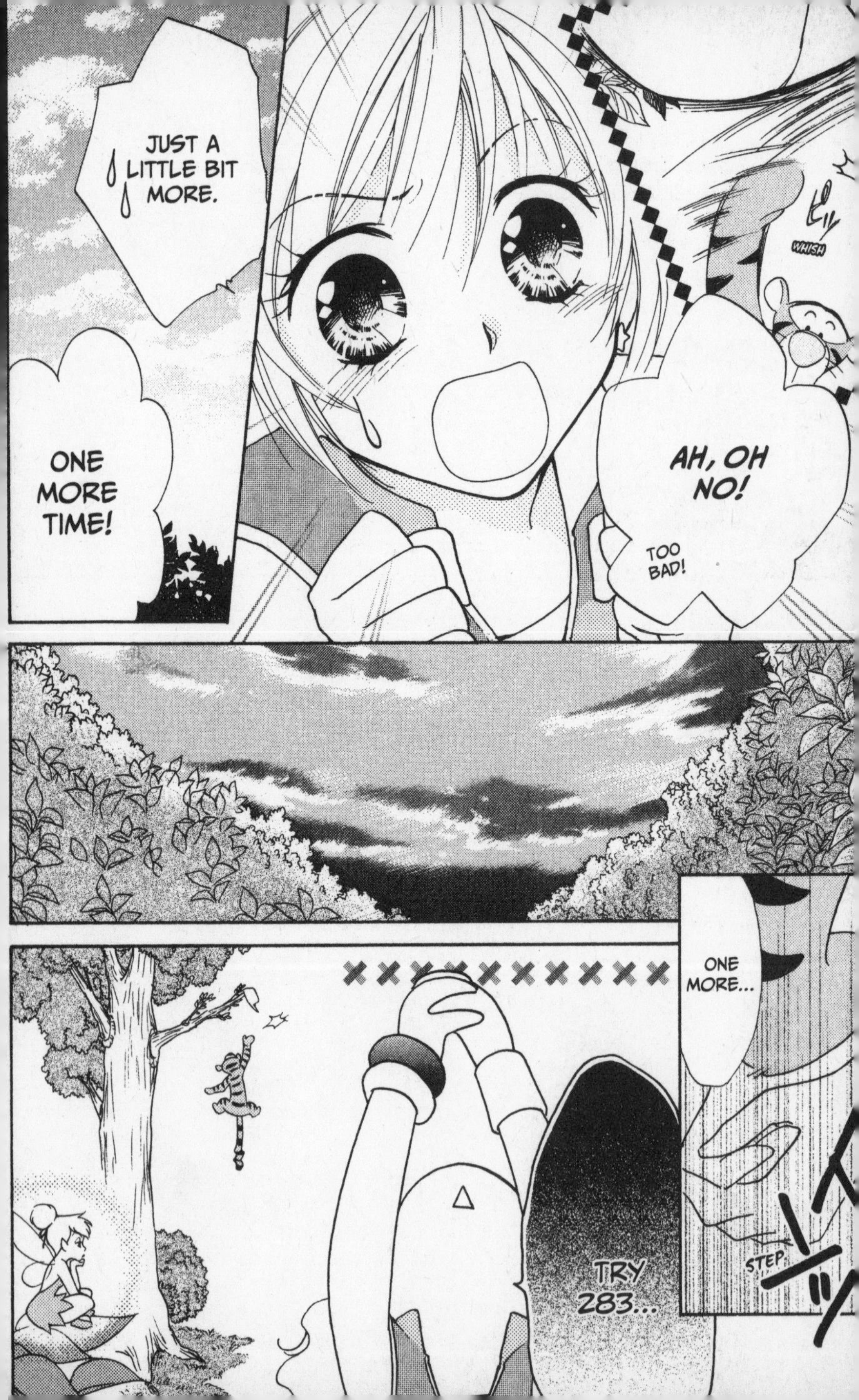
WHISH
AH, OH NO!
TOO BAD!
JUST A LITTLE BIT MORE.
ONE MORE TIME!
ONE MORE...
STEP
TRY 283...

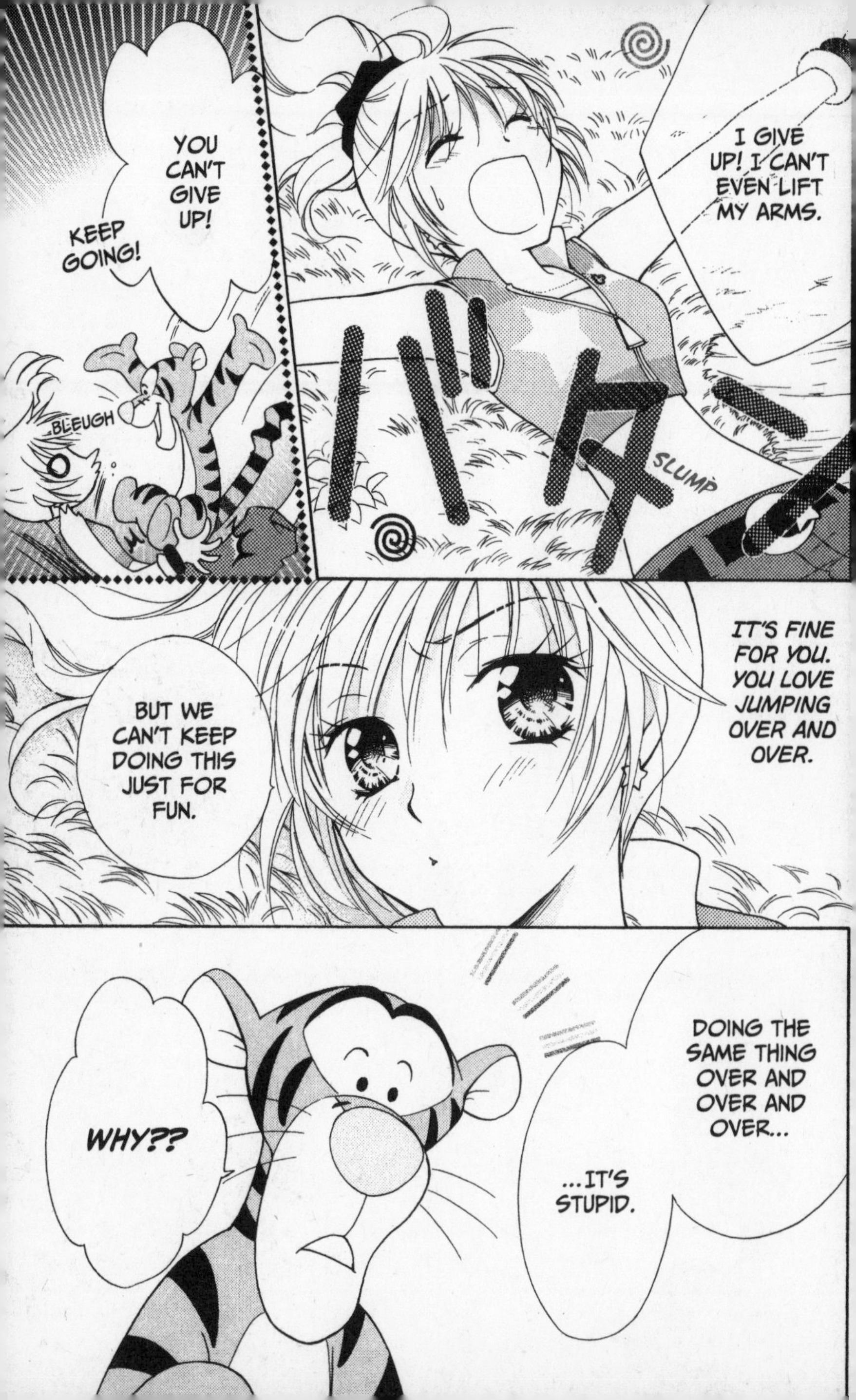
I GIVE UP! I CAN'T EVEN LIFT MY ARMS.
SLUMP
YOU CAN'T GIVE UP!
KEEP GOING!
BLEUGH
IT'S FINE FOR YOU. YOU LOVE JUMPING OVER AND OVER.
BUT WE CAN'T KEEP DOING THIS JUST FOR FUN.
DOING THE SAME THING OVER AND OVER AND OVER...
...IT'S STUPID.
WHY??

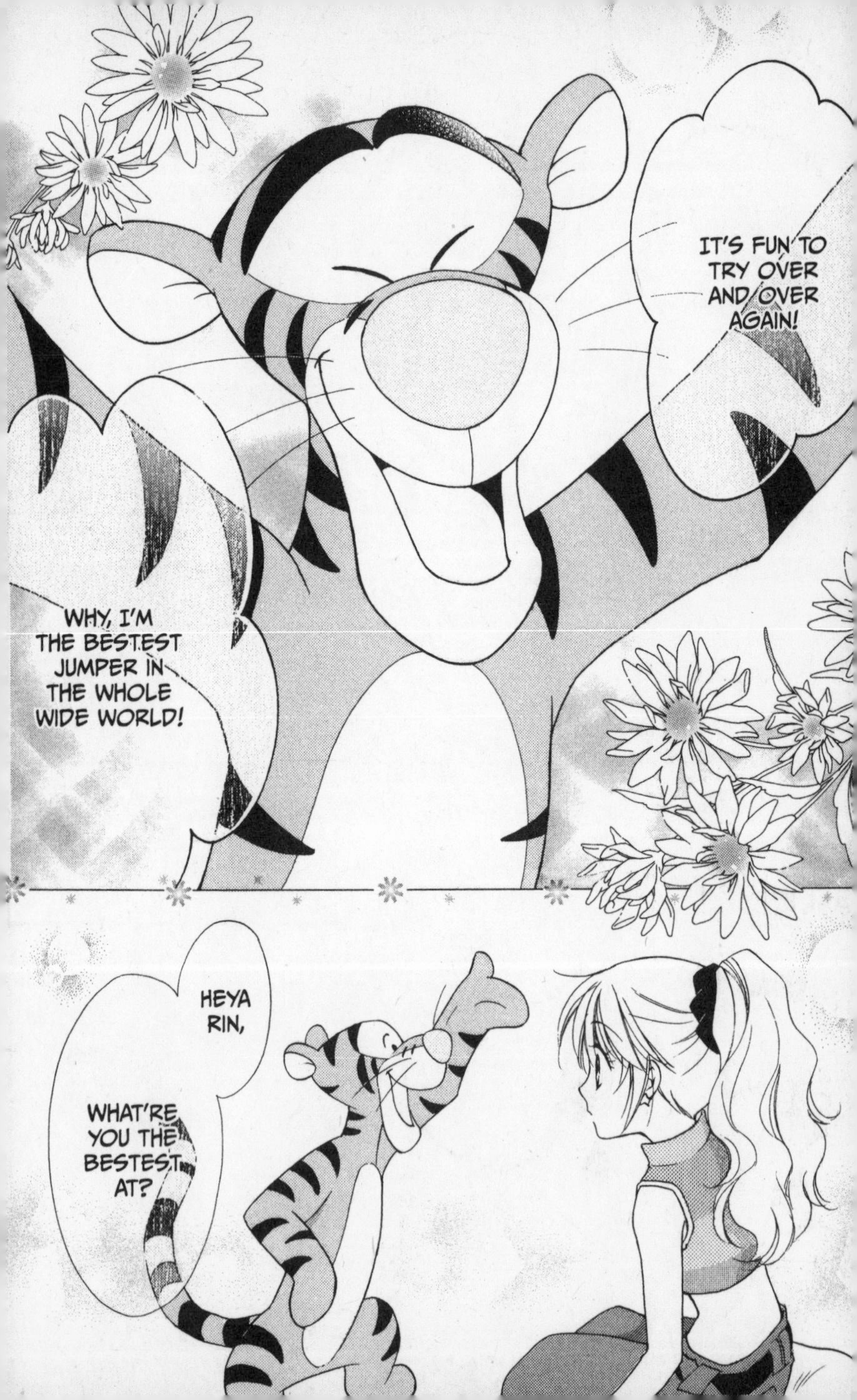
IT'S FUN TO TRY OVER AND OVER AGAIN!
WHY, I'M THE BESTEST JUMPER IN THE WHOLE WIDE WORLD!
HEYA RIN,
WHAT'RE YOU THE BESTEST AT?

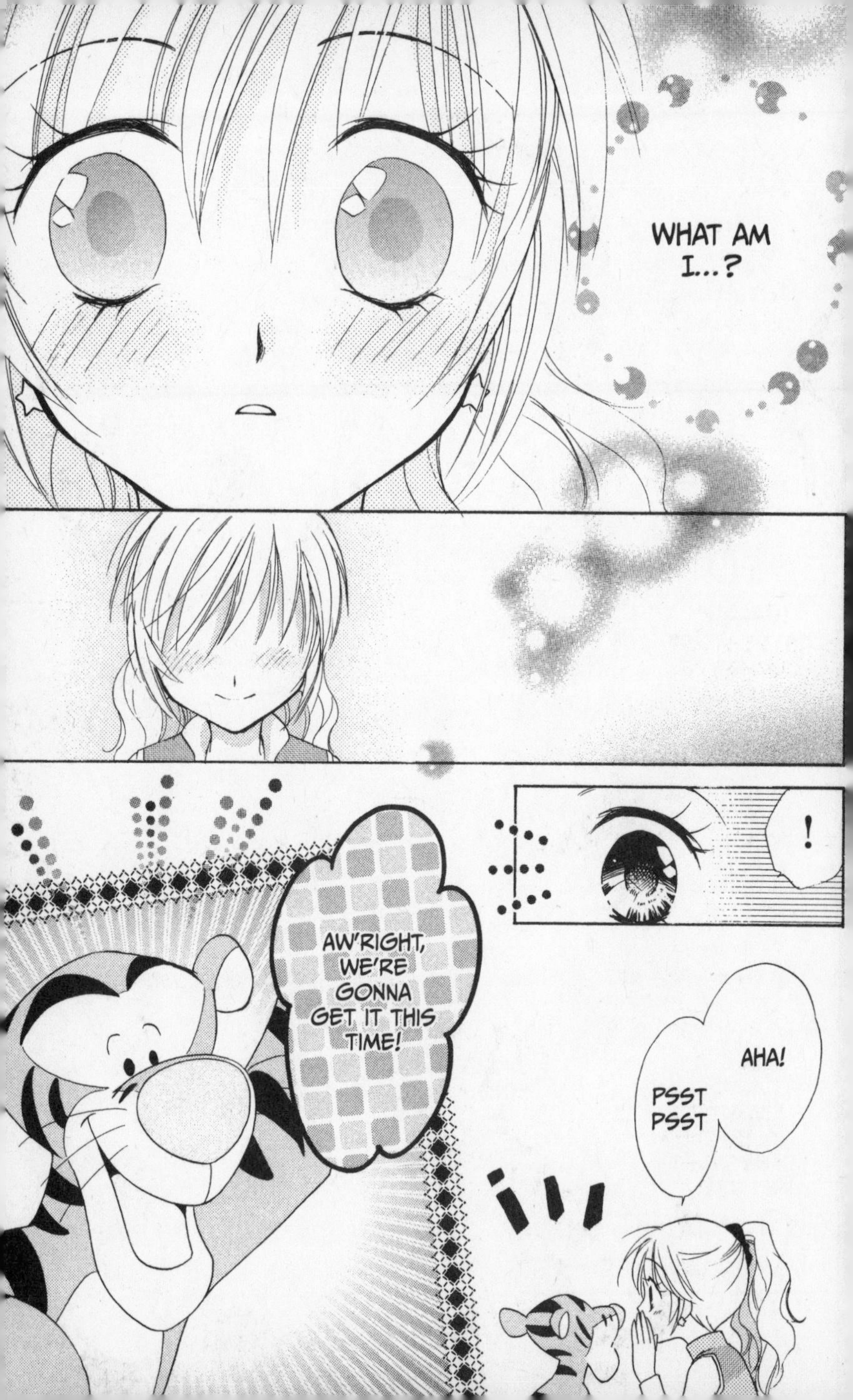
WHAT AM I...?
!
AHA!
PSST PSST
AW'RIGHT, WE'RE GONNA GET IT THIS TIME!

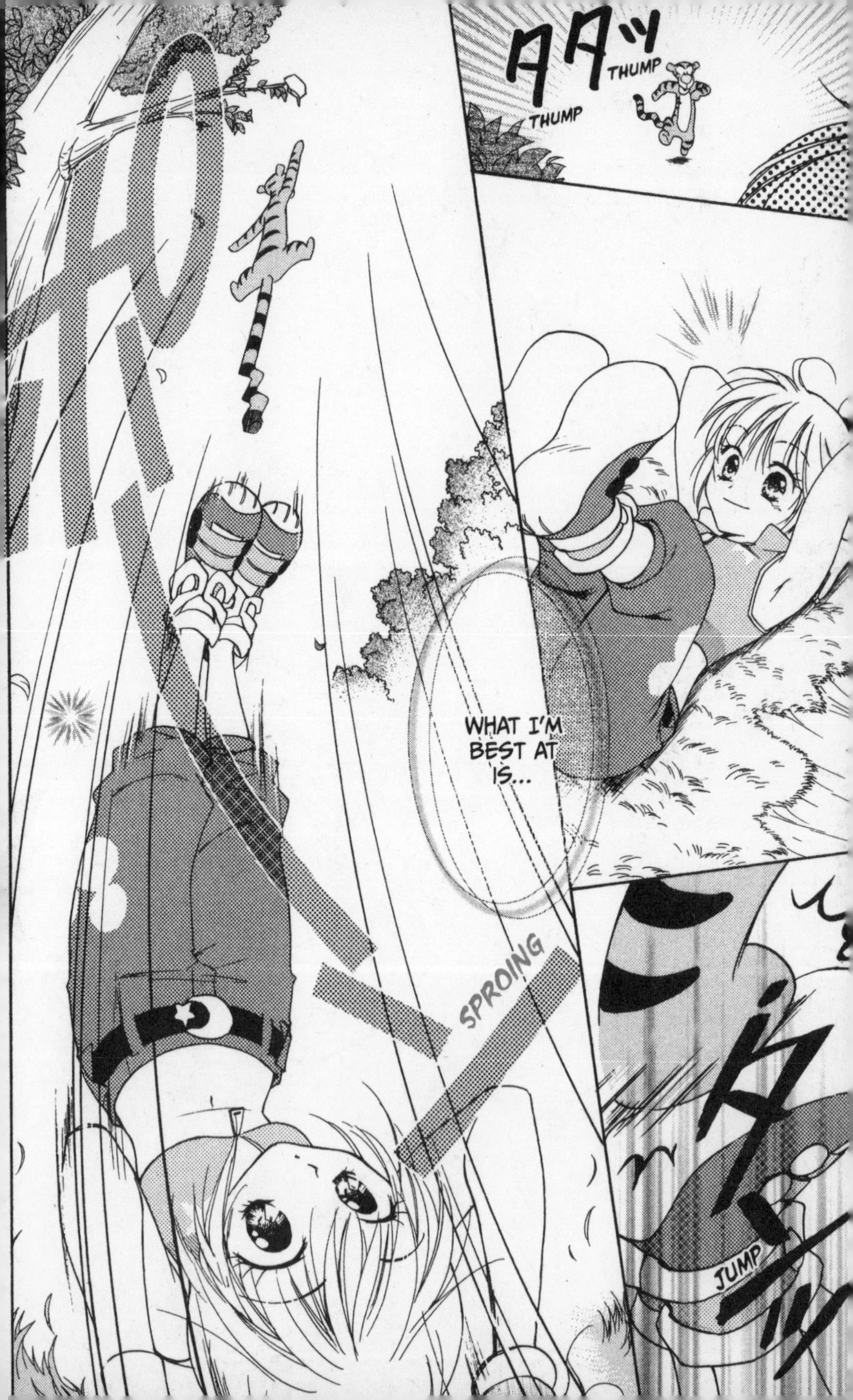

タタッ
THUMP
THUMP
WHAT I'M BEST AT IS...
JUMP
SPROING

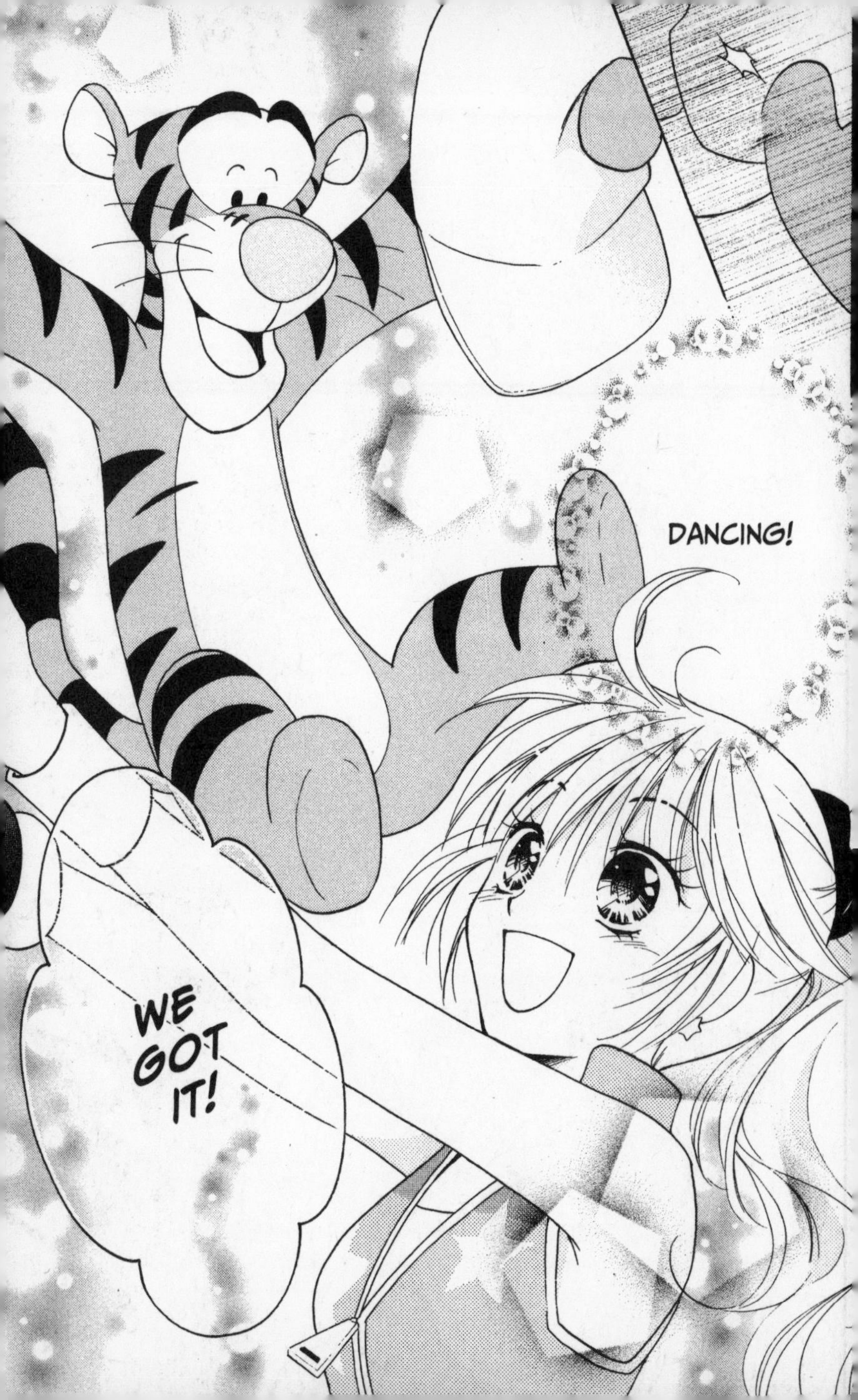
DANCING!
WE GOT IT!

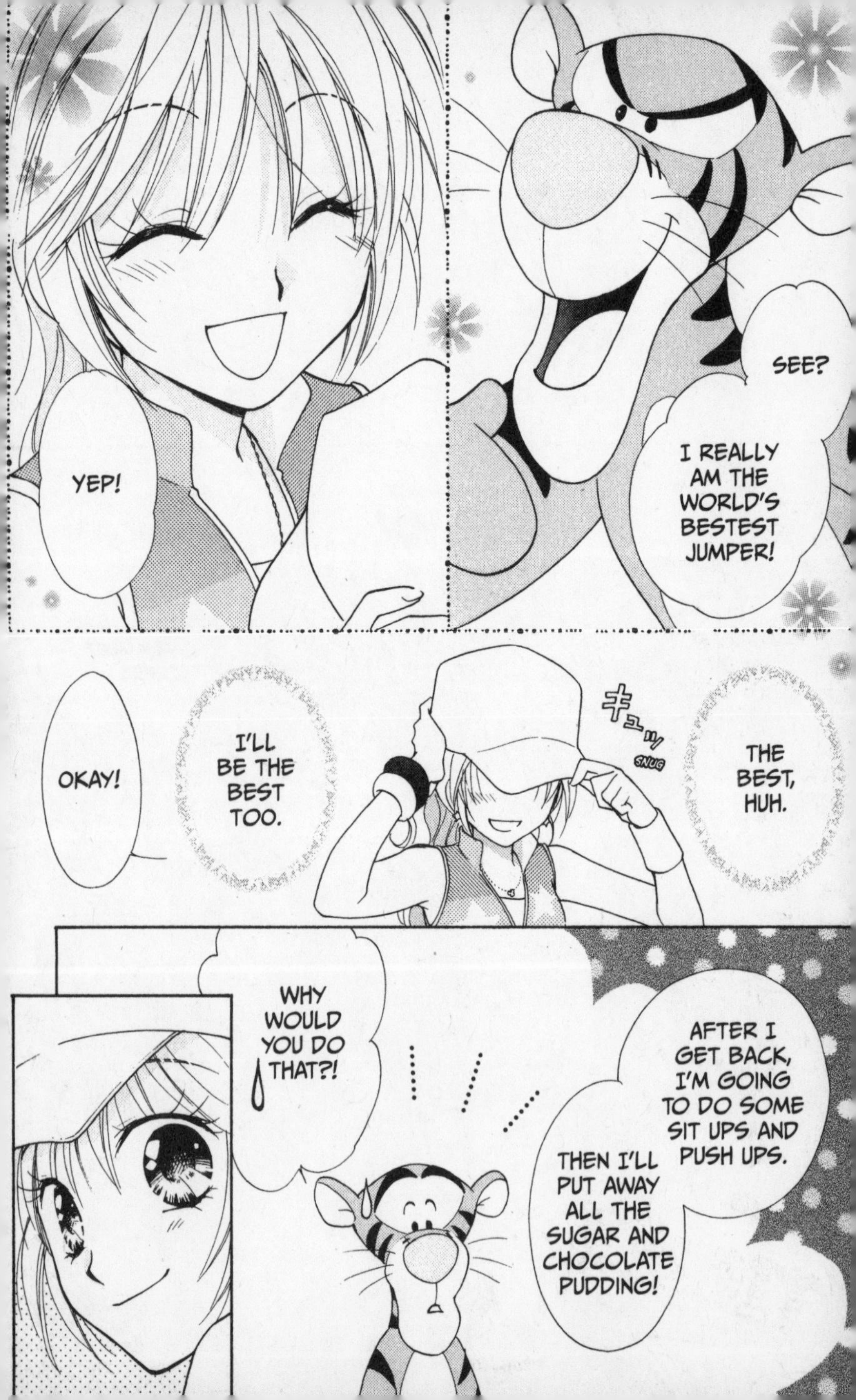
SEE?
I REALLY AM THE WORLD'S BESTEST JUMPER!
YEP!
THE BEST, HUH.
キュッ
SNUG
I'LL BE THE BEST TOO.
OKAY!
AFTER I GET BACK, I'M GOING TO DO SOME SIT UPS AND PUSH UPS.
THEN I'LL PUT AWAY ALL THE SUGAR AND CHOCOLATE PUDDING!
WHY WOULD YOU DO THAT?!

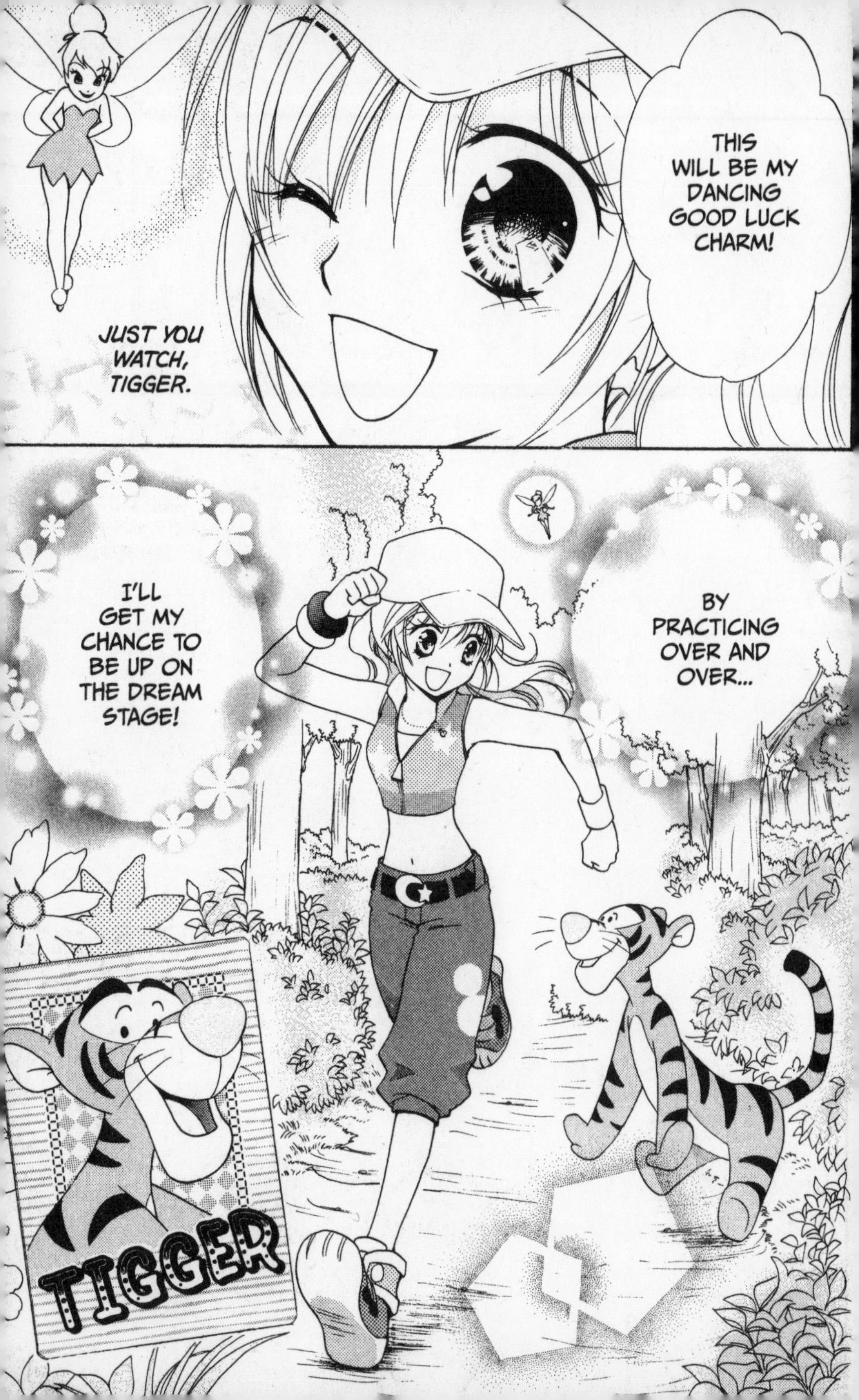
THIS WILL BE MY DANCING GOOD LUCK CHARM!
JUST YOU WATCH, TIGGER.
BY PRACTICING OVER AND OVER...
I'LL GET MY CHANCE TO BE UP ON THE DREAM STAGE!
TIGGER

SIDE STORY ★ COMIC (3)

LET'S DO THE MICKEY MOUSE MARCH! ♪
MAGICAL DANCING!!
YAHOO!
LEAVE IT TO US!
IT'S CHIP AND DALE!
YOU'RE SO TINY
I HOPE I DON'T STEP ON YOU!
WHADDYA MEAN HOPE??
IT'S FINE!
I HAVE A SAFE PLACE IN MIND.
HUH...?
GET OFF!

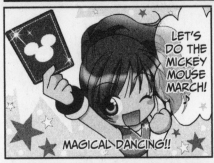

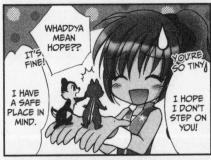

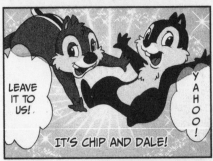

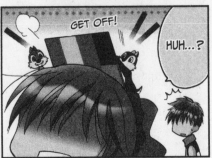

CONTINUED ON P. 146

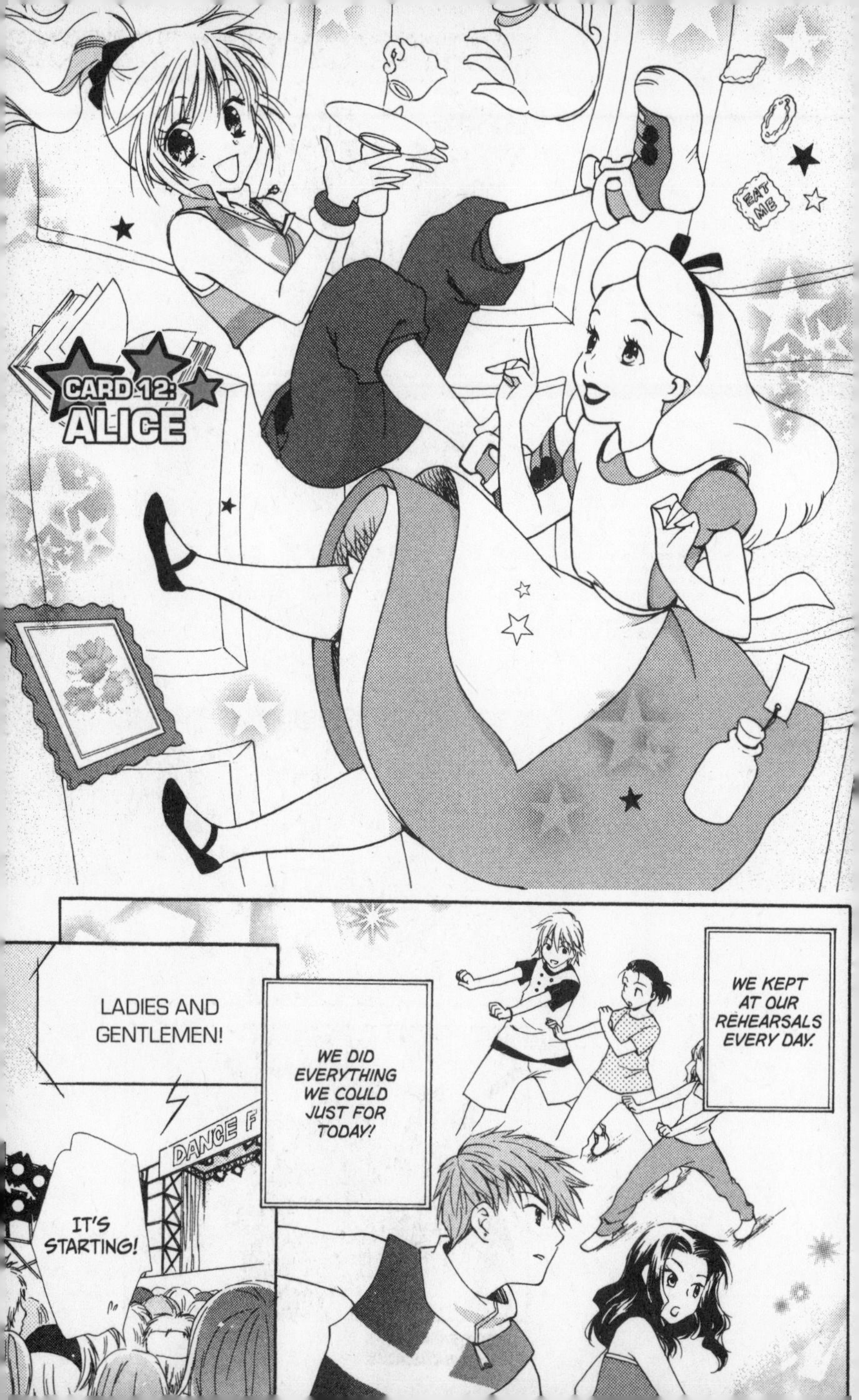
EAT ME
CARD 12:
ALICE
WE KEPT AT OUR REHEARSALS EVERY DAY.
WE DID EVERYTHING WE COULD JUST FOR TODAY!
LADIES AND GENTLEMEN!
DANCE F
IT'S STARTING!

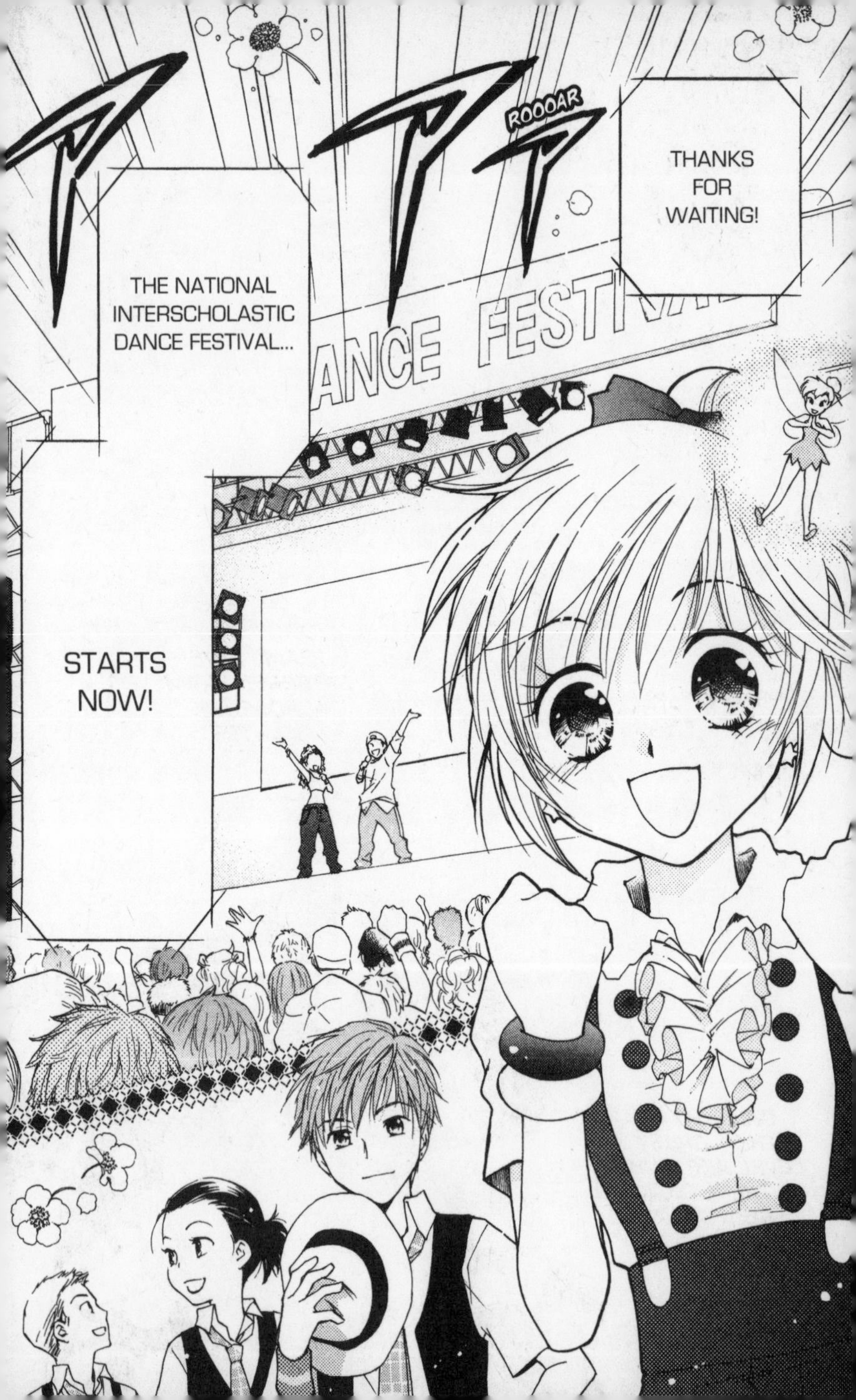
THANKS FOR WAITING!
ROOOAR
THE NATIONAL INTERSCHOLASTIC DANCE FESTIVAL...
STARTS NOW!

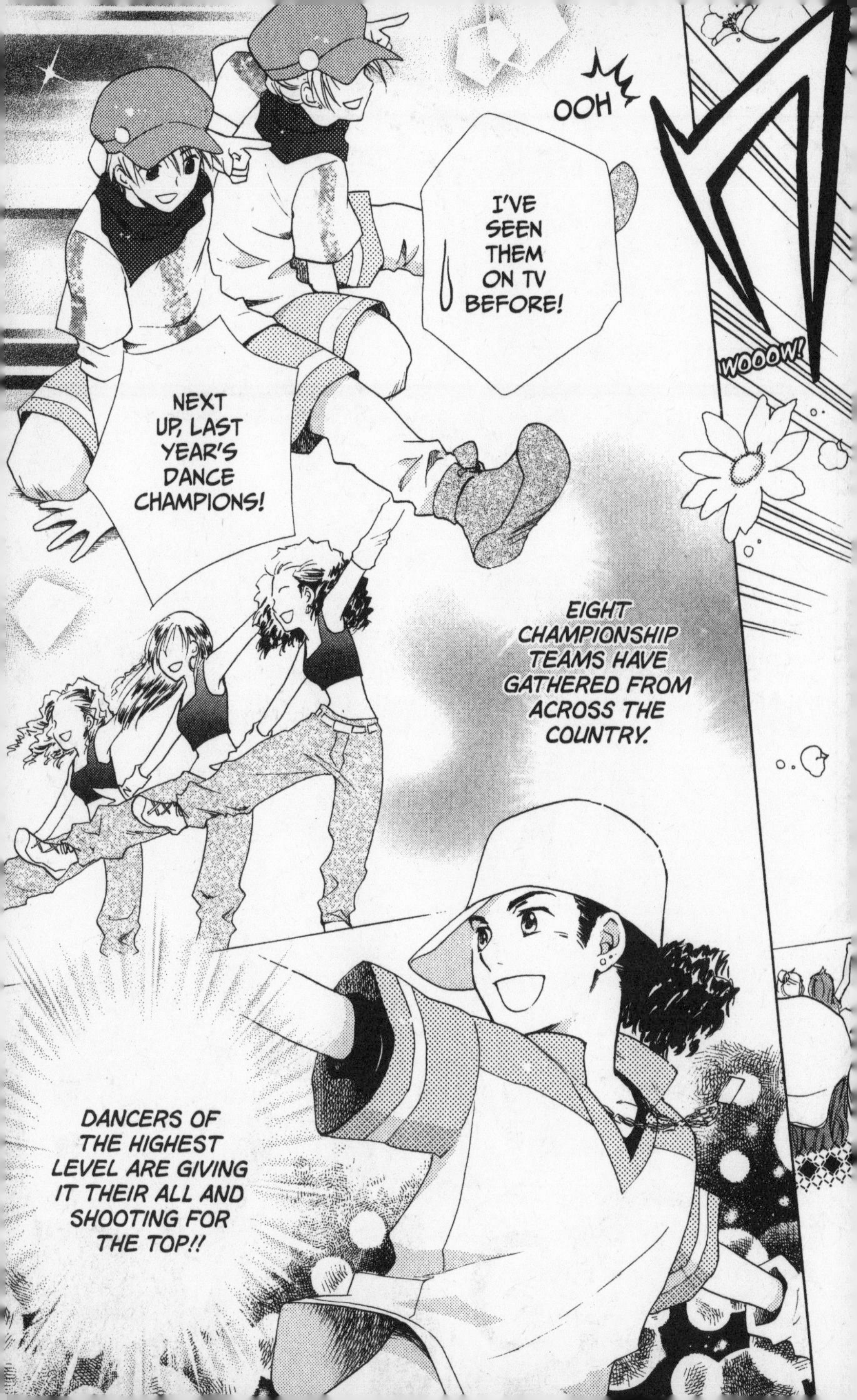
OOH
WOOOW!
I'VE SEEN THEM ON TV BEFORE!
NEXT UP, LAST YEAR'S DANCE CHAMPIONS!
EIGHT CHAMPIONSHIP TEAMS HAVE GATHERED FROM ACROSS THE COUNTRY.
DANCERS OF THE HIGHEST LEVEL ARE GIVING IT THEIR ALL AND SHOOTING FOR THE TOP!!

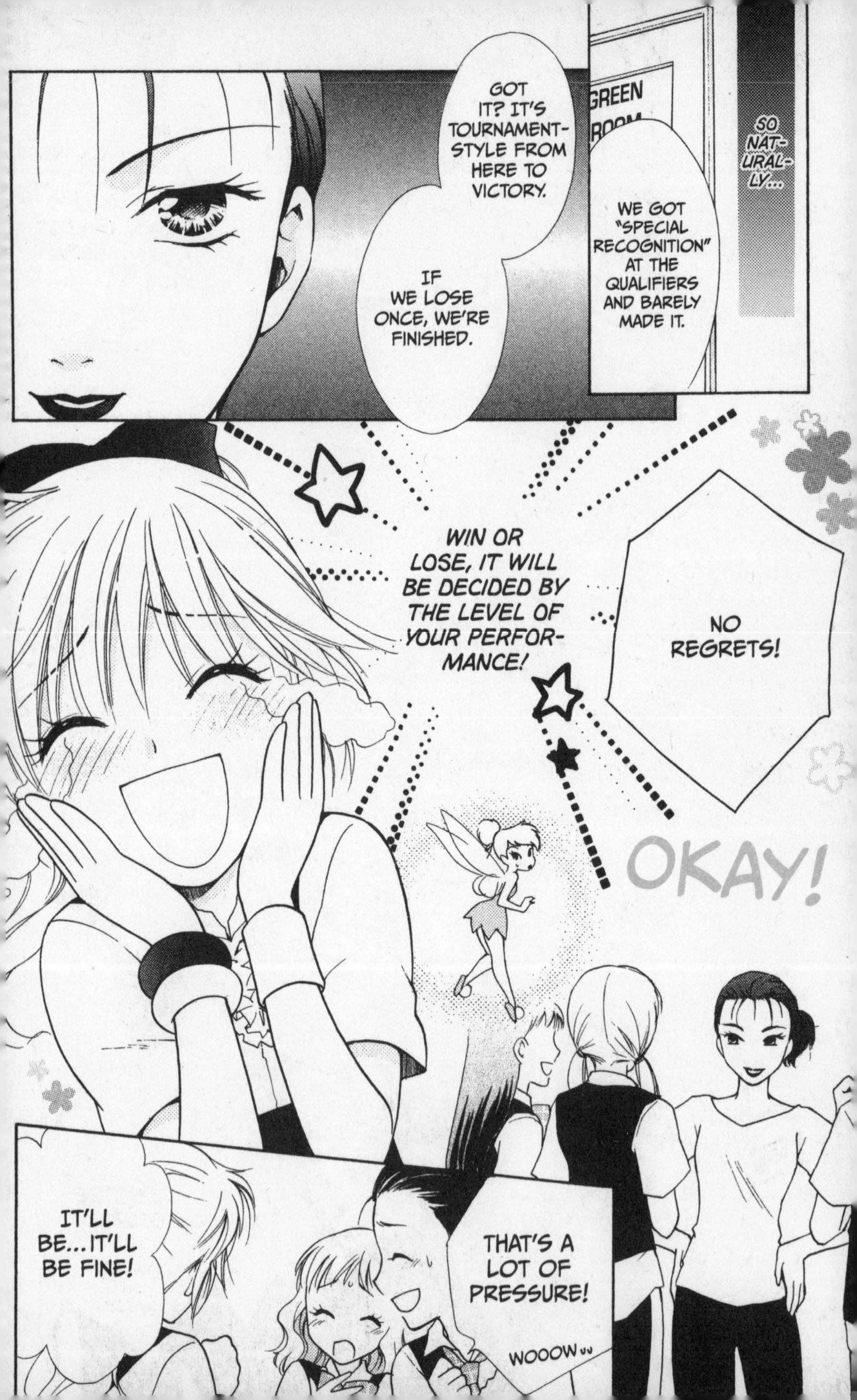
GREEN
SO NAT-URAL-LY...
WE GOT "SPECIAL RECOGNITION" AT THE QUALIFIERS AND BARELY MADE IT.
GOT IT? IT'S TOURNAMENT-STYLE FROM HERE TO VICTORY.
IF WE LOSE ONCE, WE'RE FINISHED.
WIN OR LOSE, IT WILL BE DECIDED BY THE LEVEL OF YOUR PERFOR-MANCE!
NO REGRETS!
OKAY!
THAT'S A LOT OF PRESSURE!
WOOOW
IT'LL BE...IT'LL BE FINE!

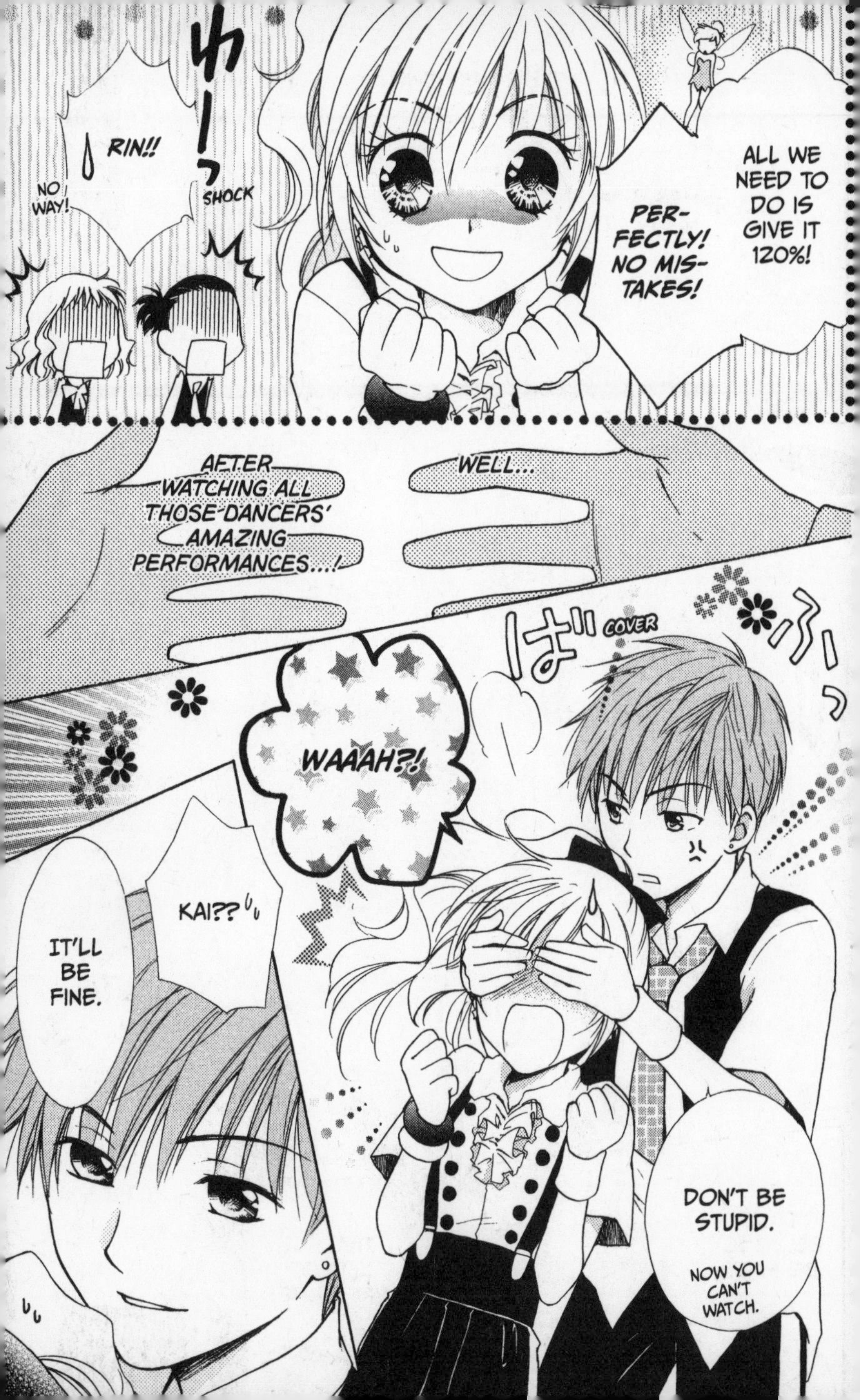
ALL WE NEED TO DO IS GIVE IT 120%!
PER-FECTLY! NO MIS-TAKES!
SHOCK
RIN!!
NO WAY!
WELL...
AFTER WATCHING ALL THOSE DANCERS' AMAZING PERFORMANCES...!
ばふっ COVER
WAAAH?!
DON'T BE STUPID.
NOW YOU CAN'T WATCH.
KAI??
IT'LL BE FINE.

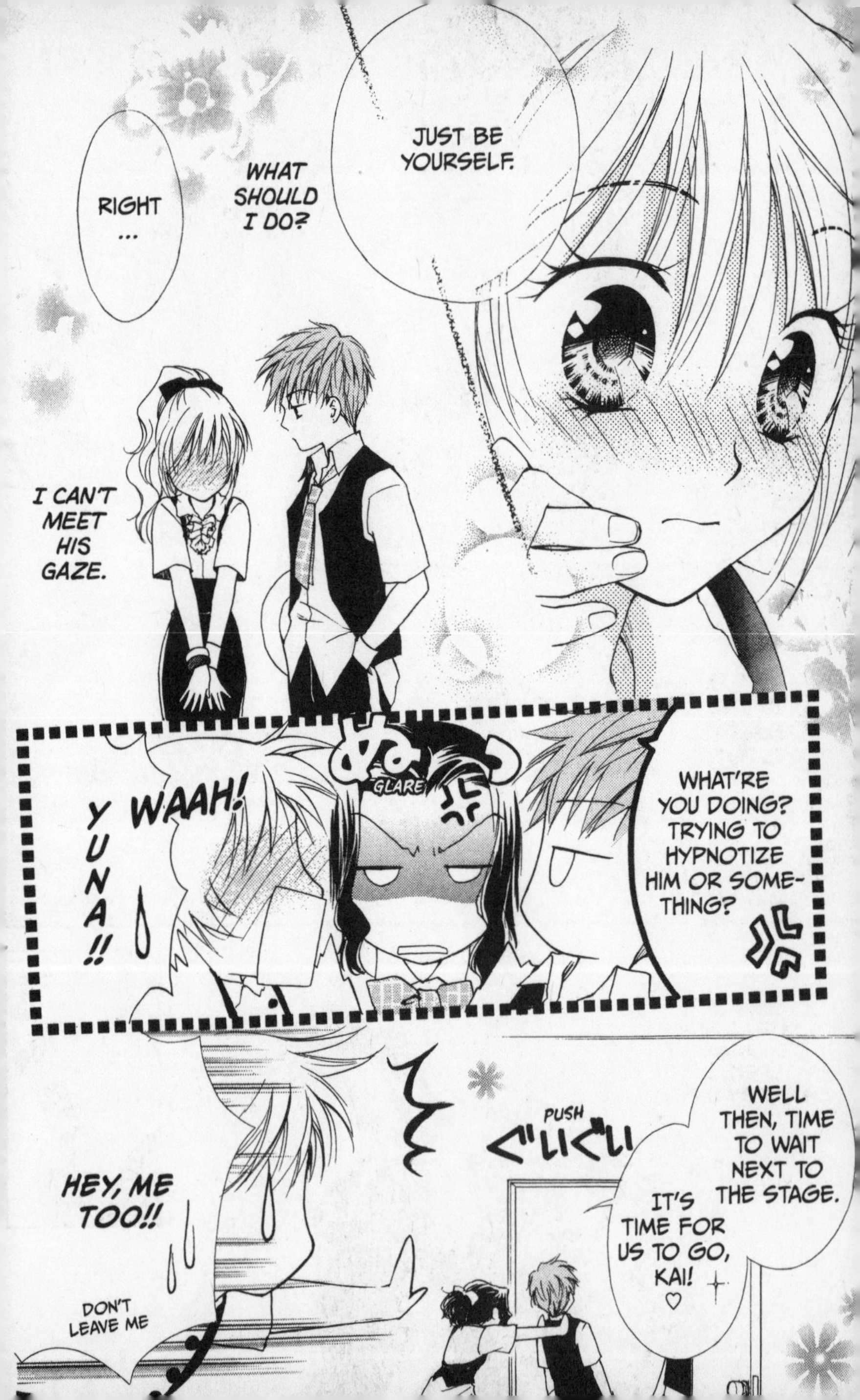
JUST BE YOURSELF.
WHAT SHOULD I DO?
RIGHT ...
I CAN'T MEET HIS GAZE.
WHAT'RE YOU DOING? TRYING TO HYPNOTIZE HIM OR SOME-THING?
GLARE
WAAH!
YUNA!!
WELL THEN, TIME TO WAIT NEXT TO THE STAGE.
IT'S TIME FOR US TO GO, KAI! ♡
ぐいぐい
PUSH
HEY, ME TOO!!
DON'T LEAVE ME

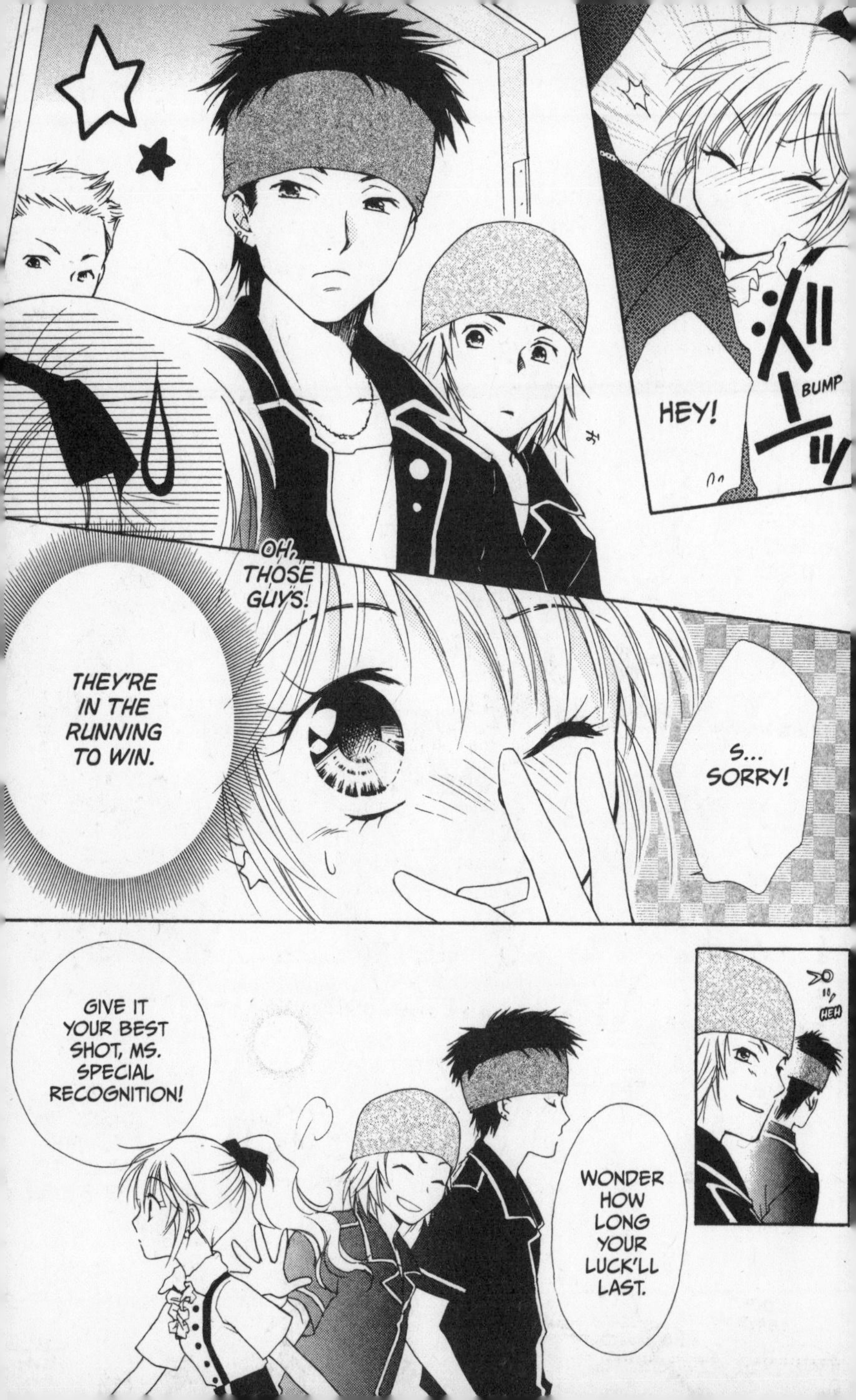
HEY!
BUMP
S... SORRY!
OH, THOSE GUYS!
THEY'RE IN THE RUNNING TO WIN.
HEH
GIVE IT YOUR BEST SHOT, MS. SPECIAL RECOGNITION!
WONDER HOW LONG YOUR LUCK'LL LAST.

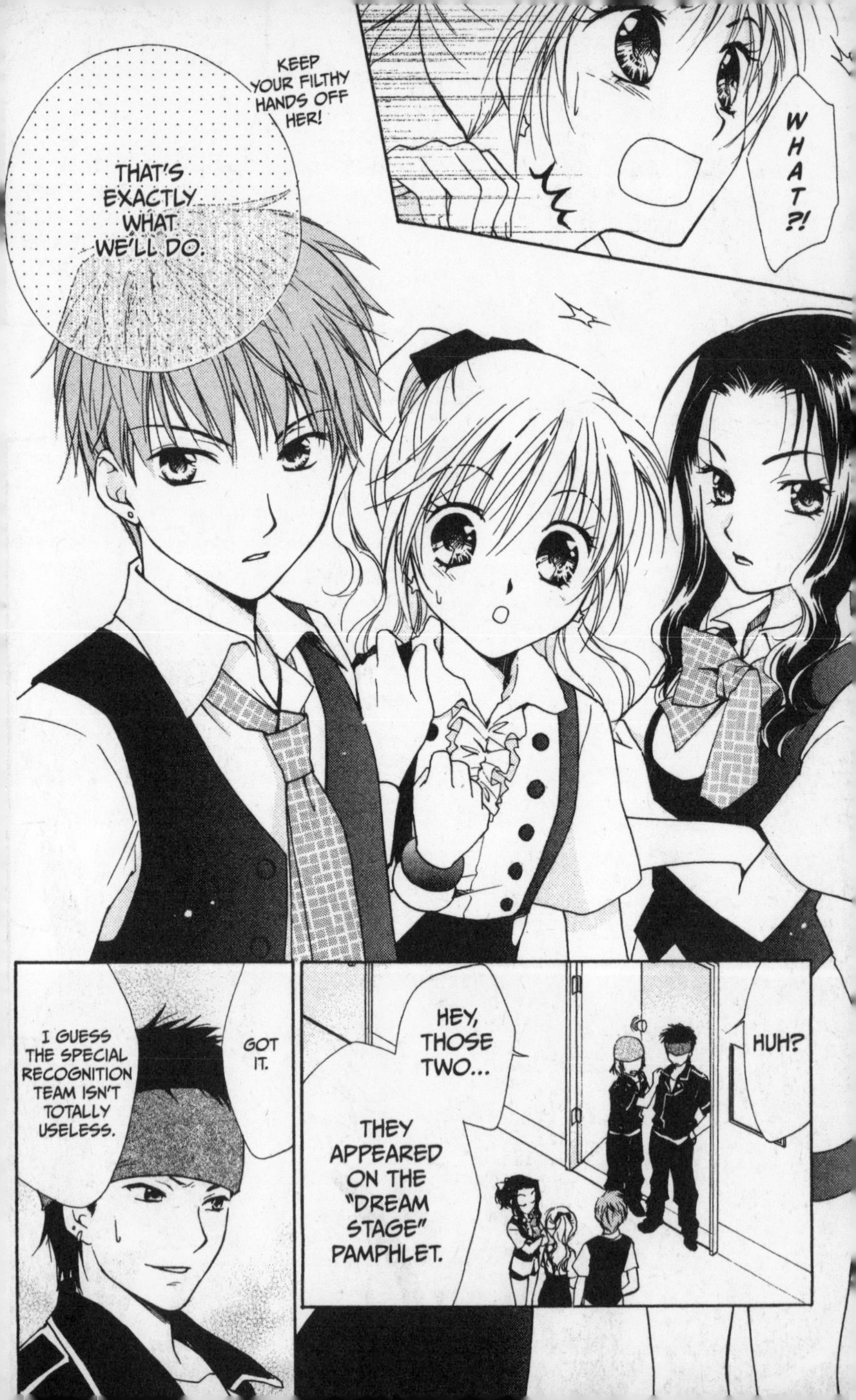
KEEP YOUR FILTHY HANDS OFF HER!
WHAT?!
THAT'S EXACTLY WHAT WE'LL DO.
HUH?
HEY, THOSE TWO...
THEY APPEARED ON THE "DREAM STAGE" PAMPHLET.
GOT IT.
I GUESS THE SPECIAL RECOGNITION TEAM ISN'T TOTALLY USELESS.

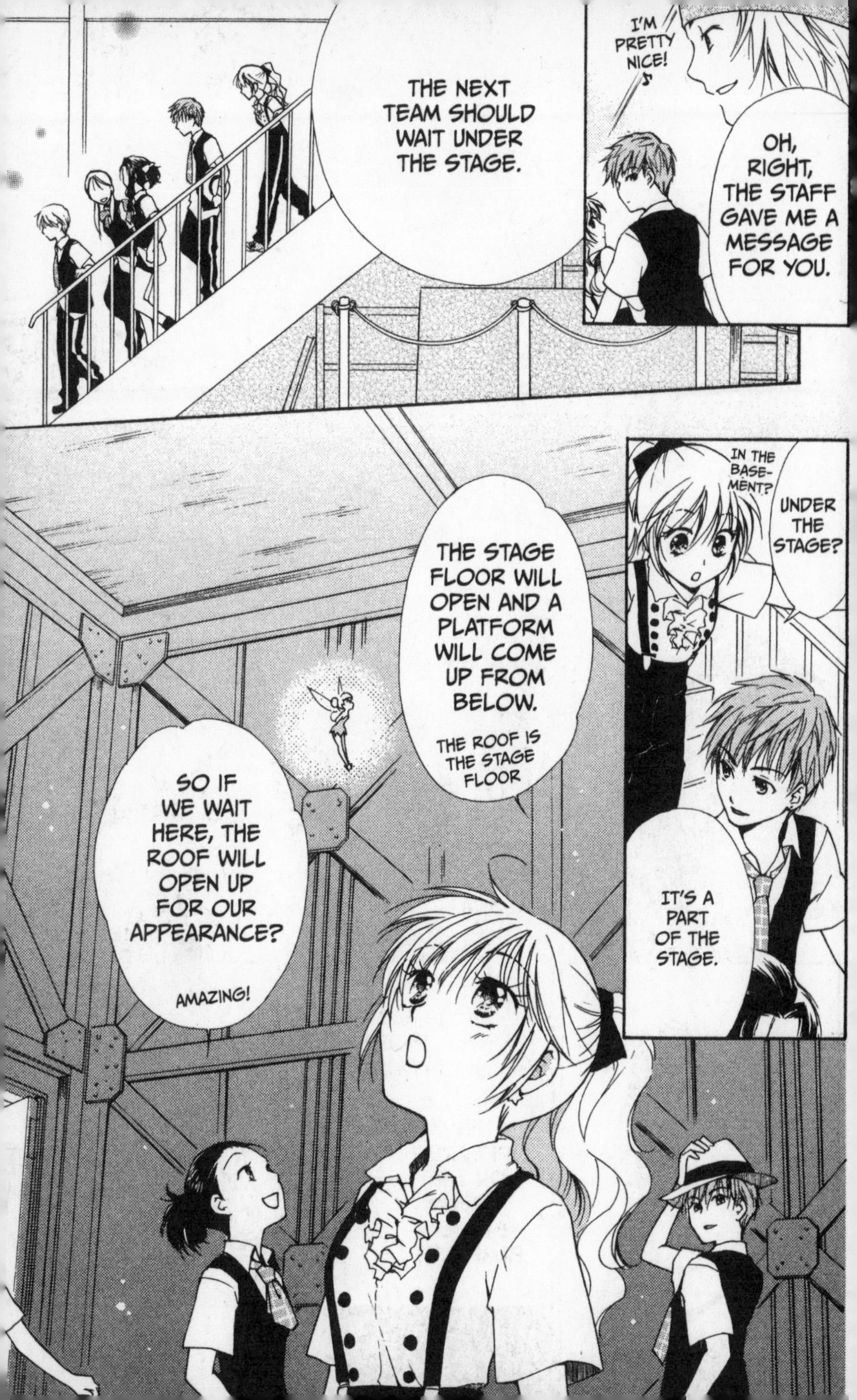
I'M PRETTY NICE! ♪
OH, RIGHT, THE STAFF GAVE ME A MESSAGE FOR YOU.
THE NEXT TEAM SHOULD WAIT UNDER THE STAGE.
UNDER THE STAGE?
IN THE BASEMENT?
IT'S A PART OF THE STAGE.
THE STAGE FLOOR WILL OPEN AND A PLATFORM WILL COME UP FROM BELOW.
THE ROOF IS THE STAGE FLOOR
SO IF WE WAIT HERE, THE ROOF WILL OPEN UP FOR OUR APPEARANCE?
AMAZING!

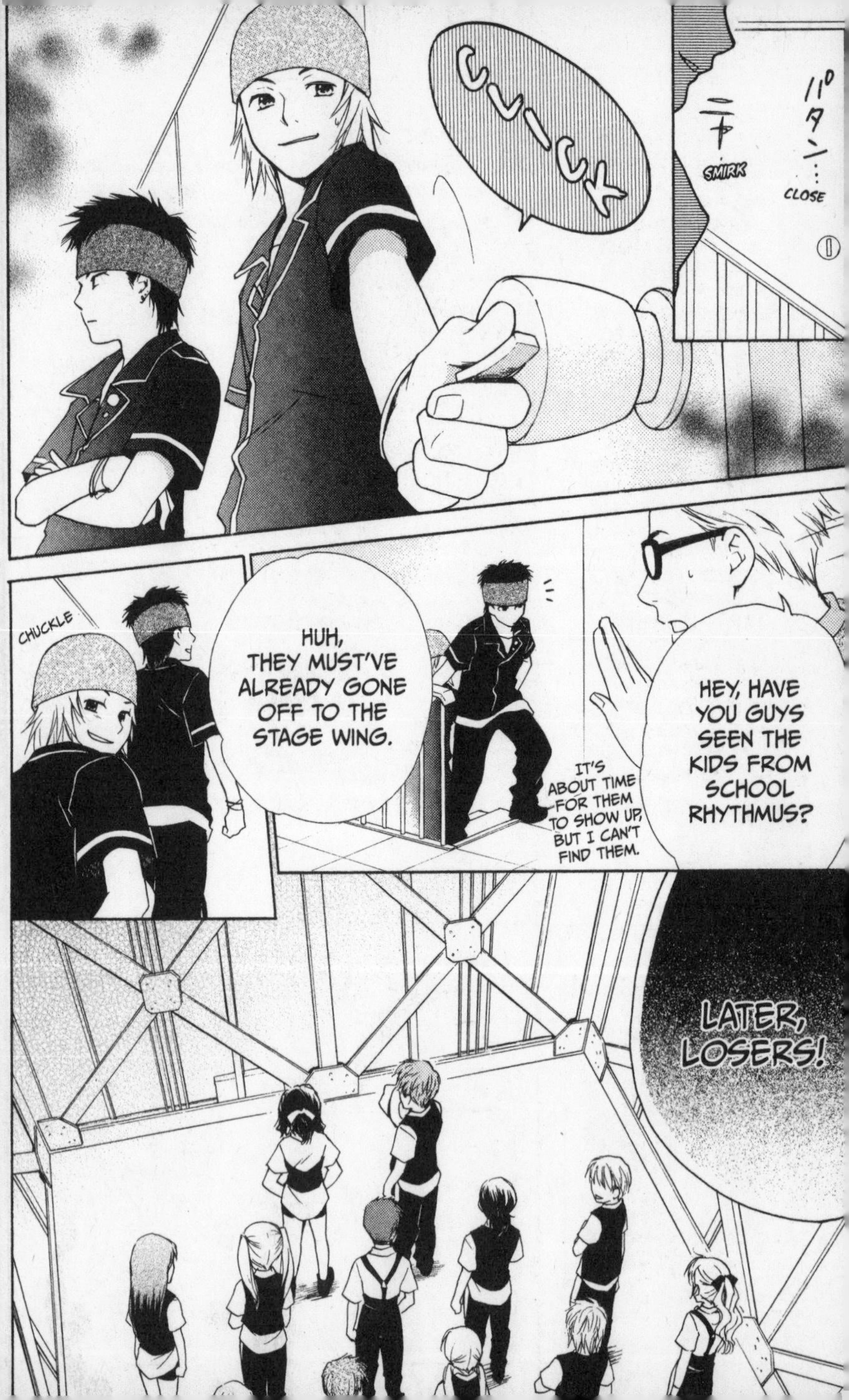
パタン…
CLOSE
ニヤ
SMIRK
CLICK
HEY, HAVE YOU GUYS SEEN THE KIDS FROM SCHOOL RHYTHMUS?
IT'S ABOUT TIME FOR THEM TO SHOW UP, BUT I CAN'T FIND THEM.
HUH, THEY MUST'VE ALREADY GONE OFF TO THE STAGE WING.
CHUCKLE
LATER, LOSERS!

READ THIS WAY

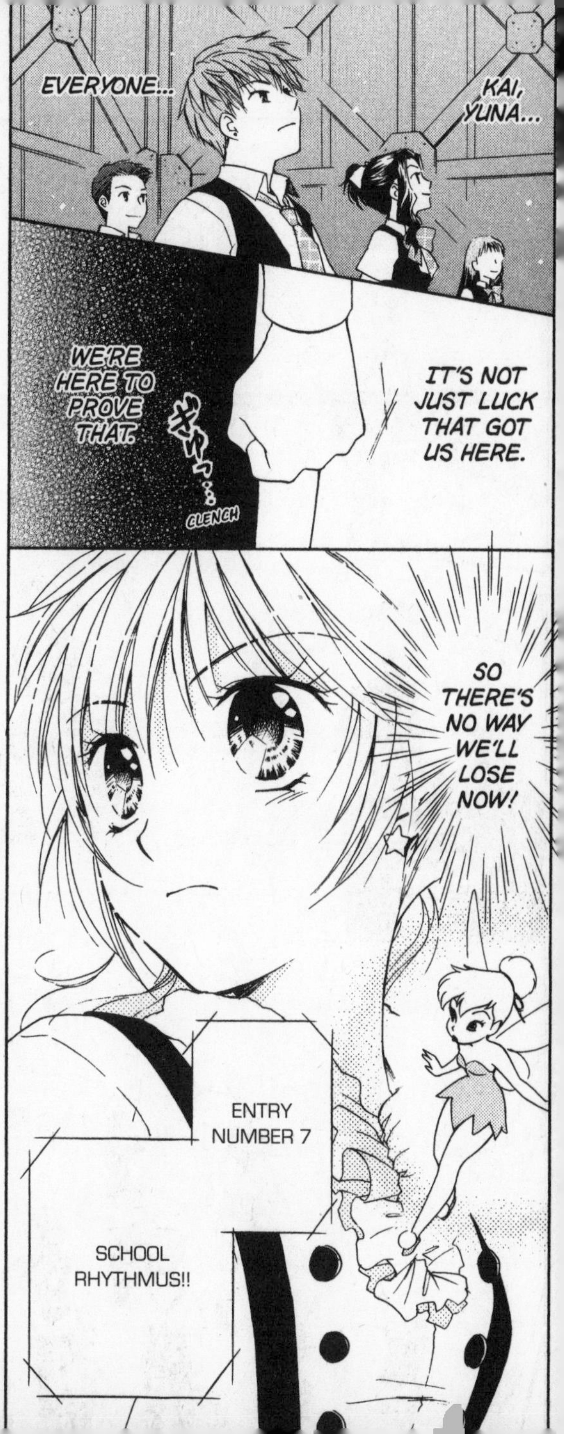
KAI, YUNA...
EVERYONE...
IT'S NOT JUST LUCK THAT GOT US HERE.
WE'RE HERE TO PROVE THAT.
CLENCH
SO THERE'S NO WAY WE'LL LOSE NOW!
ENTRY NUMBER 7
SCHOOL RHYTHMUS!!

THIS IS THE END, BUT I'M SO HAPPY THAT EVERYONE HAS DONE SO MUCH TO HELP ME. TO SEGA (WHO PLANNED AND DEVELOPED THE GAME,) TO THOSE AT DISNEY (WHO BACKED ME UP SO MUCH,) TO THE CHIEF EDITOR AND MY MANAGER AT THE NAKAYOSHI EDITORIAL GROUP (WHO PROVIDED ME WITH A LOT OF ADVICE AND HELPED FOLLOW THROUGH,) TO MY ASSISTANT GODDESSES (WHO CAME THROUGH EVERY MONTH TO LEND ME A HAND,) TO MY SISTER AND FAMILY (WHO LOOKED OUT AND SUPPORTED ME,) AND TO YOU, THE READER: THANK YOU SO MUCH!

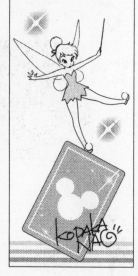

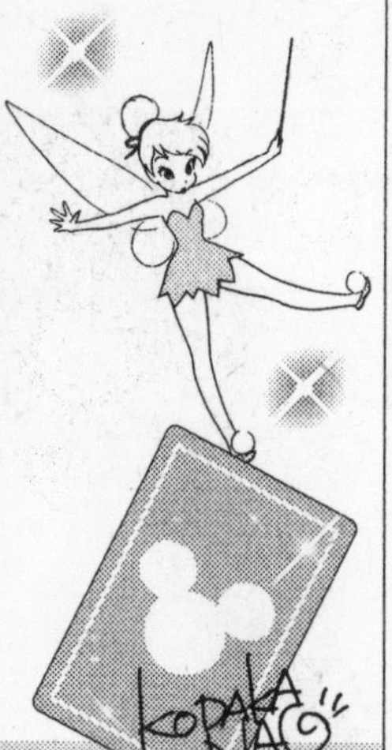
KODAKA NAO

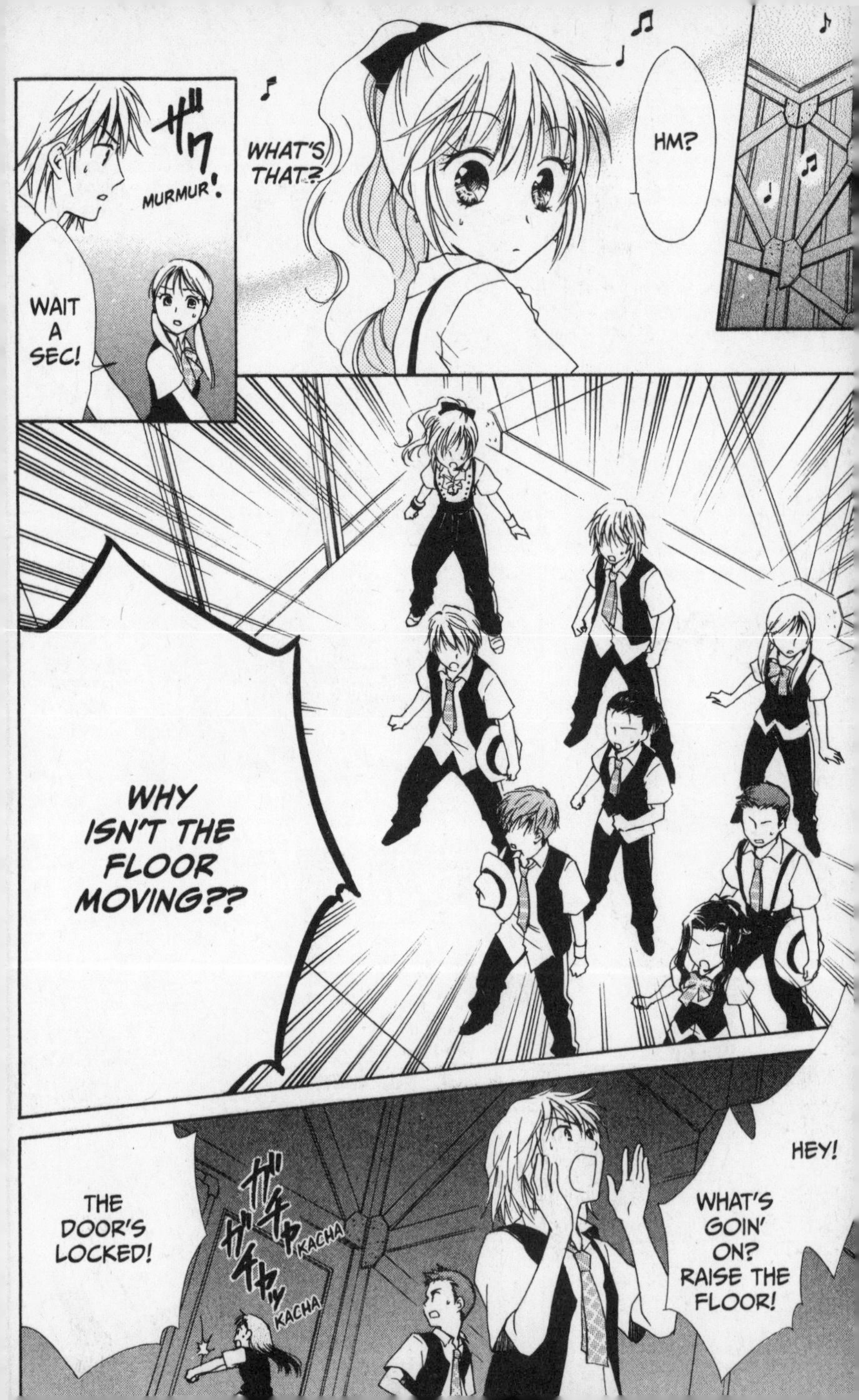
HM?
WHAT'S THAT?
ザワ
MURMUR!
WAIT A SEC!
WHY ISN'T THE FLOOR MOVING??
HEY!
WHAT'S GOIN' ON? RAISE THE FLOOR!
ガチャ KACHA
ガチャッ KACHA
THE DOOR'S LOCKED!

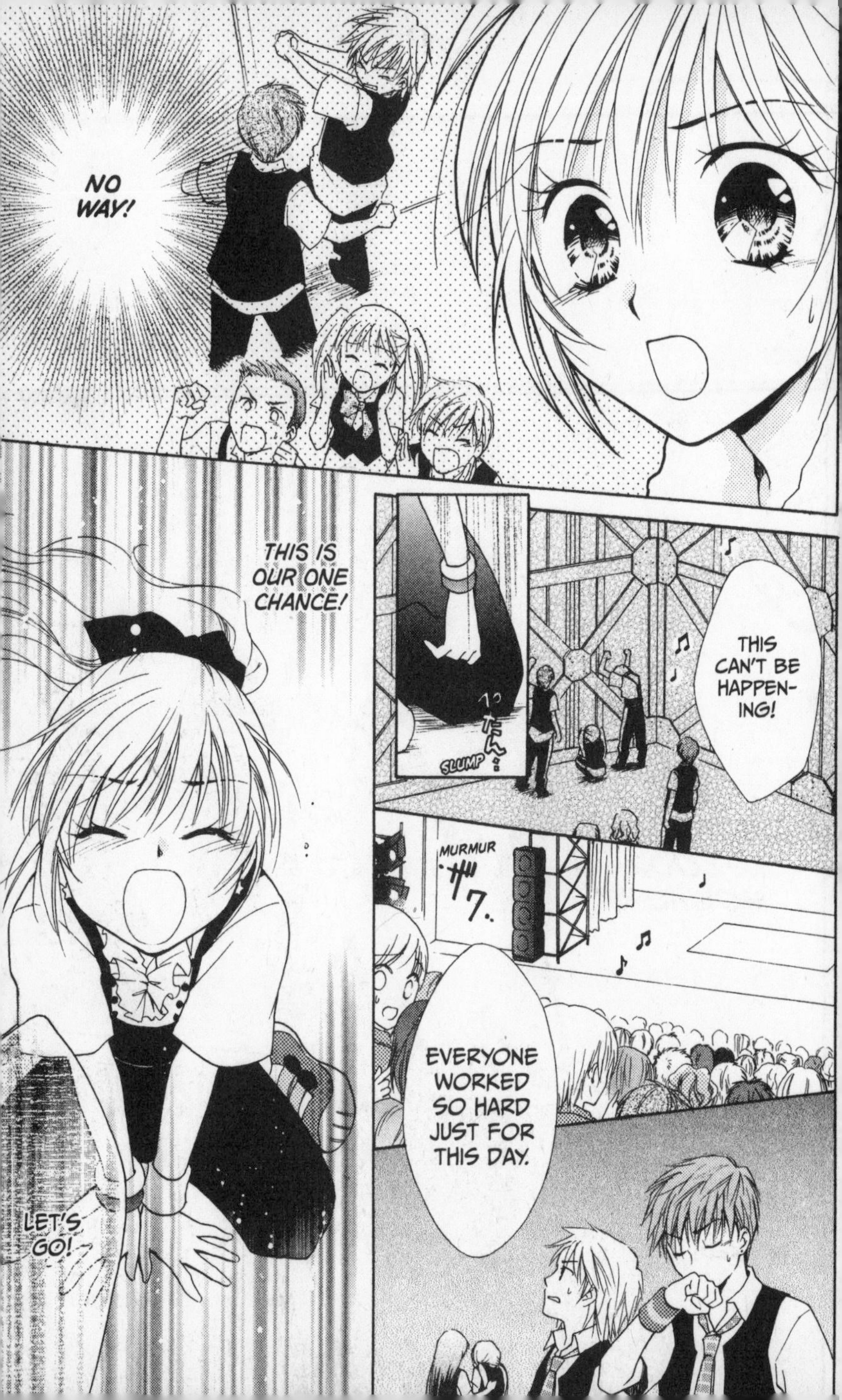
NO WAY!
SLUMP
THIS CAN'T BE HAPPENING!
MURMUR
EVERYONE WORKED SO HARD JUST FOR THIS DAY.
THIS IS OUR ONE CHANCE!
LET'S GO!

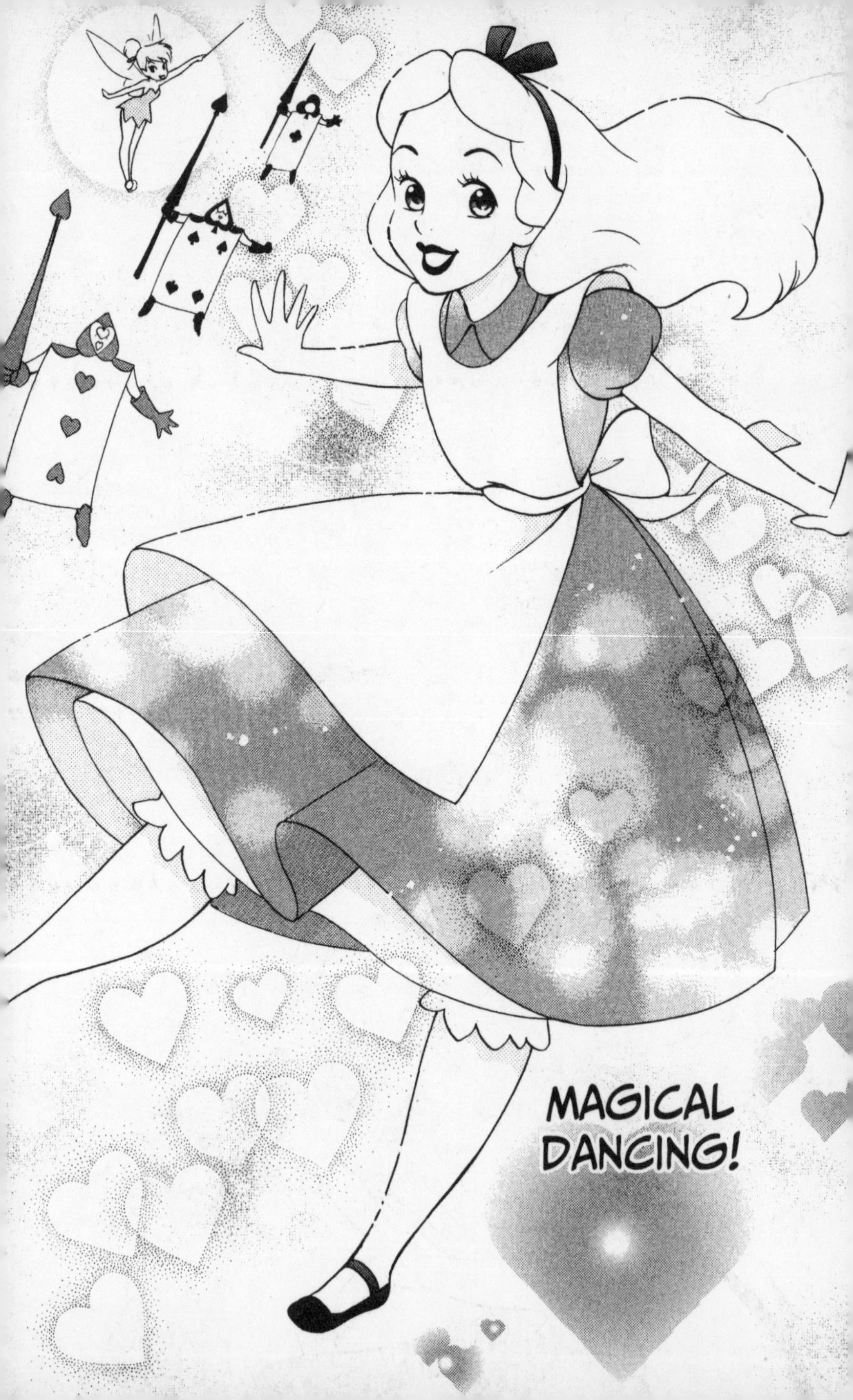
MAGICAL DANCING!

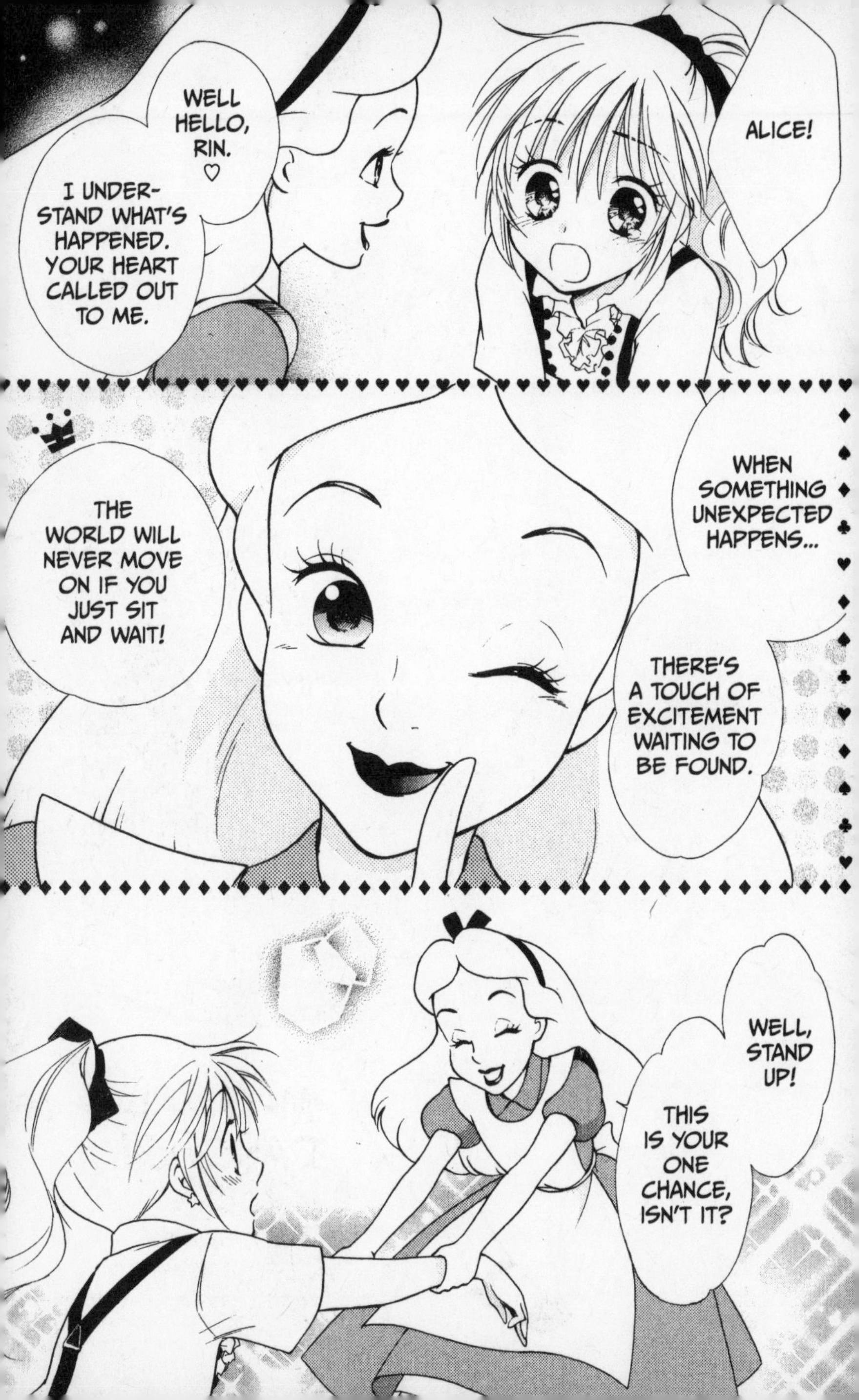
ALICE!
WELL HELLO, RIN. ♡
I UNDER-STAND WHAT'S HAPPENED. YOUR HEART CALLED OUT TO ME.
WHEN SOMETHING UNEXPECTED HAPPENS...
THERE'S A TOUCH OF EXCITEMENT WAITING TO BE FOUND.
THE WORLD WILL NEVER MOVE ON IF YOU JUST SIT AND WAIT!
WELL, STAND UP!
THIS IS YOUR ONE CHANCE, ISN'T IT?

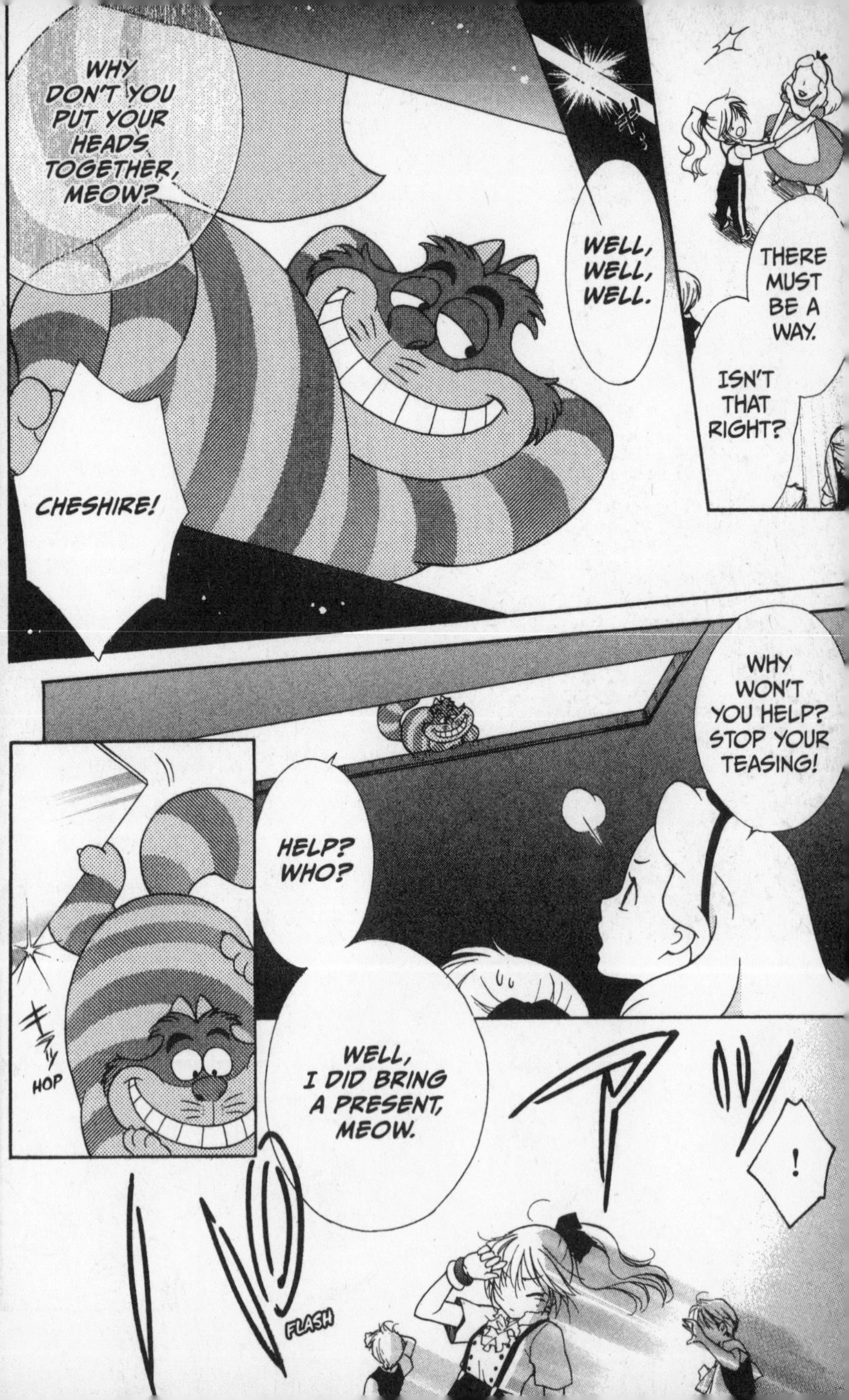
THERE MUST BE A WAY.
ISN'T THAT RIGHT?
WELL, WELL, WELL.
WHY DON'T YOU PUT YOUR HEADS TOGETHER, MEOW?
CHESHIRE!
WHY WON'T YOU HELP? STOP YOUR TEASING!
HELP? WHO?
HOP
WELL, I DID BRING A PRESENT, MEOW.
!
FLASH

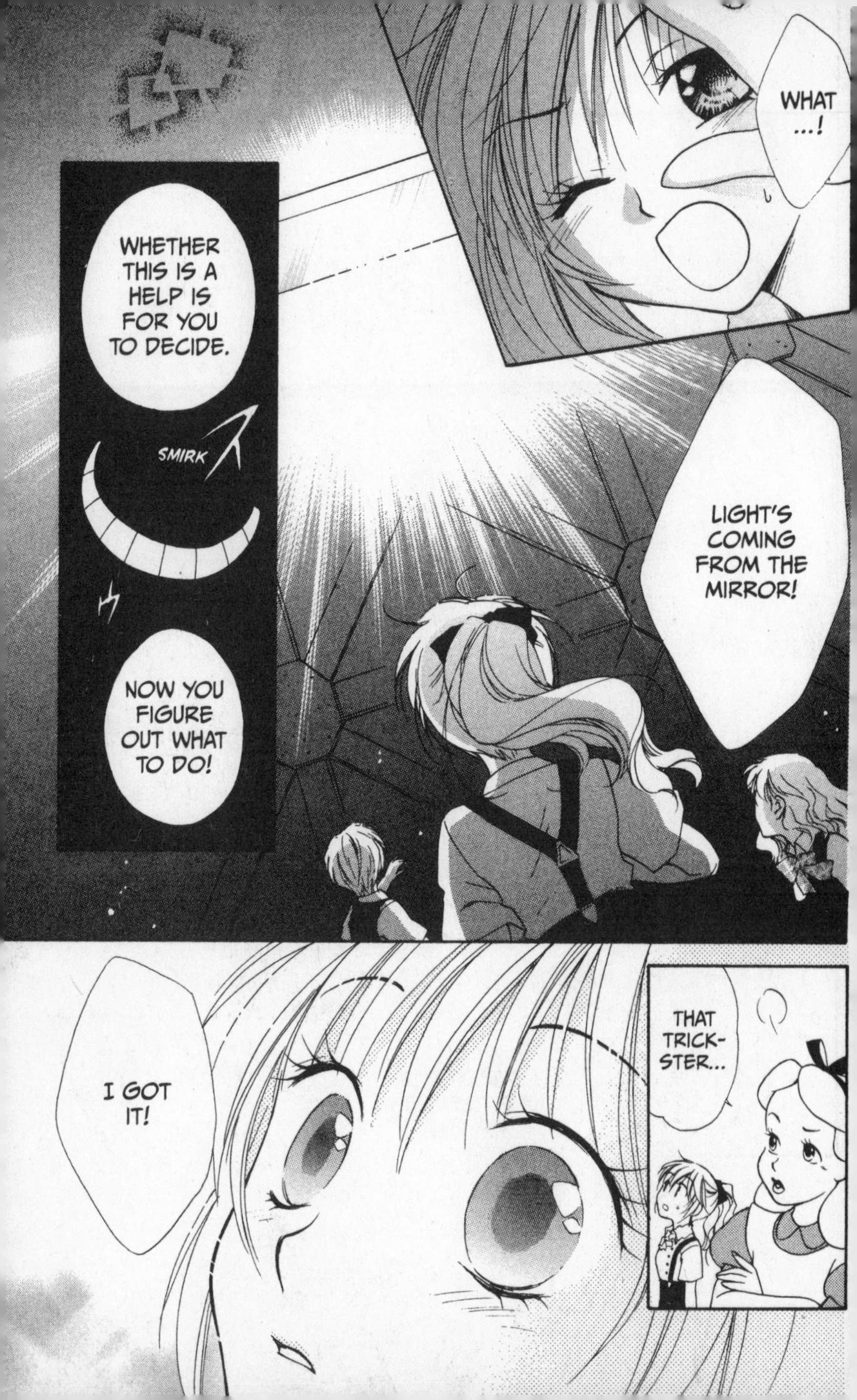
WHAT ...!
LIGHT'S COMING FROM THE MIRROR!
WHETHER THIS IS A HELP IS FOR YOU TO DECIDE.
SMIRK
NOW YOU FIGURE OUT WHAT TO DO!
THAT TRICK-STER...
I GOT IT!

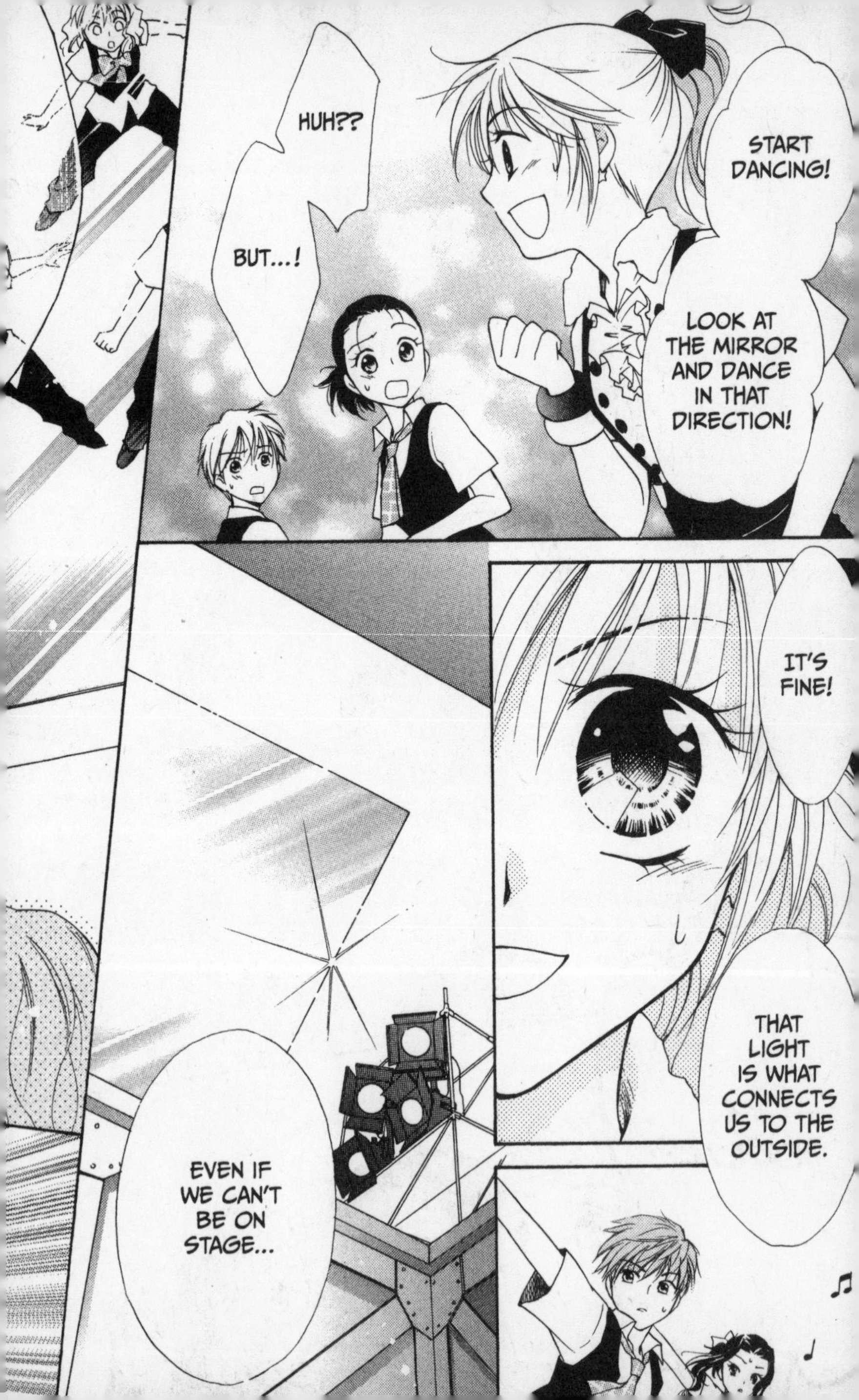
START DANCING!
LOOK AT THE MIRROR AND DANCE IN THAT DIRECTION!
HUH?? BUT...!
IT'S FINE!
THAT LIGHT IS WHAT CONNECTS US TO THE OUTSIDE.
EVEN IF WE CAN'T BE ON STAGE...

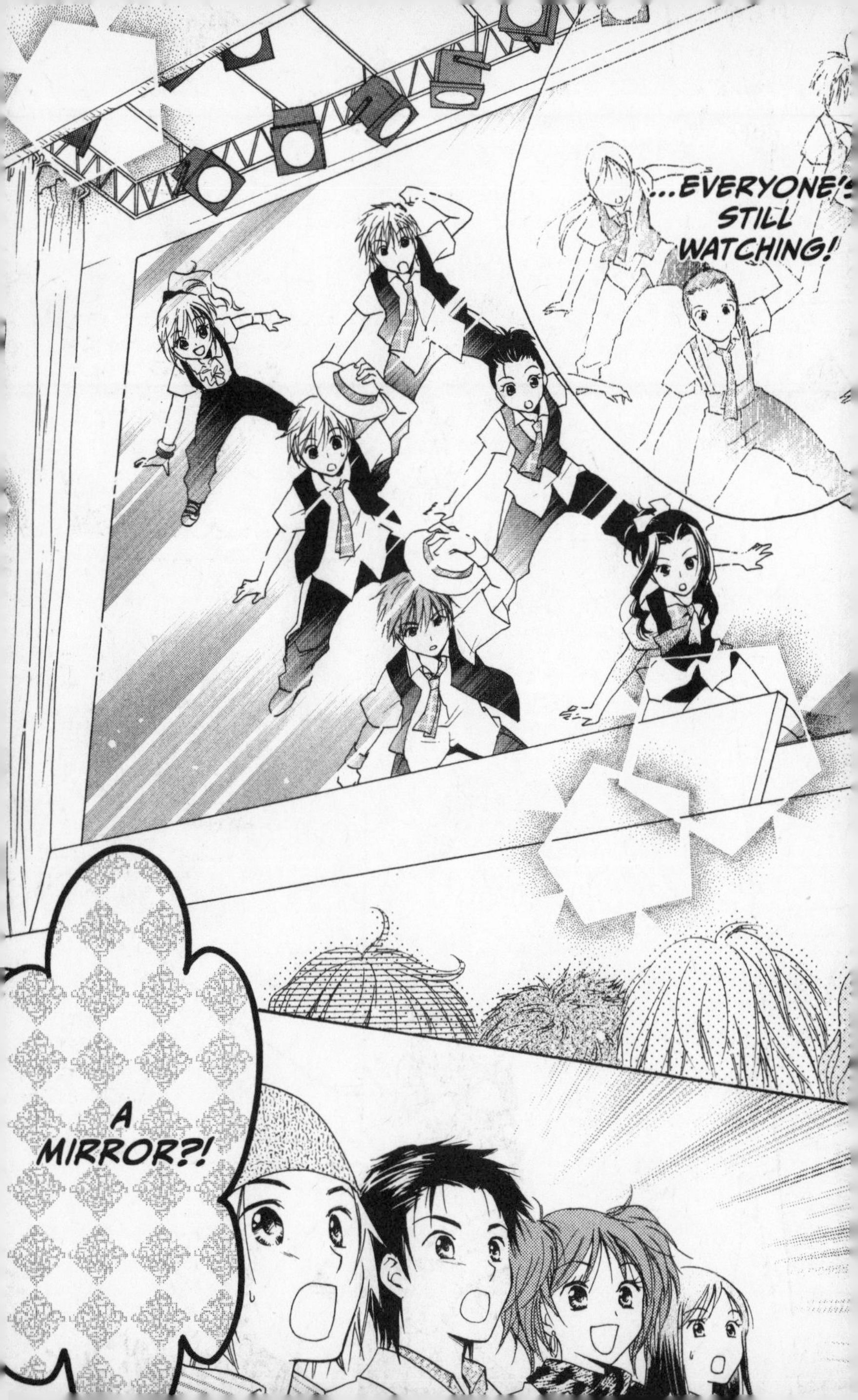
...EVERYONE'S STILL WATCHING!
A MIRROR?!

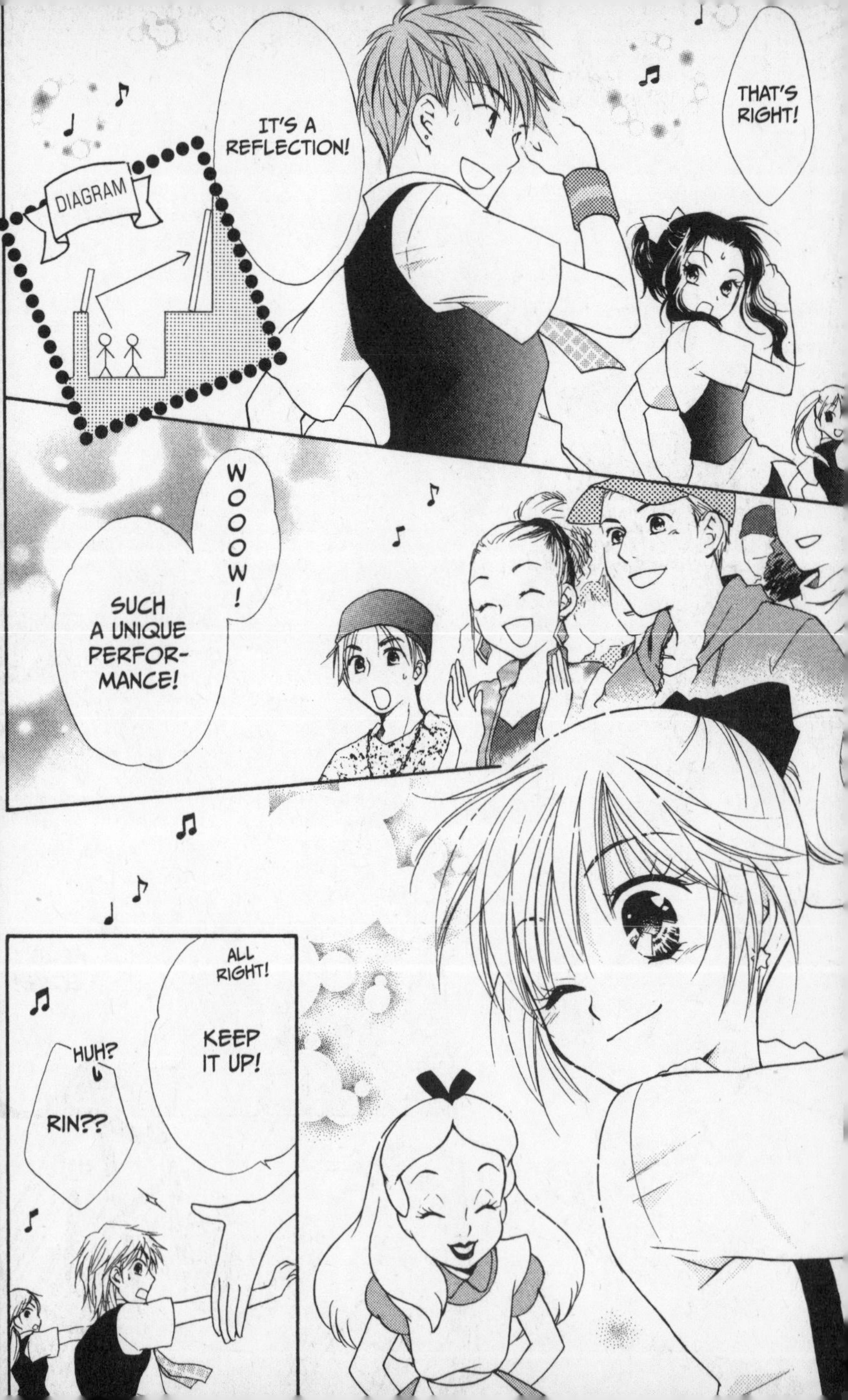
THAT'S RIGHT!
IT'S A REFLECTION!
DIAGRAM
WOOOOW!
SUCH A UNIQUE PERFORMANCE!
ALL RIGHT! KEEP IT UP!
HUH? RIN??

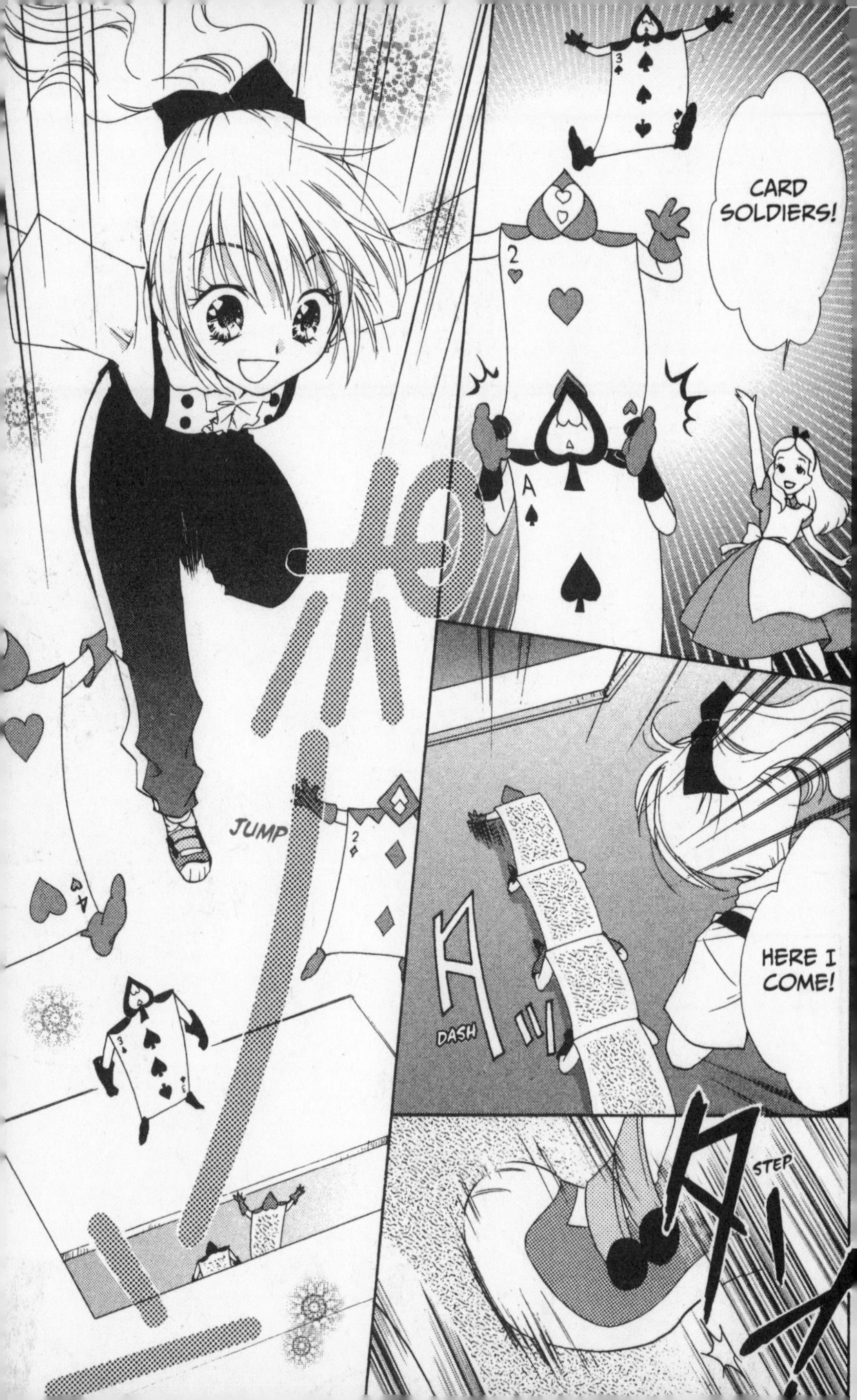
CARD SOLDIERS!
HERE I COME!
DASH
STEP
JUMP

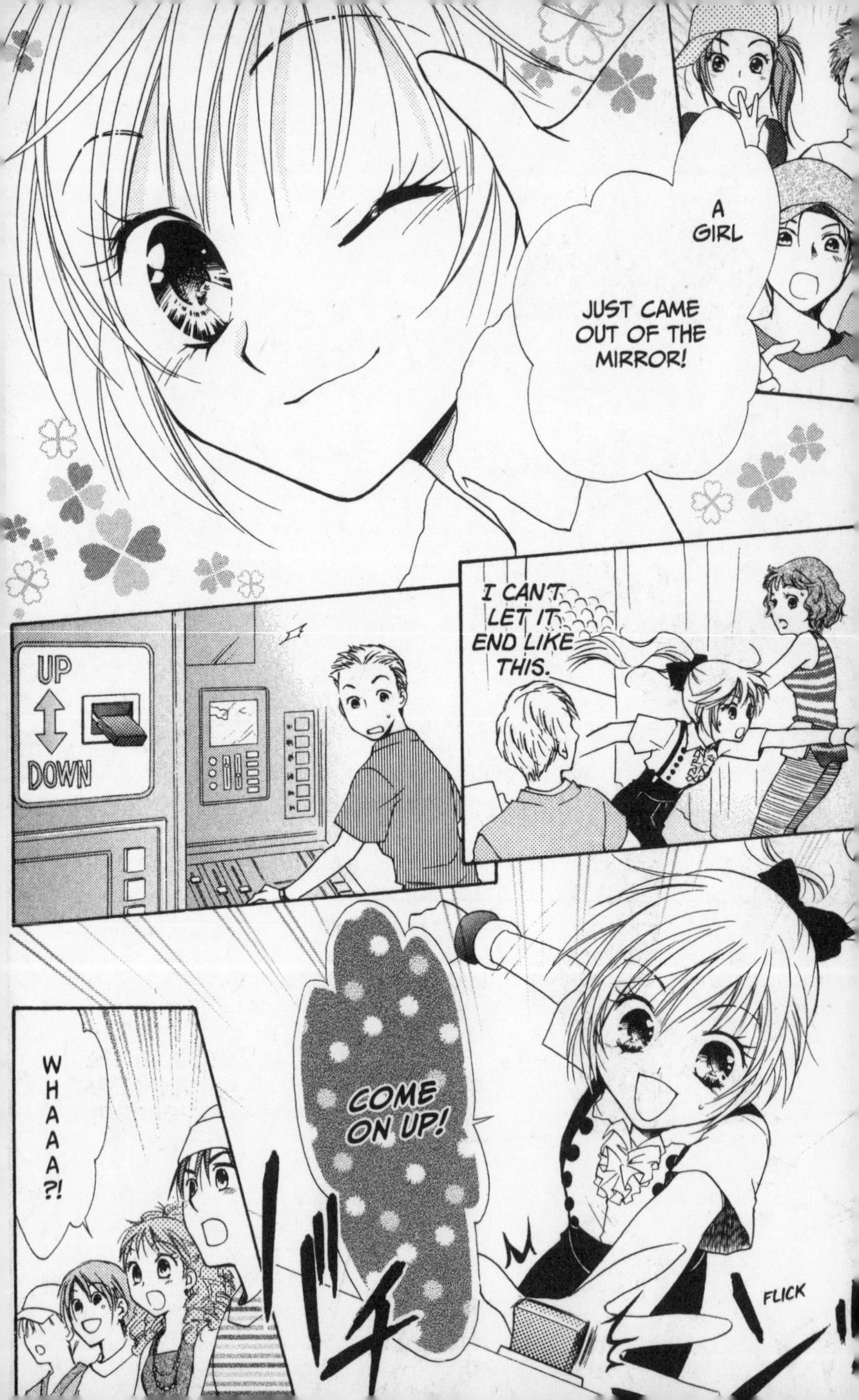
A GIRL
JUST CAME OUT OF THE MIRROR!
I CAN'T LET IT END LIKE THIS.
COME ON UP!
FLICK
WHAAAA?!

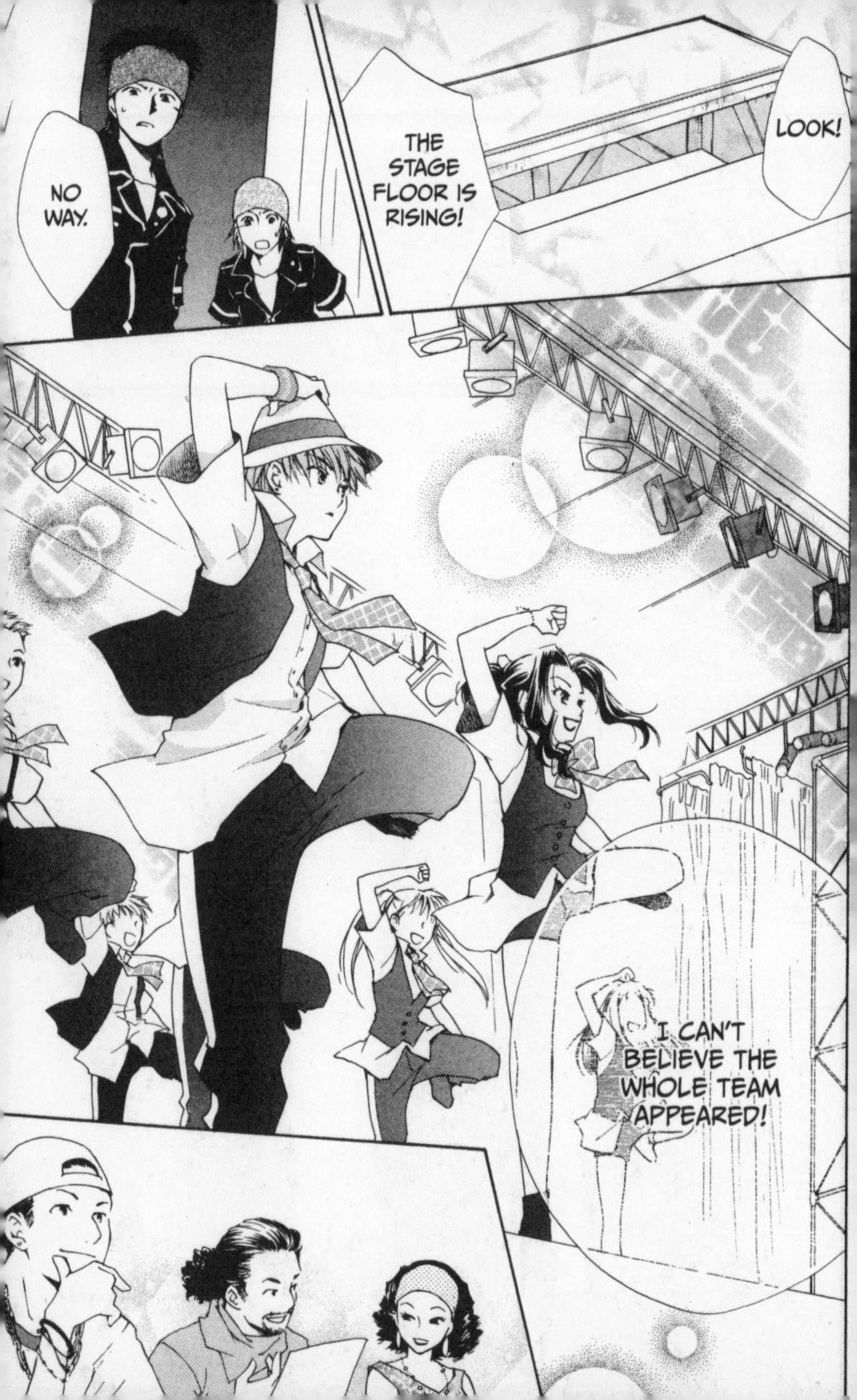
LOOK!
THE STAGE FLOOR IS RISING!
NO WAY.
I CAN'T BELIEVE THE WHOLE TEAM APPEARED!

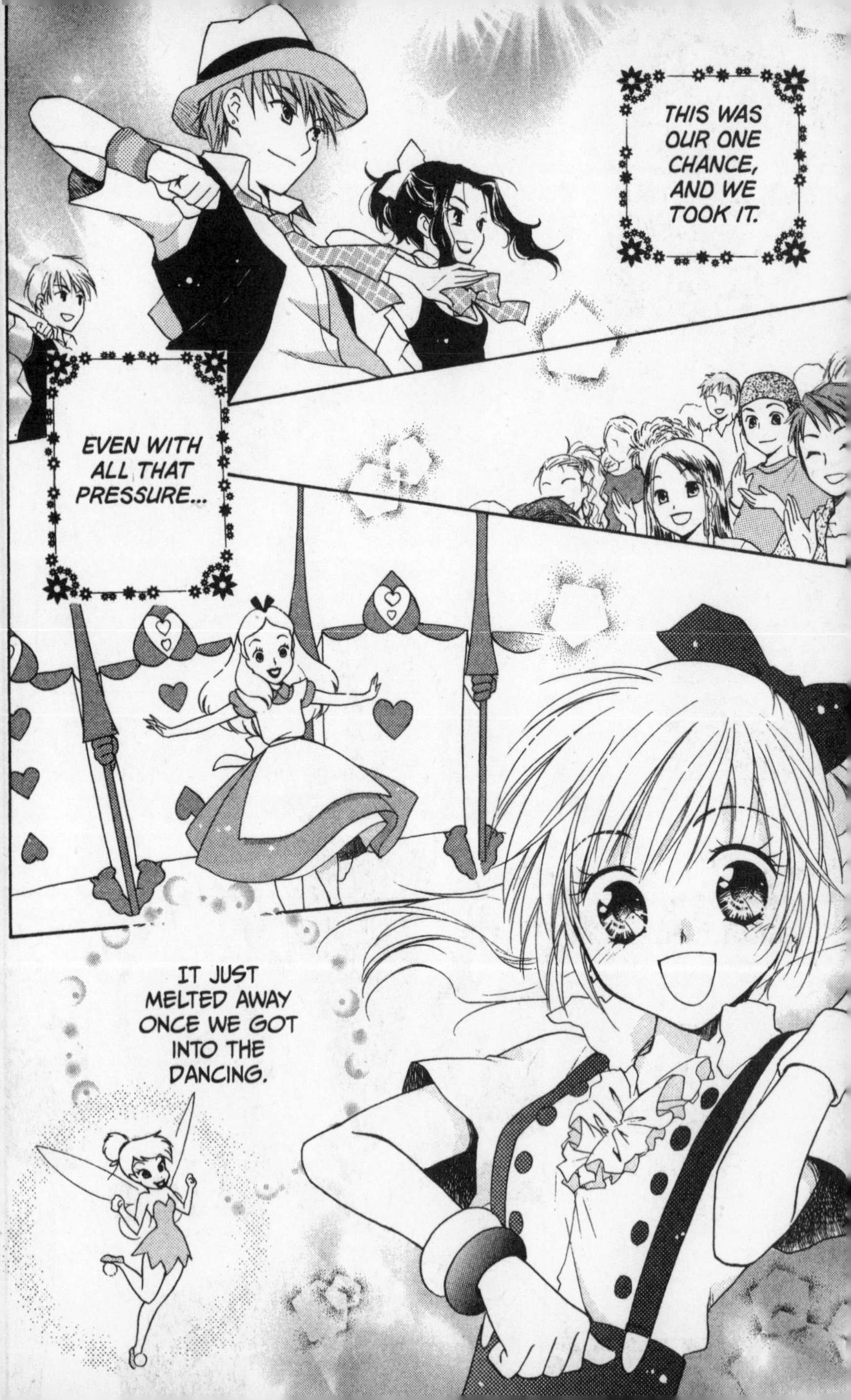
THIS WAS OUR ONE CHANCE, AND WE TOOK IT.
EVEN WITH ALL THAT PRESSURE...
IT JUST MELTED AWAY ONCE WE GOT INTO THE DANCING.

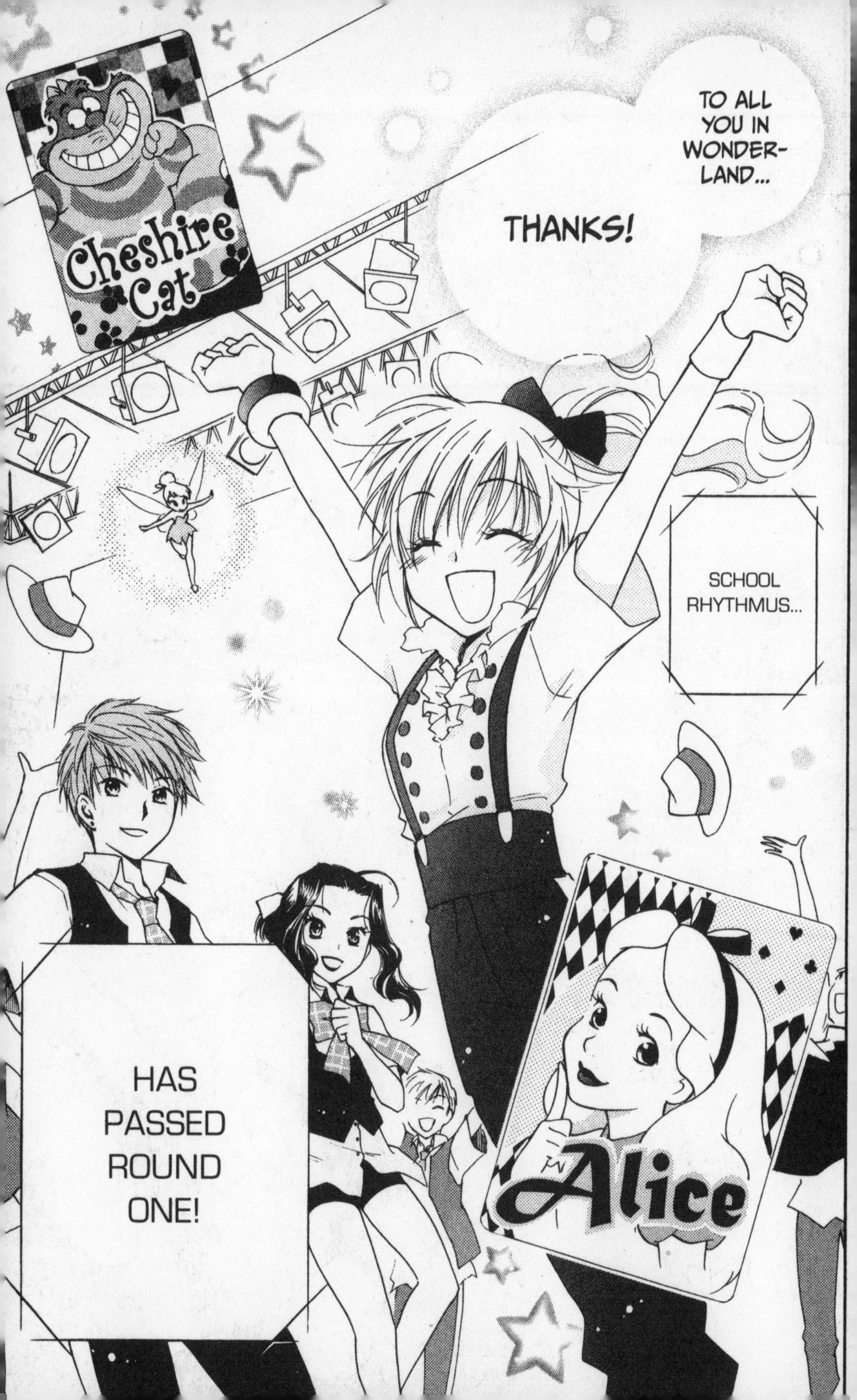
TO ALL YOU IN WONDER-LAND...
THANKS!
Cheshire Cat
SCHOOL RHYTHMUS...
Alice
HAS PASSED ROUND ONE!

SIDE STORY ★ COMIC (4)

THERE'S A DRESS-UP PARTY AT THE CASTLE. ♡
WOW!
YOU DANCE SO BEAUTIFULLY, ARIEL!
THANK YOU! ♡
HUMAN FEET ARE FANTASTIC!
YOU CAN DANCE, WALK, RUN...
AND SIT CROSS-LEGGED, PLAY GAMES ...!
AND EVEN GRAB STUFF!
HUH?

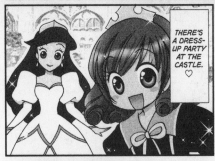

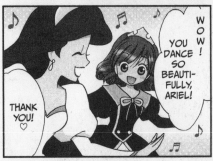

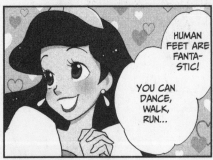

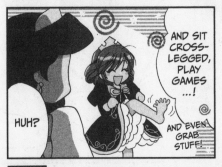

THE END

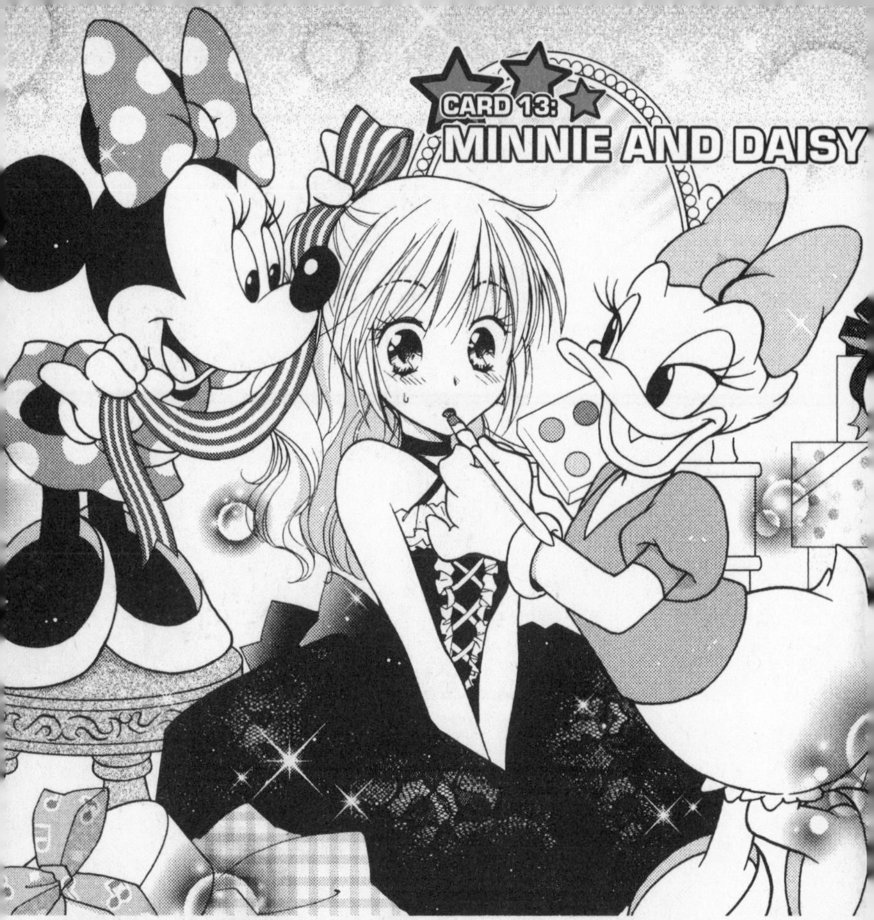
CARD 13:
MINNIE AND DAISY
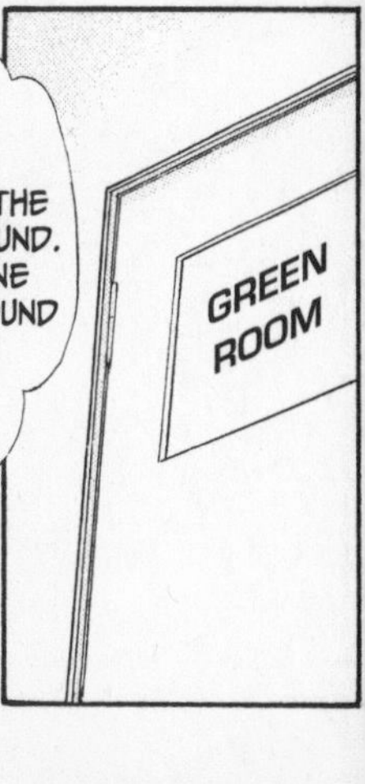
GREEN ROOM
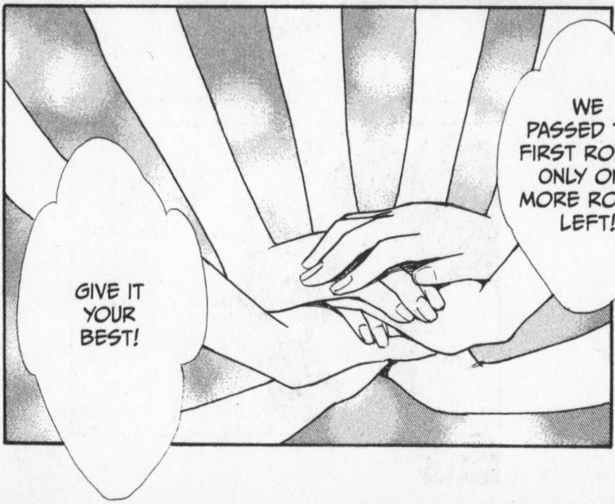
WE PASSED THE FIRST ROUND. ONLY ONE MORE ROUND LEFT!
GIVE IT YOUR BEST!

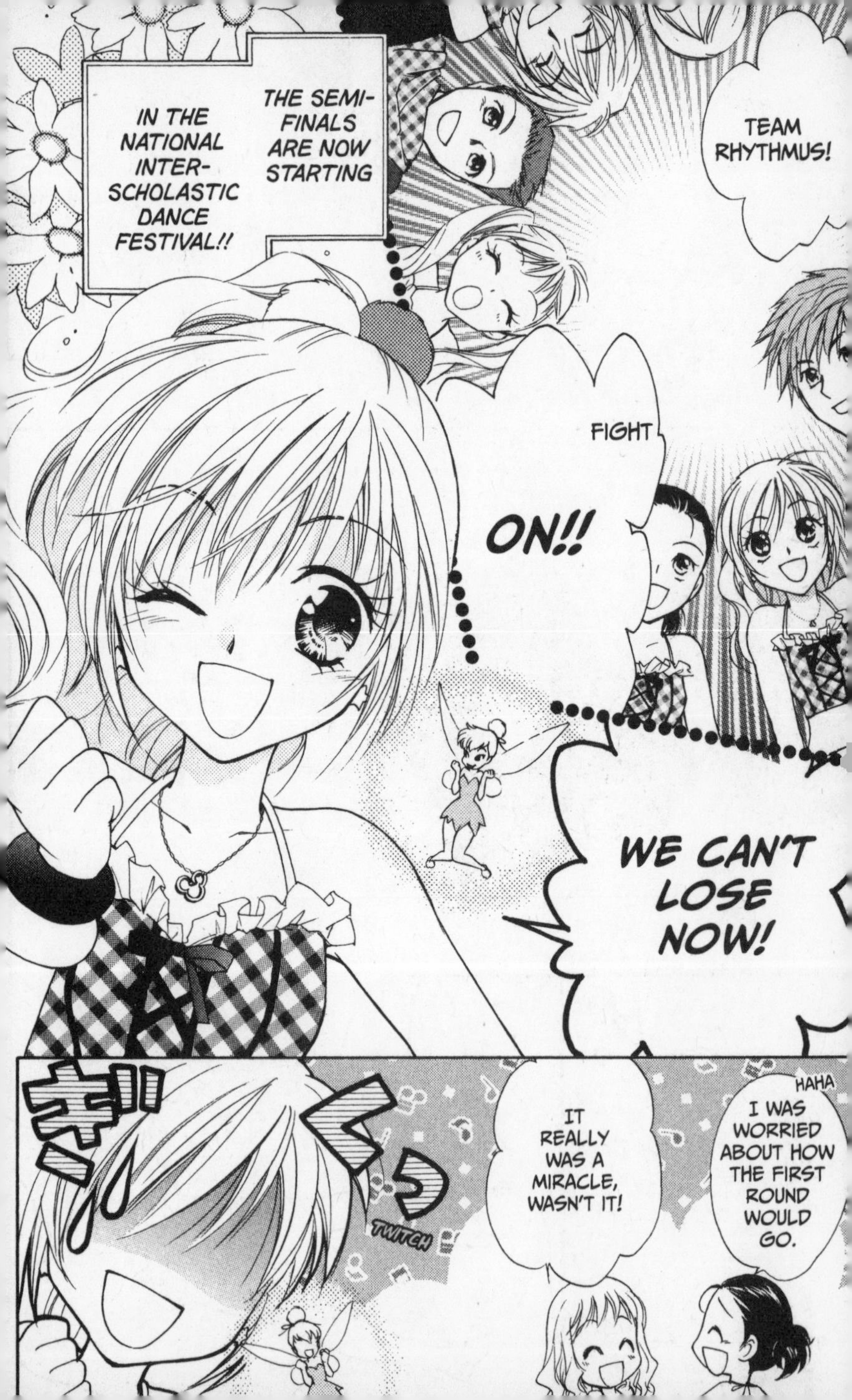

THE SEMI-FINALS ARE NOW STARTING
IN THE NATIONAL INTER-SCHOLASTIC DANCE FESTIVAL!!
TEAM RHYTHMUS!
FIGHT
ON!!
WE CAN'T LOSE NOW!
HAHA
I WAS WORRIED ABOUT HOW THE FIRST ROUND WOULD GO.
IT REALLY WAS A MIRACLE, WASN'T IT!
TWITCH

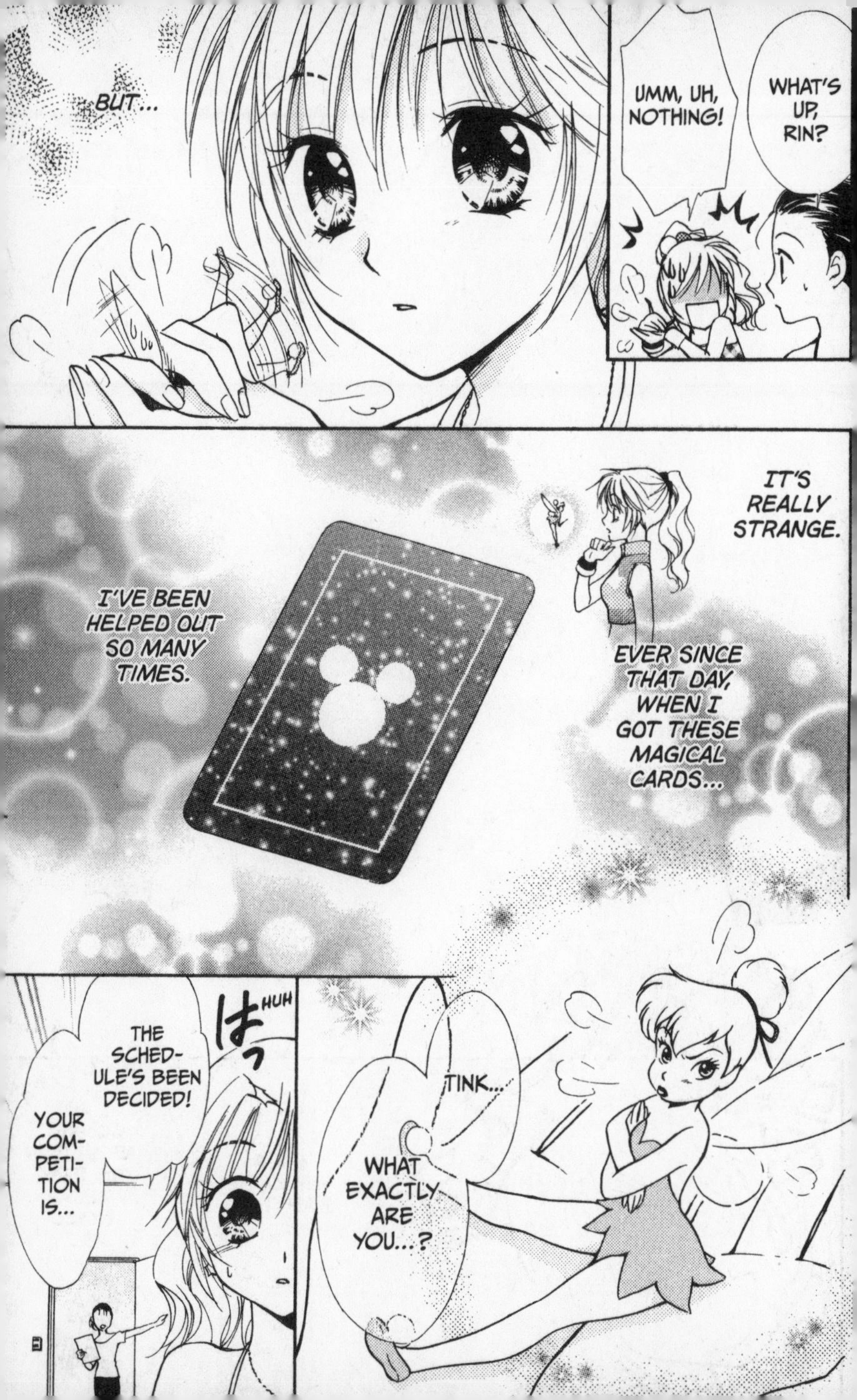
WHAT'S UP, RIN?
UMM, UH, NOTHING!
BUT...
IT'S REALLY STRANGE.
EVER SINCE THAT DAY, WHEN I GOT THESE MAGICAL CARDS...
I'VE BEEN HELPED OUT SO MANY TIMES.
TINK...
WHAT EXACTLY ARE YOU...?
はっ
HUH
THE SCHED-ULE'S BEEN DECIDED!
YOUR COM-PETI-TION IS...

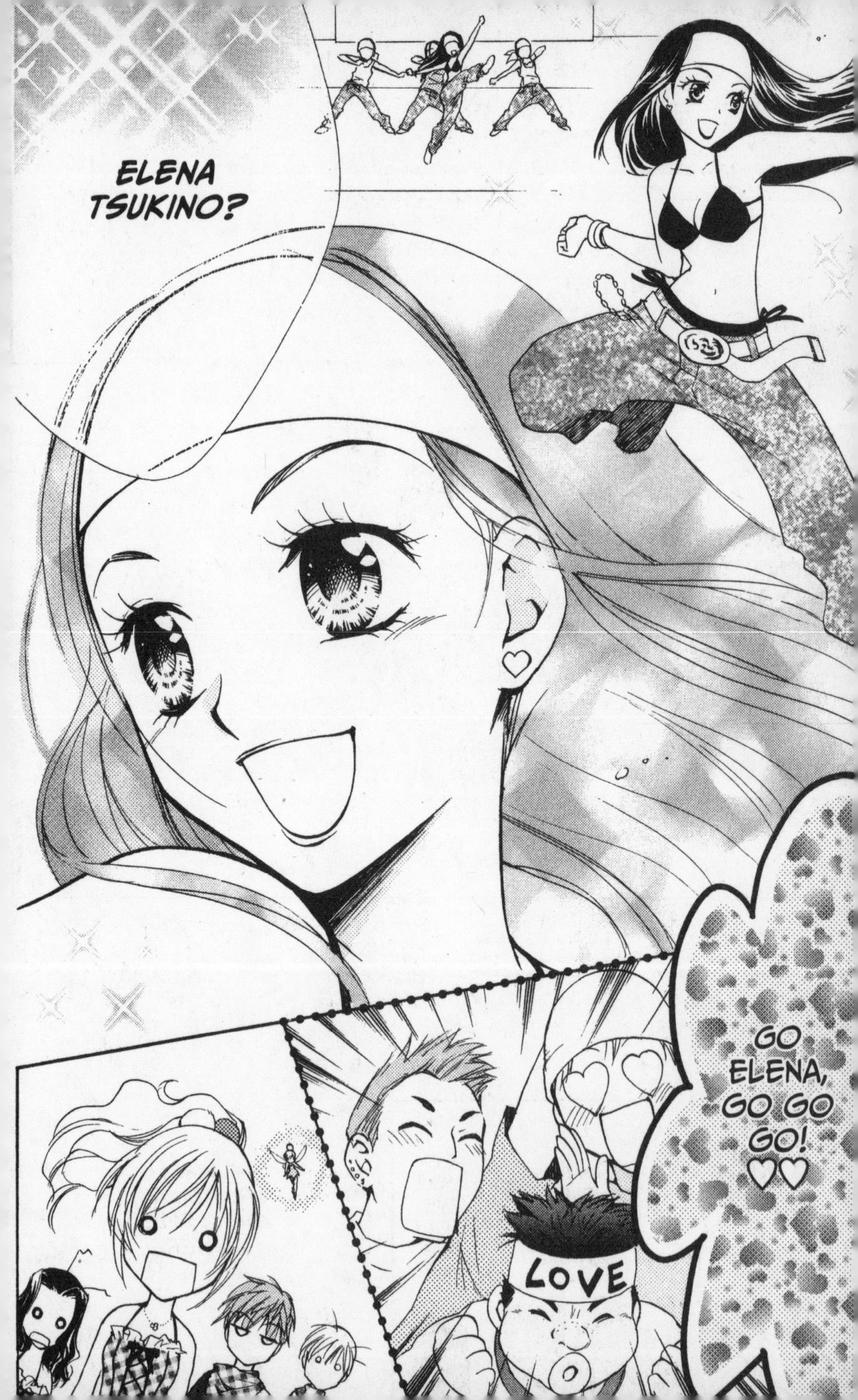
ELENA TSUKINO?
GO ELENA, GO GO GO! ♥♥
LOVE

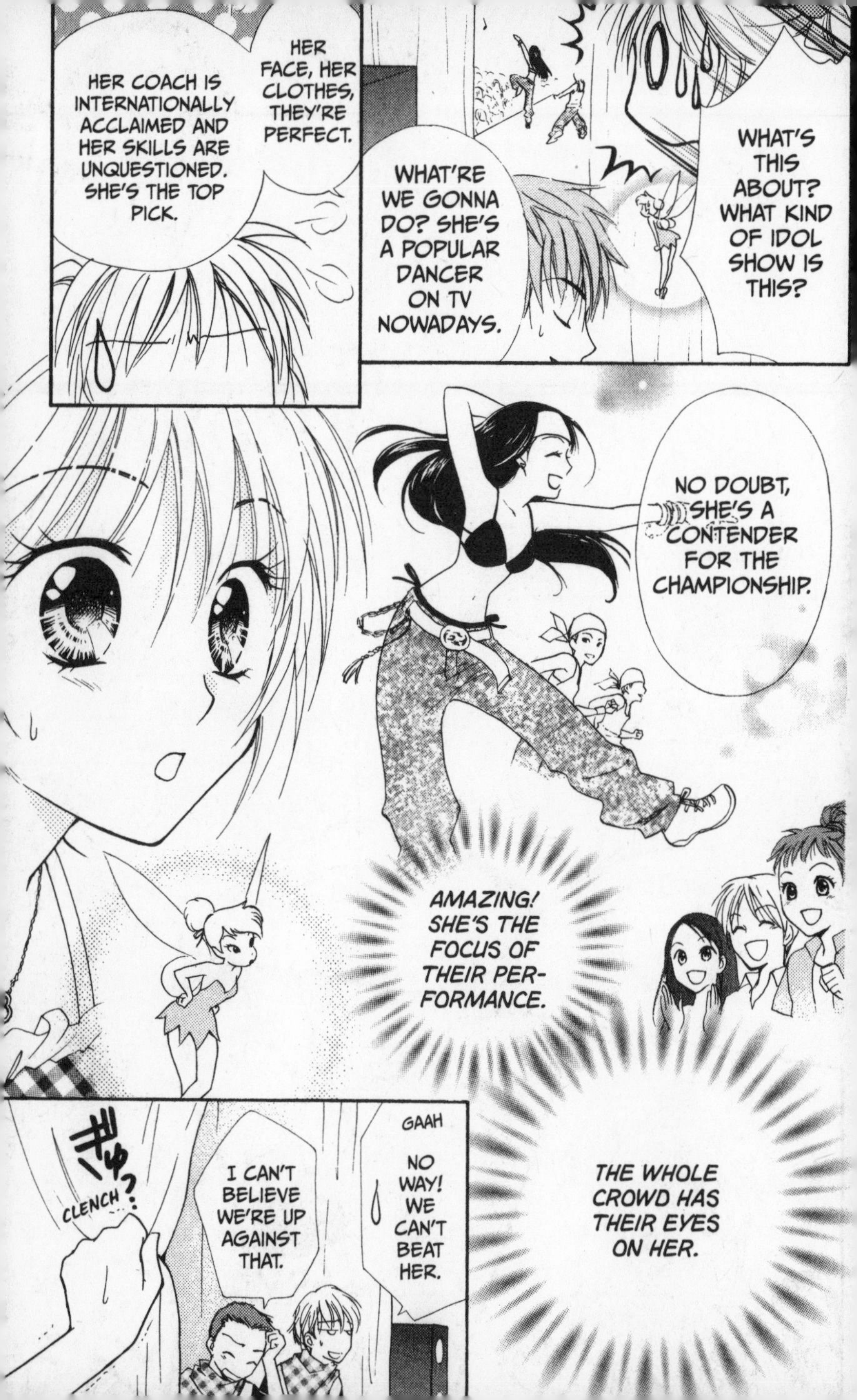
WHAT'S THIS ABOUT? WHAT KIND OF IDOL SHOW IS THIS?
WHAT'RE WE GONNA DO? SHE'S A POPULAR DANCER ON TV NOWADAYS.
HER FACE, HER CLOTHES, THEY'RE PERFECT.
HER COACH IS INTERNATIONALLY ACCLAIMED AND HER SKILLS ARE UNQUESTIONED. SHE'S THE TOP PICK.
NO DOUBT, SHE'S A CONTENDER FOR THE CHAMPIONSHIP.
AMAZING! SHE'S THE FOCUS OF THEIR PER-FORMANCE.
THE WHOLE CROWD HAS THEIR EYES ON HER.
GAAH
NO WAY! WE CAN'T BEAT HER.
I CAN'T BELIEVE WE'RE UP AGAINST THAT.
ぎゅっ
CLENCH

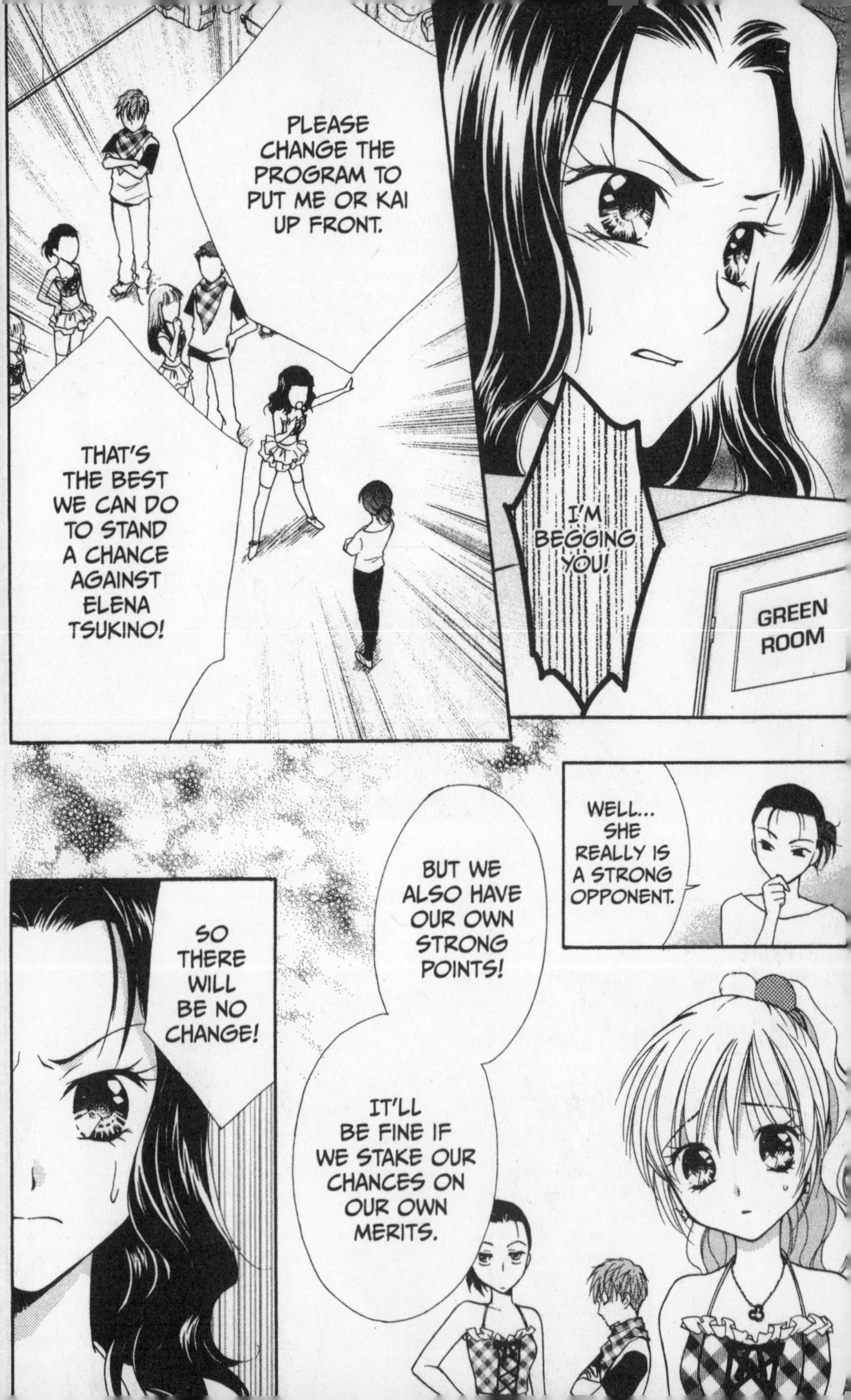
I'M BEGGING YOU!
GREEN ROOM
PLEASE CHANGE THE PROGRAM TO PUT ME OR KAI UP FRONT.
THAT'S THE BEST WE CAN DO TO STAND A CHANCE AGAINST ELENA TSUKINO!
WELL... SHE REALLY IS A STRONG OPPONENT.
BUT WE ALSO HAVE OUR OWN STRONG POINTS!
IT'LL BE FINE IF WE STAKE OUR CHANCES ON OUR OWN MERITS.
SO THERE WILL BE NO CHANGE!

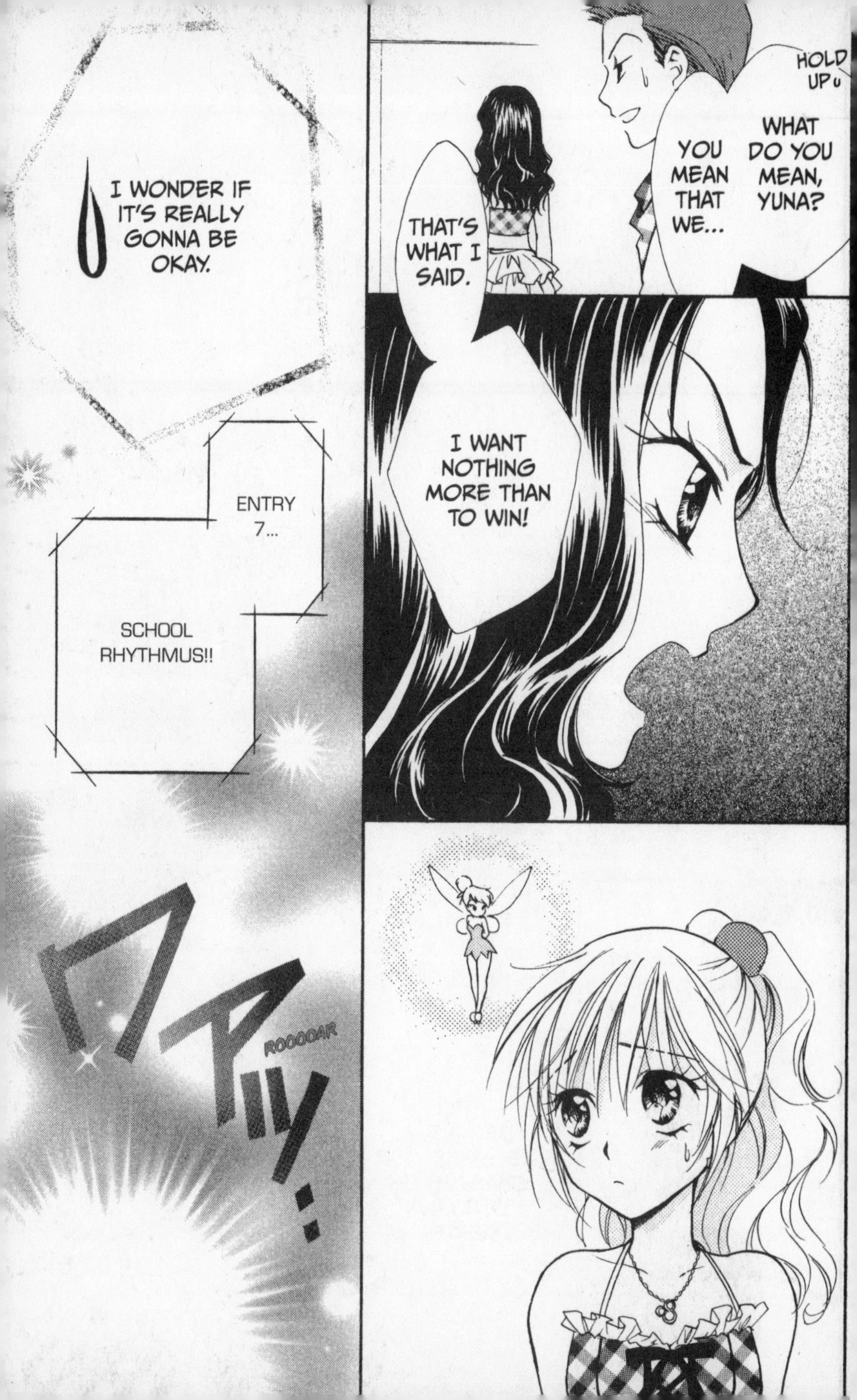
HOLD UP
WHAT DO YOU MEAN, YUNA?
YOU MEAN THAT WE...
THAT'S WHAT I SAID.
I WANT NOTHING MORE THAN TO WIN!
I WONDER IF IT'S REALLY GONNA BE OKAY.
ENTRY 7...
SCHOOL RHYTHMUS!!
ROOOOAR

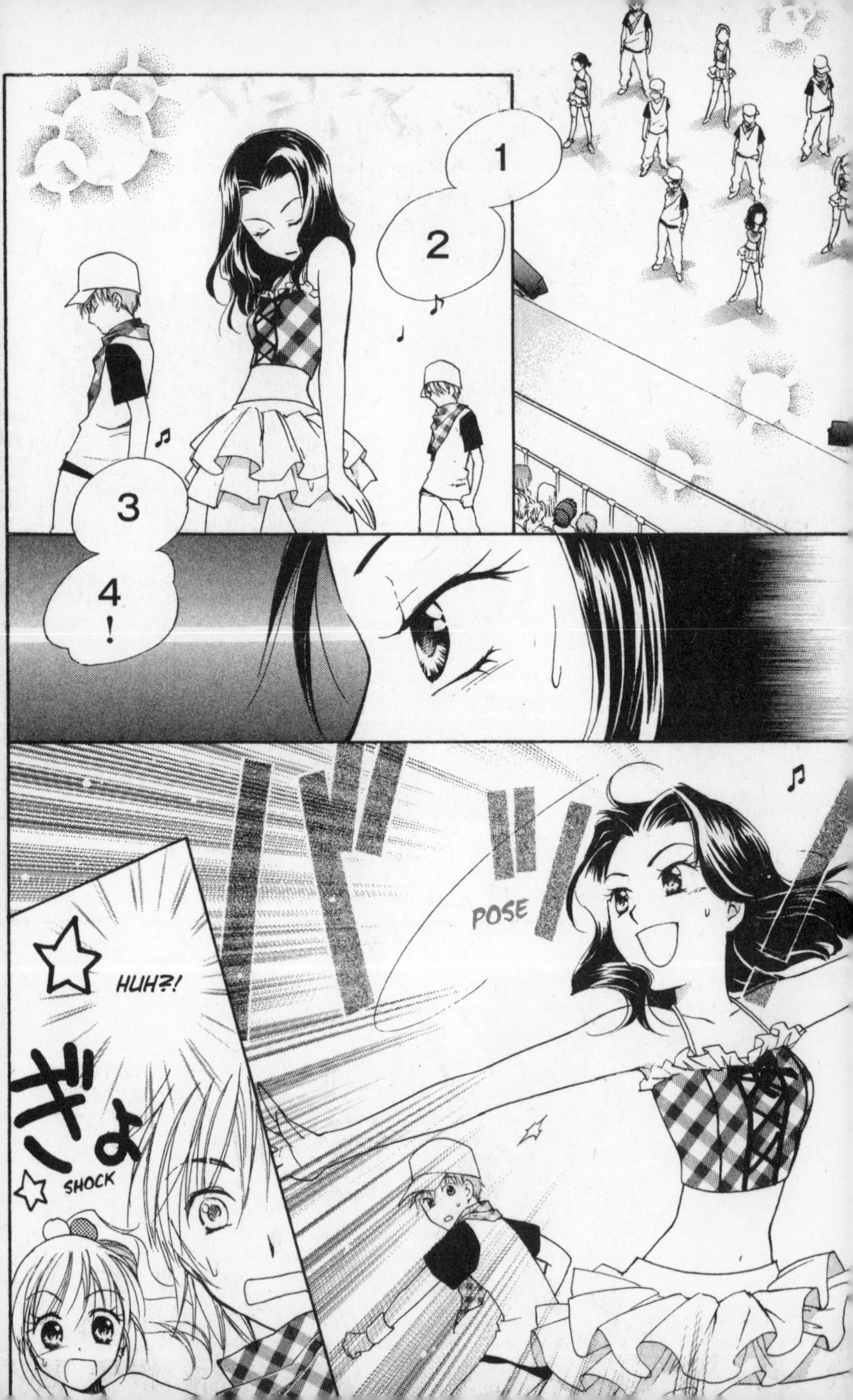
1
2
3
4!
POSE
HUH?!
ぎょ
SHOCK

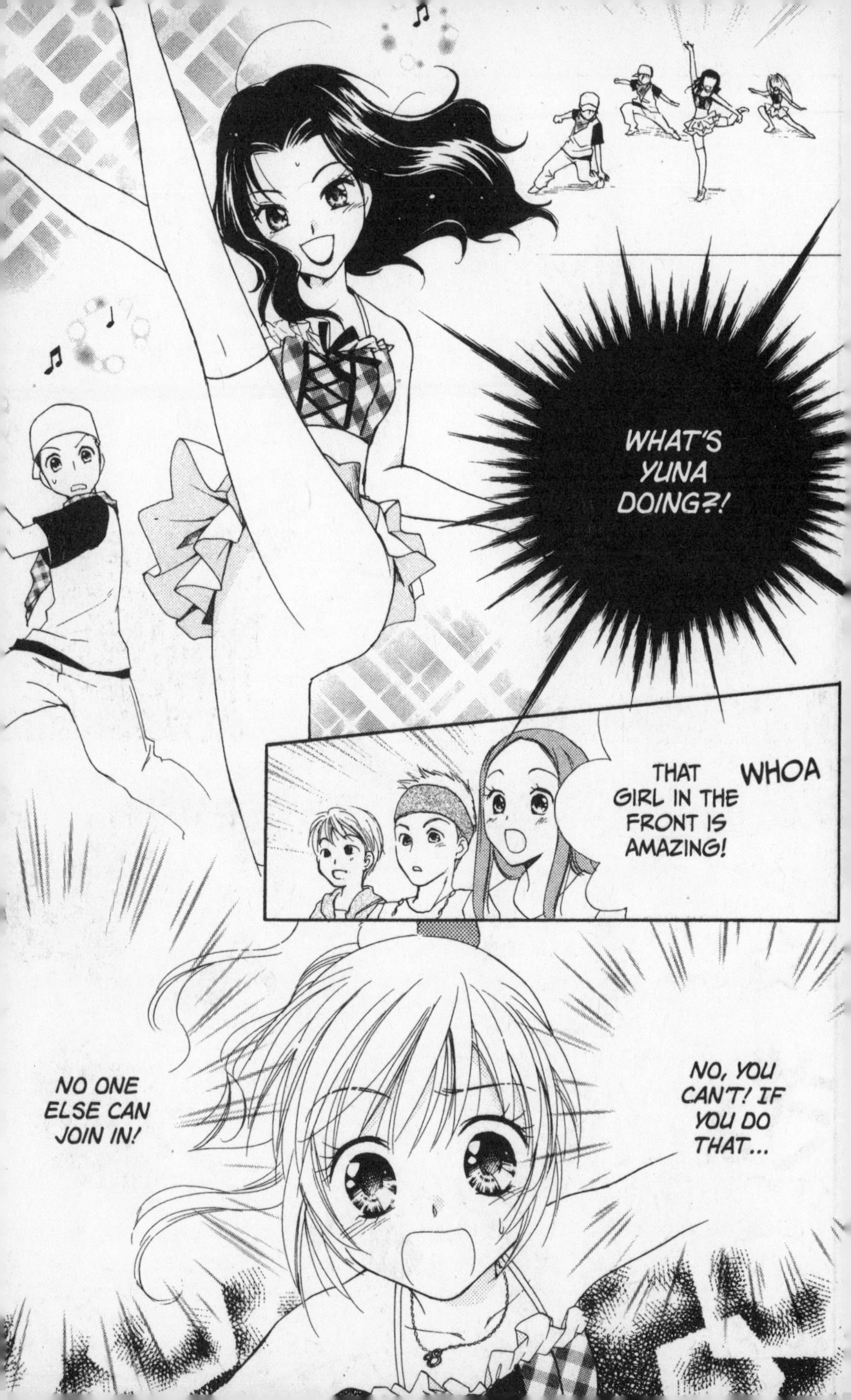
WHAT'S YUNA DOING?!
WHOA
THAT GIRL IN THE FRONT IS AMAZING!
NO, YOU CAN'T! IF YOU DO THAT...
NO ONE ELSE CAN JOIN IN!

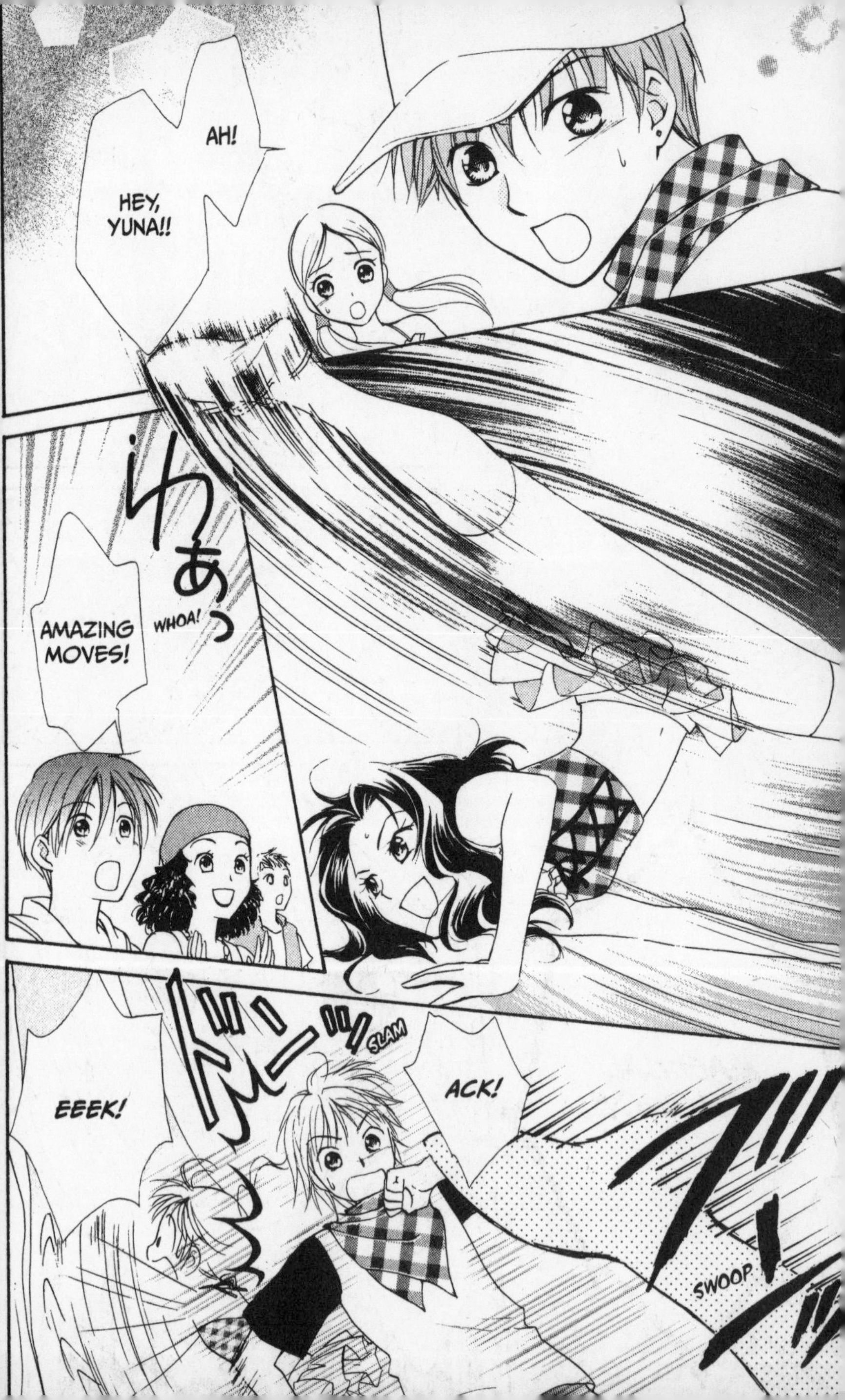
AH!
HEY, YUNA!!
WHOA!
AMAZING MOVES!
ACK!
SLAM
EEEK!
SWOOP

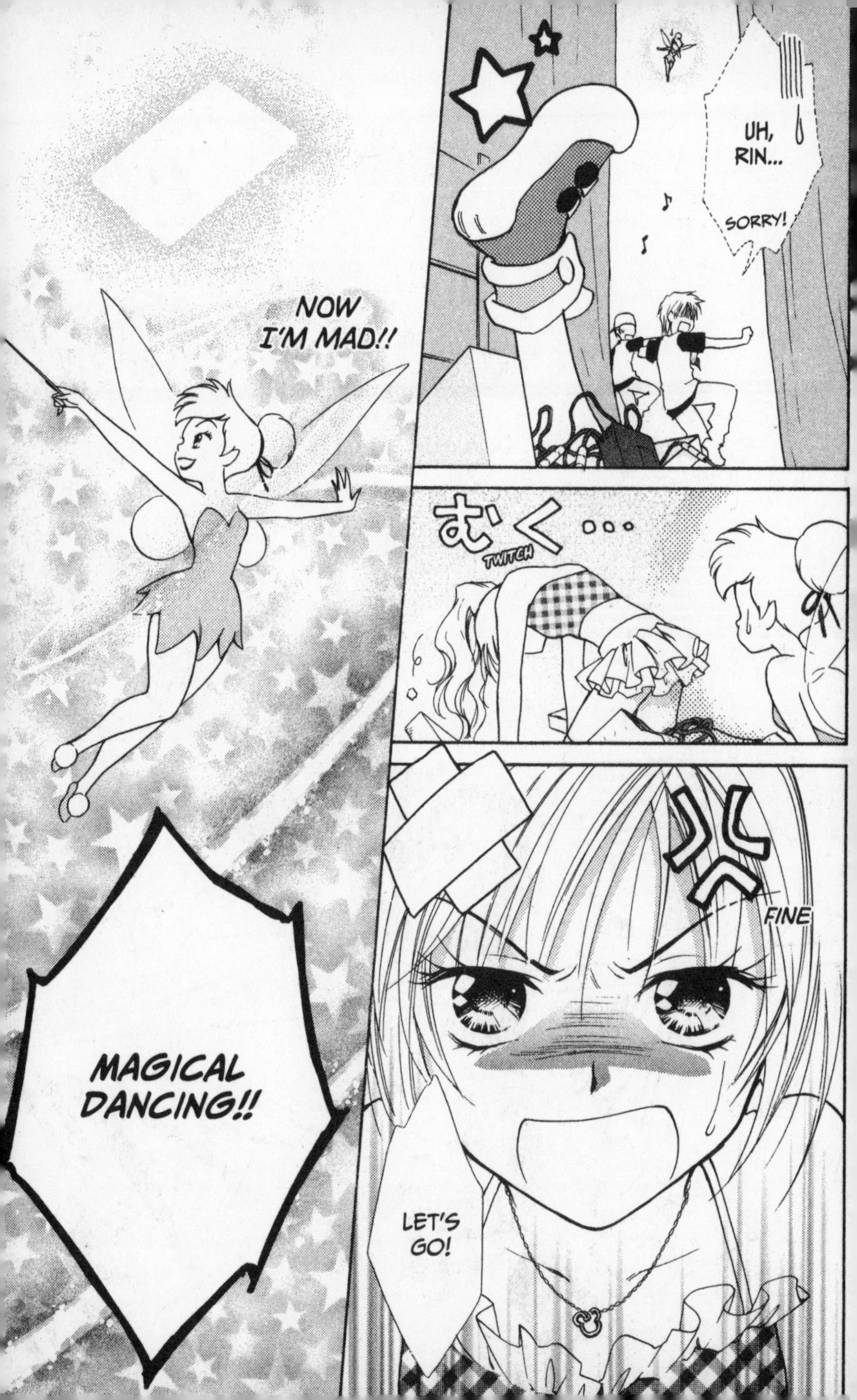
UH, RIN...
SORRY!
むく…
TWITCH
FINE
LET'S GO!
NOW I'M MAD!!
MAGICAL DANCING!!

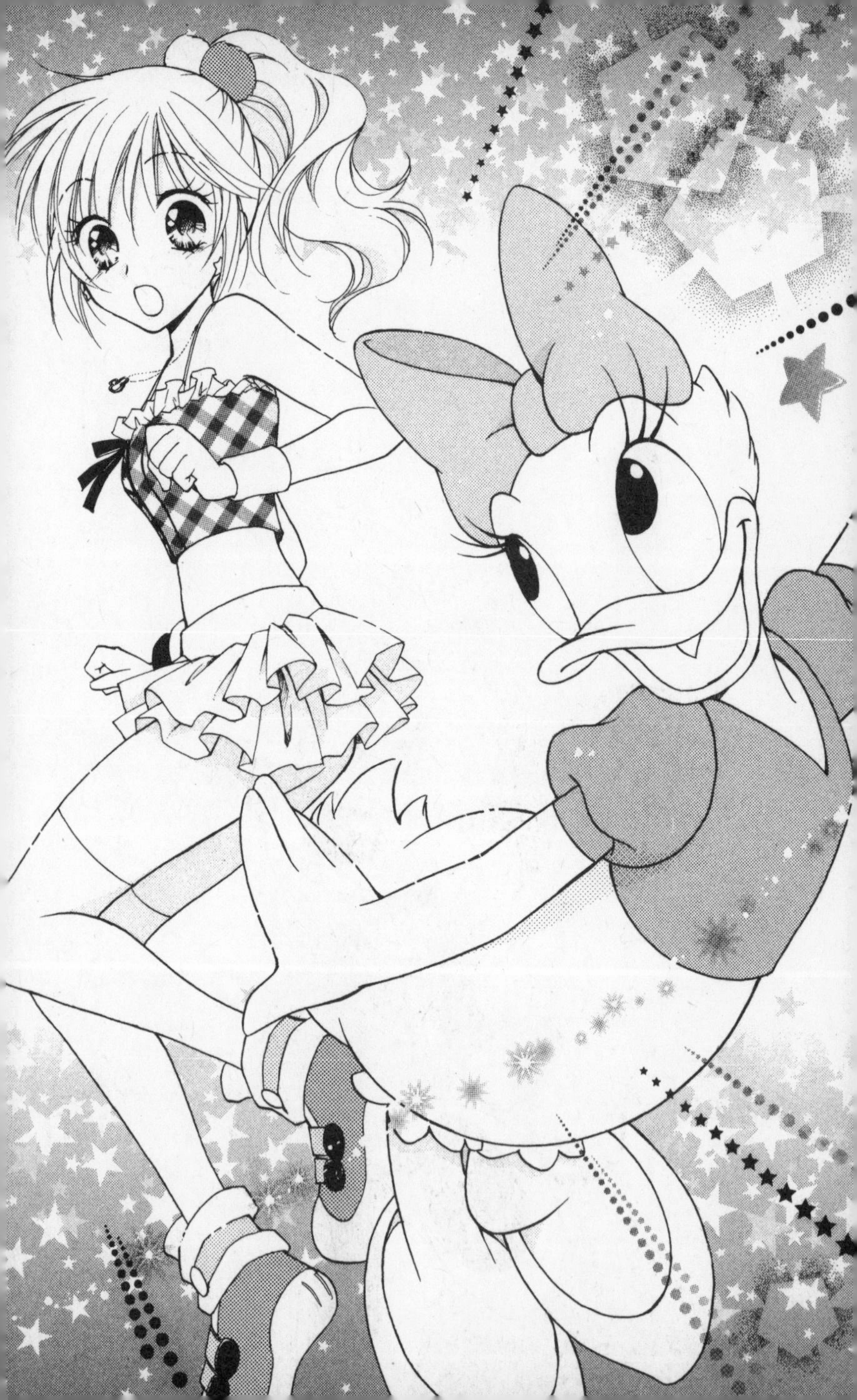

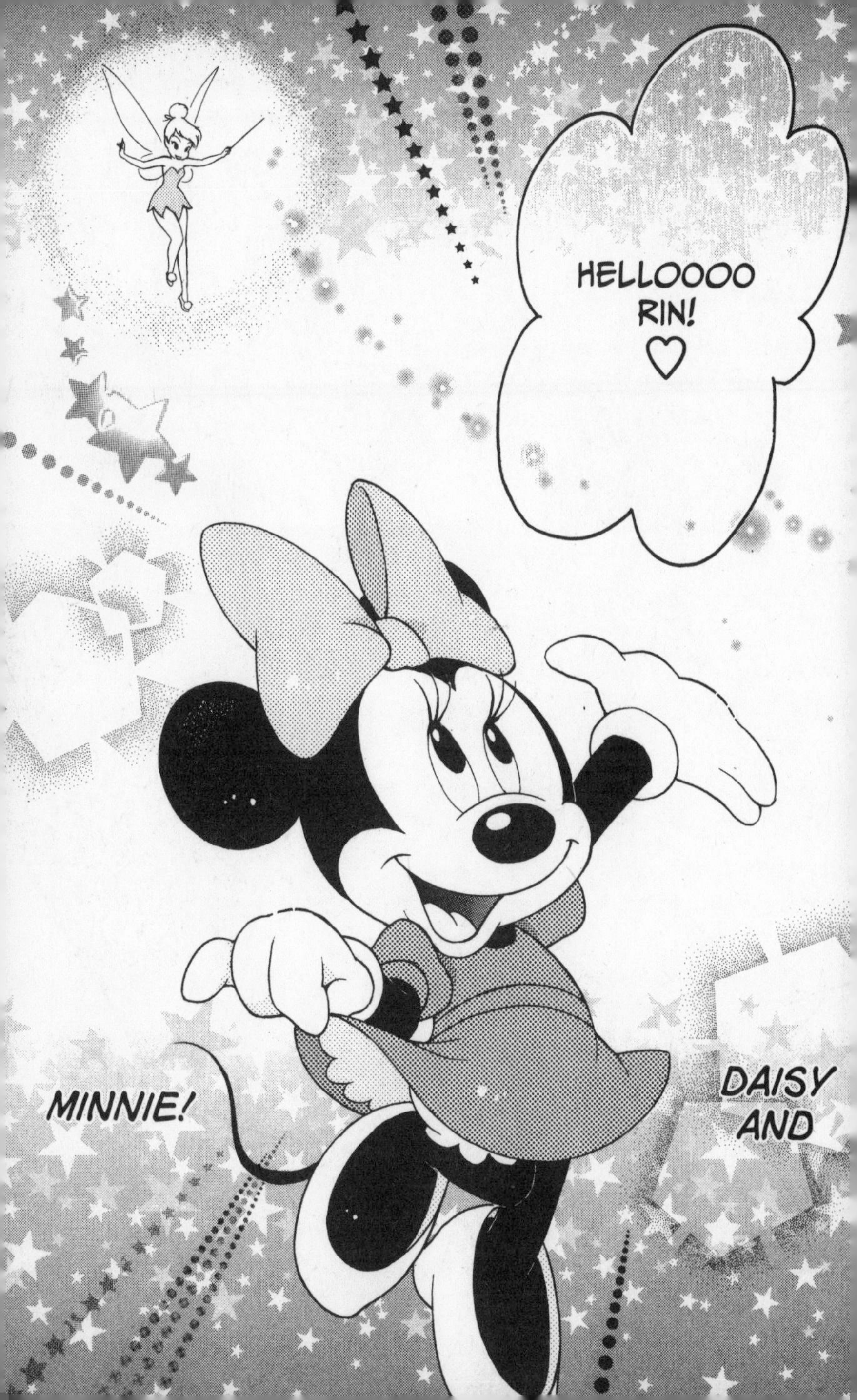
HELLOOOO RIN! ♡
DAISY AND
MINNIE!

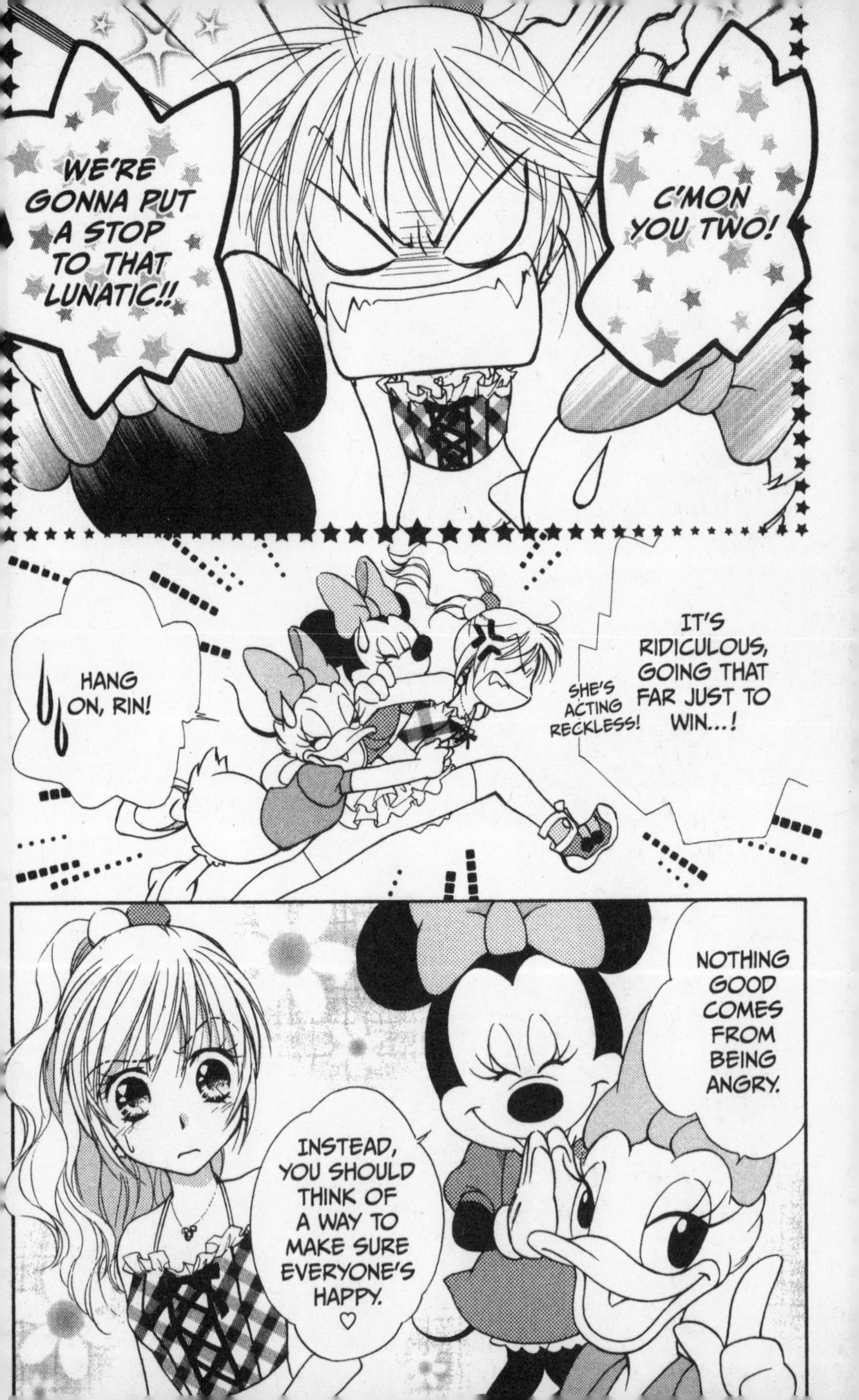
C'MON YOU TWO!
WE'RE GONNA PUT A STOP TO THAT LUNATIC!!
IT'S RIDICULOUS, GOING THAT FAR JUST TO WIN...!
SHE'S ACTING RECKLESS!
HANG ON, RIN!
NOTHING GOOD COMES FROM BEING ANGRY.
INSTEAD, YOU SHOULD THINK OF A WAY TO MAKE SURE EVERYONE'S HAPPY. ♡

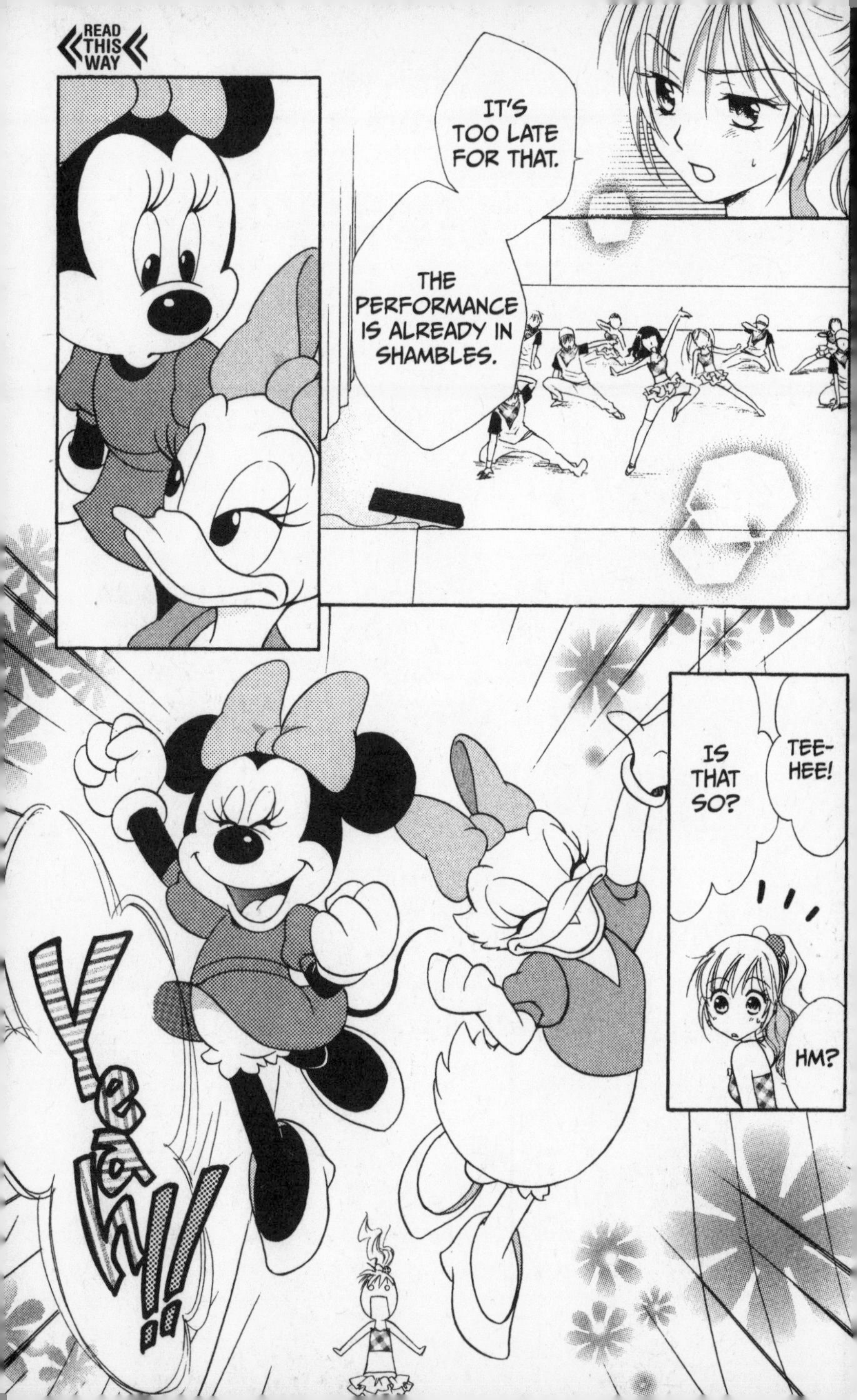
READ THIS WAY
IT'S TOO LATE FOR THAT.
THE PERFORMANCE IS ALREADY IN SHAMBLES.
TEE-HEE!
IS THAT SO?
HM?
Yeah!!

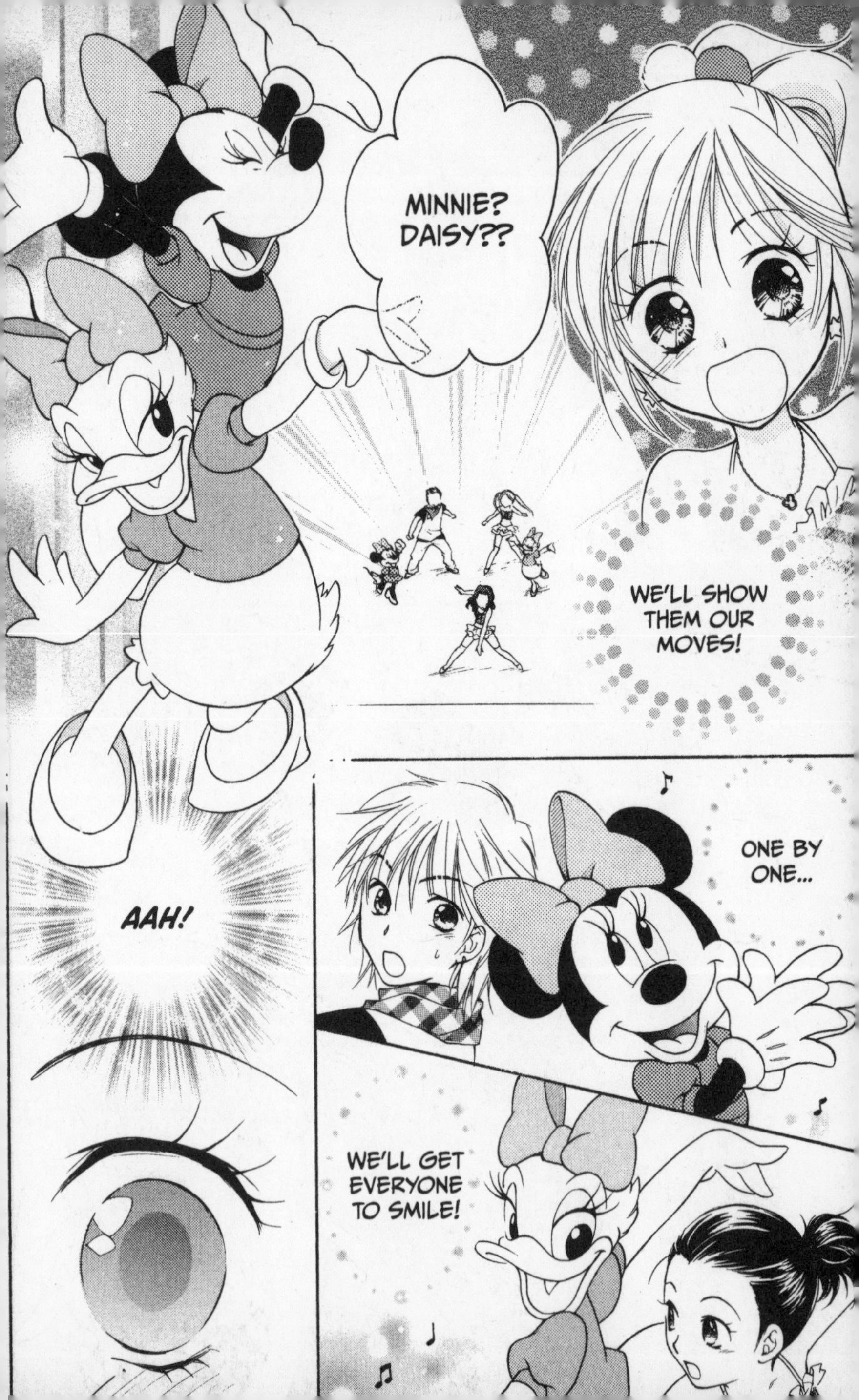
MINNIE? DAISY??
WE'LL SHOW THEM OUR MOVES!
ONE BY ONE...
WE'LL GET EVERYONE TO SMILE!
AAH!

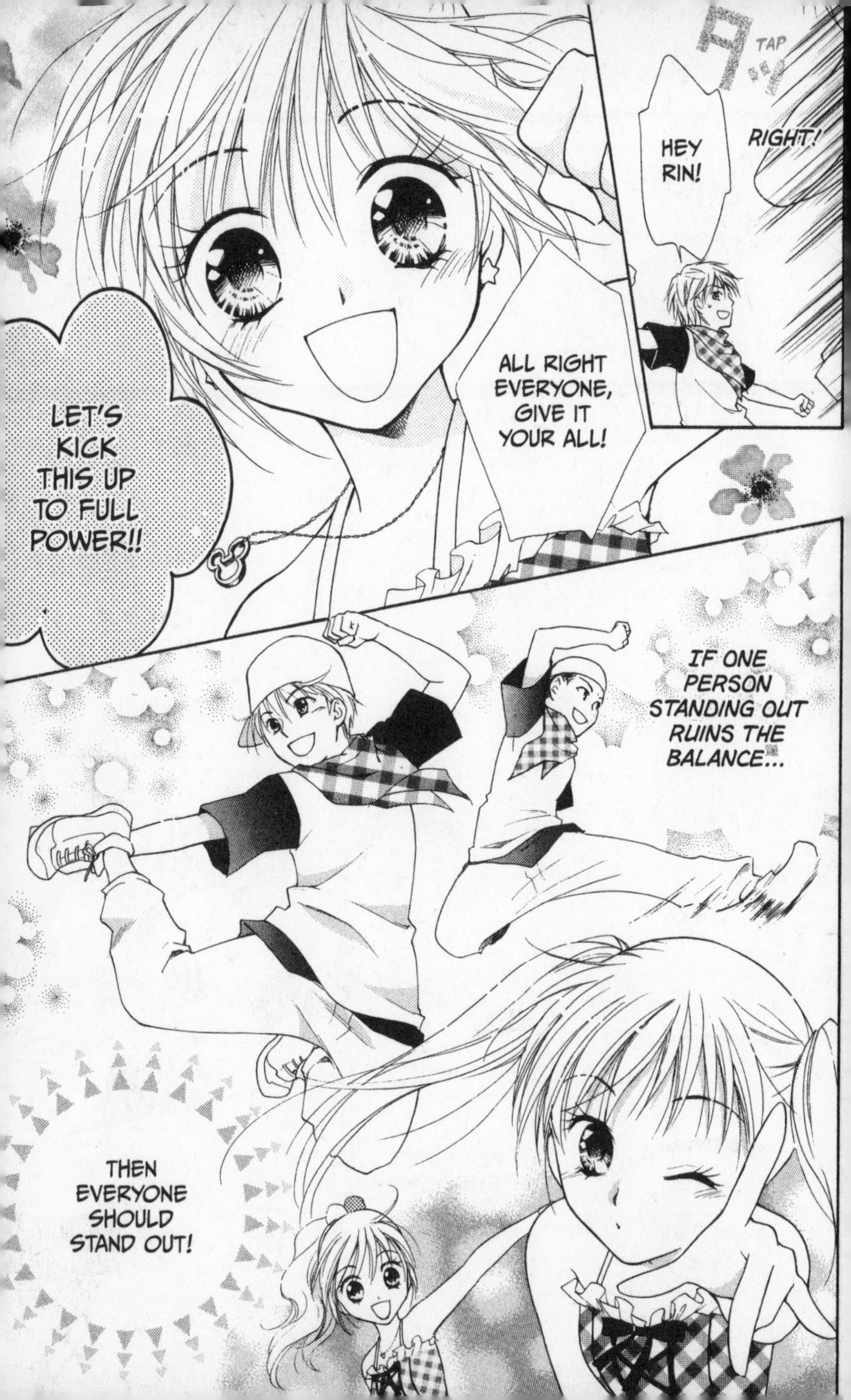
TAP
RIGHT!
HEY RIN!
ALL RIGHT EVERYONE, GIVE IT YOUR ALL!
LET'S KICK THIS UP TO FULL POWER!!
IF ONE PERSON STANDING OUT RUINS THE BALANCE...
THEN EVERYONE SHOULD STAND OUT!

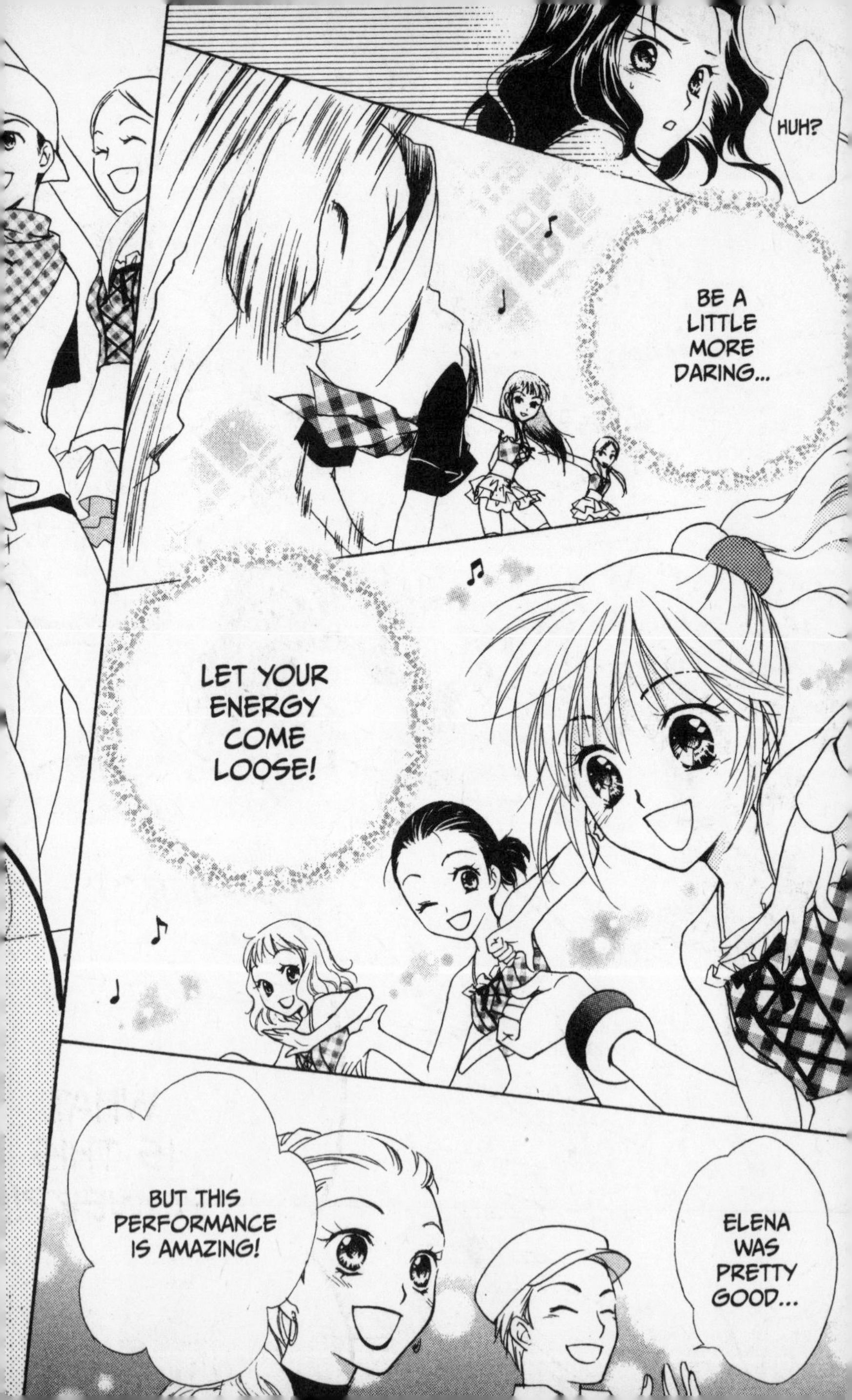
HUH?
BE A LITTLE MORE DARING...
LET YOUR ENERGY COME LOOSE!
ELENA WAS PRETTY GOOD...
BUT THIS PERFORMANCE IS AMAZING!

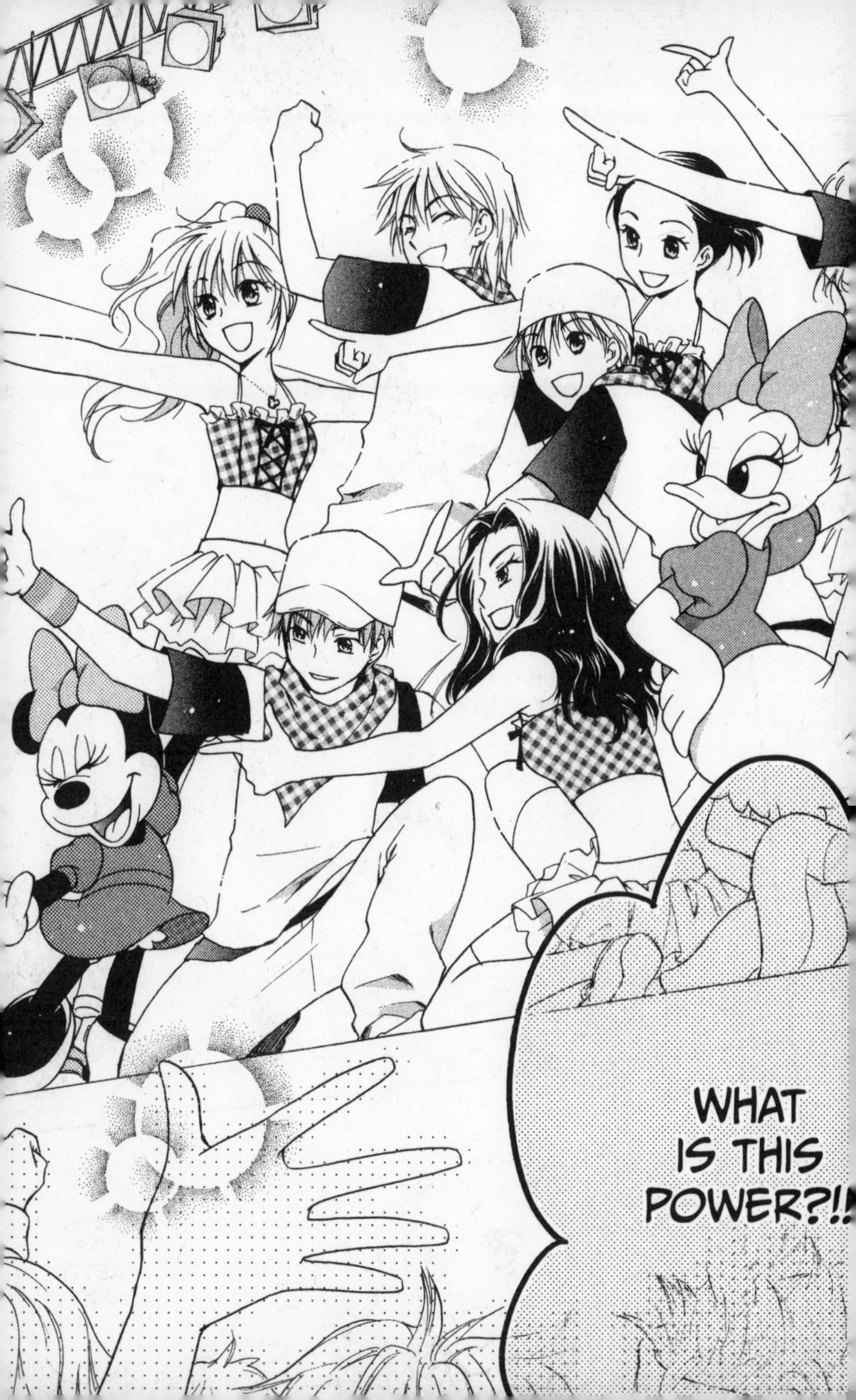
WHAT IS THIS POWER?!!

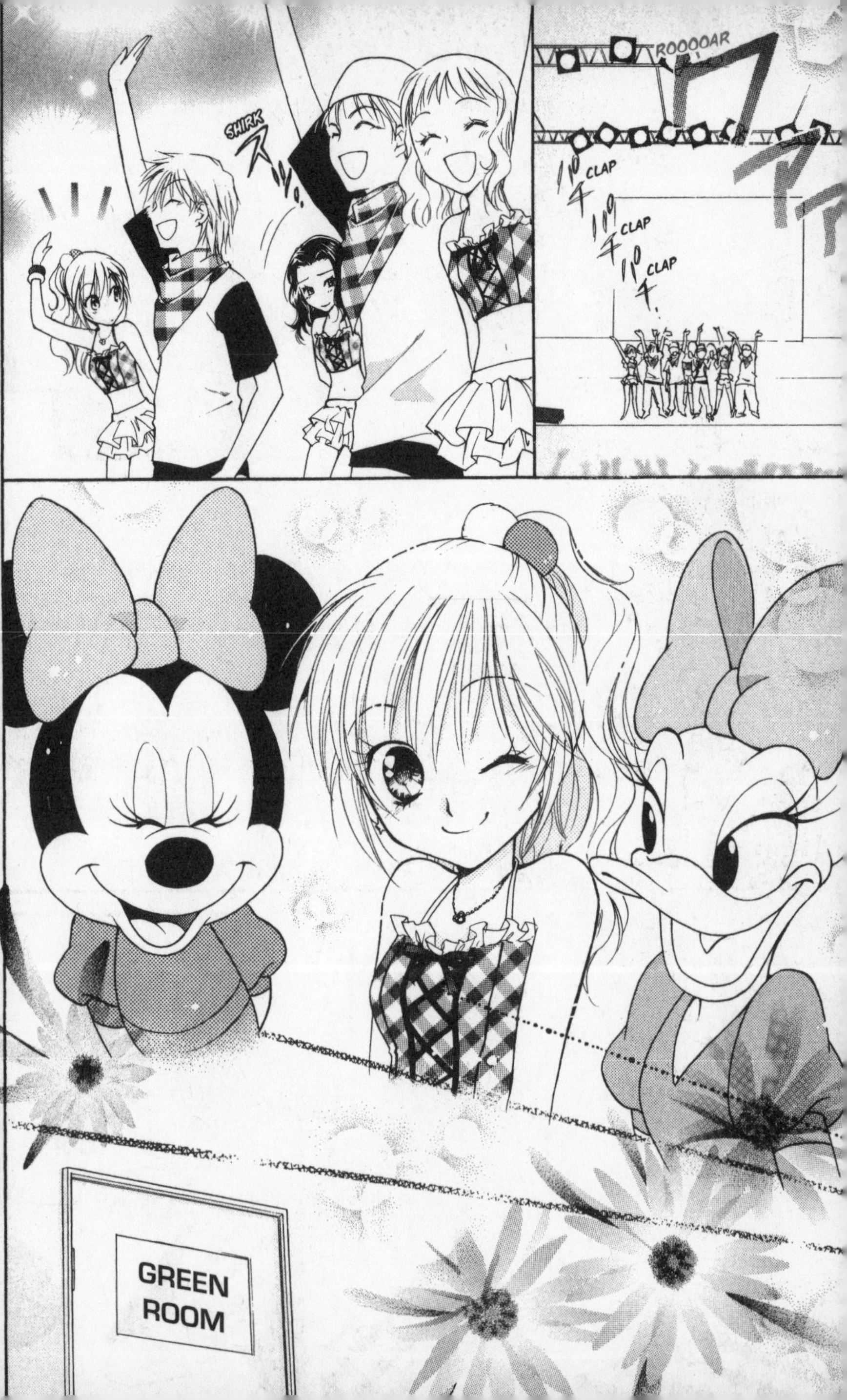
ROOOOAR
CLAP
CLAP
CLAP
SHIRK
GREEN ROOM

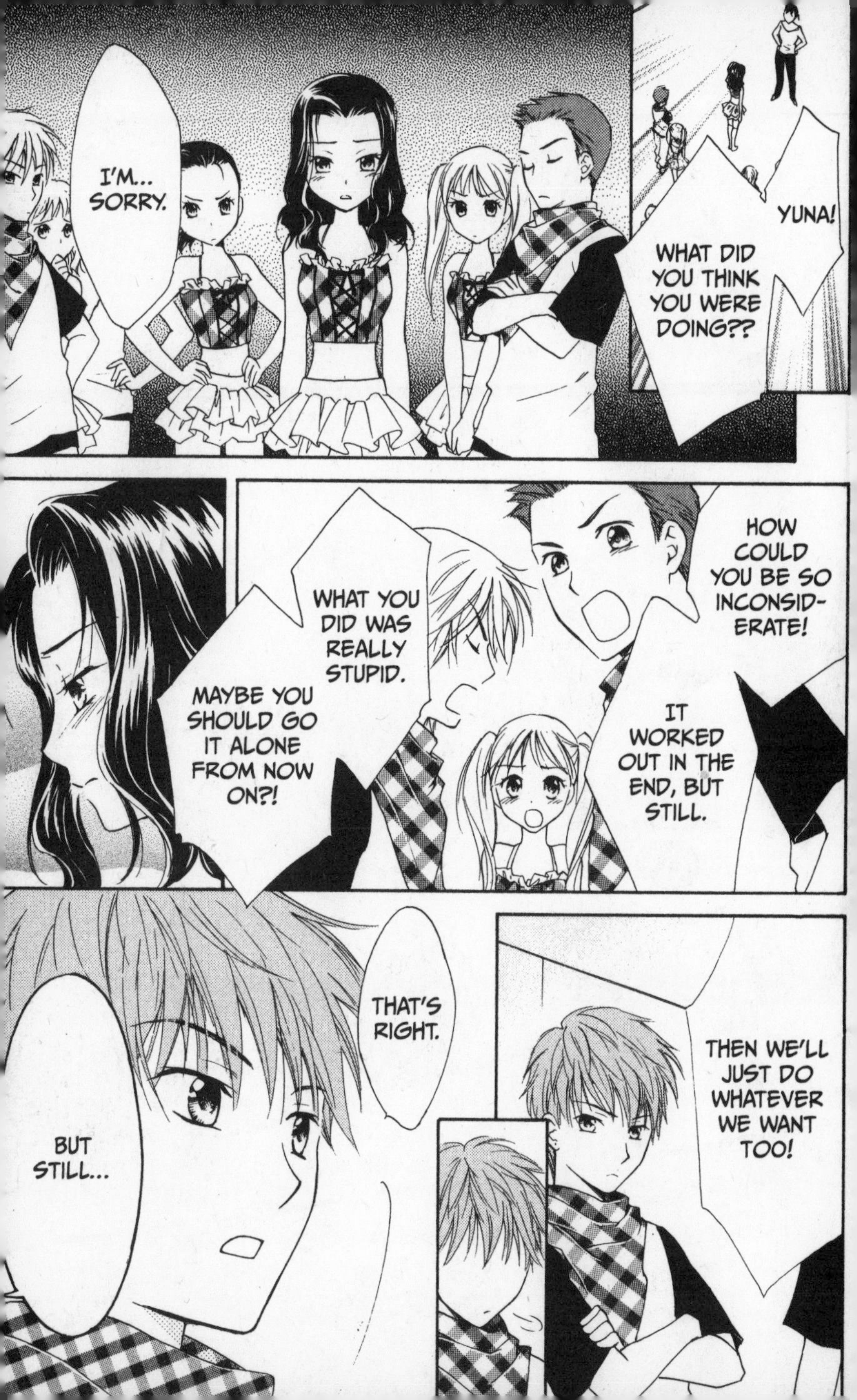
YUNA!
WHAT DID YOU THINK YOU WERE DOING??
I'M... SORRY.
HOW COULD YOU BE SO INCONSID-ERATE!
IT WORKED OUT IN THE END, BUT STILL.
WHAT YOU DID WAS REALLY STUPID.
MAYBE YOU SHOULD GO IT ALONE FROM NOW ON?!
THEN WE'LL JUST DO WHATEVER WE WANT TOO!
THAT'S RIGHT.
BUT STILL...

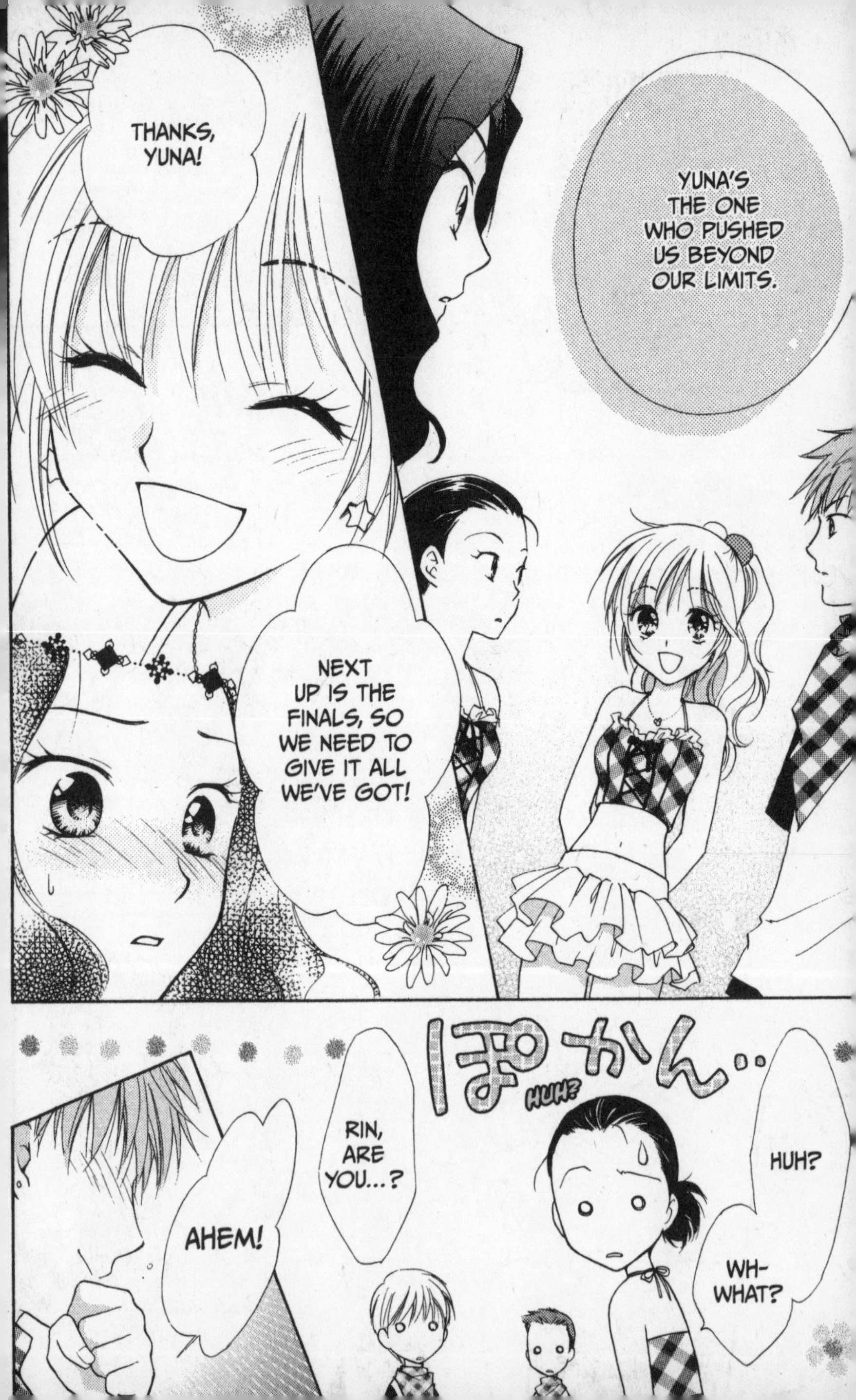
YUNA'S THE ONE WHO PUSHED US BEYOND OUR LIMITS.
THANKS, YUNA!
NEXT UP IS THE FINALS, SO WE NEED TO GIVE IT ALL WE'VE GOT!
ぽかん..
HUH?
HUH?
WH- WHAT?
RIN, ARE YOU...?
AHEM!

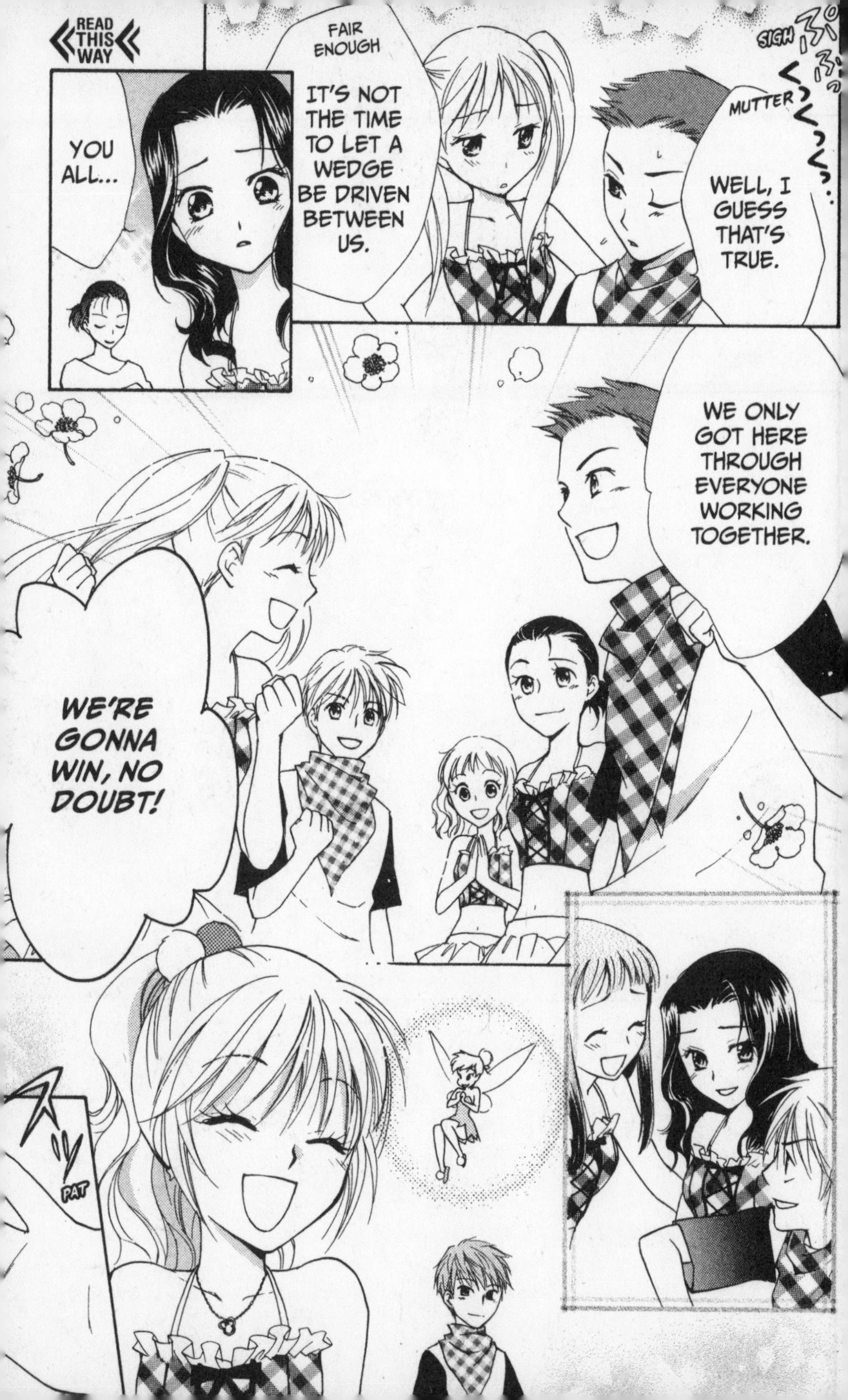
READ THIS WAY
SIGH
MUTTER
WELL, I GUESS THAT'S TRUE.
FAIR ENOUGH
IT'S NOT THE TIME TO LET A WEDGE BE DRIVEN BETWEEN US.
YOU ALL...
WE ONLY GOT HERE THROUGH EVERYONE WORKING TOGETHER.
WE'RE GONNA WIN, NO DOUBT!
PAT

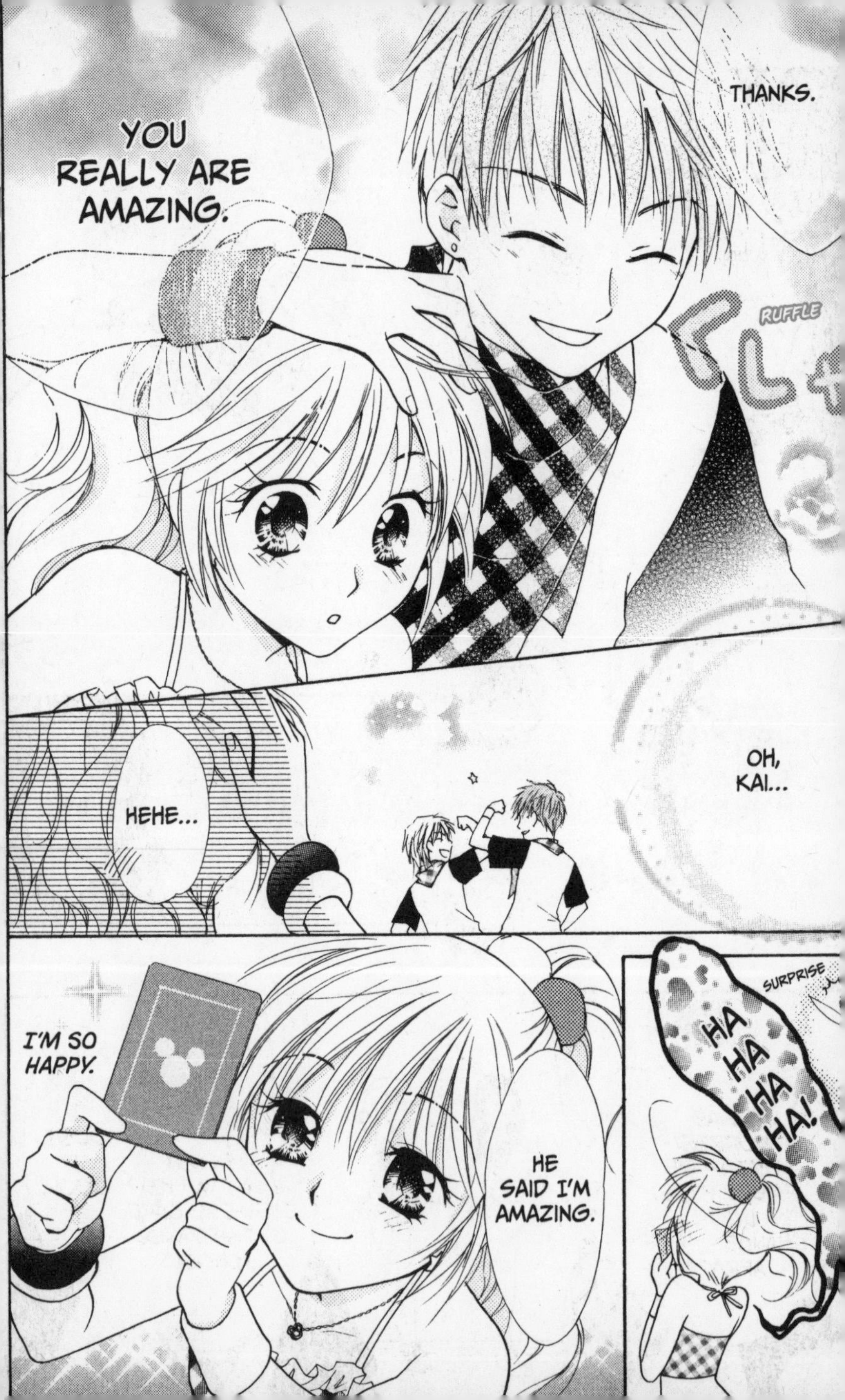
THANKS.
RUFFLE
YOU REALLY ARE AMAZING.
OH, KAI...
HEHE...
SURPRISE
HA HA HA HA HA!
HE SAID I'M AMAZING.
I'M SO HAPPY.

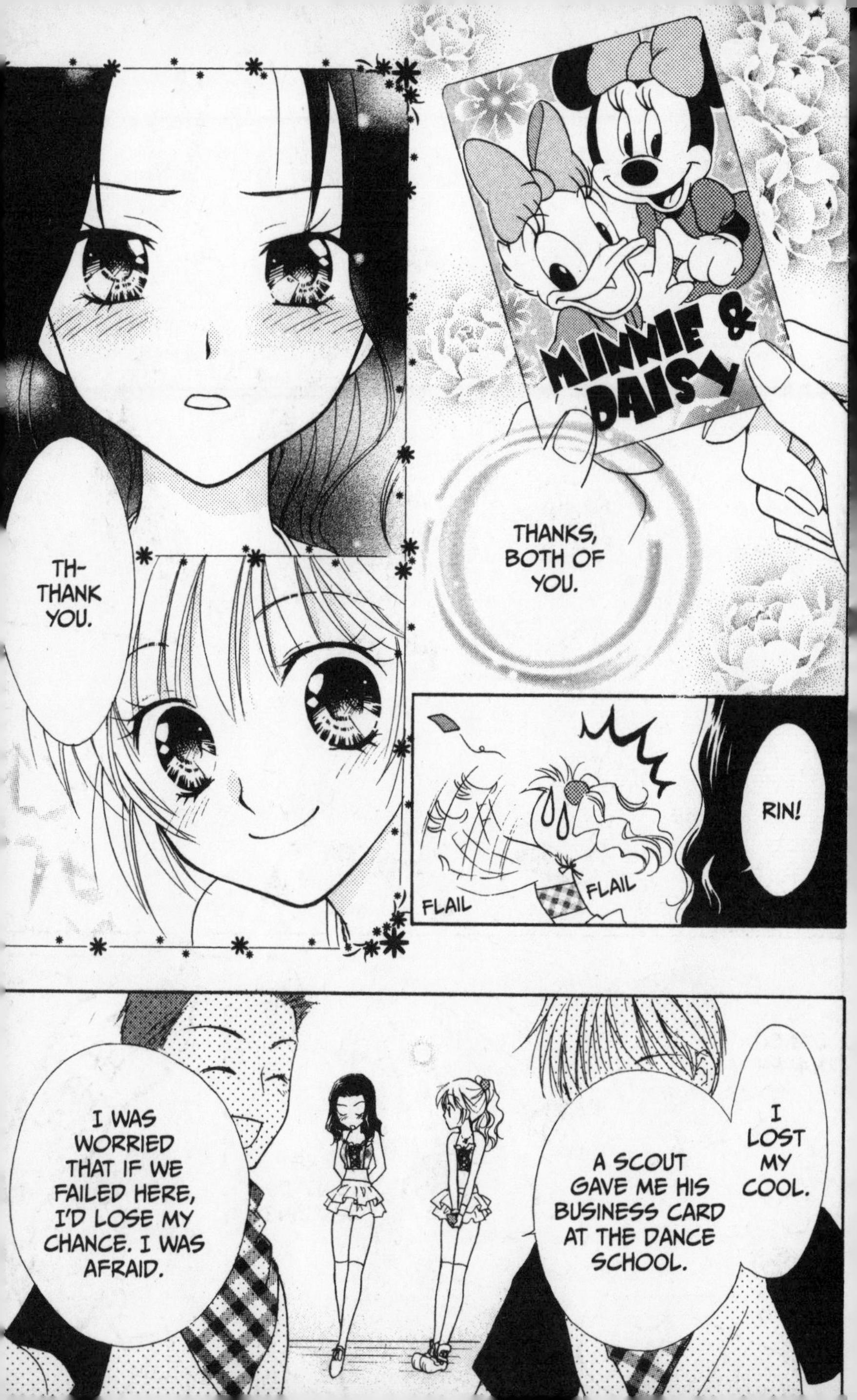

MINNIE & DAISY
THANKS, BOTH OF YOU.
RIN!
FLAIL
FLAIL
TH-THANK YOU.
I LOST MY COOL.
A SCOUT GAVE ME HIS BUSINESS CARD AT THE DANCE SCHOOL.
I WAS WORRIED THAT IF WE FAILED HERE, I'D LOSE MY CHANCE. I WAS AFRAID.

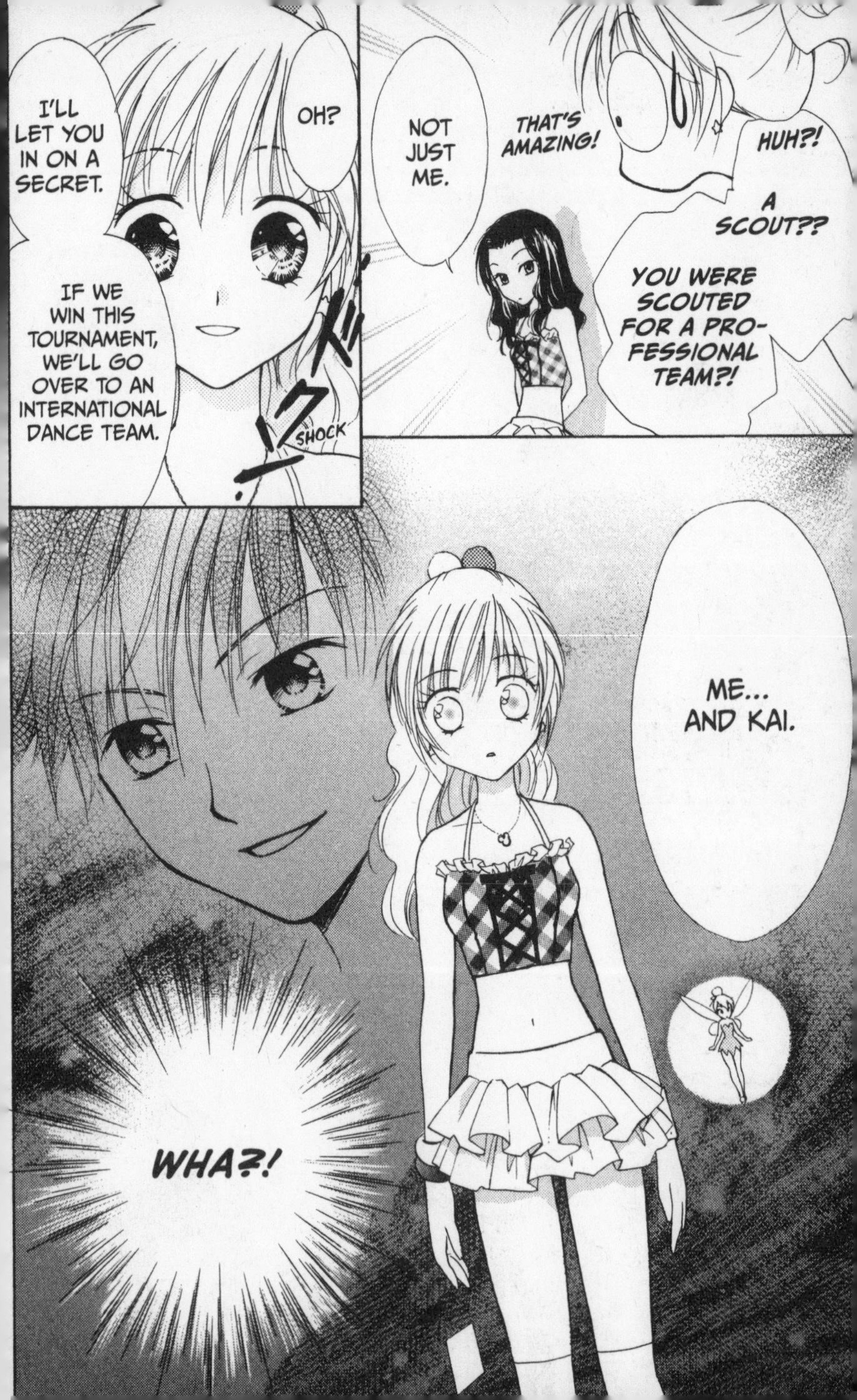
HUH?!
A SCOUT??
YOU WERE SCOUTED FOR A PRO-FESSIONAL TEAM?!
THAT'S AMAZING!
NOT JUST ME.
OH?
I'LL LET YOU IN ON A SECRET.
IF WE WIN THIS TOURNAMENT, WE'LL GO OVER TO AN INTERNATIONAL DANCE TEAM.
SHOCK
ME... AND KAI.
WHA?!

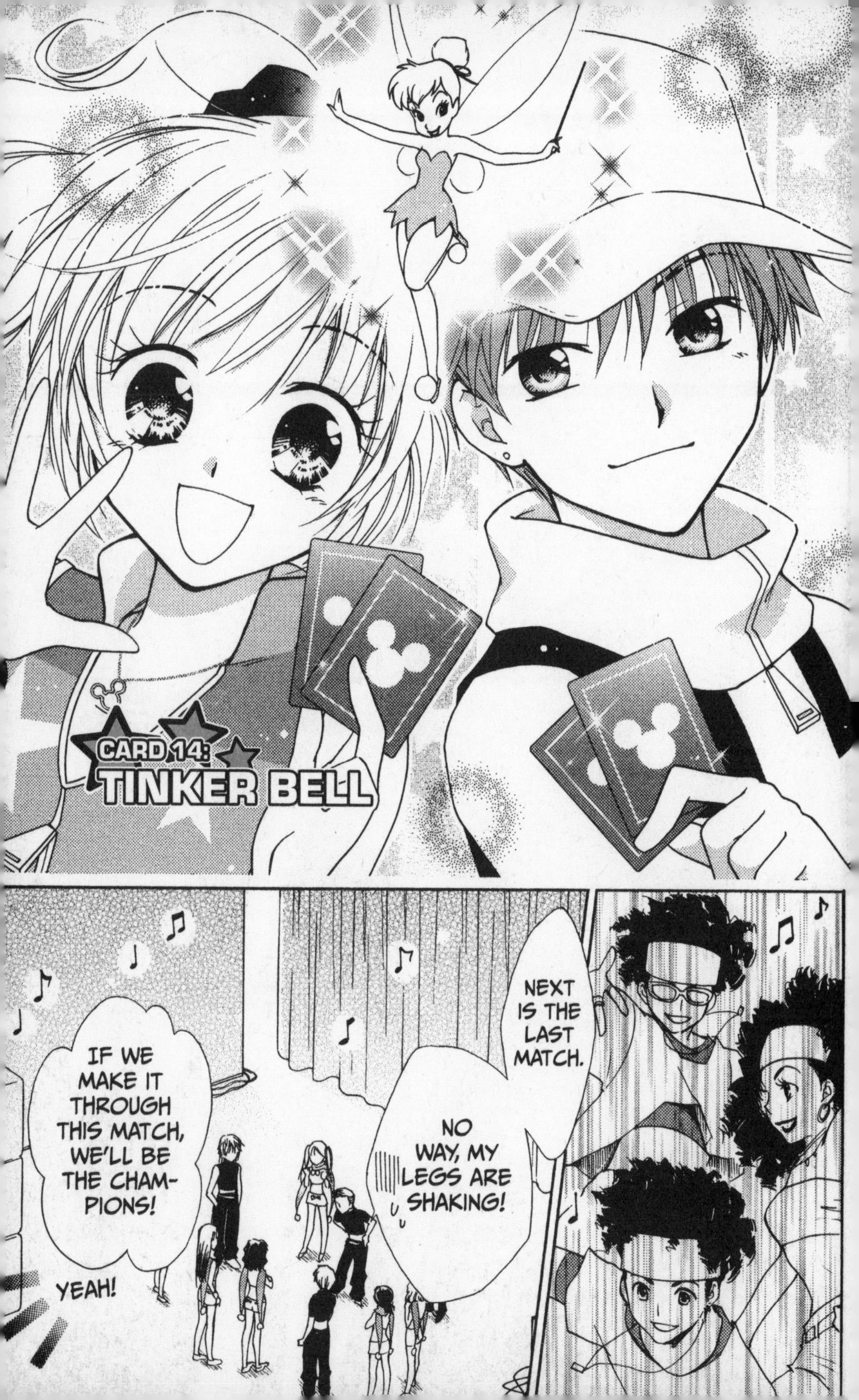
CARD 14:
TINKER BELL
NEXT IS THE LAST MATCH.
NO WAY, MY LEGS ARE SHAKING!
IF WE MAKE IT THROUGH THIS MATCH, WE'LL BE THE CHAMPIONS!
YEAH!

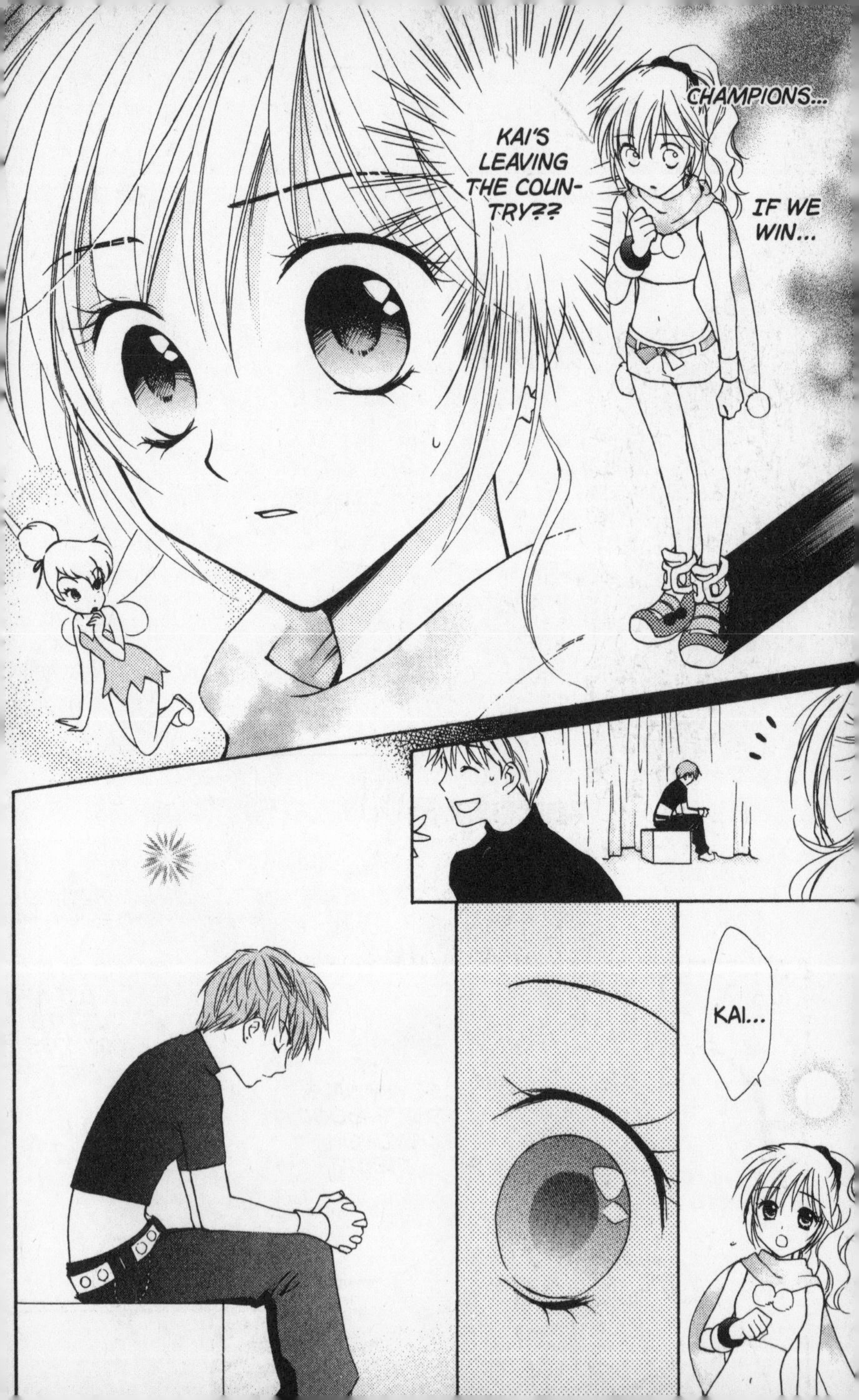
CHAMPIONS...
IF WE WIN...
KAI'S LEAVING THE COUN-TRY??
KAI...

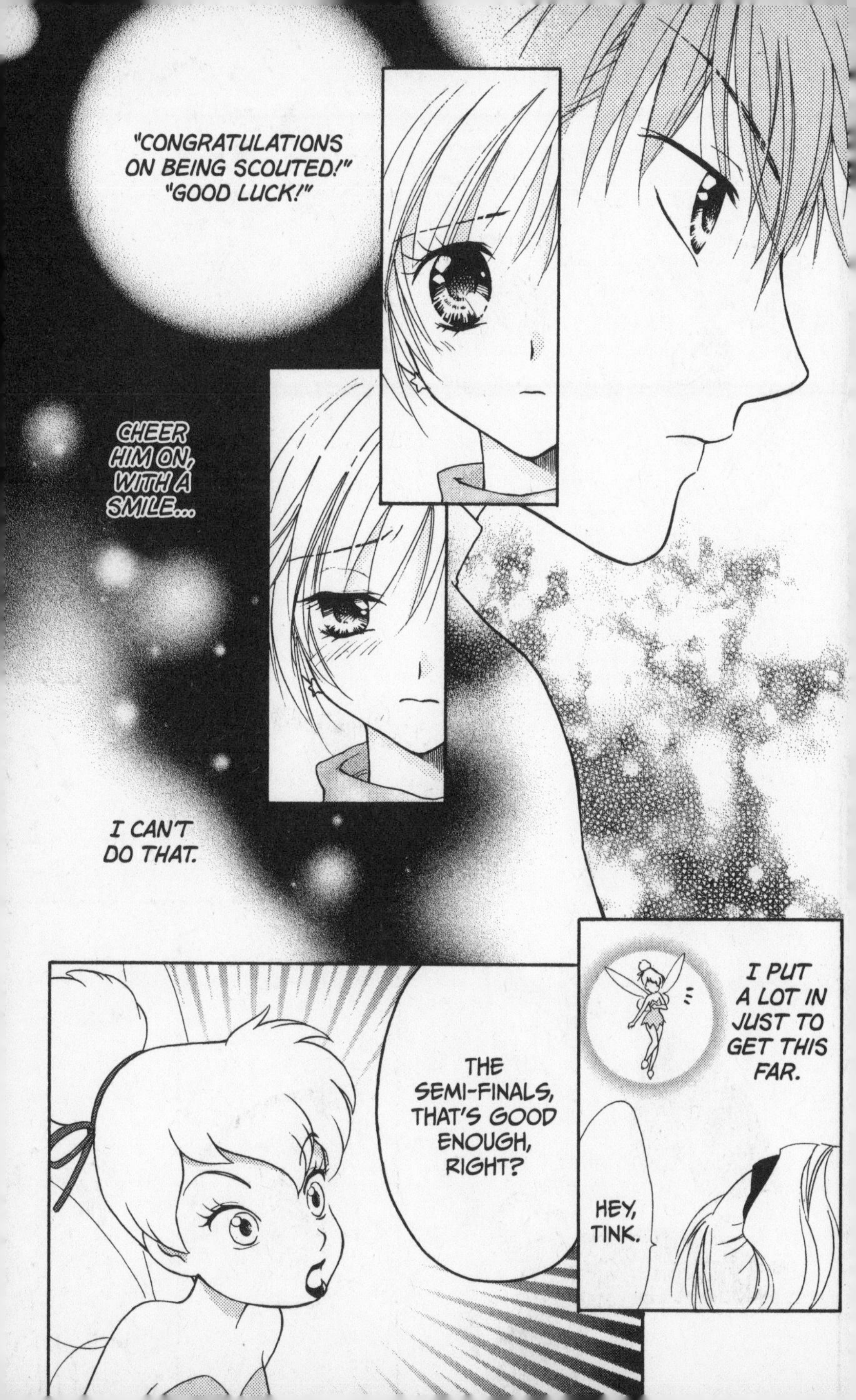
"CONGRATULATIONS ON BEING SCOUTED!"
"GOOD LUCK!"
CHEER HIM ON, WITH A SMILE...
I CAN'T DO THAT.
I PUT A LOT IN JUST TO GET THIS FAR.
HEY, TINK.
THE SEMI-FINALS, THAT'S GOOD ENOUGH, RIGHT?

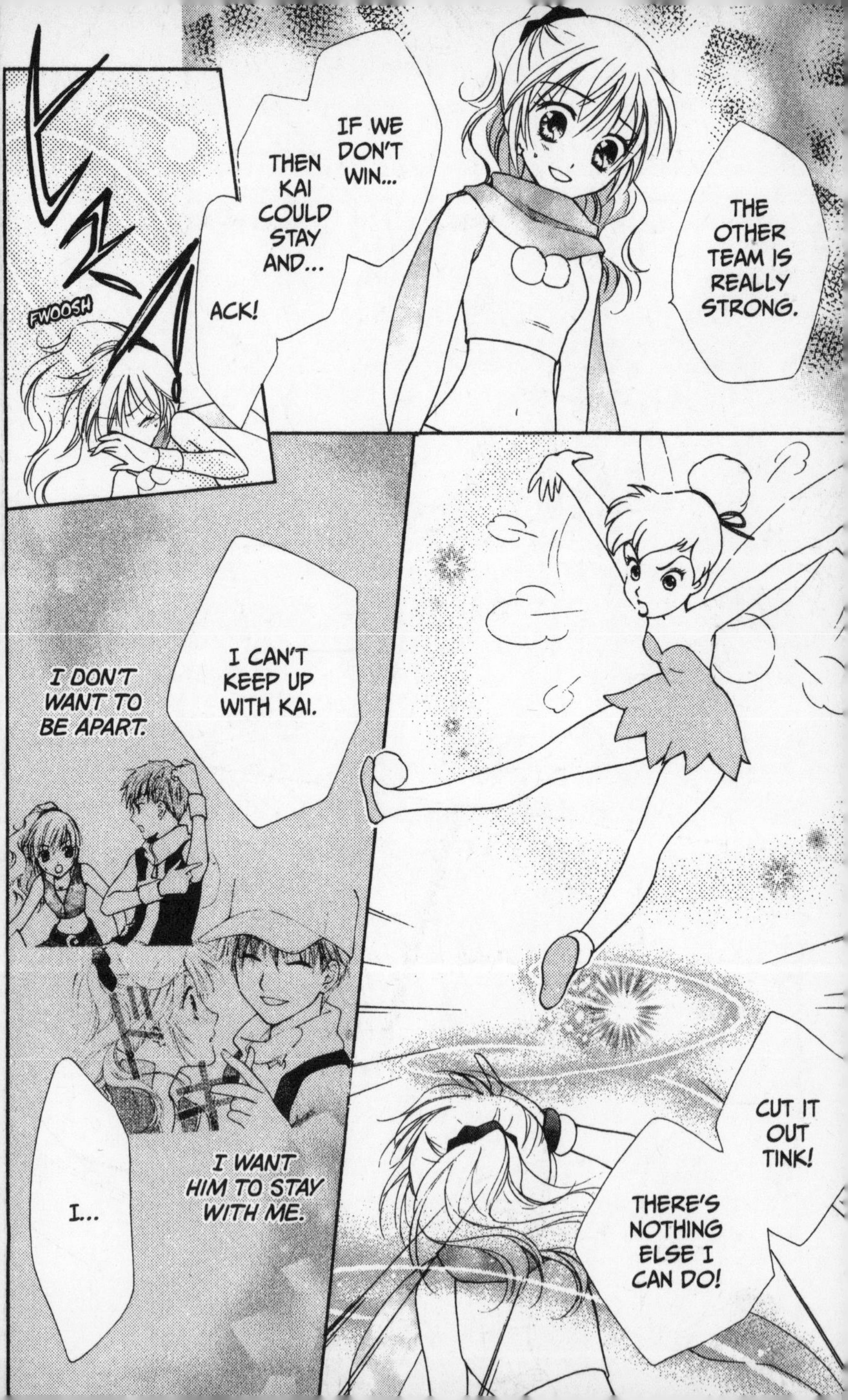
THE OTHER TEAM IS REALLY STRONG.
IF WE DON'T WIN...
THEN KAI COULD STAY AND...
ACK!
FWOOSH
CUT IT OUT TINK!
THERE'S NOTHING ELSE I CAN DO!
I CAN'T KEEP UP WITH KAI.
I DON'T WANT TO BE APART.
I WANT HIM TO STAY WITH ME.
I...

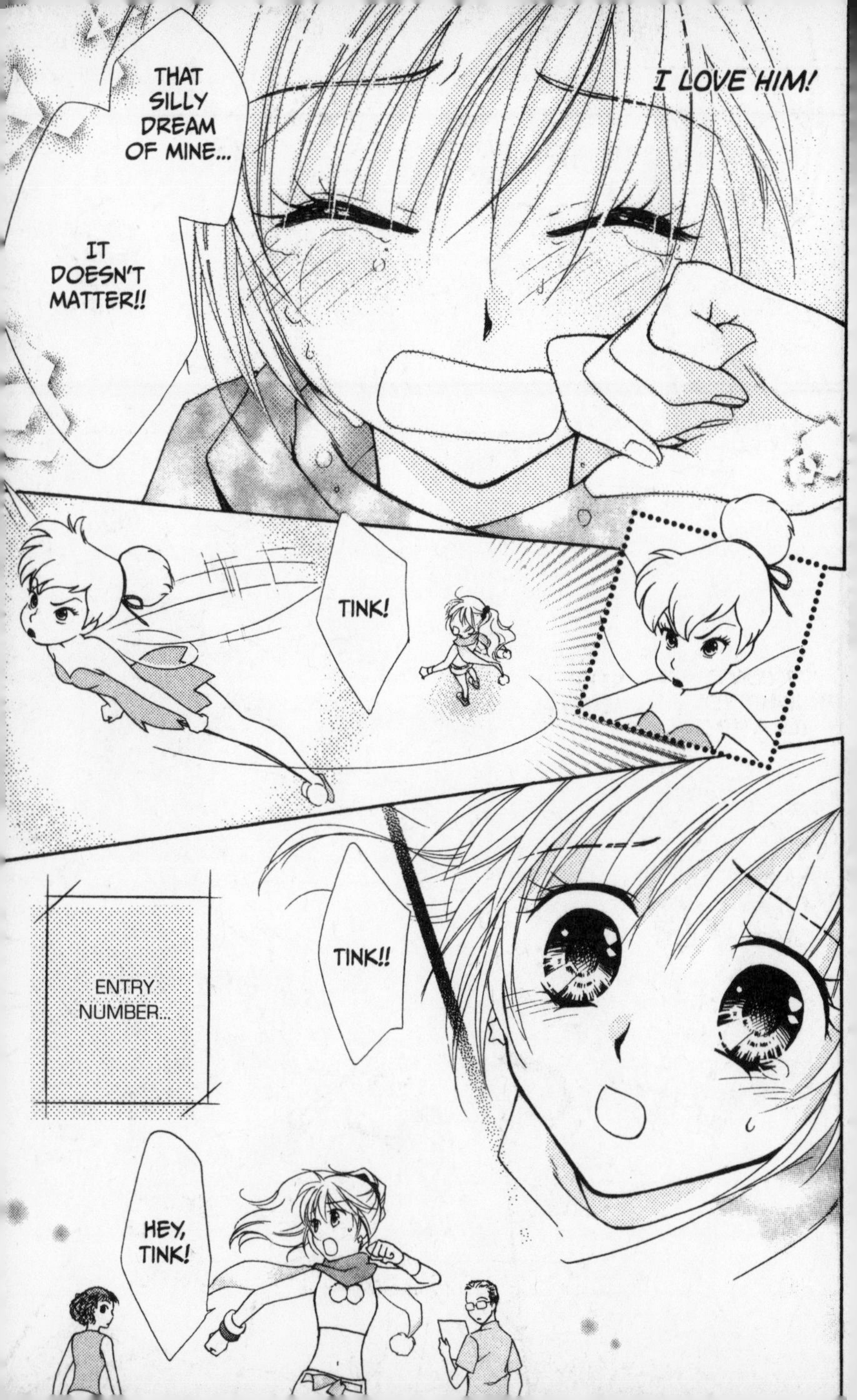
I LOVE HIM!
THAT SILLY DREAM OF MINE...
IT DOESN'T MATTER!!
TINK!
TINK!!
ENTRY NUMBER...
HEY, TINK!

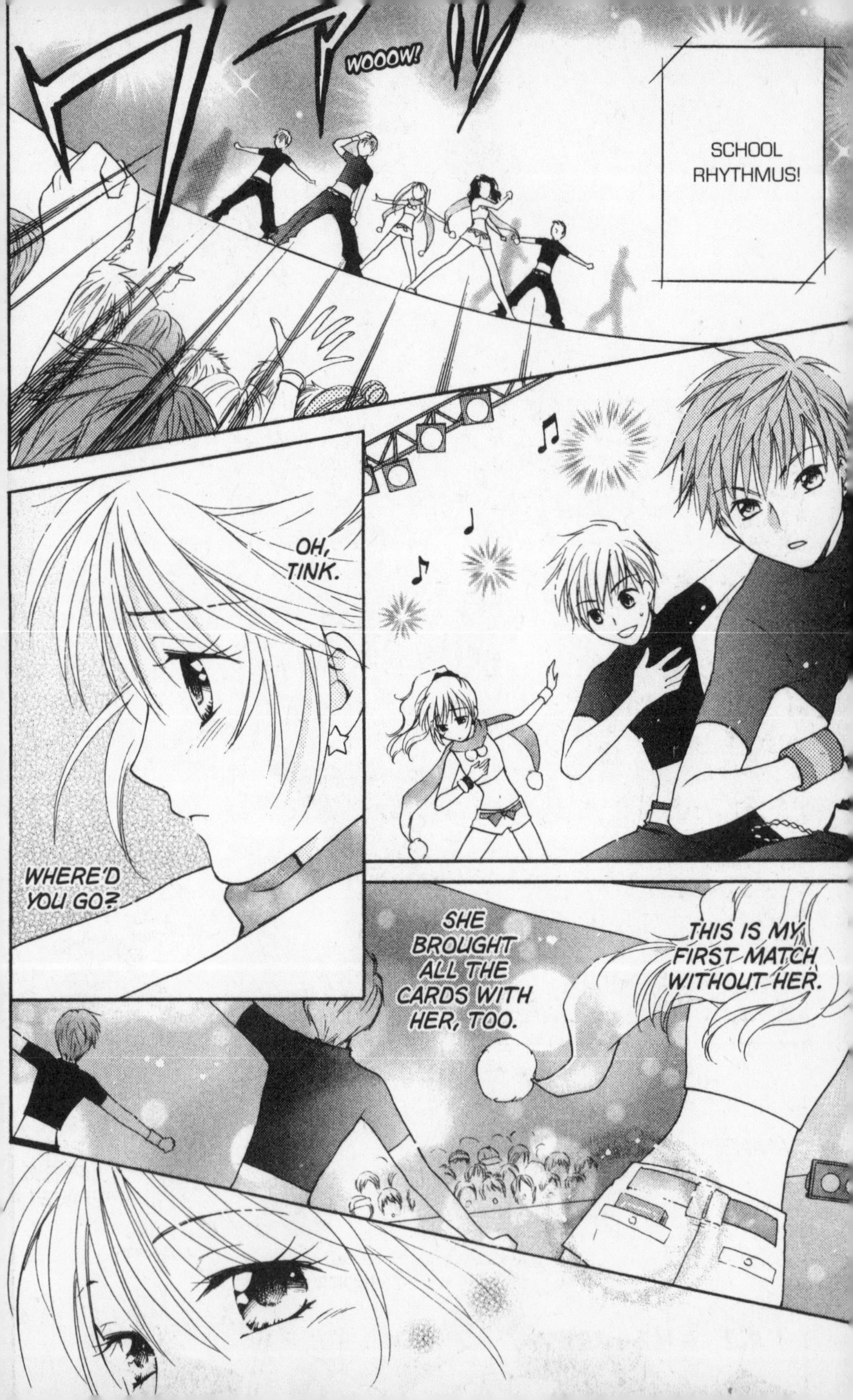
SCHOOL RHYTHMUS!
WOOOW!
OH, TINK.
WHERE'D YOU GO?
THIS IS MY FIRST MATCH WITHOUT HER.
SHE BROUGHT ALL THE CARDS WITH HER, TOO.

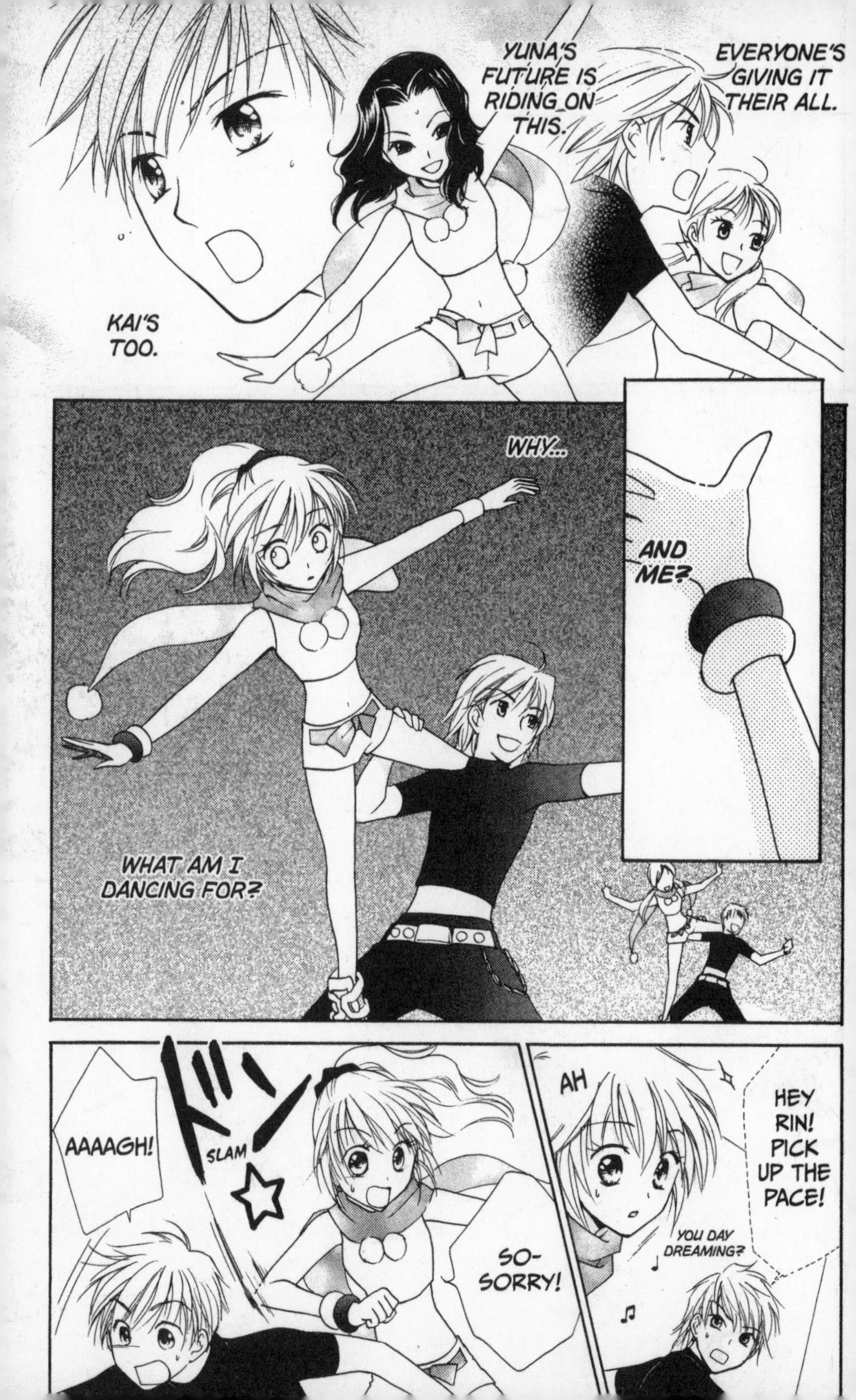
EVERYONE'S GIVING IT THEIR ALL.
YUNA'S FUTURE IS RIDING ON THIS.
KAI'S TOO.
AND ME?
WHY...
WHAT AM I DANCING FOR?
HEY RIN! PICK UP THE PACE!
YOU DAY DREAMING?
AH
SLAM
AAAAGH!
SO-SORRY!

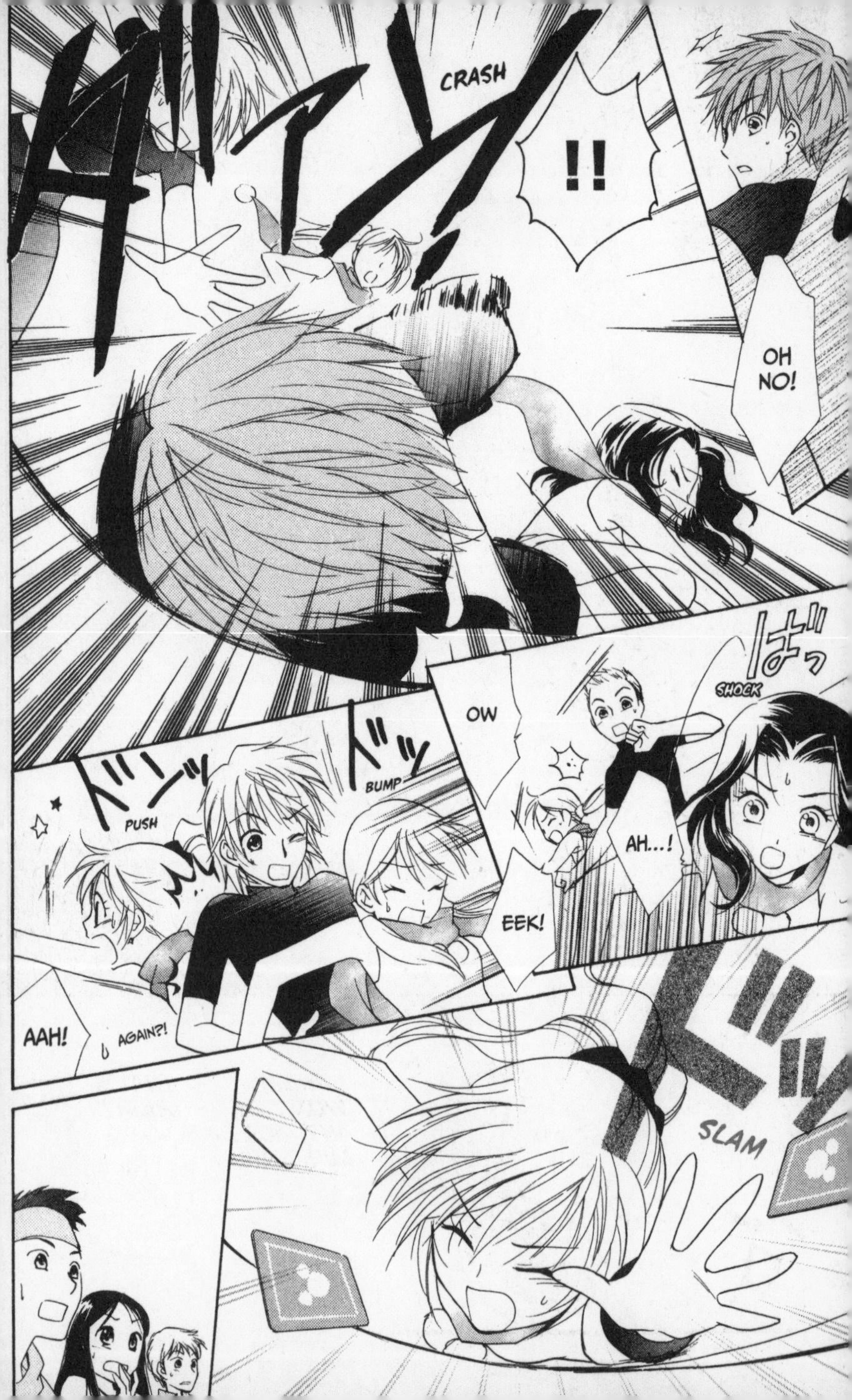

OH NO!
!!
CRASH
ばっ
SHOCK
AH...!
OW
EEK!
ドッ
BUMP
ドンッ
PUSH
AGAIN?!
AAH!
SLAM

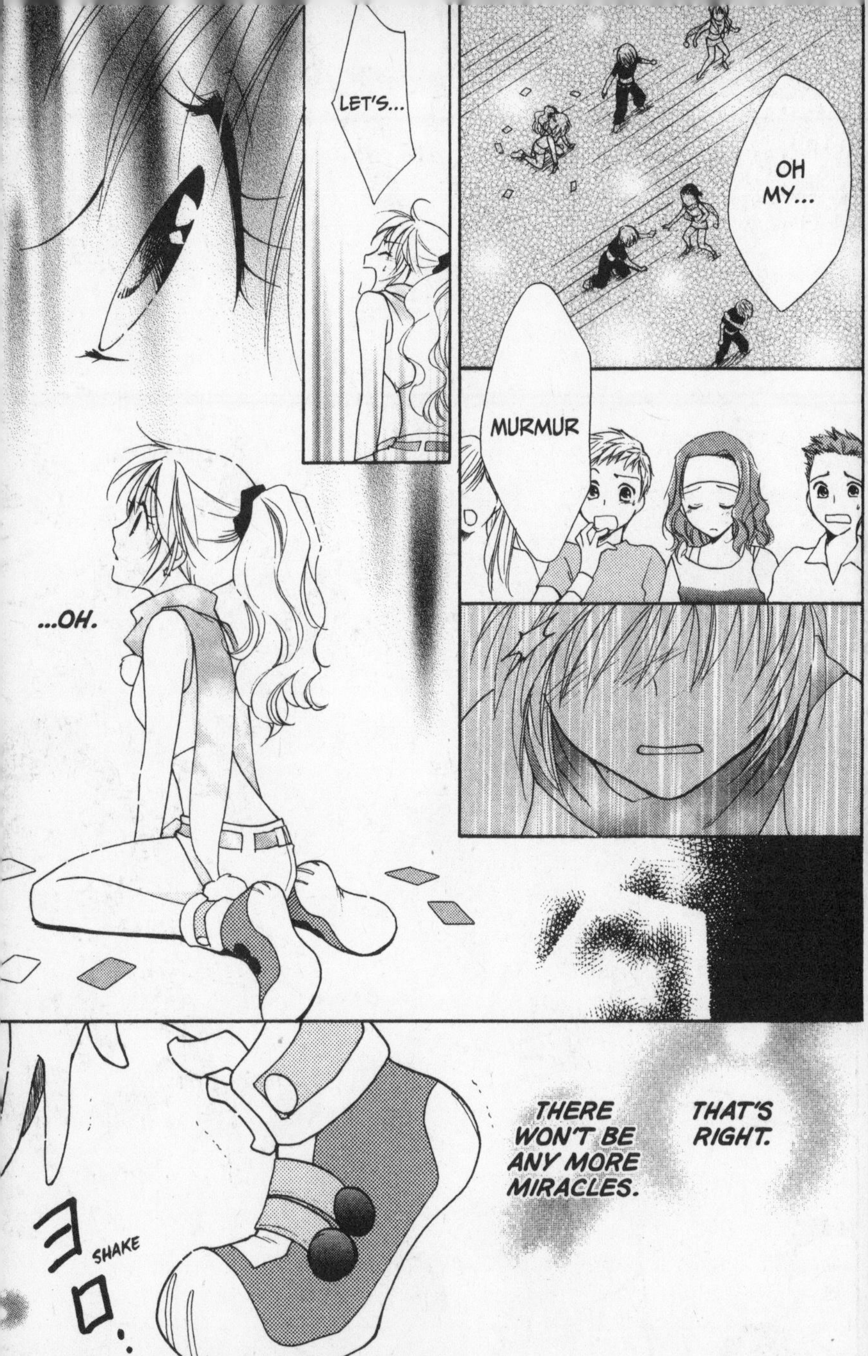
OH MY...
MURMUR
LET'S...
...OH.
THAT'S RIGHT.
THERE WON'T BE ANY MORE MIRACLES.
SHAKE

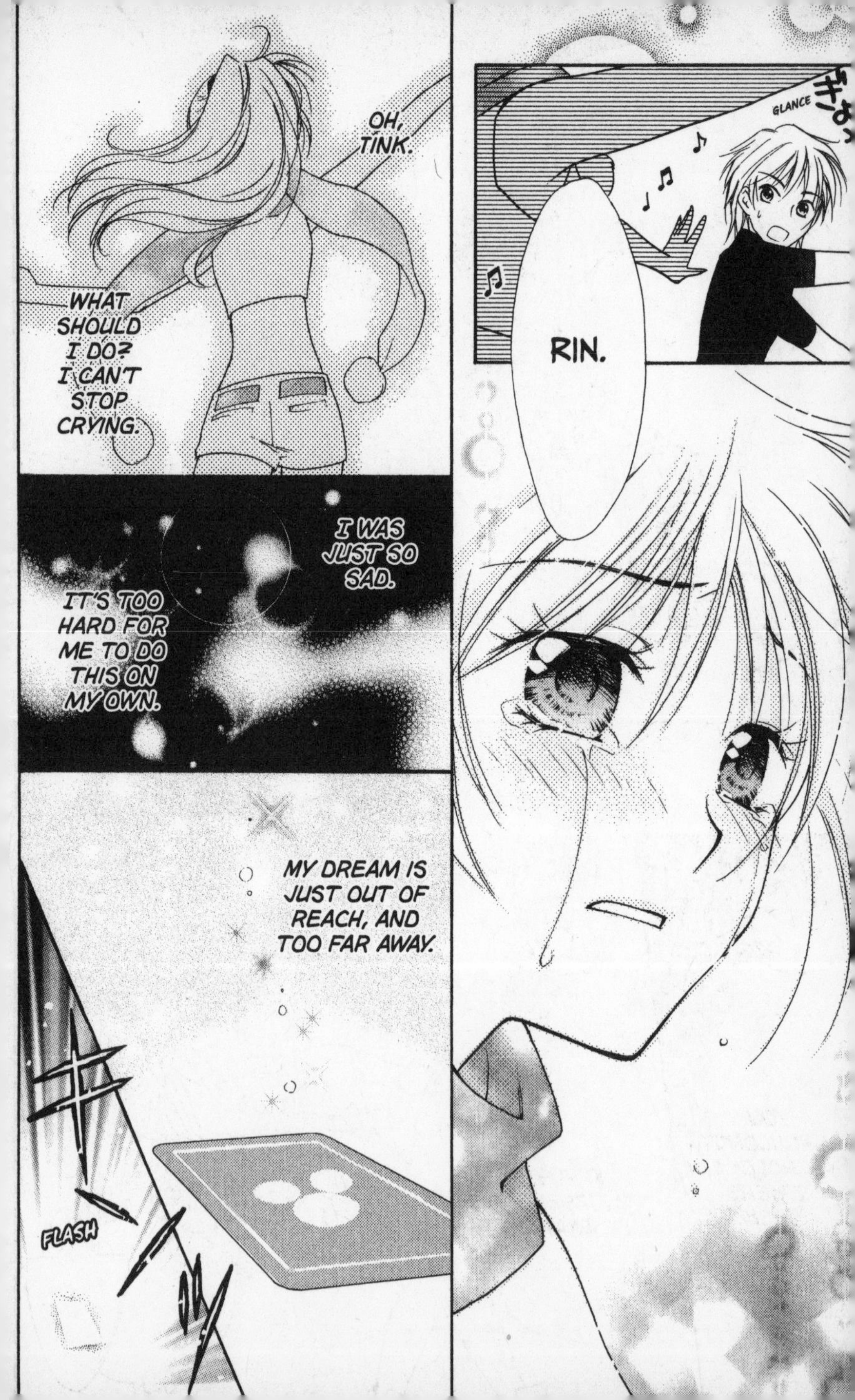
GLANCE
RIN.
OH, TINK.
WHAT SHOULD I DO? I CAN'T STOP CRYING.
I WAS JUST SO SAD.
IT'S TOO HARD FOR ME TO DO THIS ON MY OWN.
MY DREAM IS JUST OUT OF REACH, AND TOO FAR AWAY.
FLASH

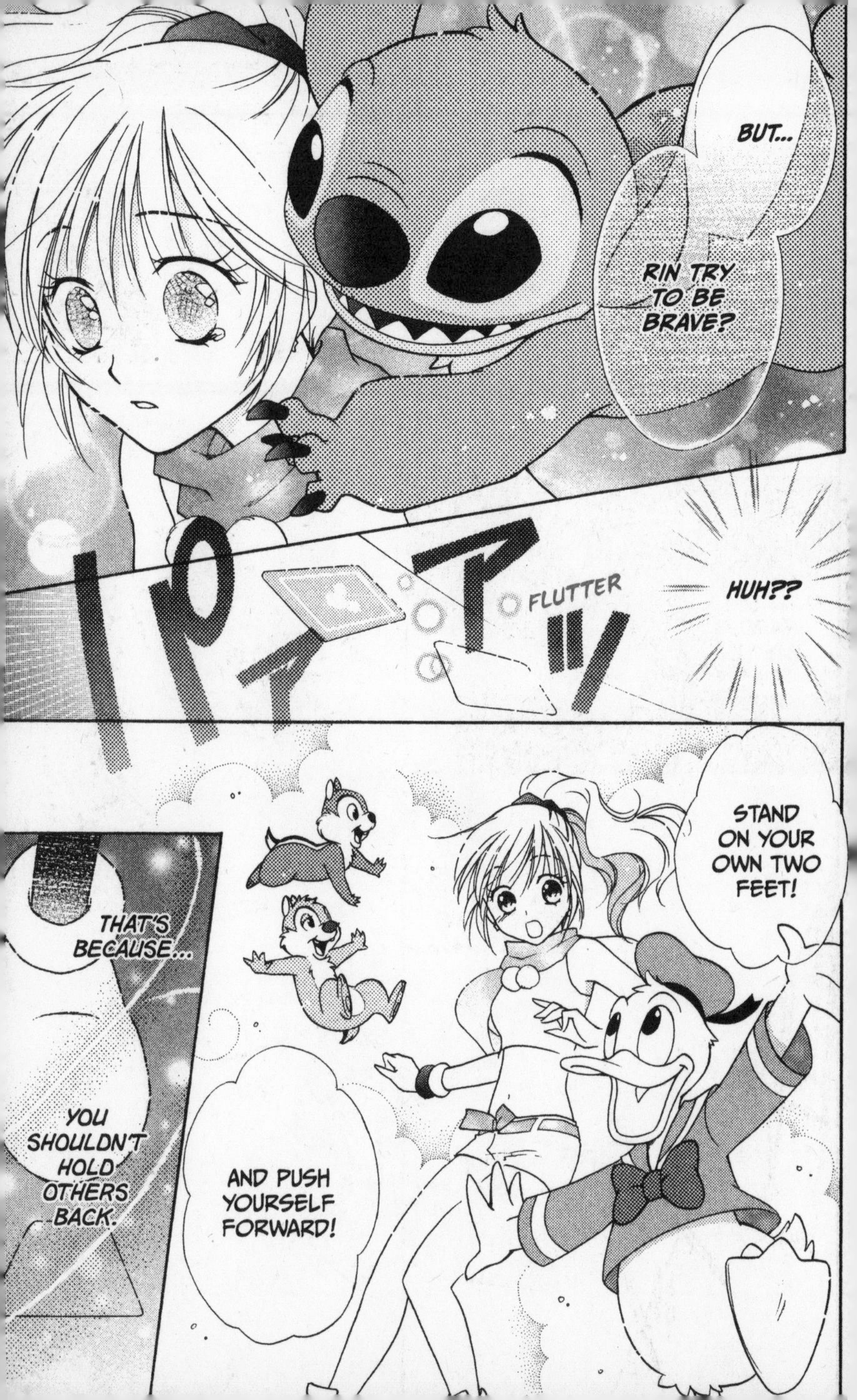
BUT...
RIN TRY TO BE BRAVE?
HUH??
パアッ
FLUTTER
STAND ON YOUR OWN TWO FEET!
AND PUSH YOURSELF FORWARD!
THAT'S BECAUSE...
YOU SHOULDN'T HOLD OTHERS BACK.

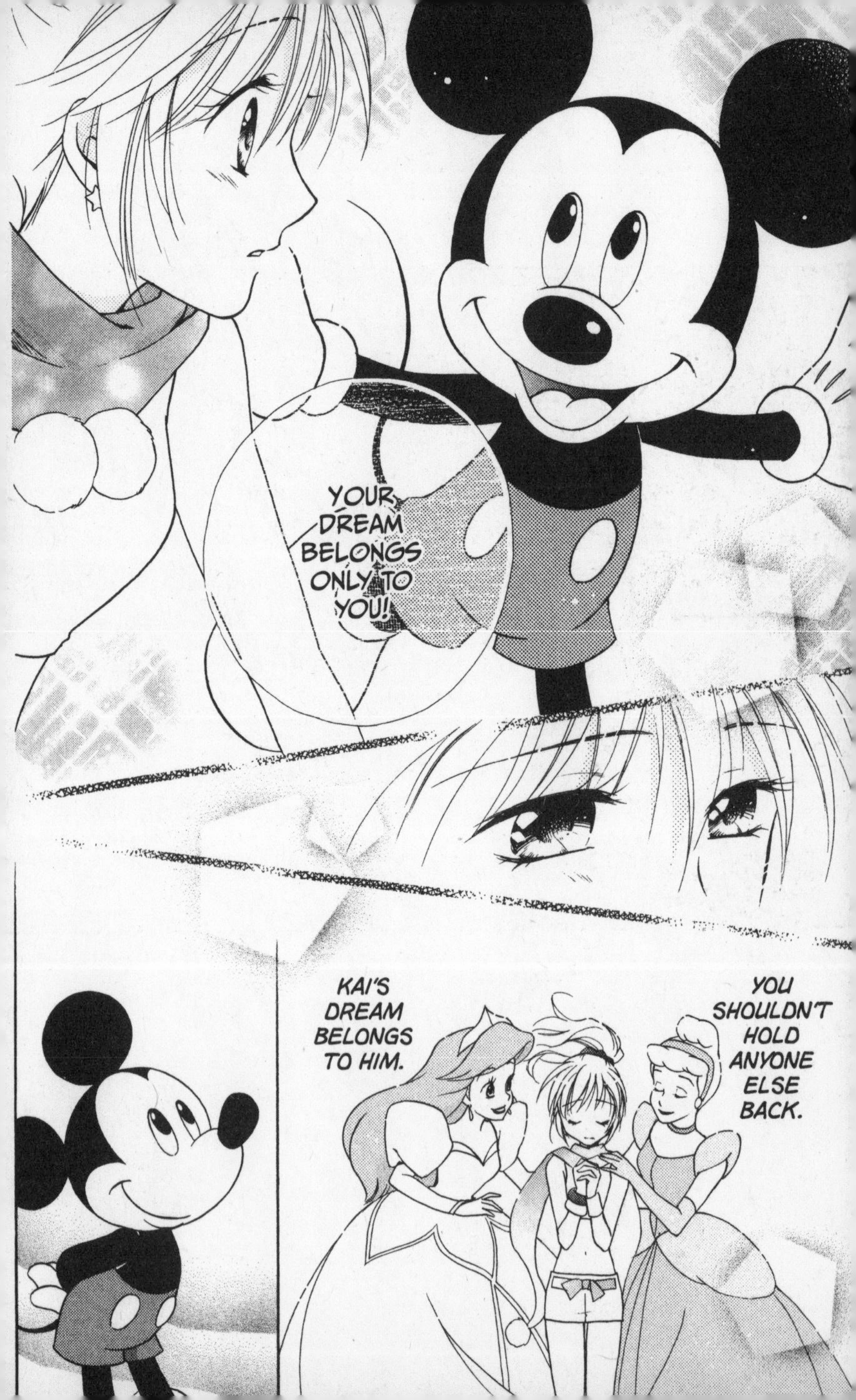
YOUR DREAM BELONGS ONLY TO YOU!
YOU SHOULDN'T HOLD ANYONE ELSE BACK.
KAI'S DREAM BELONGS TO HIM.

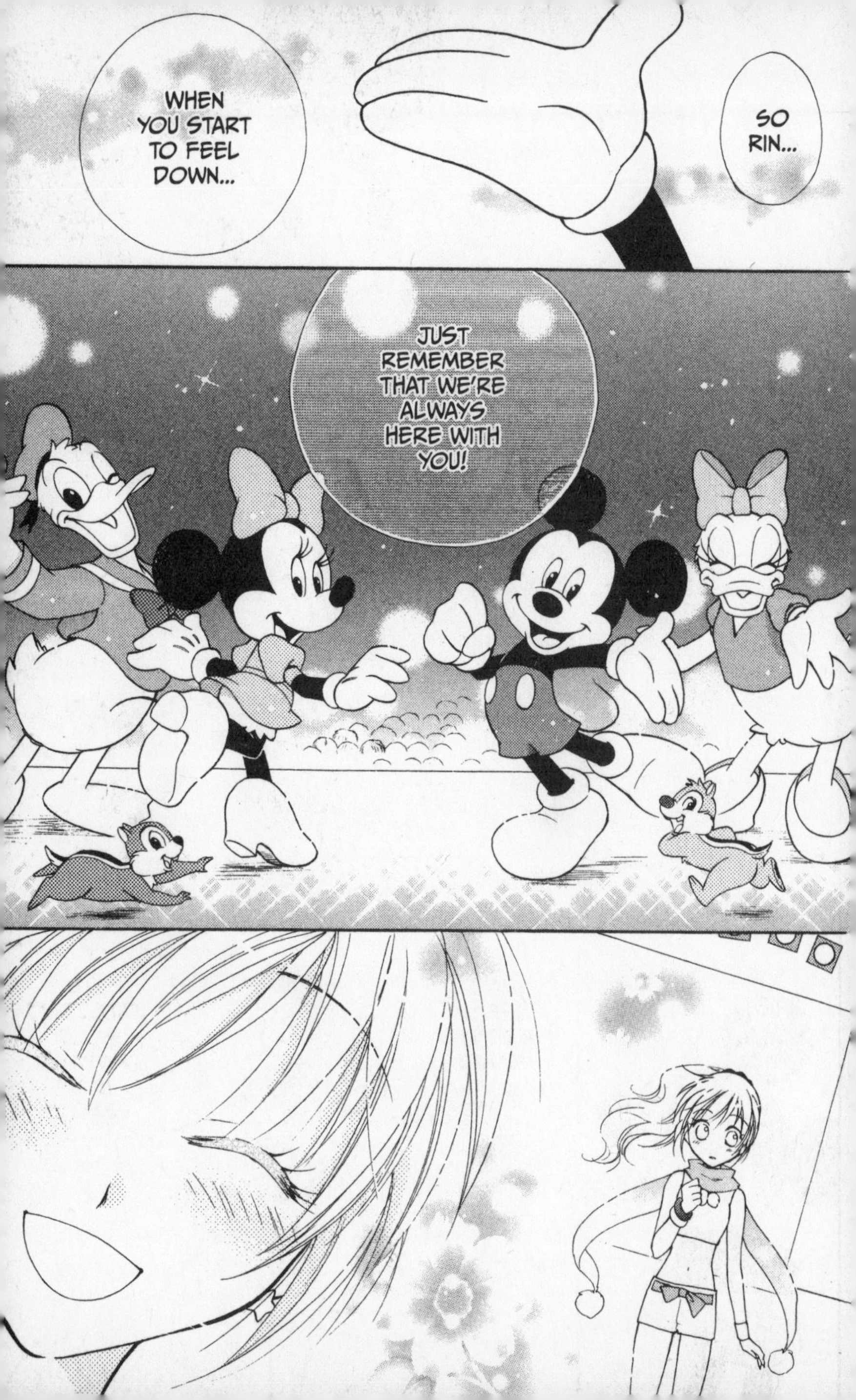
SO RIN...
WHEN YOU START TO FEEL DOWN...
JUST REMEMBER THAT WE'RE ALWAYS HERE WITH YOU!

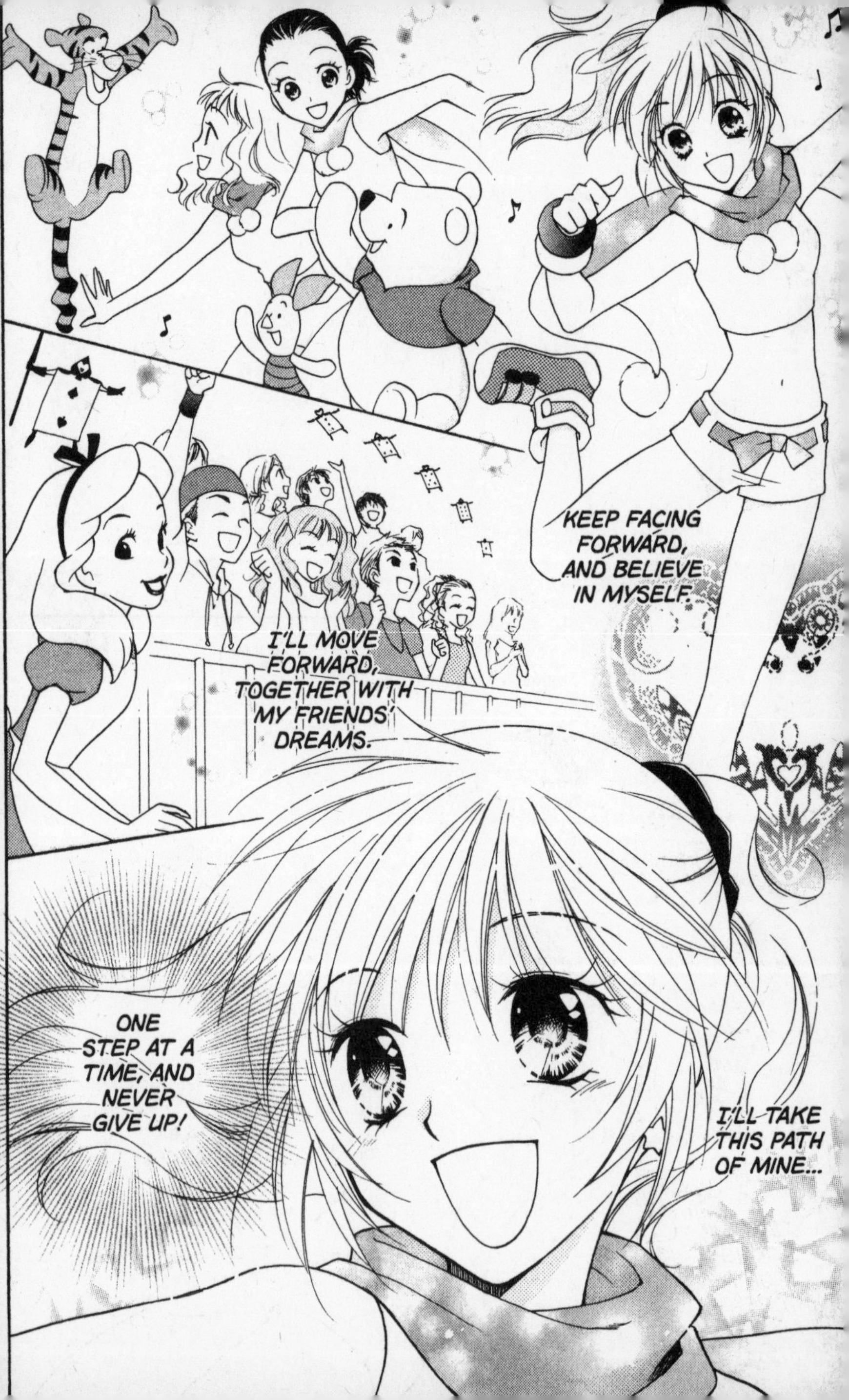

KEEP FACING FORWARD, AND BELIEVE IN MYSELF.
I'LL MOVE FORWARD, TOGETHER WITH MY FRIENDS' DREAMS.
I'LL TAKE THIS PATH OF MINE...
ONE STEP AT A TIME, AND NEVER GIVE UP!

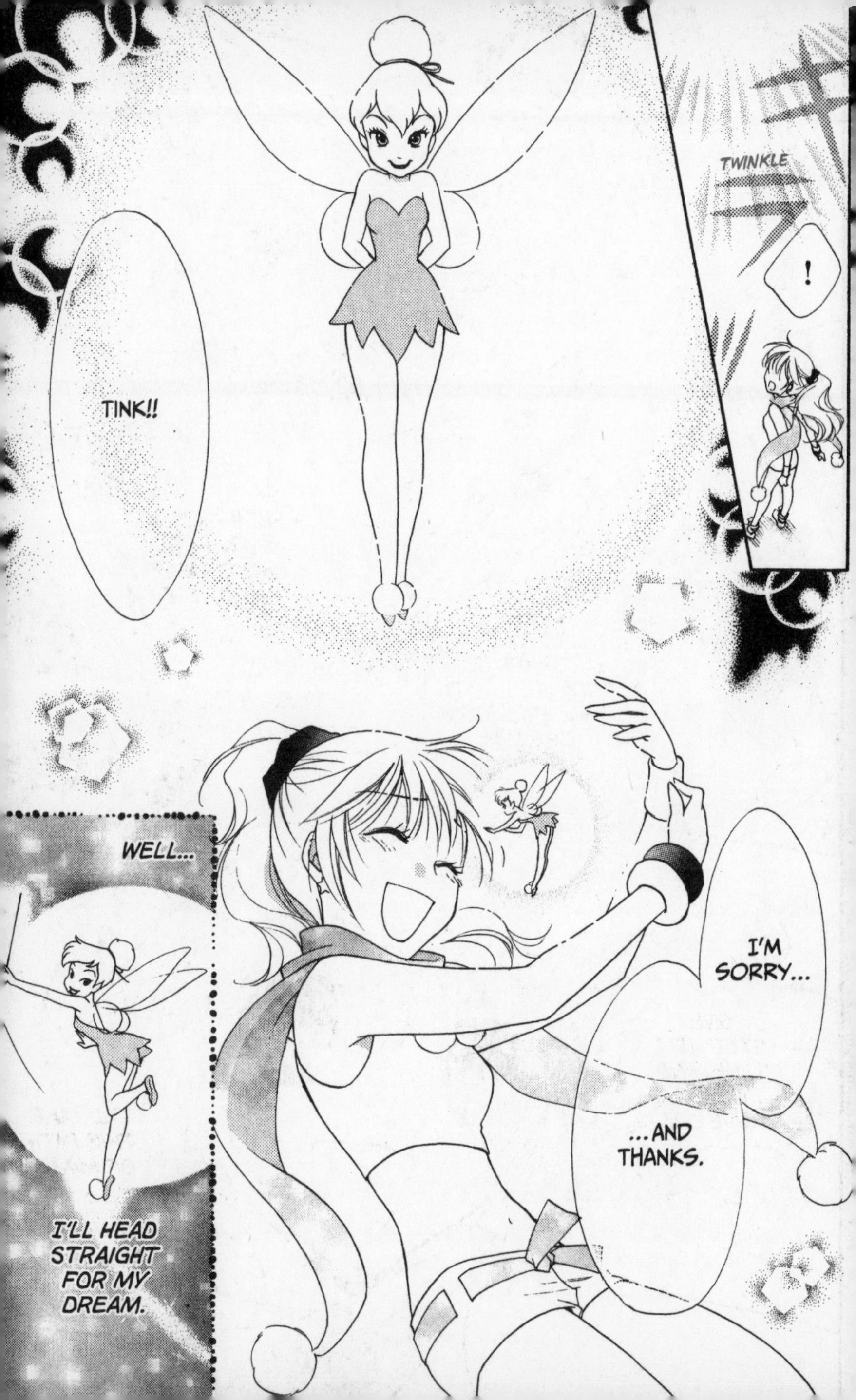
TWINKLE
!
TINK!!
I'M SORRY...
...AND THANKS.
WELL...
I'LL HEAD STRAIGHT FOR MY DREAM.

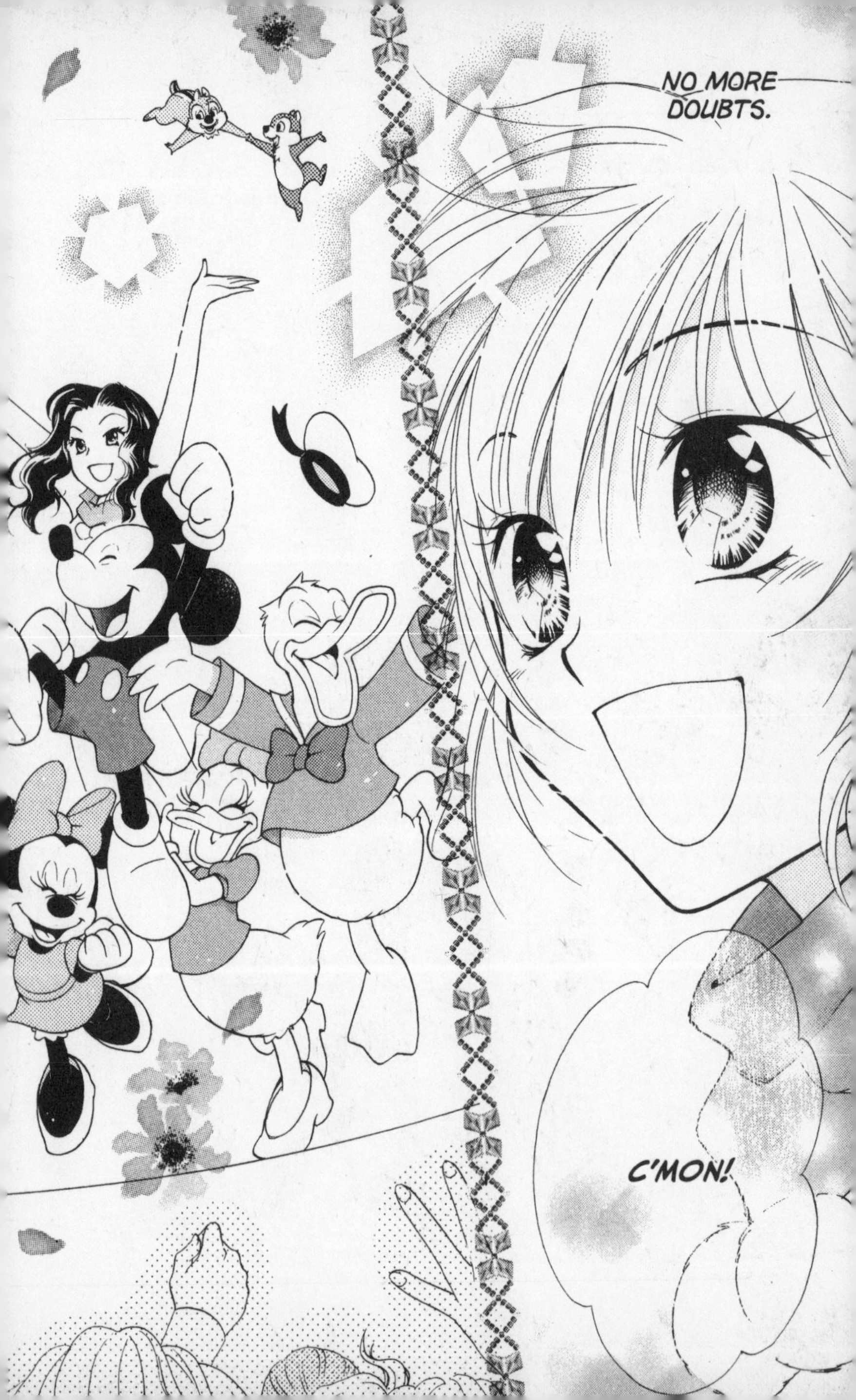
NO MORE DOUBTS.
C'MON!

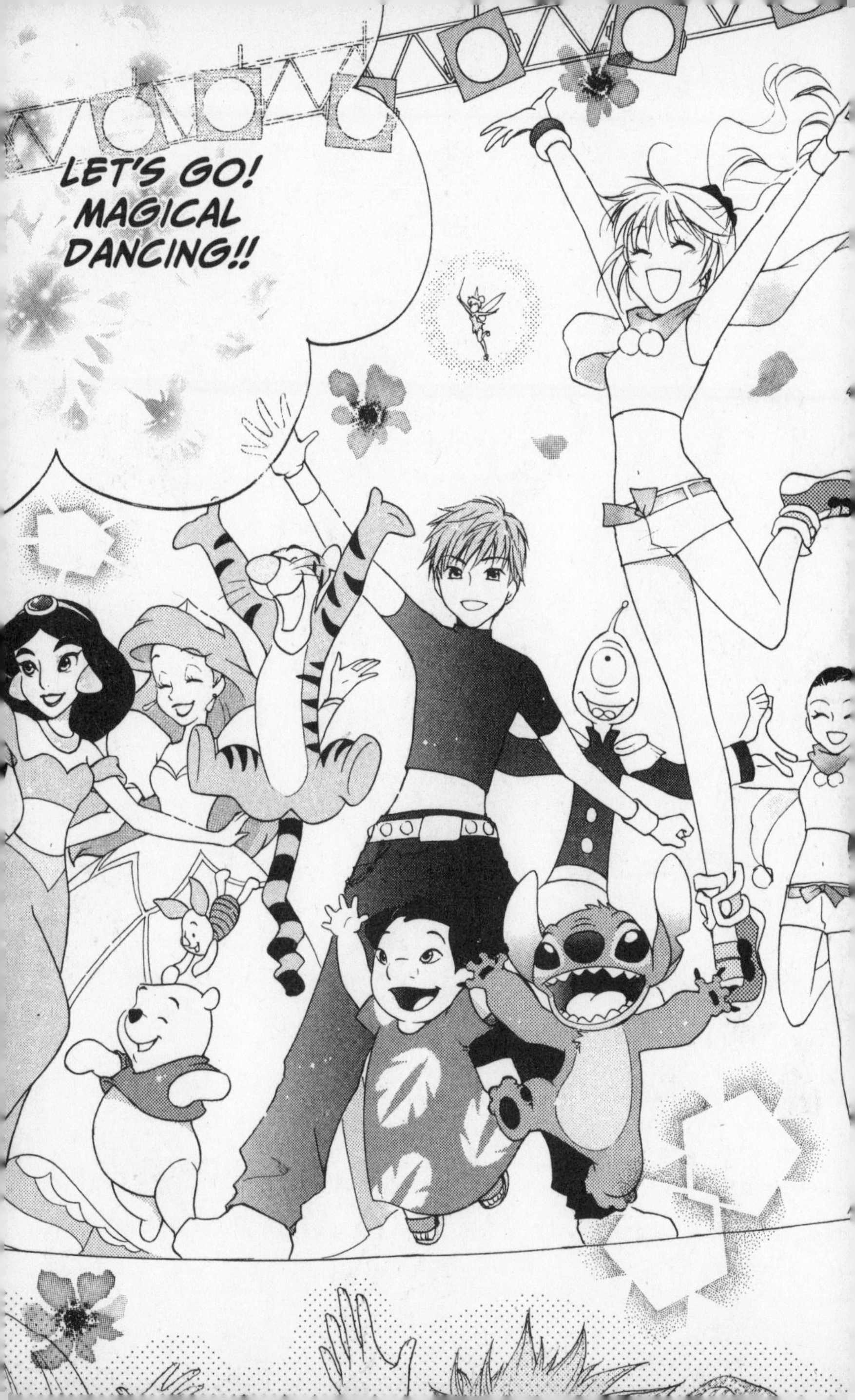
LET'S GO! MAGICAL DANCING!!

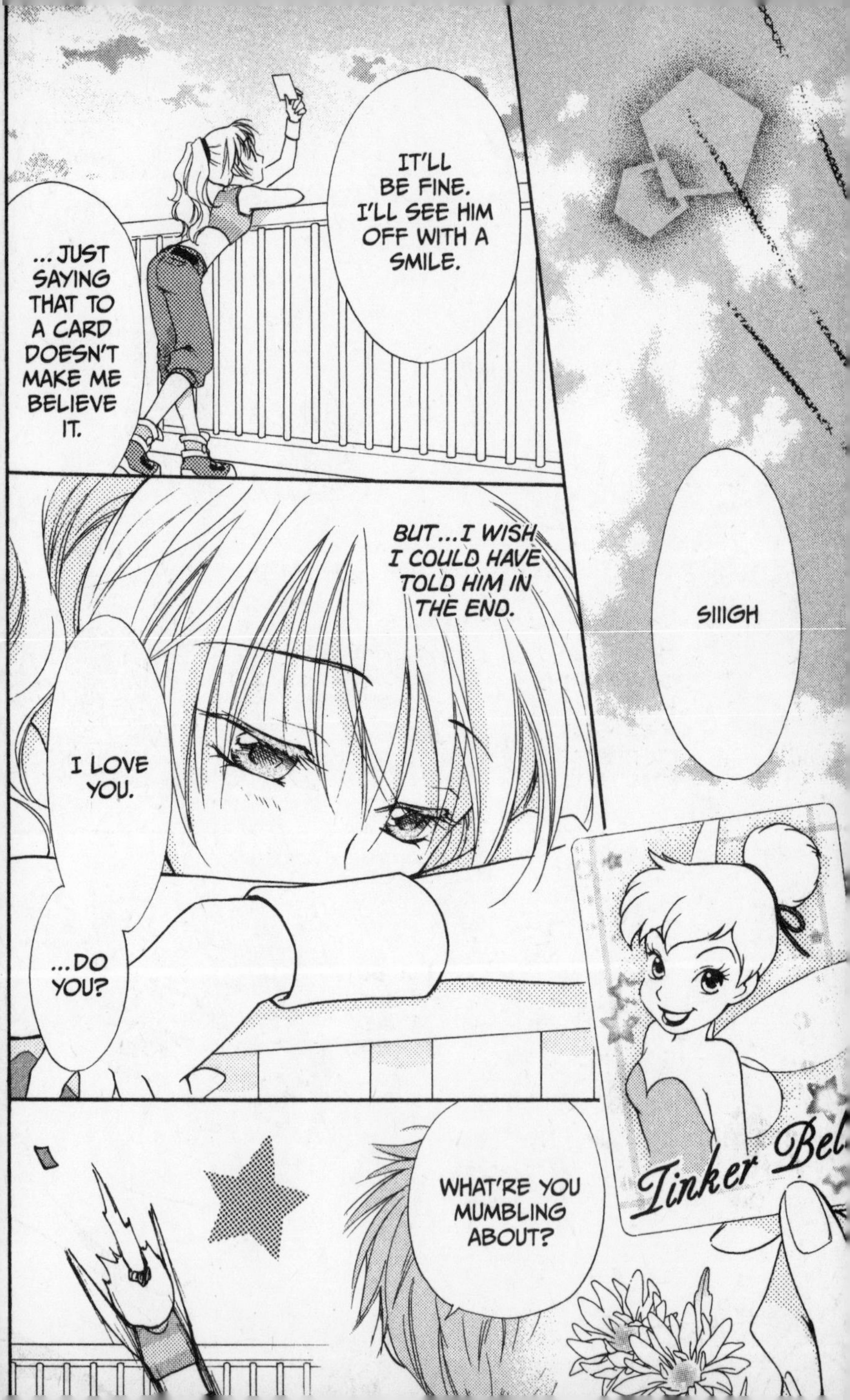
SIIGH
IT'LL BE FINE. I'LL SEE HIM OFF WITH A SMILE.
...JUST SAYING THAT TO A CARD DOESN'T MAKE ME BELIEVE IT.
BUT...I WISH I COULD HAVE TOLD HIM IN THE END.
I LOVE YOU.
...DO YOU?
Tinker Bel
WHAT'RE YOU MUMBLING ABOUT?

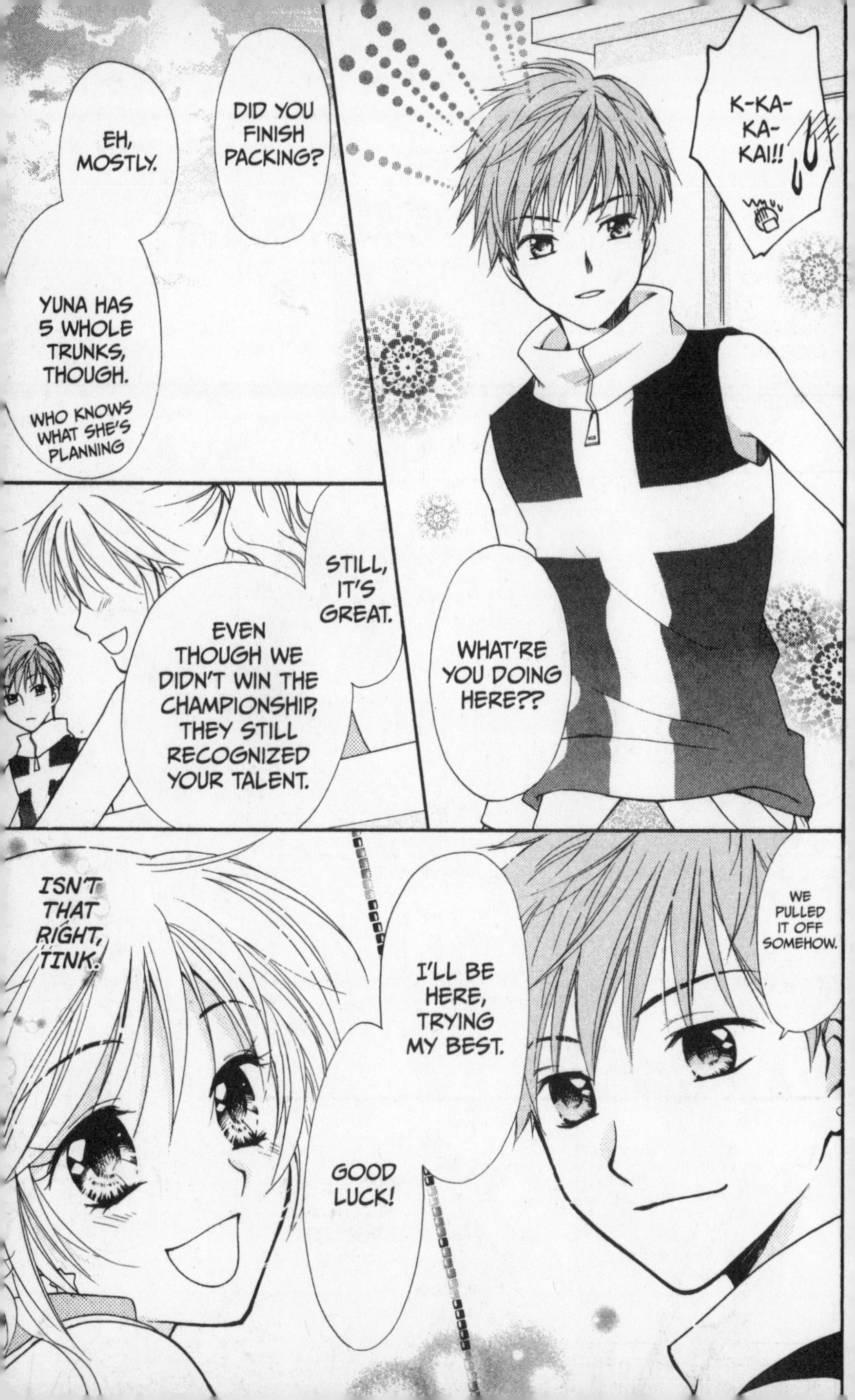
K-KA-KA-KAI!!
WHAT'RE YOU DOING HERE??
DID YOU FINISH PACKING?
EH, MOSTLY.
YUNA HAS 5 WHOLE TRUNKS, THOUGH.
WHO KNOWS WHAT SHE'S PLANNING
STILL, IT'S GREAT.
EVEN THOUGH WE DIDN'T WIN THE CHAMPIONSHIP, THEY STILL RECOGNIZED YOUR TALENT.
WE PULLED IT OFF SOMEHOW.
I'LL BE HERE, TRYING MY BEST.
GOOD LUCK!
ISN'T THAT RIGHT, TINK.

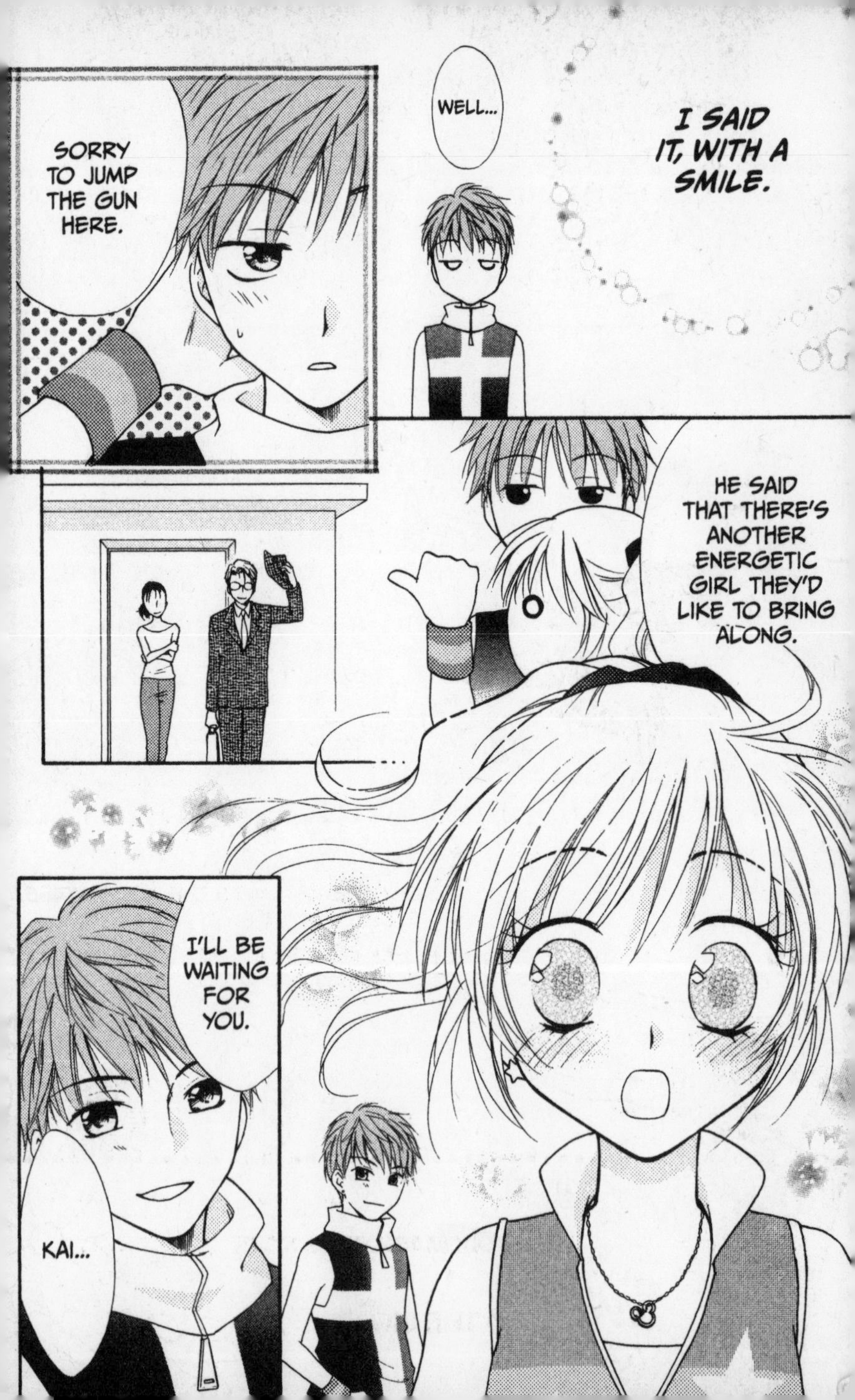
I SAID IT, WITH A SMILE.
WELL...
SORRY TO JUMP THE GUN HERE.
HE SAID THAT THERE'S ANOTHER ENERGETIC GIRL THEY'D LIKE TO BRING ALONG.
I'LL BE WAITING FOR YOU.
KAI...

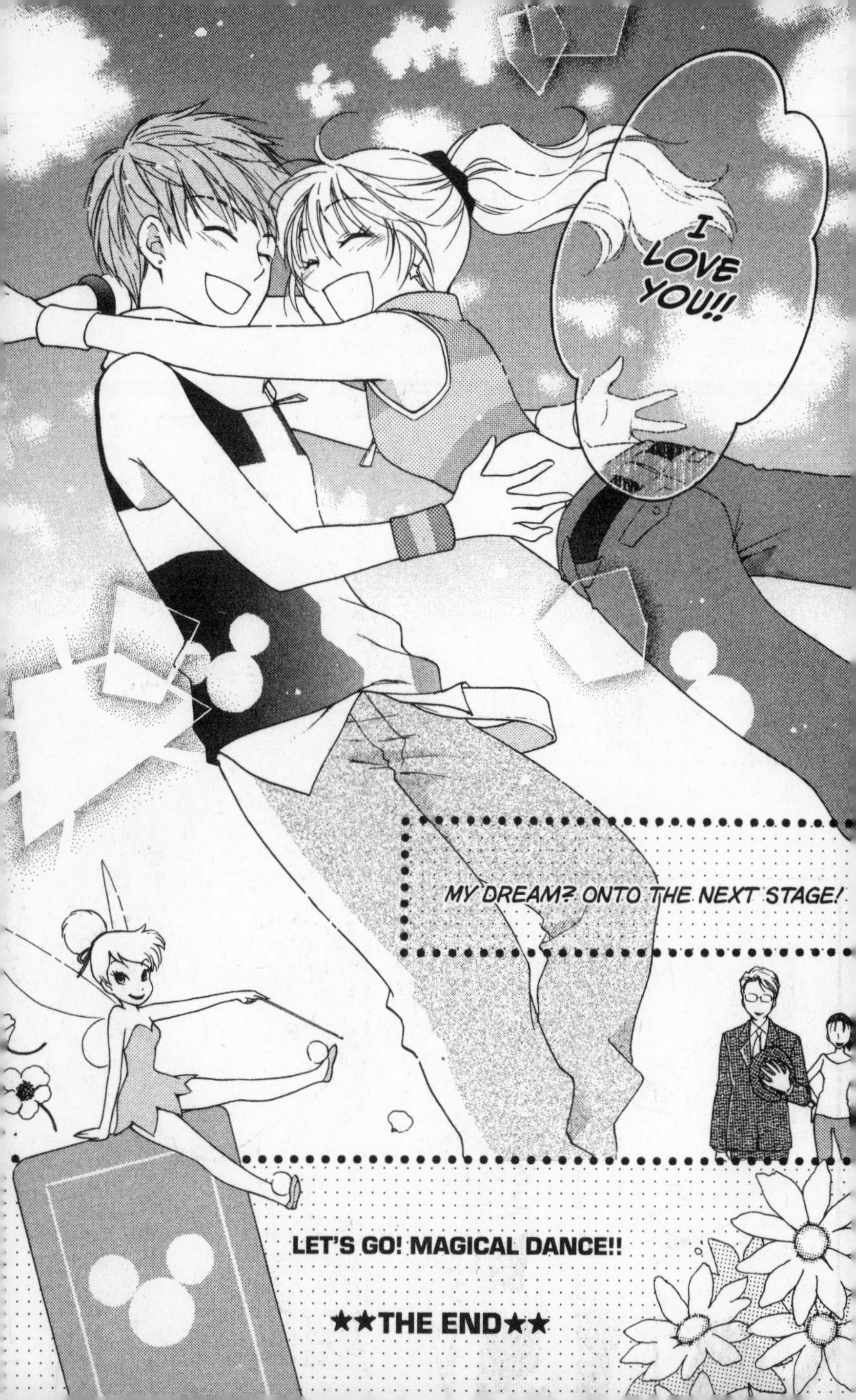
I LOVE YOU!!
MY DREAM? ONTO THE NEXT STAGE!
LET'S GO! MAGICAL DANCE!!
★★THE END★★

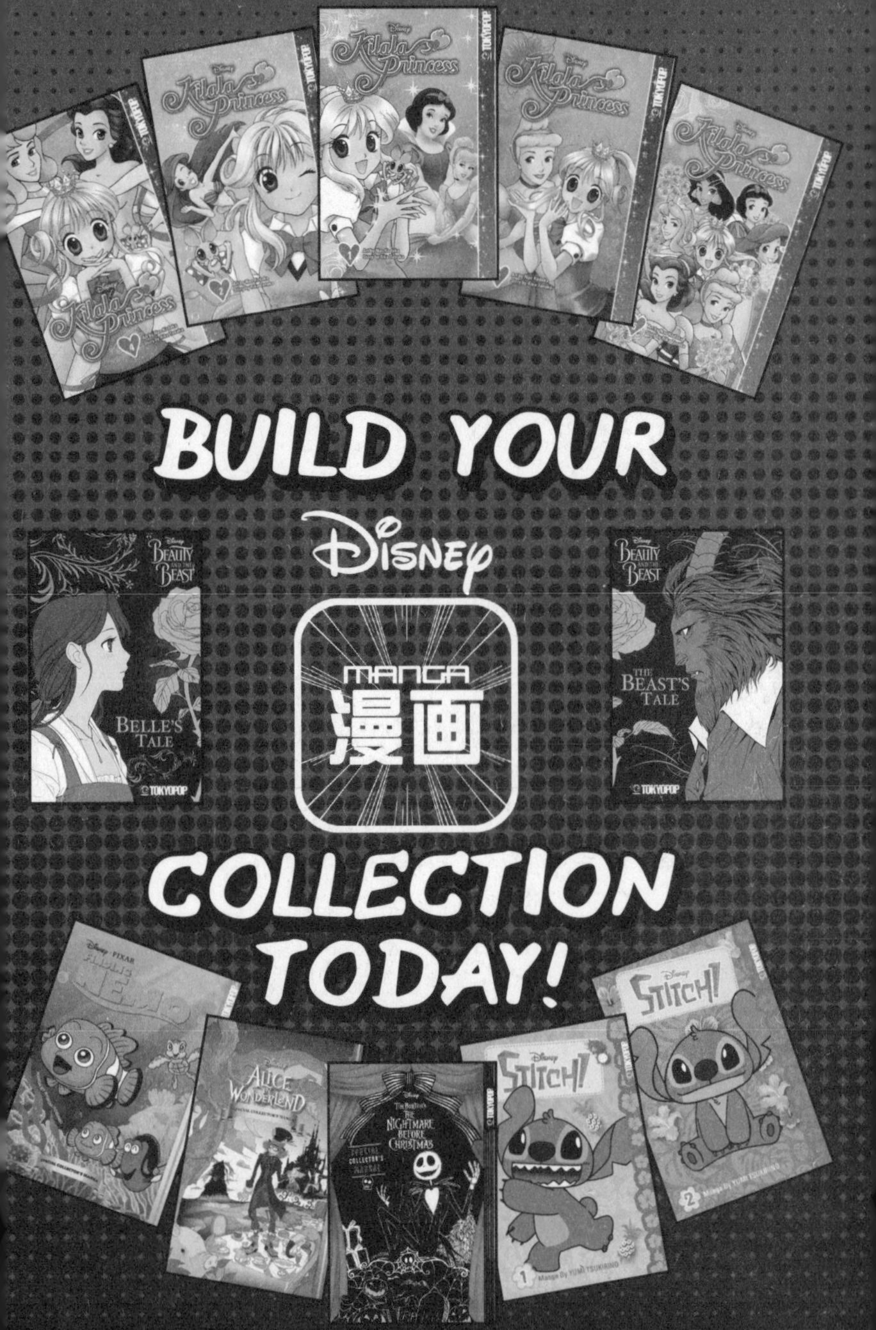
BUILD YOUR
DISNEY
MANGA
漫画
COLLECTION
TODAY!
Kilala Princess
Beauty and the Beast
Belle's Tale
The Beast's Tale
TOKYOPOP
Alice in Wonderland
The Nightmare Before Christmas
Stitch!

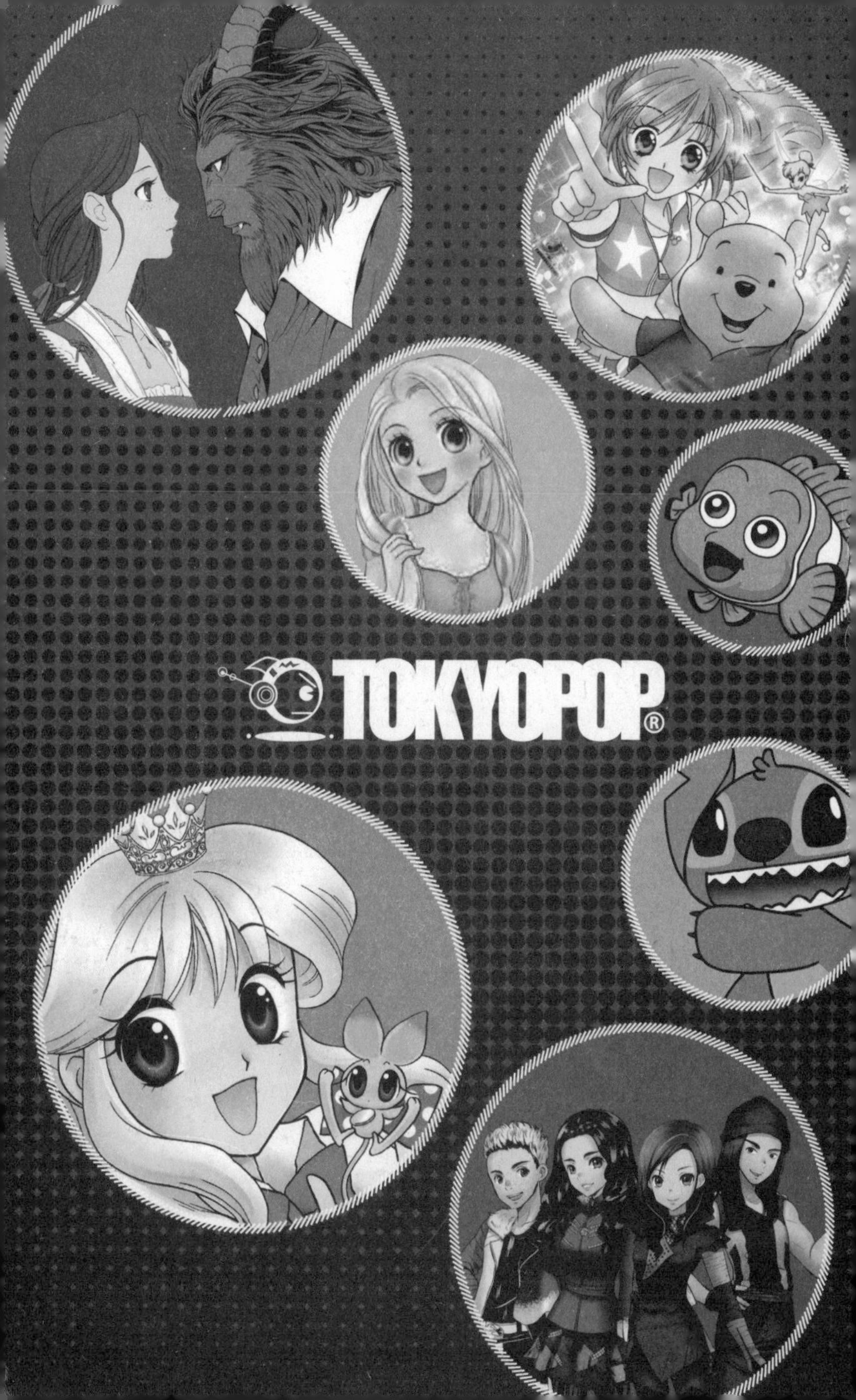
TOKYOPOP®

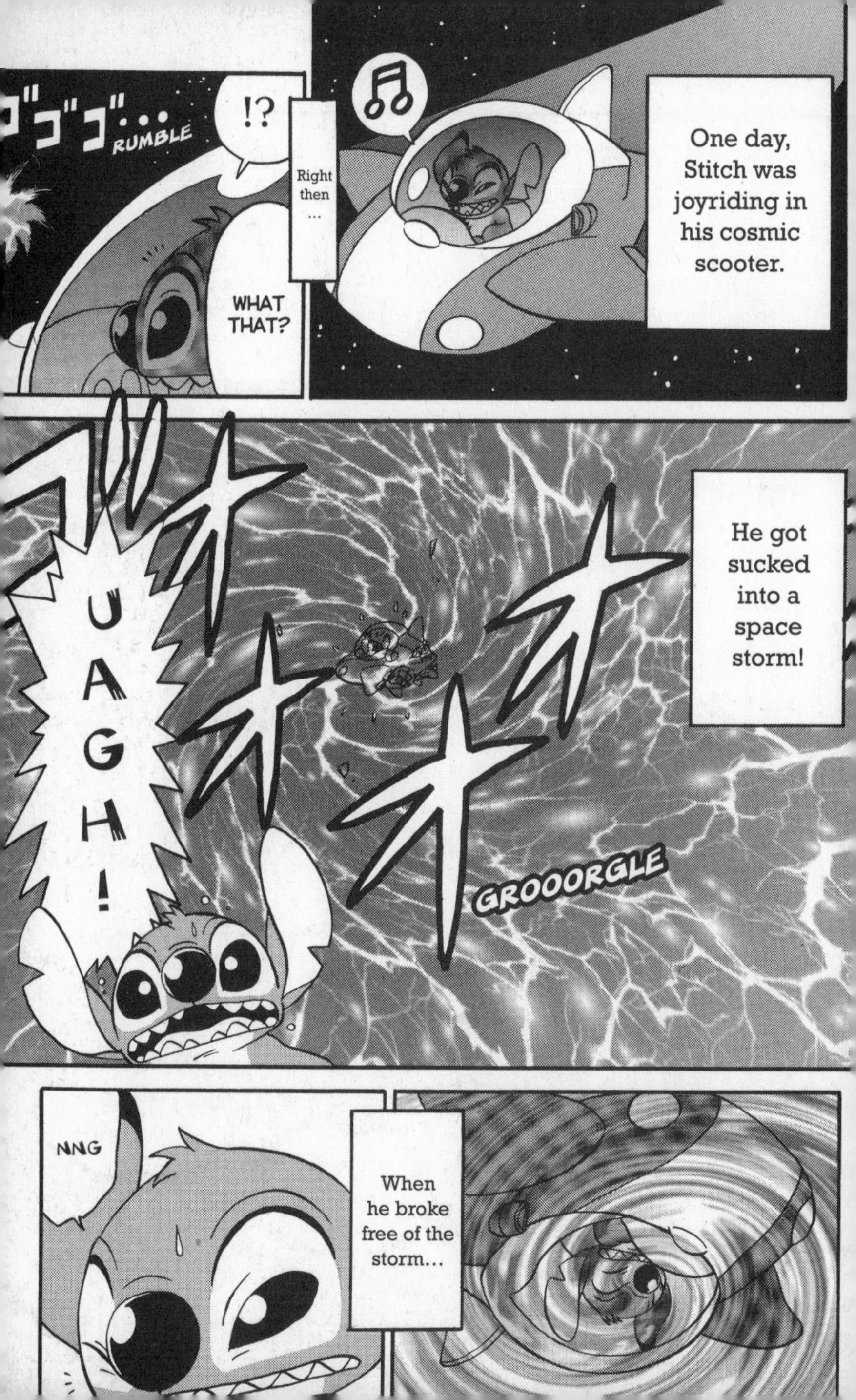
One day, Stitch was joyriding in his cosmic scooter.
Right then ...
!?
ゴゴゴ...
RUMBLE
WHAT THAT?
He got sucked into a space storm!
UAGH!
GROOORGLE
When he broke free of the storm...
NNG

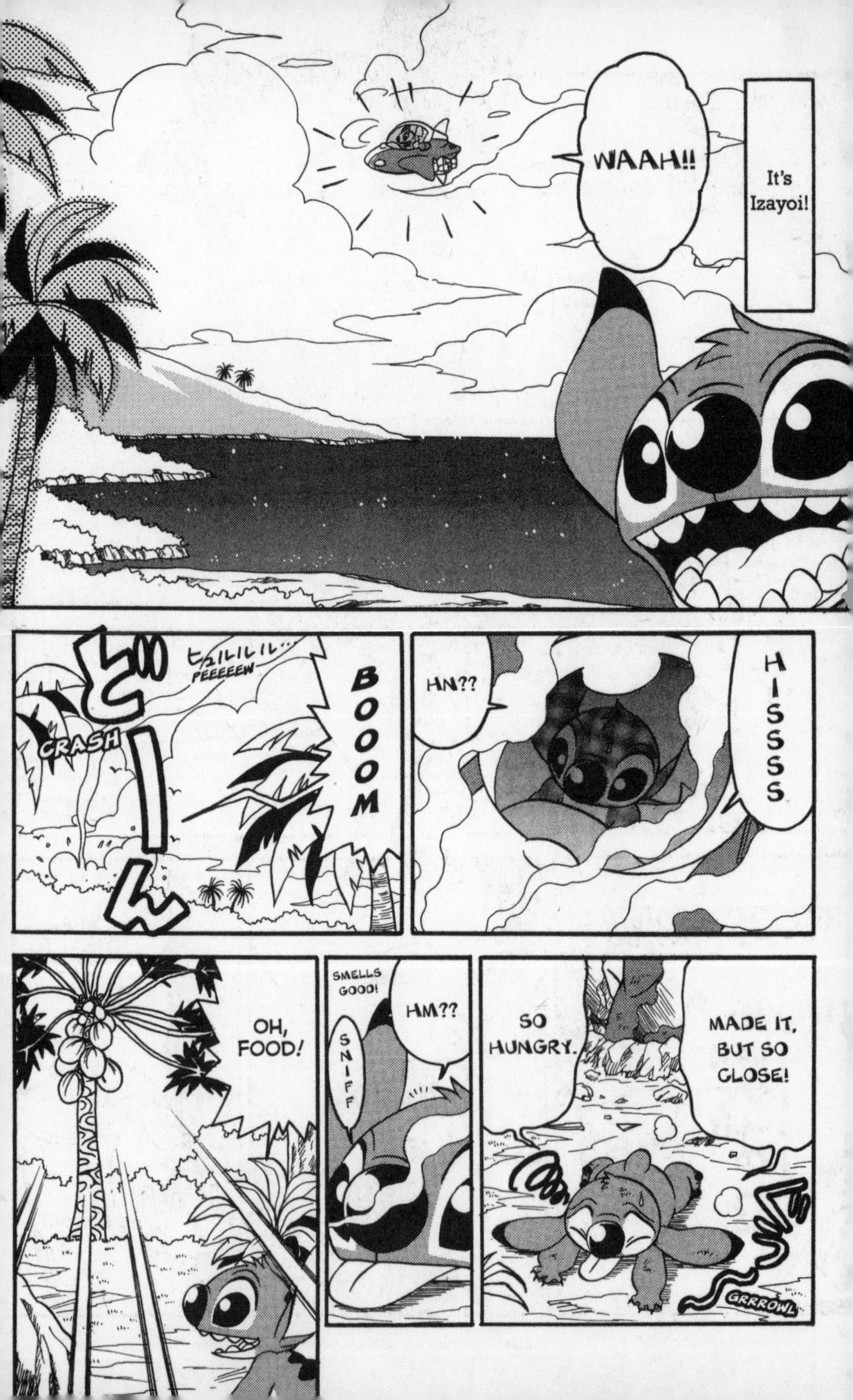
It's Izayoi!
WAAH!!
HISSSS
HN??
BOOOOM
ヒュルルル…
PEEEEEW
どーん
CRASH
MADE IT, BUT SO CLOSE!
SO HUNGRY.
GRRROWL
HM??
SMELLS GOOD!
SNIFF
OH, FOOD!

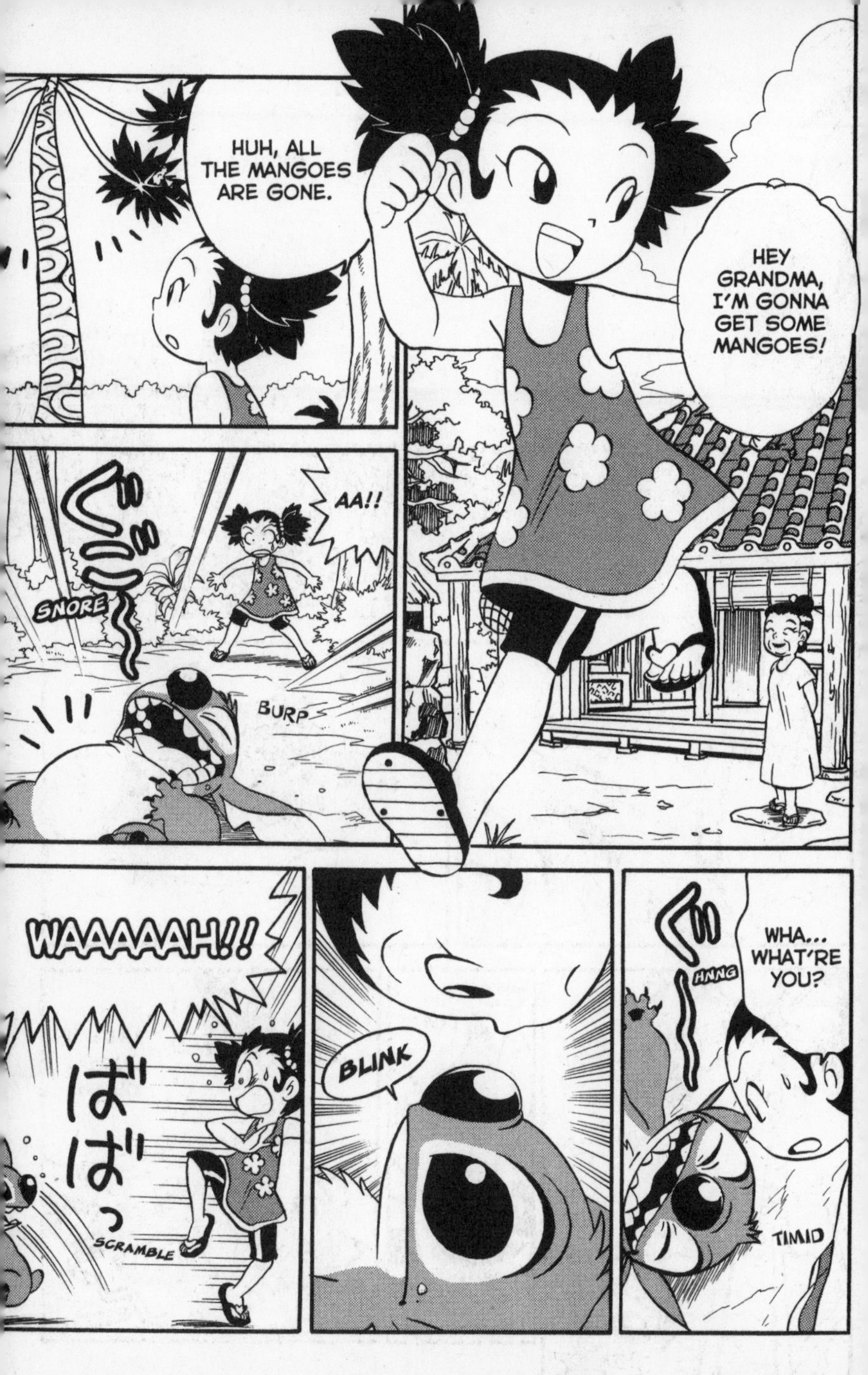
HEY GRANDMA, I'M GONNA GET SOME MANGOES!
HUH, ALL THE MANGOES ARE GONE.
AA!!
SNORE
BURP
WHA... WHAT'RE YOU?
HNNG
TIMID
BLINK
WAAAAAH!!
ばばっ
SCRAMBLE

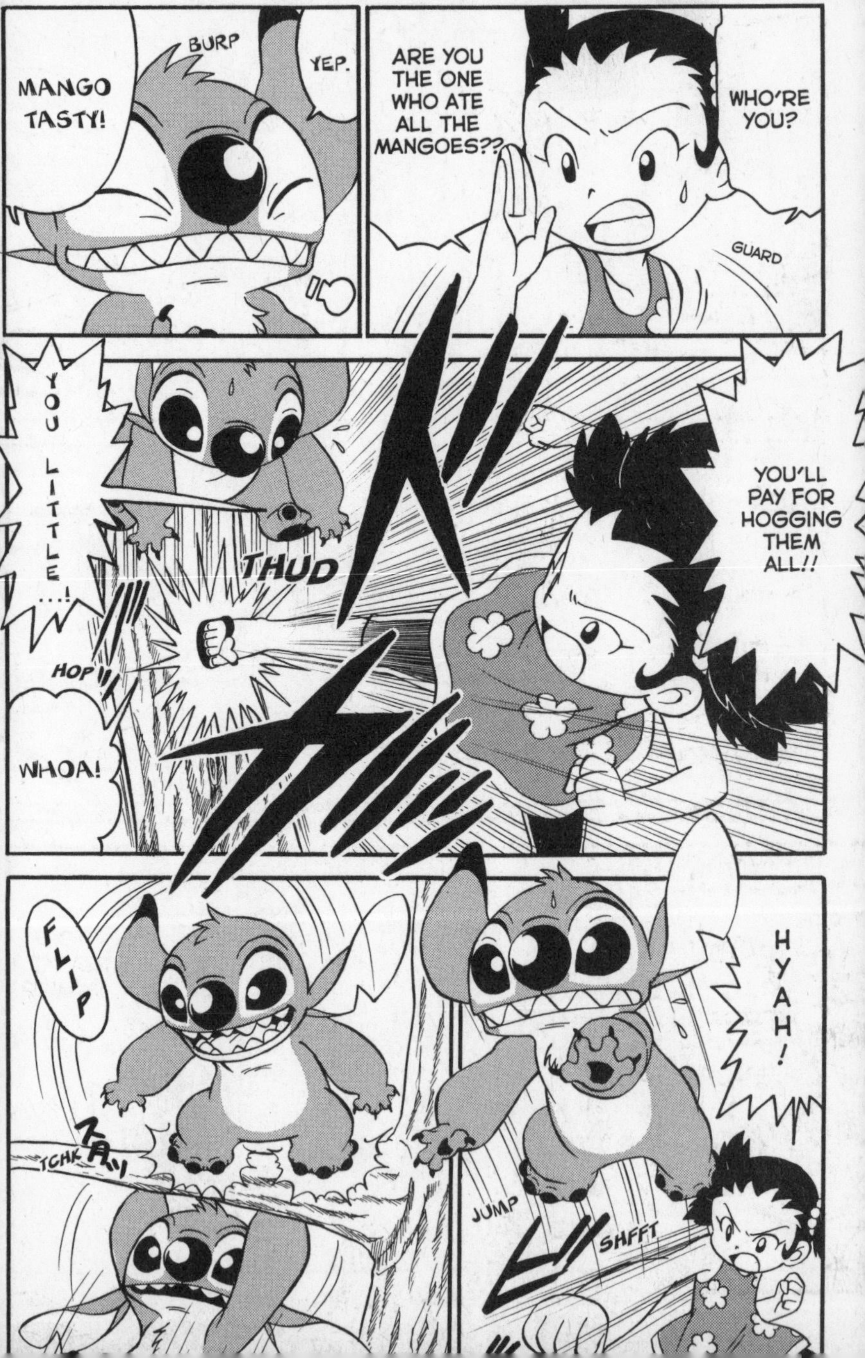
WHO'RE YOU?
ARE YOU THE ONE WHO ATE ALL THE MANGOES??
GUARD
YEP.
BURP
MANGO TASTY!
YOU'LL PAY FOR HOGGING THEM ALL!!
THUD
YOU LITTLE ...!
HOP
WHOA!
HYAH!
JUMP
SHFFT
FLIP
TCHK

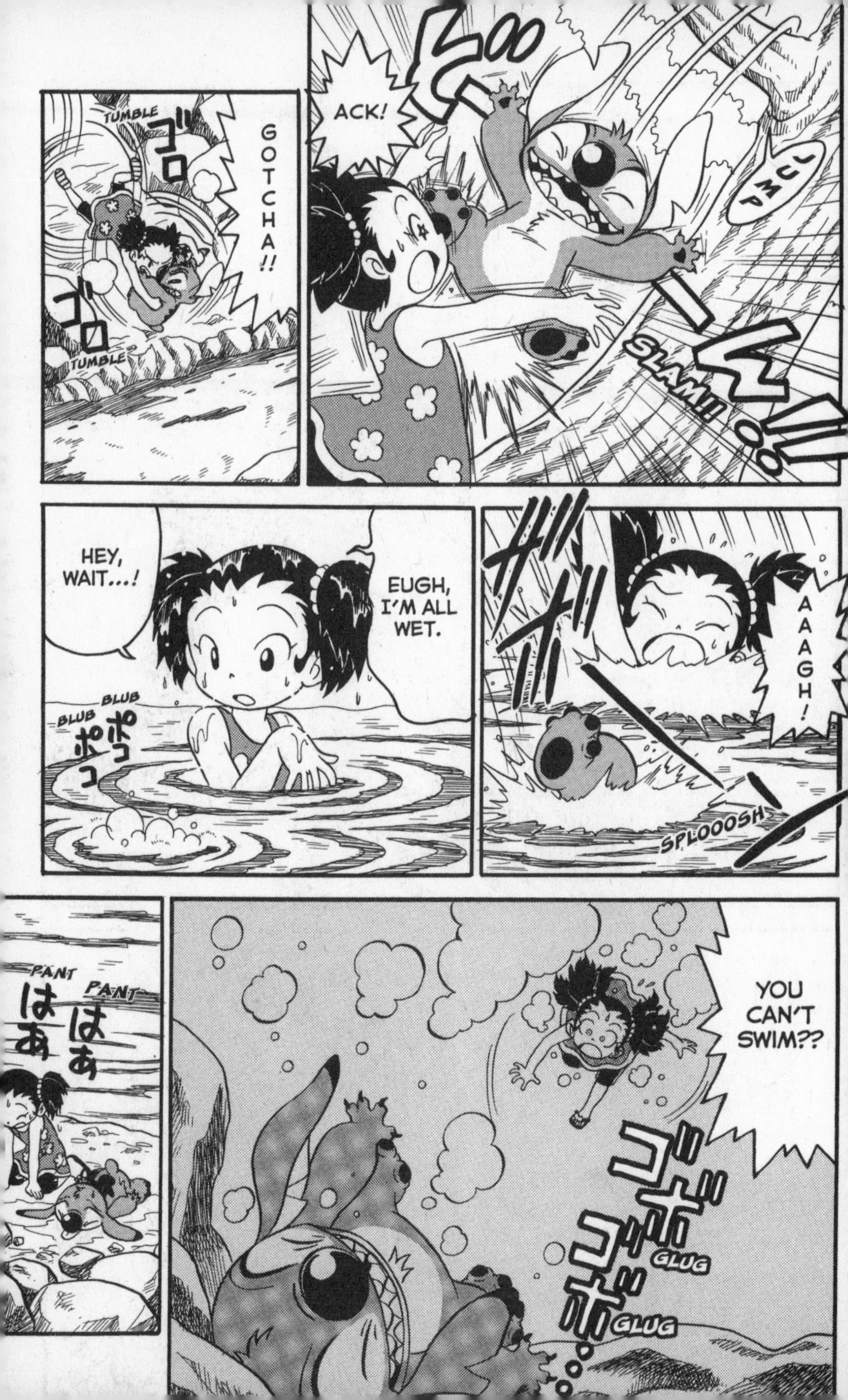

JUMP
ACK!
SLAM!!
GOTCHA!!
TUMBLE ゴロ
TUMBLE ゴロ
AAAGH!
SPLOOOSH
EUGH, I'M ALL WET.
HEY, WAIT...!
BLUB BLUB ポコポコ
YOU CAN'T SWIM??
GLUG ゴボ
GLUG ゴボ
PANT PANT はぁ はぁ

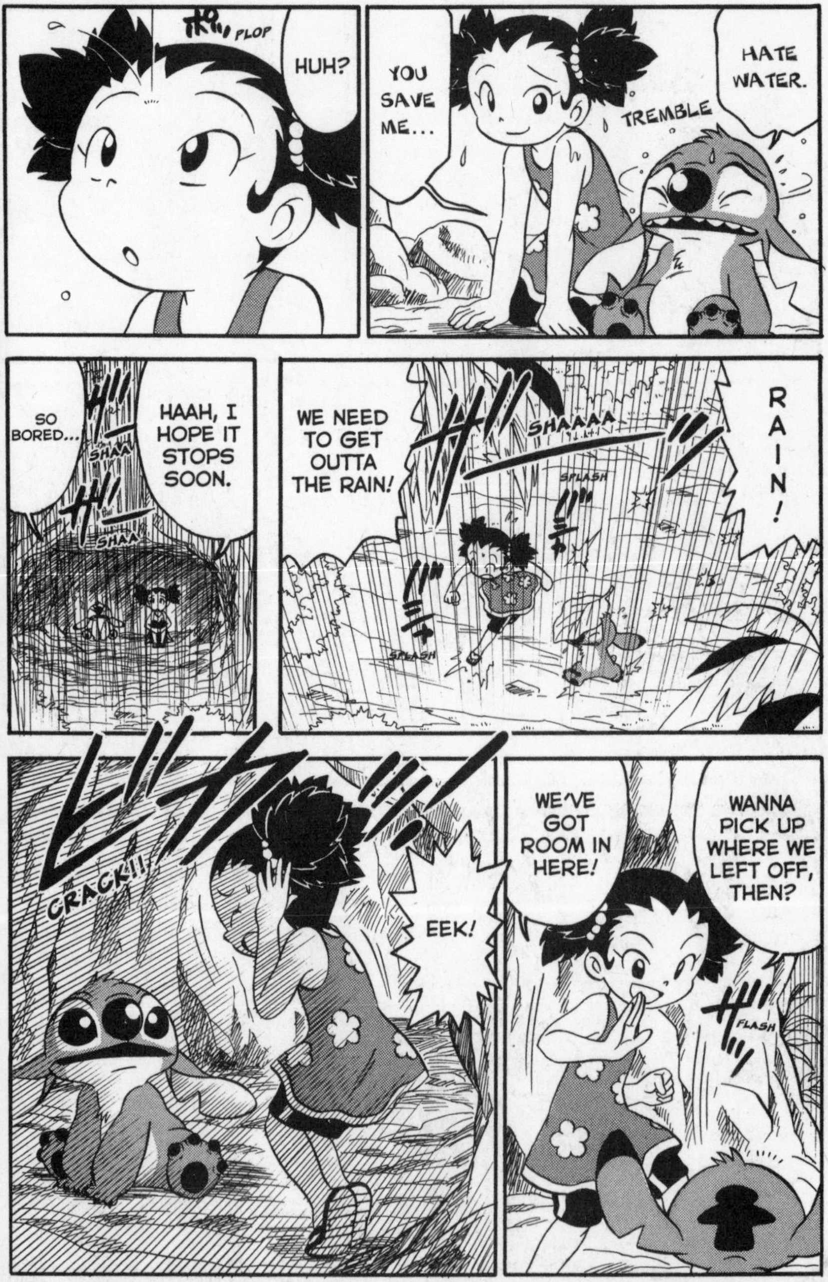
HATE WATER.
TREMBLE
YOU SAVE ME...
HUH?
PLOP
RAIN!
SHAAAA
WE NEED TO GET OUTTA THE RAIN!
SPLASH
SPLASH
HAAH, I HOPE IT STOPS SOON.
SO BORED...
SHAA
SHAA
WANNA PICK UP WHERE WE LEFT OFF, THEN?
WE'VE GOT ROOM IN HERE!
FLASH
EEK!
CRACK!!

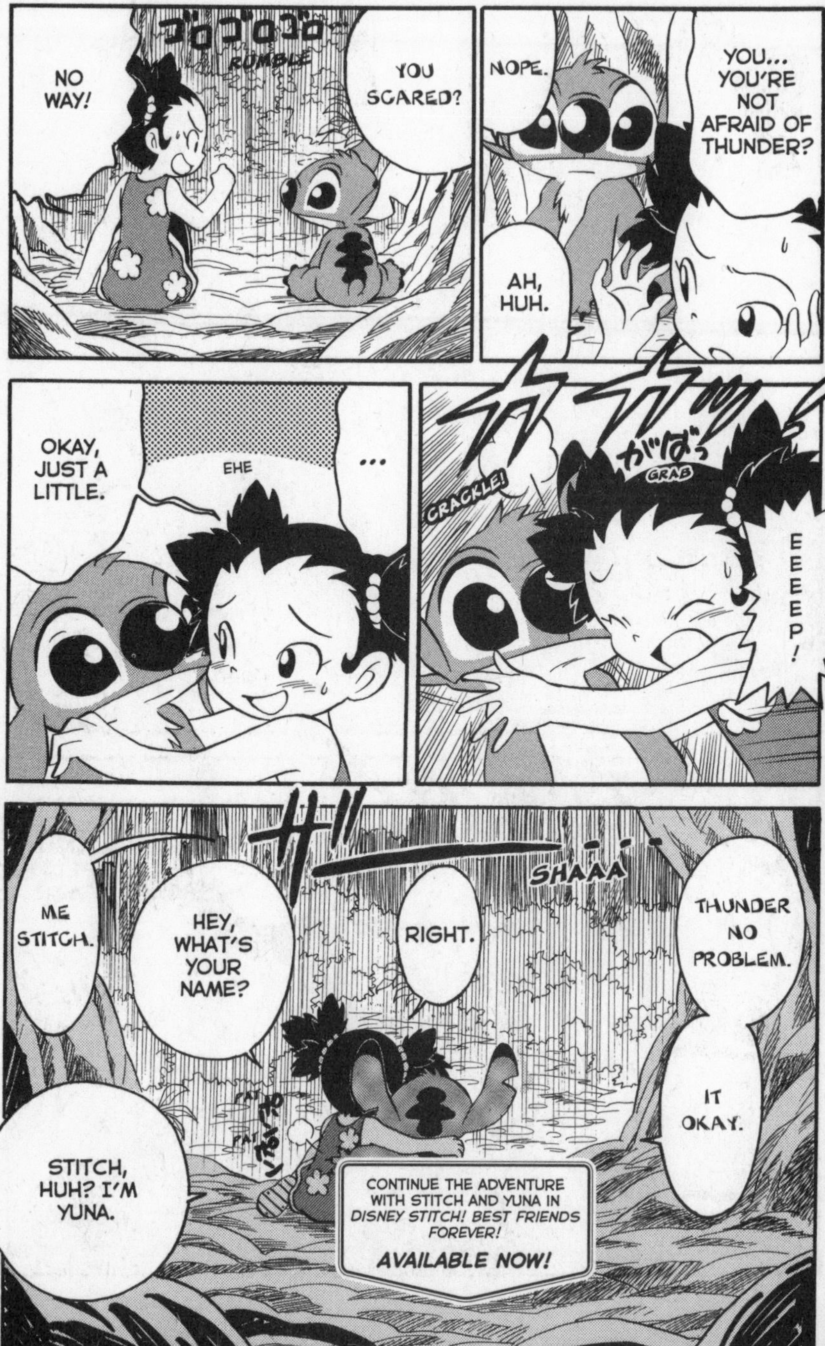
YOU... YOU'RE NOT AFRAID OF THUNDER?
NOPE.
AH, HUH.
ゴロゴロゴロ
RUMBLE
YOU SCARED?
NO WAY!
CRACKLE!
GRAB
EEEEEP!
...
EHE
OKAY, JUST A LITTLE.
SHAAA
THUNDER NO PROBLEM.
IT OKAY.
RIGHT.
HEY, WHAT'S YOUR NAME?
ME STITCH.
PAT
PAT
STITCH, HUH? I'M YUNA.
CONTINUE THE ADVENTURE WITH STITCH AND YUNA IN *DISNEY STITCH! BEST FRIENDS FOREVER!*
AVAILABLE NOW!

DISNEY FAIRIES MANGA

BELOVED DISNEY CHARACTERS IN A CUTE MANGA STYLE!

LEARN MORE ABOUT TINKER BELL AND HER FRIENDS!

FAMILY FRIENDLY FANTASY MANGA SERIES WITH VALUABLE LESSONS FOR CHILDREN!

DESCENDANTS

Full color manga trilogy based on the hit Disney Channel original movie

Inspired by the original stories of Disney's classic heroes and villains

Experience this spectacular movie in manga form!

Magical Dance Volume 2
Story and Art by Nao Kodaka

Publishing Assistant - Janae Young
Marketing Assistant - Kae Winters
Technology and Digital Media Assistant - Phillip Hong
Retouching and Lettering - Vibrraant Publishing Studio
Translations - Jason Muell
Graphic Designer - Phillip Hong
Copy Editor - Daniella Orihuela-Gruber
Editor-in-Chief & Publisher - Stu Levy

A  Manga

TOKYOPOP and 🐢 are trademarks or registered trademarks of TOKYOPOP Inc.

TOKYOPOP inc.
5200 W Century Blvd
Suite 705
Los Angeles, CA 90045 USA

E-mail: info@TOKYOPOP.com
Come visit us online at www.TOKYOPOP.com

f www.facebook.com/TOKYOPOP
🐦 www.twitter.com/TOKYOPOP
▶ www.youtube.com/TOKYOPOPTV
📌 www.pinterest.com/TOKYOPOP
📷 www.instagram.com/TOKYOPOP
t TOKYOPOP.tumblr.com

ISBN: 978-1-4278-5679-1
First TOKYOPOP Printing June 2017
10 9 8 7 6 5 4 3 2 1
Printed in Canada

STOP

THIS IS THE BACK OF THE BOOK!

How do you read manga-style? It's simple! To learn, just start in the top right panel and follow the numbers:

MAY -- 2018